A CHANGE OF HEART

"See you tomorrow!" Julia called. "Good night!"

But instead of leaving, Ben closed the door behind her and stepped inside again—much too close to her. She tried to back away, but he reached out to touch her.

"Stay here, Julia," he said softly.

"No. Go home."

He didn't go. He folded her into his arms. She stood mesmerized, unwilling to escape even though she felt she should resist.

"I don't want to do this," she said.

"I think you do." His mouth grazed the side of her cheek; her heart raced.

"I'd like you to leave, Ben," she managed to say.

He tilted her chin up toward him. "Tell me you don't want one kiss, Julia."

"I don't," she began, "want. . . ." Her words were silenced by the soft pressure of his mouth closing over hers. Then the kiss deepened.

She truly wanted to stay lost in that kiss forever, but common sense nagged at her. She stepped backward into her living room, putting space between them.

"Will you tell me to go away again, Julia?"

No, don't go away. She didn't speak the words. She simply turned and made the imperceptible movement that slid her smoothly, easily, back into his waiting arms.

IT'S NEVER TOO LATE FOR LOVE AND ROMANCE

JUST IN TIME (4188, $4.50/$5.50)
by Peggy Roberts

Constantly taking care of everyone around her has earned Remy Dupre the affectionate nickname "Ma." Then, with Remy's husband gone and oil discovered on her Louisiana farm, her sons and their wives decide it's time to take care of her. But Remy knows how to take care of herself. She starts by checking into a beauty spa, buying some classy new clothes and shoes, discovering an antique vase, and moving on to a fine plantation. Next, not one, but two men attempt to sweep her off her well-shod feet. The right man offers her the opportunity to love again.

LOVE AT LAST (4158, $4.50/$5.50)
by Garda Parker

Fifty, slim, and attractive, Gail Bricker still hadn't found the love of her life. Friends convince her to take an Adventure Tour during the summer vacation she enjoys as an English teacher. At a Cheyenne Indian school in need of teachers, Gail finds her calling. In rancher Slater Kincaid, she finds her match. Gail discovers that it's never too late to fall in love . . . for the very first time.

LOVE LESSONS (3959, $4.50/$5.50)
by Marian Oaks

After almost forty years of marriage, Carolyn Ames certainly hadn't been looking for a divorce. But the ink is barely dry, and here she is already living an exhilarating life as a single woman. First, she lands an exciting and challenging job. Now Jason, the handsome architect, offers her a fairy-tale romance. Carolyn doesn't care that her ultra-conservative neighbors gossip about her and Jason, but she is afraid to give up her independent life-style. She struggles with the balance while she learns to love again.

A KISS TO REMEMBER (4129, $4.50/$5.50)
by Helen Playfair

For the past ten years Lucia Morgan hasn't had time for love or romance. Since her husband's death, she has been raising her two sons, working at a dead-end office job, and designing boutique clothes to make ends meet. Then one night, Mitch Colton comes looking for his daughter, out late with one of her sons. The look in Mitch's eye brings back a host of long-forgotten feelings. When the kids come home and spoil the enchantment, Lucia wonders if she will get the chance to love again.

COME HOME TO LOVE (3930, $4.50/$5.50)
by Jane Bierce

Julia Delaine says good-bye to her skirt-chasing husband Phillip and hello to a whole new life. Julia capably rises to the challenges of her reawakened sexuality, the young man who comes courting, and her new position as the head of her local television station. Her new independence teaches Julia that maybe her time-tested values were right all along and maybe Phillip does belong in her life, with her new terms.

GARDEN OF LOVE

EILEEN HEHL

ZEBRA BOOKS
KENSINGTON PUBLISHING CORP.

ZEBRA BOOKS are published by

Kensington Publishing Corp.
850 Third Avenue
New York, NY 10022

First Printing: February, 1995

Printed in the United States of America

To my husband, Tony, for 35 years of love,

and to all the Anthonys in my life:
Anthony Aquina, my Dad;
Anthony Hehl, Jr., my son;
John Anthony Aquina, my brother;
Robert Anthony Berardi, my godson/nephew.

One

"A tour of classical Greece and all the islands, absolutely," Julia Maxwell said, thumbing through a stack of folders so high it threatened to keel over. "I've wanted this my whole life, Sara. To see Athens, Delphi, Mykonos—"

"Mykonos is a must!" Her travel agent, Sara Miles, yanked yet another glossy brochure from a rack. "Behold. All the rich and famous vacation at Mykonos."

It was April, with a weak spring sunlight streaming in through the glass windows of All Seasons Travel Bureau. Julia was in her glory buried in travel folders, knowing that—at long last—she had ample summer vacation time and enough money saved for her dream trip.

"Corfu," Julia said in an awed voice. "And Santorini." She scanned page after page of vivid color photos in the Grecian tourbooks, marveling at the oceanic hues of the books—a whole spectrum of blues for the Aegean, the

Ionian, and the Sea of Crete. Her heart was already there.

"The Acropolis . . . Olympia, Delos, Nauplia . . . I can't tell you how many courses I've taken on Grecian art, philosophy, and architecture." Julia grinned at the red-haired woman by the travel computer. "This is finally my year to do it, Sara."

"You'll have a wonderful time." Sara flashed a sincere smile. "There's so much to see. You can include Turkey if you like, Julia."

Julia shook her head. "No. I want two full weeks just for Greece alone."

"You're not traveling by yourself, are you?" Sara asked.

"No. My co-worker Selena is definitely going, and there are two others who might be able to make it." Julia sighed with pleasure, anticipating long days in the hot sun, sightseeing, swimming, tasting Greek delicacies. . . .

"Best of all," Julia added, "an old college friend of mine is living in Athens right now. So it's a perfect time to go."

"I'm happy for you, Julia."

"Thanks! And you know what I plan to do when I get back?" Julia spoke on a sudden impulse. "Sell my house. It's time now. I've decided to get a compact condo near town."

"No kidding?" Sara looked surprised. "I thought you loved that house."

"Oh, I do, in one way, but it's too big now. My two older girls are married and Cristy's away at college most of the time."

Sara frowned. "Julia, forgive me for saying this, but don't they usually advise new widows to wait an interval of two years before making drastic lifestyle changes?"

Julia felt her spine stiffening. "It's one year they recommend. But my Jay has been gone more than two years."

"Hard to believe." Uncomfortably, Sara shifted her weight in the chair. "I'd never have guessed it was two years already."

Julia knew it was time to change the subject. "Anyway, will you work up the total costs on these tours? I'll stop back tomorrow after work to make a decision."

"Of course." Sara looked up from her computer. "Oh, I envy you! I can't imagine having a whole block of time free like that for travel."

Julia managed a bright smile. She wanted to say, *You envy me? You still have your healthy, loving husband and your three kids at home. . . .*

But no one wanted to hear that, Julia knew from experience. She stood up and smoothed the skirt of her suit. "Thanks. Talk to you tomorrow."

She stepped out into the blustery cold April air, her mind already filled with what clothes to pack and which sturdy shoes to take for long hikes along the Grecian shores.

The afternoon was waning, though it was sunny and barely four. She considered dinner: stop at the nearest salad bar or not? She decided instead to go home and heat up yesterday's chili. She settled into her aqua Saturn and, still grinning, drove toward Camelot Road.

The trip to Greece had her excited. This was the first time she'd felt truly elated about anything in—well, in this whole two years, frankly. She was the first to admit she'd been totally destroyed after Jay died.

It was amazing. That one's brain and intellect could possibly come back to life after such numbing grief—that gave a whole new meaning to the words "recovery" and "moving on."

She made a right turn into the driveway of her home. The brick two-story Georgian sat back on an acre of rocky Connecticut lawn, looking, as always, sedate. Julia frowned slightly. A house that big was meant for a growing family. "Moving on" for Julia would involve selling the house she'd lived in for a quarter of a century.

Settling into her own small condo would be heavenly, she thought, parking in the garage and pressing the automatic door button. Imagine never worrying about a lawn or snow shoveling as long as you lived! And Willowset Condos, her place of choice, had several swimming pools—she'd made sure of that when she went browsing—pools to which you'd never have to add one bit of algaecide or Supershock. Maintenance would do it all for you.

She was surprised to find herself still smiling as the big, quiet house closed around her. She refused to dwell on the silence, though it was so deep a person could hear every swish of the lilac bushes her husband had planted outside. So? Silence never killed anyone, she thought fiercely, and placed her good coat in the hall closet.

Yes, all in all life was beginning to look good again. Not perfect. It would never be perfect, without Jay . . . but Julia was making progress every day, in many small areas. She'd always felt as long as you could look forward to *something,* you were on the right track.

"I'm definitely on the right track this spring," she said aloud, even though she knew only certified crazies talked to themselves. She'd slip out of her work clothes—a good raspberry suit that Jay had loved on her—and then settle down with her nuked bowl of chili and the six o'clock news.

Her smile widened. Greece was waiting for her. The language she'd studied, the art and travel books she'd perused—now it would all come together for her. By September she'd be a woman who knew all about classical Greece, and not just some small-town grandmother who'd never ventured beyond the U.S.

Look out world, she thought, because here comes a globe-hopping Julia!

It was almost dark.

A tidy brown car had been parked across the street a long time, though its occupant didn't move a muscle.

A pair of eyes narrowed as they glared at the Maxwell house.

Then the occupant of the car saw some-one—a man?—walking up the driveway of the Maxwell house. Swiftly, the motor was gunned and the small brown car drove away.

"Sara'll tell us the full cost tomorrow," Julia was saying at that moment into the dining room telephone. "But it does sound like one fantastic voyage, Selena." Julia stood by her sliding glass doors, gazing out at a bleak backyard filled with spring mud, winter-dead grass, and clumps of fallen maple leaves that nobody had bothered to rake in November.

"Well, I'm in, no matter what." The voice on the other end of the phone was Selena Mulroony, Julia's co-worker at Marble Street School, and closest friend. Selena had also lost her husband so the two women had much in common now. "All that antiquity over there in Greece—it's bound to make me look younger, right?"

"Count on it." Julia chuckled and was just about to draw her drapes closed to shut out the sloppy exterior landscape—when she spotted movement in one corner of her yard.

"For heaven's sakes," she whispered. "You won't believe this. There's an absolute stranger in my backyard."

"But—that's awfully odd. You have your property all fenced in, don't you?"

"Of course."

"Then he came in the gate. Must be a burglar, or someone up to no good. You ought to dial 9-1-1 right this minute, Julia."

"You might be right." Julia was myopic and without her glasses could barely see as far as the property's corner. She squinted; what she could discern seemed to be a large, man-shaped intruder pushing some sort of appliance. A wheelbarrow, possibly?

But it wasn't *her* wheelbarrow. Hers, she knew, was safely locked up in Jay's gardening shed. So why was this giant of a person pushing a strange wheelbarrow into Julia's yard?

"Let's hang up," she said to Selena. "I do need the police here." Selena complied.

Julia took one last look: he was still there, and busy doing something with that wheelbarrow that she couldn't figure out. She promptly dialed 9-1-1.

"I need a police car right away." She tried to keep her voice low so the intruder wouldn't hear. "My address is 134 Camelot Road—and please tell them to hurry." She put down the phone. Yes, he was still there and he still looked threatening.

She pressed her nose to the cold glass. He was a huge man, no doubt about that. He was swathed in such a big furry jacket you couldn't tell his actual size. Not only that—she had an impression of a furry face, too. A beard of some sort?

Fortunately the police in Stonewell, Connecticut, were known for showing up quickly, and Julia was glad when two officers appeared at her front door. She escorted them out to the backyard, where the man still was.

"Hold it right there, buddy," the taller cop yelled, about to reach for his revolver. "Police. Raise both hands and—"

"I'm under arrest?" The intruder's shoulders were shaking with what looked like laughter.

"Get those hands up, pal," said the shorter cop, moving swiftly across the muddy lawn toward the corner.

The large hands went up but the intruder never stopped laughing. "It's now a crime to transport a sundial?" he asked.

"Huh?" All three of them, the two officers and Julia, moved closer to the spot near the old stone wall where the man had been busy doing something.

"What's going on here?" demanded the tall policeman. "Did you say you're stealing a sundial?"

"He can't be stealing a sundial," Julia said. "I don't own a sundial!"

"You do now." The suspect himself said that, in between his fits of barely controlled laughter.

Two

Inside her kitchen, Julia busied herself fixing a pot of coffee while the crime story was being unraveled.

"So you say you're a neighbor of Mrs. Maxwell?" The tall cop had his notebook out on Julia's kitchen table and was trying to form some sort of report.

"Yes, he is, Officer." Julia knew her face must be beet-red. "Now that I get a closer look at him, I see that he's Mr. Wilson. He lives right down the street."

"My name is Ben Wilson," the man said, pulling out a pocketful of identification.

The second officer checked out the driver's license. "Benjamin T. Wilson." He frowned with authority. "Would you care to explain now why you're trespassing in Mrs. Maxwell's yard?"

"Of course." Because the kitchen was warm, Ben Wilson pushed back the hood of his big fuzzy parka. Julia saw that he was indeed a giant of a man, even sitting on her kitchen chair, and that he did indeed wear a beard. He was at least her age—fifty or so—but the sandy-colored hair on his head and beard was barely streaked with silver. His large green eyes were set in a tanned, sun-bronzed face, and he looked remarkably cheerful for a man on the verge of being arrested.

"Sorry for all the trouble, really." Wilson addressed all three of them. "None of this would have happened if Cristy had called you first, Mrs. Maxwell."

"Cristy? My daughter?"

"Why, yes. She was supposed to tell you—a few things." The soft green eyes turned to look at her with great innocence. "Could she have called and left you a message?"

"I don't know." Truthfully she hadn't checked her answering machine when she had come home; she'd been too excited about her trip to Greece to think of anything else. She turned now to where the machine sat on top of an old butcher block.

The signal light was flashing. Certain that she was about to be humiliated in some uniquely Cristy way, Julia adjusted the controls to *Rewind Message* and then *Play*.

"Hi, there, Mom?" The saucy voice of her

youngest daughter piped out from the speaker. "Guess you're not home yet, hmm?"

"That's Cristy," Julia told the police officers. "She's a student at the University of Connecticut."

"Her senior year," Ben Wilson added, as though that were somehow relevant. Julia shot him a look of annoyance.

"Mom, please call me the minute you get in, because my friend Ben Wilson, will be showing up in your yard any minute—"

"She got that right, anyway," the tall cop commented with a smile.

"I asked him to help us with a project," Cristy went on. "I need to explain it all to you. Call me immediately. I'll be in my room, waiting."

"You'd better call her, Mrs. Maxwell," Ben Wilson suggested politely. "She's the only one who can tell you this news."

Julia dialed the dorm and Cristy picked up the phone as though she'd been sitting there just waiting for it to ring.

"You'd better have a good explanation for this sundial caper," Julia said. "Because we've got the law here and your friend Ben Wilson ready to be handcuffed."

"Oh my God," Cristy howled. "I should have known! But I can explain. Mom, this is going to be a major shock, I know—" She hesitated.

"Maybe you ought to sit down, Mrs. Maxwell, before she tells you," Ben Wilson said.

"No thank you," Julia's heart was beating rapidly and she wondered why the man seemed to anger her with every word he spoke.

"Mom, I'd much rather tell you this in person—"

"Just tell me, Cristy."

"Well, Jeremy and I have been unofficially engaged, as you know." Cristy's voice managed to be both whimsical and musical. "But now that graduation's only a month away for both of us, we started talking seriously. Little did we know we'd decide to set the wedding date soon—"

"Cristy, please get to the point." Julia was aware of the three men watching her as she conversed with her daughter.

"We've decided on this coming September, Mom."

Julia felt her knees go weak. Stunned, she slid down into a chair after all. September? Who on this earth could pull together a wedding by September?

"Sorry about that, Mom, but it's what we decided, since it would help us careerwise starting out as a married couple. Are you okay?"

"Cristy, please just explain about the sundial!"

"Okay, but you might not like it. Anyway—here's the real kicker and I hope you'll go along with it."

Cristy seemed to take a deep breath before going on. "We'd like to have a garden wedding right there in our backyard in Stonewell."

"Garden wedding? What are you talking about? We have no gardens, Cristy."

"No, not yet. It could be gorgeous. . . . Now don't faint and don't die, Mom, we'll talk about this ASAP. The thing is, Ben Wilson offered to help us and so that's why he came into the yard today. He's lending us that sundial as the beginning of our gardens . . ."

The beginning of our gardens . . .

Julia shook her head in astonishment. Now she had to retell this whole tale to the police officers, who needed it for their official report.

How do you make them understand that your youngest daughter is a total flake living in some sort of fantasy land?

"I'll get back to you, Cristy Lynn," she said quite rationally and with firmness. "Stay right where you are." She put down the telephone.

* * *

After the police had left, Julia felt two distinct things: annoyance (still) with Ben Wilson, and embarrassment that she'd almost had him arrested.

But annoyance was right on the top of her list, though she couldn't explain why, exactly. She didn't really know the man, except for the fact that he'd been at Jay's funeral as a friend of Cristy's. She remembered him as a tall, quiet, respectful man in a dark suit, she'd grant him that. For some reason she'd always disliked Benjamin T. Wilson.

Or what he stood for: endless gardening.

Cristy had liked him very much and spent countless hours over there at Wilson's house, especially right after Jay's death. Julia that whole summer had resented the time Cristy spent at the neighbor's home, and somehow thought it was unnecessary for Cristy to become enamored of all that gardening nonsense.

Call me a control freak if you want to, she thought now, pouring a second cup of coffee for herself and Ben Wilson. I just don't seem to like the man and I always managed to let Cristy know it. . . .

But she had to be polite.

"I apologize again, Mr. Wilson," she said in her most gracious voice, "for the police fiasco. I can't imagine why I didn't recognize you."

"Oh, nobody would." He grinned good-naturedly. "I'm sure I look like Nanook of the North Pole in my Arctic jacket. . . . Mrs. Maxwell, you seem quite upset by Cristy's news."

"I am," she said truthfully.

"You needn't entertain me at a time like this. I'll go on along home so you can take care of matters."

"That's thoughtful of you." She bit her lower lip momentarily. "I guess I am a bit shaken by this wedding idea. It's too sudden and impulsive."

"A garden wedding could be very lovely, as she said." Ben Wilson's face radiated an enthusiasm that Julia seldom saw in a man half his age. "Those two kids are brimming with schemes. I think she truly has a beautiful idea there."

"I don't agree." She stirred her coffee. "The truth is we have no garden here. I don't know where she gets these romantic notions—certainly not from me, because I've never been a gardener, and certainly not from her two older sisters because they had quite traditional weddings."

Her voice was beginning to take on a slightly cold edge, and she didn't like the sound of it. She stopped and inhaled a deep, calming breath. Why was she wasting her arguments on this person, anyway? It would be Cristy and Jeremy she had to convince.

"Cristy told me you had no garden to speak of." His voice was soft, calm, reassuring. Why was it she felt like strangling him?

"That's why she phoned me a while ago," Ben Wilson said. "She'd like my help in planting, and setting up some landscaping items such as the sundial I just wheeled over here."

"Mr. Wilson." Julia knew she was speaking in icy tones again but there was no help for it. "I appreciate what you say but, to be honest, I doubt there will be any wedding here in September. So I'm sorry we've wasted your time—"

He grinned. "And almost got me a police record, too, hmm?"

"That, too." She stood up in a dismissive way. "I really do need to call my daughter now and try to reason with her."

He stood also. "Of course. I'll be on my way with no further fuss. Except—"

"Yes?"

His large, fuzzy face softened, a blend of

optimism and entreaty. "I hope you'll keep an open mind, Mrs. Maxwell."

"I'll try."

"I saw many wonderful possibilities in your backyard. I suppose I'm a romantic, too, but I can picture Cristy floating along a flowery flagstone path in her bridal gown—"

Julia tried to smile but her head had begun to ache. "I thank you for your insight. It makes an intriguing picture, I'm sure, but—"

"I know. It's absolutely none of my business," he said quietly. His face remained cheerful, his green eyes sparkling with energy. "Thanks so much for the coffee."

He slipped out the sliding glass doors and headed for his wheelbarrow. Julia watched him until he disappeared around the corner. Then she raced to the oval antique mirror above her sideboard to see whether she looked as stressed out as she felt.

The woman looking back at her was unusually pale with big, worried blue eyes and an unruly mop of short, dark curls. Was this the same woman who was smiling and dreaming of ancient Greece only half an hour ago?

She hoisted a comb and did battle with the recalcitrant curls even as she planned her strategy.

Definitely, she'd get in the car right now,

and go to see the kids in person. That was always preferable to a phone call.

She had to find a way to change their plans. A wedding instead of her trip to Greece? A wedding in September when at least a year was needed to plan a decent wedding?

And a wedding in a garden when they literally had no garden?

No way, José!

The campus of the University of Connecticut had always fascinated Julia. It was a place of contrast. Some of the old buildings were covered with ivy while others were brand new and modernistic. There were sloping green lawns even in muddy April, old cow barns as well as a giant library, mature maple trees and many new, baby plantings. She thought it a beautiful campus, and she was glad all three of her girls had been educated there.

She breathed a sigh of relief when she entered Storrs. She'd been driving for an hour and it was now dark, of course. She was to meet Cristy and Jeremy at a coffee shop on the edge of campus. Driving to it with precision, she thought, *Here we go,* upon seeing her daughter speedwalking toward the car.

"Hey, Momserina!" Cristy, tall and slim

with long hair gleaming in the light from the coffee shop, smiled broadly. "We could've talked on the telephone, you know. You didn't have to drive all this way!"

"I love taking drives," Julia said, setting her emergency brake. She stepped out and enveloped her daughter in a warm hug. "Honey, I'm so happy for both of you . . . being engaged is a very special time."

"Thanks." Cristy hugged back with great fervor. "I love him so much, and we have so much in common, both being in horticulture."

"But Cristy, we do have to do some talking—"

"Oh boy, do I know that!" Cristy now spotted Jeremy coming out of the coffee shop. "We're over here, Jer."

Now they had a three-way hug while Julia said again how delighted she was about their engagement. "You're the cutest-looking couple I've ever seen," she said, standing back for a second to study them: Both tall and dark-haired with very dark eyes, they did look spectacular together. Tears misted Julia's eyes suddenly, and she kissed Jeremy's cheek.

"Sorry about the whole Ben Wilson thing, Mom," Cristy said.

"Never mind that, honey. Let's get to a table so we can talk about you—both of you—and decide what's going on here."

They settled at a table near a veritable jungle of potted green plants, and Jeremy ambled over to the coffee bar to get three cups of designer coffee.

"You look stressed out," Cristy said right away. "What's up?"

Julia took a deep breath. "Honey, it's this plan of yours. It isn't going to work. I hope I can make you listen to reason."

"Why?" Cristy's slender face looked genuinely puzzled. "I know you hate gardening but you don't have to do a thing, really. Jeremy and I are the aggie majors and we'll plant whatever's needed. The wedding should be fairly easy."

Julia sighed. "Cristy, it's not just the idea of turning our property into a—a Garden of Eden. That sounds impossible enough, but there's even more to consider."

"Such as?"

"Money problems, for one thing. I do have some saved but a wedding is an enormous expense—"

"Oh, Mom. Are you saying there isn't enough money for a small, simple wedding in the yard?"

"Yes frankly. I've been saving for two whole years but I don't think there's enough. . . ."

Cristy leaned forward, visibly upset. "I'll never understand why you're not one of those rich widows we always hear about in our town."

"Well, I'm not, as you know. Your Dad was always so healthy, he was underinsured. That house is a big drain on my money."

"Plus you've had college expenses for all of us." Cristy's silver earrings dangled as she spoke. "I realize you've had to keep working hard and I do feel bad about that."

"No." Julia waved her hand. "No, I don't mind working at all, it's what keeps me going. But as for extra money . . . honey, there just isn't enough for a quick wedding like this."

Jeremy came back with the coffees just then.

"I have everything all figured out, Mom," Cristy went on. "We're going to do this wedding El Cheapo style. Picnic tables and a barbecue where we can throw on hot dogs and beans. It won't cost much at all. It'll be like a big picnic!"

Julia shuddered. *Keep an open mind,* that man Ben Wilson had said, but she was finding it very difficult.

"An El Cheapo wedding? Is that what you truly want?"

"Sure. Don't we, Jer?" Cristy and Jeremy nuzzled their faces together for an impromptu kiss.

"Cristy, I don't think . . ."

"Just remember this, Mom: Daddy promised all three of us we could have exactly whatever kind of wedding we wanted."

Julia felt the blood drain from her face. "Yes, he did promise that, but what he meant was—well, like April and Bethany had. Traditional church weddings and a lavish reception at the country club."

"Cristy decided she's not the country club type, Mrs. Maxwell," said Jeremy.

"Daddy said whatever kind we wanted," Cristy repeated with slow emphasis. "Whatever kind. Jeremy and I have decided to say our vows under the maple tree that my Dad planted."

"Under the maple tree?" Julia was stunned; she could still see Jay planting that tree when Cristy was born.

"Mom, this is exactly what we choose." Cristy's dark eyes glittered with unshed tears. "If Daddy were here, he'd grin and tell us to go for it. You know he would."

If Daddy were here . . .

The lump that formed in Julia's throat threatened to choke her. Through a mist of blurred vision, she stared at her youngest child and tried to form some kind of statement. It seemed virtually impossible at the moment.

"I'm not asking for much, Momacita. Just a few dollars to buy some chrysanthemums, that's all, to make the yard kinda pretty. And a short white dress with a veil and the fixin's for a picnic."

Jeremy put in, "We'd pay for it all ourselves if we could. We have no money right now, but after we work all summer maybe we can manage some."

"No." Julia found her voice and it came out with firm authority. "Absolutely not. You do not pay for your own wedding and you do not say your vows among a couple of mums."

"But that's what we've been dreaming of—"

"Listen to me." Julia squared up her shoulders. Thank God Cristy hadn't known of her mother's plans to tour Greece. "Now that I think about it, I can scrape together enough money. . . . The only important thing is your wedding, and it shall be exactly when and where you want it."

"Really?" Cristy's heart-shaped face beamed with surprise.

"Of course. But I should hope we'd do it with a little more style and grace than a family picnic."

"Now we don't need anything fancy, Mom."

"We do. Even if you are both aggies and you think outdoor life is the only way to go—" Julia smiled broadly. "It'll be your only wedding! We'll have many beautiful touches."

"You mean like tablecloths?" Grinning with mischief, Cristy adopted a bogus hillbilly twang. "Real *cloth* ones, Mammy, just like Hillary has at that there White House in Washington D.C.?"

Julia pretended to swat her. "Yes, real cloth ones, you devil! And a canopy, and pots of wonderful flowers everywhere, and the most beautiful bridal chinaware, and—"

"Ooooh, this is beginning to sound like Princess Di's wedding day."

"Better. It's going to be better," said her mother with pride. Julia took a sip of her French vanilla coffee, feeling both exhilarated and terrified. "Your Dad would have been very pleased about all this, you know."

"I do know." Now it was Cristy's turn to have tears spilling from her eyes. "He sure would. Daddy always loved a great party, didn't he?"

"Absolutely." Julia felt tears streaming quietly down her cheeks. "He always said his middle name was 'Party!' "

"My Dad," Cristy said to Jeremy, who had been mostly silent all throughout the negotiations. "Wish you could've known my father better, because he loved being a host. Especially for the weddings of his daughters."

"I don't know who will give you away," Julia whispered as the thought occurred to her. At the moment it seemed unthinkable that it wouldn't be Jay himself. "But we'll worry about that some other time. Meanwhile—"

"Meanwhile, there's a lot to do this summer, Mom."

"And we're going to do this wedding right, honey." Julia pulled out a notepad for beginning her lists. It promised to be a summer full of lists, she realized ruefully.

Wedding lists instead of the Parthenon, Mykonos, Crete, or Santorini. "We'll make this the loveliest garden wedding anyone ever had," Julia vowed aloud. "We'll stage this party just as if we were doing it with Daddy."

The great salty tears continued to roll, unwanted but unstoppable. There was something healing in crying for Jay at this particular moment, here in a UConn coffeeshop. It seemed to bring Jay closer to them, if that were at all possible.

Cristy pressed a kiss to her mother's cheek. "Thanks, Mom."

Three

Ben Wilson loaded up his fireplace with four nicely split applewood logs, pushed them into place with the brass poker, then settled back to watch the gradual buildup of crackling flames. He had a massive brick fireplace in his log home, bigger than any he'd ever seen anywhere else. Well, he'd built this place to be his final dream house, the bachelor digs to end all bachelor digs. And after five years here, he still felt he'd done his planning exactly right.

Settling back on a dark-brown leather couch, he surveyed the room, deriving pleasure from the bachelor trappings: bookcases that covered three walls, hanging green plants, a shelf full of antique pewter mugs, a wall of Ansel Adams prints showing snowy scenes in Yosemite. His beagle, Ivan the Terrible, settled at his feet, curled up, and enjoyed the fire.

Ben's mind drifted to this afternoon, and

the woman named Julia Maxwell who had almost had him arrested.

Cristy's mother. Cristy was a bright, de-
lightful girl who'd visited him often in the
past two or three years, on her vacations from
college. "I'm insane about gardening," she'd
often said, "but there's no point tilling my
own home soil because my Mom's going to
sell the homestead. I can tell. Mom needs a
whole new life somewhere else."

Julia Maxwell, he thought now, was an interesting woman. Pretty, vivacious, determinedly
upbeat from what he'd seen. She had dusky
blue eyes, that wealth of short, curling black
hair, and a face that was as honest as it was
finely sculpted. She was still in the grip of a
widow's deep grieving, he had recognized that,
too; not surprising, only two years after losing
her husband.

Still, Ben couldn't help wondering whether
he'd ever stand a chance with Julia. He
grinned. He knew he was a big, lumbering
bear of a guy who didn't make great first impressions. Maybe not even seconds or thirds.
Usually when people got to know him, however, they saw beneath the muscle and bulk
and fuzzy beard, and sensed the depth of
Benjamin Wilson.

Would that happen with Julia?

He stared, mesmerized, into the hissing fire, daring to daydream about having a lady friend as fine and attractive as Julia Maxwell. Pipe dreams, maybe.

Unless he was being unusually sensitive, she seemed to actively dislike him for some reason. Anyway they probably had nothing at all in common. But they would be thrown together quite a lot this year—more than Julia knew, at this point.

The woman had no idea, he was sure, just how much Cristy had asked him to renovate the property at 134 Camelot Road. He'd be charging into Julia's backyard a great many times between now and September.

He smiled slowly. "Well, Ivan, I can tell you one thing. If she agrees to that garden wedding, it ought to be a very interesting summer."

Ivan snorted with supreme disinterest. What was the big deal?

"Don't you think the whole idea is slightly CRAZY?"

"We'll have margaritas all around," said April Tanner, nee Maxwell, to their waiter who wore a gigantic gold Mexican sombrero and a south-of-the-border belt. "My mother probably needs a double."

"I do not." Julia waved away the idea and tried to take control of the family meeting. It was the following Sunday and was her oldest daughter April's thirtieth birthday celebration at El Toreador Restaurant. April and Bethany had elected to come without their families, so it was just Julia and her blond daughters, the girls who looked most like Jay's side of the family. Cristy couldn't get away from college this particular weekend.

"Cristy's a nutcase, Mom," declared the middle sister, Bethany. "Why would a Catholic girl want to get married on the lawn in back of her house? Does that sound sane?"

"Remember we're talking about Cristy." Julia sat back in her pseudo-Spanish chair and took on an appearance of calm. "It's not so terribly crazy. I admit it threw me for a loss at first, but then—it occurred to all of us that your father would have loved it."

April and Bethany fell silent. In the background, Mexican music blared cheerily, with Mariachi band sounds that made you want to leap up to dance around one of the decorative sombreros.

"Think about it," Julia went on. "If Cristy can pull this off—and she does plan to work all summer creating nice gardens—it will be a last big hurrah. The very final party to be held at the house where you all grew up."

"So you're truly planning to sell the place, Mom?" asked April, wide-eyed.

"Definitely. I know you'll all be sad but it's the best thing for me, both financially and— otherwise."

"Probably true." Bethany reached out for a large taco chip and dipped it into some greenish salsa. "Memories of Daddy are everywhere in that house. Must be like living with a ghost. Once you get rid of that big ark you'll be able to do all the traveling you always wanted."

"We don't mean to be interfering," April said. She was the first of Jay Maxwell's A-B-C girls; he'd picked the names for each of the babies, thinking it original to follow the alphabet. He'd hoped, no doubt, to continue on to J or K eventually. "Mom, I know it sounds like we're against all of Cristy's plans—"

"We're not, but we're just afraid it could be a fiasco." Bethany broke off and smiled when the margaritas arrived—small frosted glasses with the correct amount of salt around the rims. "Mmmm. I just love birthday lunches."

"Especially when we leave the kids at home with their fathers." April smiled brightly, her face transformed like a sudden spring day after weeks of rain. It was odd how much April and Bethany looked alike, even though their personalities were different. April was the worry-wart individual and Bethany the official peacemaker in the family. Cristy was the only tall, dark-haired one who most resembled her mother.

"This is heaven, without my kids," Bethany agreed.

"I don't know." Julia frowned. "I wish they'd joined us. I really enjoy seeing my grandchildren. The daddies, too."

"Well, I'm the birthday girl and I got my wish this time." April was still smiling happily. "Let them eat peanut butter and jelly at home this one time!"

"Speaking of the daddies," Bethany said, "Daniel wants me to get the whole story about the police visit at your house, Mom."

"How did he know about that?"

"He listens faithfully to the police scanner. They mentioned an intruder at your address, and later said it was a false alarm, but we haven't heard any of the juicy details yet."

Both daughters stared expectantly at Julia.

"The juicy details, hmm?" She proceeded to tell the events of that fateful afternoon, leaving out the fact that she'd taken a distinct and unreasonable dislike for Mr. Ben Wilson.

"Is he that gardener guy Cristy thinks is so fabulous?" April sounded slightly sneering. "She manages to collect some of the weirdest characters, I swear. I always say, she's so *different* from us—are you sure she's not adopted, Mom?"

"Of course I'm sure," Julia said with a frown.

"Wilson's not so bad," Bethany said. "Once Cristy took me to see the guy's house and gardens. It's like a paradise over there. He has about two acres, and every inch of it is landscaped like—oh, like a wealthy estate. It's amazing."

"I don't know anything about the man." Julia took a healthy swig of her frosted margarita. "He did deposit some kind of a sundial in my backyard, however. God knows what else they're planning."

"Great. A sundial."

"A sundial?" April shook her head. "Now what's that got to do with anything? Isn't that just typical of Cristy!?"

"Cristy probably has a stage plan all drawn up," Bethany said wisely. "Better be prepared for anything, Mom."

"No doubt the bridesmaids will be wearing Druid costumes," added her sister.

"And instead of a priest she'll have some guru from a local tree farm."

"Now you're being sarcastic, girls," Julia said firmly. "And it's not necessary. Cristy's wedding day will be every bit as nice as yours were."

She took another sip of her margarita and wished she'd ordered a double, after all. She had plenty of doubts herself, though she wouldn't voice them to April and Bethany.

Just for instance: How were they ever going to turn that plain old green lawn backyard into a "garden?"

How would they manage to deal with the vagaries of weather; September, by definition, could be Indian summer hot or prematurely cold. And what if it rained?

And above all, how was Julia going to deal with that man—that great big unavoidable man Ben Wilson from down the street?

The intruder in the dark brown raincoat had recently been pacing the back of the Maxwell property, and was now standing across the street from the Maxwell home, watching as Julia Maxwell returned home.

The person walked on.

Four

A light spring rain was drifting down when Julia decided to step out her back door later that day. Gunmetal skies made the afternoon dark, and shadows from Jay's border bushes seemed deeper than usual.

She walked briskly across her yard, hearing the scrunch of wet grass beneath her feet. Inclement though the day was, Julia felt the need to survey her property. She'd been feeling somehow as though she'd lost all control lately, essentially in regard to this wedding date that was racing along toward her at breakneck speed.

And besides—she scanned the yard with a critical eye, making an instant inventory—there were absolutely no flowers.

She'd known that, and it had been fine all these years. Jay had loved floral gardens but with his newspaper career, he'd had little time to devote, so they'd lived with the plainest of yards possible. Julia always told him they weren't outdoor people, and they certainly didn't want the bother of messing around with soil, fertilizer, and weeds. That only sounded like work—and who needed extra work?

Her gaze took in the property lines, because their neighbors' houses were not terribly far away. When they first moved in, Jay had made sure hedge plantings were installed. That at least gave them a dense screen of privacy that had always been appreciated.

There were trees for shade, the maples and oaks, and a few trees for a feathery-green winter display, like the hemlocks. But the rock wall was falling down in a couple of places and even the tulips or daffodils never came up any more.

Not much of a setting for a so-called garden wedding, she thought with brittle clarity, circling around the new sundial as rain gently pelted her face. It's awfully stark here.

"Penny for your thoughts," said a deep masculine voice from the direction of the south-side garden gate.

"They're not worth a penny, I'm afraid." Julia knew without looking that Ben Wilson had appeared once again on her land. She sighed with resignation. Showing up unexpectedly was getting to be a habit of his. And she was supposed to be polite to him even though there was no escape.

Ben Wilson unlatched the gate and came through it. "I heard you said yes to the garden party."

"Word gets around fast, doesn't it?"

"I hope you're not feeling discouraged, Mrs. Maxwell."

She turned to face him, forcing a smile. He stood there looking as large as a mountain, with sun-browned skin and that thick, sandy hair flying around in the rainy breeze.

"I'm trying to think positively," she said.

He ran a hand through the flyaway hair and circled around her. "I know it seems like a gigantic mission, but we can do it."

"Can we?" She really didn't want to get into a discussion with him, but she recognized her need to talk to someone at this moment. "Cristy uses the word garden, but all I see is a flat lawn—not even a great lawn at that, just one that's full of crabgrass. Oh, and one falling-down stone wall over there in that corner. Period."

"It's a start. If you're wondering about the sundial—"

"Yes, I am."

"Cristy wants to use it as the central focus in a bed of late summer perennials. She has a plan all drawn up. Maybe I should have brought it to show you."

"No, that's all right. It can wait." She felt a stab of annoyance that he should know Cristy's plans before she did.

"The plans are quite extensive, Mrs. Maxwell," he said slowly. "I hope she's going to run them by you before things get under way."

"I hope so, too." Her eyes widened. "What do you mean, extensive?"

"Well—" He swept one large arm in an arc to designate a curved area. "For instance, right here she wants a pathway . . . that'll be either flagstones or bricks, whatever you ladies decide. She wants it flanked with flowers and just wide enough so she can walk down the aisle, so to speak, toward her wedding ceremony."

"Well . . ." Julia could picture that. "That sounds like a tall order, but it would be beautiful."

"Oh, but that's just the beginning. Over here—" He strode with long legs to another section of the yard where a copse of maples stood. "Here she wants a shaded bank garden, with inset rocks and some colorful plants that like the cool shade."

"Oh. A rock garden, then?"

"Yes. She wants several statues in it, too." Here he had the grace to look embarrassed, at least. "A cupid, several large bunnies—and a classic birdbath."

"Good Lord," Julia said. "She wants the Bronx Botanical Gardens and the Museum of Modern Art, no less!"

He grinned and his big face looked years younger. He had a cheery look behind that fuzzy beard, with soft green eyes that glistened in the rain and seemed to hold inner peace and good will.

"She does want a lot," he agreed. "Have we mentioned the seven-tiered fountain and the lily ponds yet?"

Julia's mouth dropped in total shock.

"Just teasing, honestly," Ben Wilson quickly reassured her. "None of it's going to be that terrible, Mrs. Maxwell. You'll see. It can go quite smoothly."

Julia reached over to pull out a scraggly weed left over from last summer. "I'm not a gardener, Mr. Wilson, nor have I ever wanted to be."

"I can tell that."

She looked sharply at him to see if he meant it as an insult. It didn't seem so.

"What I mean is, I'm sure you've been busy with other things," he added hastily. "Your

job, your home, your daughters and grandchildren—"

"You certainly know a lot about me," she
said coldly.

A red flush crept up from beneath his coat
collar. "I've been friends with Cristy quite a
long time. She likes to talk. . . . she's a regu-
lar chatterbox, and she sometimes spills out
all sorts of family information."

And I find that extremely irritating, Julia
thought but didn't say it aloud.

"Well," she said, "thanks for the tour and
the rundown on the prospective plans. It
helps me to be somewhat prepared for what's
coming."

"My pleasure." His voice was husky and
his green eyes stared straight at Julia. She
squirmed with discomfort.

"Well, good evening, Mr. Wilson." She
started toward her door.

"Excuse me, but would you—?" He stopped
mid-sentence.

"What?"

"Oh, I guess not. I was going to ask, would
you like to share a bite of dinner . . . with
me. At a restaurant?"

Julia stiffened in absolute terror. "Thank
you, but no."

"I see."

"In the first place, I don't really do that type of thing yet. I'm not ready for any sort of—dating. You must understand, it's only been a short time since Jay died."

"I do realize that, and I understand." His face softened with empathy. "What I suggested wouldn't be a date, as such, but two friends who have a lot to discuss."

Darn the man! Since when were they friends? She wished she didn't feel quite so attuned to Ben Wilson; she was so terribly aware of him—his large, alarming presence, his deep and soothing voice, his penetrating gaze. Damn, she felt uncomfortable!

"Like it or not," he said with an apologetic little smile, "we seem to be involved in a partnership of sorts. Wedding Central, you might call it."

Julia laughed nervously. "I guess you're right about that. Cristy has you signed on for all the floral decorations, not even asking whether it's an inconvenience for you."

"It's not." The lines of his face were relaxed, yet firm. "I've already told her I'd be delighted to take on this challenge. I'm basically retired from my normal line of work."

"And what was that?"

"I was a landscape architect. I designed

golf courses, industrial park gardens, projects like that."

"Impressive," she murmured.

"Now I write and I teach at the local college, just a few landscaping courses, and mostly I putter in my own gardens at home."

"I see. So you really didn't mind that Cristy burdened you with all her wedding-garden plans?"

"Not one bit. In fact, I'm honored. I consider both Cristy and Jeremy good friends. I really do feel like a partner in this major endeavor."

"That's kind of you," Julia said because she didn't quite know what else to say. "I'm sure Cristy is lucky to have a friend such as you, Mr. Wilson.

"Even so," she said primly, "I must pass on your invitation to dinner. But thank you for the thought." She pulled her coat tightly around her and hurried away from him. She needed to put some distance between them. Why was she so tempted to say "yes" to his outrageous dinner invitation?

"Good night, then, Mrs. Maxwell," he called out amiably.

"Yes. Good night." She rushed inside and closed the sliding glass door with a bang.

I didn't invite him here, she thought defensively. I didn't ask him to barge in and take over, knowing more about the plans of my own daughter than even I do.

She reached out to hold a photo, one of many that stood on her dining room oak sideboard. It was her wedding picture: a black and white portrait of young Jay Maxwell and even younger Julia, his bride. She stared at it though she'd committed it to memory long ago.

Jay, Mister Personality, blond and smiling. Julia, tall for a woman—in fact, almost the same height as Jay, but a contrast to Jay with her classic "Snow White" features—the pale skin and the black, curly hair.

Something way deep inside did a sad flip-over, the familiar stabbing of pain that always came when she acknowledged she no longer had Jay, her husband of more than thirty years.

"I said no to him, Jay," she whispered. "I have no intention of going to dinner with any man, not even a friend of Cristy's."

Her vision was blurred by tears as a painful lump formed in the back of her throat. Jay looked so far away in the picture, so elusive that she couldn't reach out to touch him, even though she touched his profile in the photo.

"I'm simply not ready," she whispered out

loud. Her hushed voice sounded very loud in the huge, silent house where the only other sound was the faint ticking of a grandfather clock in the hall.

"Besides, the man looks like a great big shaggy dog!" The words came bursting out even though she knew perfectly well she was lying. In truth, Ben Wilson really was surprisingly handsome, though he was a different sort of handsome from Jay's clean, sharp looks.

She could just imagine what her longtime friend Liz would say about him—"Ooh, he's a total hunk, Julia," or some such adolescent patter. But Julia was not at all like the multimarried Liz, nor was she even remotely involved in classifying hunks.

"Shaggy dog indeed," she finished, and went in search of a good mystery novel to curl up with.

Five

"The bride-to-be," Julia typed into her computer, "is the daughter of Mrs. Julia Maxwell of Stonewell, Connecticut and the late Jay Maxwell. . . ." She was at the office, should have been re-doing the annual school budget printout, and instead was putting finishing touches on an engagement announcement for *The Stonewell Weekly Star.*

"Someone's doing some personal stuff at work," chanted a slightly singsong voice from the desk adjacent to hers.

"So sue me." Julia went right on typing.

"Not *moi.*" Selena Mulroony arranged her plump, comical face into a look of angelic innocence. Although she was in her mid-fifties, Selena didn't seem to have a wrinkle anywhere; her face was as freckled and unlined as a child's. She had carefully permed brown hair that always looked neat compared to Julia's unruly natural curls.

"Then don't harass me." Julia went on typing. *"A garden wedding at the home of the bride's mother is being planned for September of this year. . . ."*

Julia wrote the society piece with confidence, having been through this routine twice before. More than twice, if you counted her own nuptials years ago. She liked to consider herself a seasoned MOB: mother of the bride.

Selena waited until Julia had finished, then asked, "So, how's it all going so far?"

"You don't really want to know." Julia readied the inkjet printer and ran off a copy of her announcement.

"I do. Tell me."

Julia looked at the older woman, the co-worker who'd quickly become a good friend when Selena was hired at Marble Street Elementary School last year. They worked side by side every day, and had gotten into the habit of sharing almost all their daily news.

"In a nutshell," Julia said, "I'm trying to be extremely cheerful about the whole wedding thing—even though I had to cancel Greece—but who's complaining?"

"Certainly not you, Jules," Selena deadpanned.

Julia sighed. "You have a right to complain, though. You ended up canceling also."

"Yeah, it was a bummer, but we'll survive."

Selena was one of the group who'd been planning to travel with Julia, but now the whole
idea had been shelved until another year.

With a half-smile, Julia went on, "And . . .
I'm trying to be a very good sport about all
the gardening that's about to take place on
my property."

"That shouldn't be a problem." Selena
would say that. She had long been a member
of the mulch-happy populace who loved digging among the earthworms. "Visualize the
floral enchantment, Julia. Any beautification
they do will only enhance the value of your
house, remember."

"True." Julia sighed and stared out the tall
office window. Sunday's rain had disappeared
and now a blustery April day was in full force,
with sharp winds and cold, relentless sunshine.

"So? What's the real problem?"

Julia turned with surprise. "What makes
you think there's a real problem? I just said
I'm making the best of the new situation. Our
trip still will happen next year or the year
after that—"

"I'm not talkin' about the trip to Greece,
sweetie." Selena dropped her voice so the
school principal, in the office adjacent to
theirs, wouldn't overhear. "I can see there's

something else about this wedding that's getting to you."

"Nonsense."

"Don't nonsense me. I know you, Jules, maybe better than anybody else at this point. After all, who sat here and handed you wads of Kleenex tissues week after week, huh?"

Julia smiled. "Have I been *that* bad?"

"You've been a grieving widow. It can get bad, I should know. I've been there myself."

"But Kleenex? Me? Week after week?"

"Don't change the subject. What's eating you? You don't like this Jeremy person?"

"Oh God, no, I love Jeremy. Those two are perfect together. I can see them running a giant nursery together someday—or the C & J Mail Order Antique Rose Catalog or something."

"So? If you love the boy, then what?"

Julia's phone rang and she pounced on it, glad of a diversion. She ended up in a long conversation with a secretary from another school system. When she hung up, Selena was busy with a small red-haired student.

"Mrs. Mulroony, do you have any band-aids in here? We can't find the nurse and I have a cut on my finger!" The little boy held it up with glee. "Do you have the kind with dinosaurs on 'em?"

"No, we have the plain old sterile kind, Ryan."

"Oh, well, okay . . ." After he'd been bandaged and gone on his way, Selena appeared to have forgotten their previous topic momentarily. She was straightening out her supply drawer of first aid materials and muttering about dinosaurs.

"Selena . . ." Julia initiated the conversation this time. "You're right, y'know. There is something bothering me."

"Do I know my friend Jules or WHAT?" Without missing a beat, Selena pulled a home-baked cake out of a desk drawer. "Let's schmooze over coffee and calories. It's time for coffee break anyway, isn't it?"

"He's the darndest man," Julia confessed a few minutes later as they sat in the teacher's lounge, the iced banana cake already cut into slices and the coffee already poured into thick mugs.

"Why do you say that?"

"Because I want to dislike him, and I can't seem to manage it!" Julia made herself laugh at that. "You know I despise gardening, so anything he does will be a pain in the neck to me. But he's such a nice guy—I don't know, it's hard to explain."

"Now wait. Let me reiterate. You want to dislike him," Selena repeated slowly. "Why would you want to dislike someone who's been a good friend to your daughter?"

"Oh, this will sound paranoid, but—sometimes I have the crazy feeling that Cristy's trying to set us up. Matchmaking."

"Oh ho." Selena's plump face broke into a wide smile. "The plot thickens."

"And I want no part of it! Can you imagine, the man actually invited me out to dinner last night?"

"The dastardly demon," Selena said solemnly. "I'm shocked."

"Don't start that. You know what it's like." Quick tears sprang to Julia's eyes. "I still feel *married*, for God's sake. I don't want to have any sort of interest in any other man. . . ."

Selena sat forward. "So wait. So you're saying you DO feel some interest in this guy?"

"No!"

"I don't believe you, Jules. I think you feel a great deal of interest in Mr.—what's his name? Ben?"

"Ben Wilson."

Selena was quiet for several moments, busying herself with cutting another slice of cake.

Her silence began to be annoying, because Julia knew exactly what was going on inside her friend's head.

"You're wrong, Selena. I'm not attracted to him."

Selena smiled and nodded, keeping her silence. It was terribly unnerving.

"You think you're so smart," Julia snapped. "You think I'm like some teenage girl who gets her head turned just because a man is helpful and sort of sweet and amiable. . . ."

"Oh, so he's all of those things? Fascinating."

"He's so big he looks like a bear. Sometimes he even looks unkempt—not dirty at all, but just so casual, the way gardeners do, as though he lived out in some tent."

"I see. A big ole cuddly bear who's charming, cheerful, single, and seems interested in you—hmmm."

"Selena, stop it. You know I have no intention of dating, or even looking at other men. Not for—oh, at least four or five years. If ever."

"Right. This is too soon. It could never work."

"Why are you mimicking me? You remember what they said in those grief workshops—that widows often make mistakes in the first couple of years. We have to be so careful!"

Selena just rolled her eyes upward. "You really must be sure to be very cautious, Julia. Heaven forbid you should find some happiness somewhere."

Julia knew it would be useless to lose her temper. An outburst would only convince Selena, more than ever, that Julia was harboring unwanted romantic feelings for Ben Wilson.

"I'll have another hunk of that banana cake," Julia said gruffly. "Instead of a trip to Greece next year, I'll probably need to do one of those Richard Simmons slimming cruises."

"Not with me, you won't," said Selena, chewing happily as she always did. "I'm satisfied with my extra poundage. But then I'm not the one being pursued by a sweet cuddly ole bear of a man."

Julia ignored her friend totally.

On Friday of that week, in a brown car on Main street, a trembling pair of hands opened the local newspaper to the Society Pages.

"MISS CRISTY MAXWELL BETROTHED," read the headline, and there was a picture, too, of both of them: Miss Cristy Maxwell with a jubilant smile, Mr. Jeremy Crenshaw

standing behind her, a hand resting lightly
on her shoulder.

The shaking hands folded the paper neatly
so that only the engagement notice was face
up.

Six

With the first flush of warm weather came a weekend visit from Cristy and Jeremy, their fists full of major renovation plans. They dragged Julia out back, positive she was every bit as enthusiastic as they were.

"What would you think of a gazebo?" Cristy asked first off, pointing to a nice flat spot near the tall rose hedges Jay had planted. "Like, right here?"

"A gazebo." Julia managed to smile calmly. "Would that be a five-thousand dollar gazebo, or a seven-thousand dollar gazebo?"

"Well, they are gorgeous. And we could have the wedding ceremony in it, or the dancing, especially if it rains or it's a very hot day. But if you think they're too expensive—"

"I'm afraid they are, dear."

"Okay, I tried. No problem, then." Cristy paced around an area as if taking measurements. "On to Plan B. We can pop up a couple of tents in case of rain, of course. And an archway right here ought to be perfect to be married under, and that won't cost a thing. Ben Wilson's offered to make it for free."

Hmmph, nothing's ever for free, Julia thought with her teeth clenched.

"Ben's really good at making things of wood." Cristy's big dark eyes looked excited as she paced across the lawn.

"And Ben said we can get the arch in early," Jeremy said. "So we can grow some vines over it all summer and it'll be flower-covered by September."

Cristy inhaled. "Imagine saying our vows beneath a canopy of morning glories? Or clematis leaves?"

"Or possibly wisteria," added Jeremy. "Sounds so romantic."

"And so horticultural." Julia sighed. The kids had been home only two hours and already she was tired of hearing about vines, perennials, flagstone walks, garden urns, and hollow logs that could be turned into planters. Good grief. She wanted to scream, "Just do whatever you want; I don't care." But as the MOB she had to care.

What's a nice Bronx girl like me doing in a place like this? she thought crazily. *I abhor gardening.*

She'd grown up in the north Bronx and had moved out here to the country only under dire protest. It would be better in Connecticut for the kids, Jay had said, and of course he'd been right. But a city dweller like Julia still longed for subways, the Guggenheim, Bloomies, sidewalk pretzel vendors, and Grand Central Station. Longings for the urban trappings like that never really dissipated.

"Ben suggested we get married right here," Cristy continued, pointing to another perfectly flat spot in the exact center of the rectangular yard. "By the time we're through with this section, Ben says, it'll be a riot of summer and fall flowers."

Ben says, Ben says, Ben says. Irritated, Julia changed the subject.

"Cristy, there are so many details we haven't worked out yet, such as how many guests you envision." Julia was sure she could steer the topic away from gardening. "And are you planning to have your sisters in the wedding party?" This at least was bridal territory with which she was more familiar.

"My sisters . . . ? Oh, sure. They're fuddy old duddies, but what the hell." Cristy smiled devilishly. "And maybe the two little pests can be flower girls."

Julia responded to that with a great grin.

"Wonderful, honey! I can just see the tiny girls in long, flowered dresses, looking like perfect angels. Emily and Danielle will be overjoyed!"

"Yeah, yeah," Cristy muttered. Kids were not her passion at this point in life, and sometimes she pretended that she barely tolerated her two sisters' offspring. "They'll be cute. They can carry baskets of rose petals or some such silliness."

"I can't wait for you to tell them this good news," Julia began, but never got to finish. Through her wooden garden gate someone was arriving—the ever-present intruder once again, Benjamin T. Wilson.

"Knock knock," he called out. "Can I enter here without getting slapped into police handcuffs?"

And then something strange happened. Julia turned and saw the big fellow gilded by the morning sunlight, his body looking vast against the dark of the hemlock trees.

Staring at him, she felt just as if something had collided against her at top speed. She was thrown off balance for half a second, and breathing was difficult, until she could regain her equilibrium.

This is unacceptable, reason screamed at her heart. You can't go to pieces every time a live male comes on the premises. He's a gardener, remember? You don't like him—remember?

"Hi, Ben!" Cristy and Jeremy ran over to hug him and shake his hand. "Thanks for coming over!"

Thanks for letting me know you invited him over, Julia thought, clenching her fists. She had to admit, though, he looked unusually good today and not as though he'd crawled out of a tent.

Instead of the big fuzzy parka, he'd switched to a new, sharp spring jacket in a deep moss green color that gave him a lean, clean appearance, as if he'd stepped from the pages of *GQ*. He'd had a haircut and the clean-cropped neckline made him look younger somehow, though the beard still glistened silky and sandy across his strong jawline.

Light green eyes, Julia thought with disdain; I never did like a man with green eyes. Jay's eyes had been a wonderful coffee-brown, always darkly expressive and full of love.

There, she'd managed to focus her concentration on Jay and it helped, though tears stung her eyelids for an unguarded moment.

"Good morning, Mrs. Maxwell," Ben said as he strode across her lawn. The damn green eyes sparkled with spring sunshine, giving him an angelic look that was ridiculous on a man over six feet two.

"Haven't you and Mom progressed to a first-name basis yet?" Cristy looked shocked. "Hey wake up, guys, this is the nineteen-nineties!"

Ben gave a long, slow smile. "She's right, you know." His eyes never left Julia. "May I call you Julia?"

"Well—" What could she say? "Yes."

His cheerful facial expression didn't change. "And you'll call me Ben?"

This time she merely nodded. *Go away*, she wanted to say; I don't want any strange men hanging out here, where my memories of Jay are strongest.

"Momserina, Ben told you about the bridal path?" Cristy asked.

"Bridal path . . . do you mean the flagstone walk?" She realized she was having trouble concentrating.

"Precisely. We're going to stake that out here today, if that's okay with you," Jeremy said.

"Everything's okay with me," Julia said, "as long as it doesn't go over our budget." She'd already told the kids exactly how much wedding money she could comfortably spare. It was a sizable amount, but wouldn't allow for a redwood gazebo or a ten-piece Philharmonic orchestra.

"Shall we give the walk a graceful curve, Cristy?" Ben Wilson had already taken out a tape measure and a length of garden twine. She supposed he was about to mark out the location of Cristy's garden path. He certainly looked as if he knew what he was doing.

She wandered away from them, studying the far corner of her property as if something quite fascinating were located there. Actually she could remember Jay planting a small flowering crabapple tree right where she was standing. It had died after three years and they never did replace it.

I'm doing all this garden wedding stuff for you, Jay, she thought, her heart twisting with poignant memories. Only because you told each of the girls they could have the wedding of their choice. . . .

When September comes, when it's all over, this Ben person will disappear from my life and things can get back to normal.

"Mom! How do you like the curve of this walkway?"

"Looks fine to me." She saw they'd been carving out the lines of the path already, chopping into sections of established lawn. With the three of them working, the project was moving along quickly.

"Will you come with us to pick out the

flagstones?" Cristy asked. "We're going down to Homestead Discount Depot in a few minutes."

"No," Julia said. "I have tons of work to do inside. And it's your wedding walk, after all, not mine, so—"

"Julia." Ben's soft voice interrupted her. "Please take a ride with us. It would mean a lot to Cristy."

She bristled. Did she have no life of her own any longer? No options? Was her very soul to disappear into the extravagant plans for this Garden of Eden?

"Please, Mom? I need you to help me decide. Do you think Daddy would have chosen an all-white path or a multicolored one?"

And there was Cristy using every trick in the book to involve her mother.

"Ben just offered to take us all for lunch," Cristy added, "and that sounded like fun."

Lunch, now. Not a date but a "working lunch" with the engaged couple as ostensible chaperones.

She must have nodded her head without realizing it, because Cristy plunked a big kiss on her cheek.

"Thanks, Moms. I know you hate the Homestead Discount Depot. We'll have you nominated for sainthood!"

Saint Julia, she thought, turning away from them and all their eager digging and measuring. Maybe we can find a statue to erect in the garden: Saint Julia of the Roses.

She'll probably be every bit as cranky as I am.

Almost a full hour wasted in that Homestead Discount Depot while the three gardeners oohed and aaahed over every flowerpot, garden brick, and flagstone in sight.

I've got to stop being so sour, Julia decided finally, even though she hated every minute in the Homestead place. You can try being pleasant if only for Cristy's sake. After all, none of this garden of paradise stuff was going to kill her.

She stared at a giant wooden windmill and wondered why they hadn't thought to buy that. They could take such amazing wedding pictures sitting on the blades of the windmill. . . .

Stop it! She knew she was going too far now. Pretty soon she'd be sounding like April and Bethany.

Cristy had a load of purchases, and expected Julia to pay for them with a genuine smile. It was all part of the Mother of the

Bride routine. The irony was that instead of dyed high-heel shoes, hoop petticoats, and pearl tiaras, they were investing in bags of organic fertilizer. Different.

Julia handed the checkbook over to Cristy and stood apart for a moment, watching her youngest girl get into line to pay for her purchases.

"You must be very proud of a daughter like that," said a quiet voice from behind her.

"I am," Julia said. "Although I was just thinking about how very—different—Cristy manages to be."

"Different can be okay." Ben Wilson was awfully close. She could actually smell him: a pleasant woodsy scent, as though he'd been using a fireplace, and a faint soapy fragrance that wasn't overpowering but smelled frankly masculine.

Something in her cringed. She didn't want to be close enough to be aware of his aromas. She stretched as if she needed a change of position, and leaned back on a counter full of small garden tools.

"Those two are going to have a good marriage," Ben said with quiet confidence. "They're not afraid of hard work, and they're full of dreams at the same time. A great combination."

"Yes," Julia said, turning again to look at her daughter. "Jay used to call Cristy the little Punkin'head, for some reason. He'd known from his own experience that it was hard to be the youngest."

"That's true."

"And he spoiled her even as he tried to teach her coping and growing-up techniques." Julia smiled. "So she's a unique blend of little-girl vivacity and . . . oh, sophisticated-woman capability. Not at all like the other two sisters—but definitely a Very Important Person."

"What a beautiful analysis," Ben said quietly. She squirmed because she felt he'd somehow moved imperceptibly closer to her once more. "No wonder she's such an individual."

"Yes," Julia said, shifting off away from him.

"Well where shall we have our lunch?" Ben asked Julia.

"I don't care. Whatever you people want to do."

"You must have some sort of preference."

"Well, no, but I do love a salad bar."

He grinned with triumph. "A salad bar it'll be, then. I know just the place."

Oh great, Julia thought, following him out of the store. The way things've been going, he'll probably find some place where they grow their own lettuce and call it Mr. McGregor's Garden.

Seven

Ben was glad he'd thought of The Steak House. The ambiance was great—a cool, dark dining room with magnificent oak ceiling beams, round tables, sturdy captain's chairs. Their homebaked bread was always superb, and he knew Julia would approve of their salad bar.

So why, he wondered as they sat down ready to order lunch, did she look so apprehensive?

"Have you got a headache or something, Mom?" Cristy asked, evidently noticing the same thing.

"No," Julia said. "Not really. I just feel—"

"What, Mom?"

Ben noticed that her face flushed a soft rose color. "Oh, not ready to be seen out in public with a man. Even though we're with you two also. I know it's crazy, but—"

Cristy placed a sympathetic hand on her mother's shoulder. "I think I get it. And don't worry, Ben understands too because he lost his wife about five or six years ago."

"I didn't know that." Ben watched as her dusky blue eyes turned toward him in surprise. "I guess I thought—"

"That I was divorced?"

"Yes, or simply a bachelor." Julia looked down at her place setting as if she were counting utensils. "Did you—do you have any children?"

"No," he said simply.

"This is a great place, Ben," Cristy interjected. "I for one am hungry, and the food here looks infinitely superior to college food."

"Anything is better than college food," Jeremy said.

"Oh yeah? Wait till we're married." Cristy chuckled. "You'll be wishing for college food after you taste some of my cooking!"

"Oh, my God." Jeremy looked terrified.

"You're in for a real treat, Jeremy." Julia spoke with heavy irony. "Wait until she does one of her tuna casseroles for dinner some night."

Ben watched as Julia smiled, and was pleased to see she was beginning to relax somewhat. Maybe she did see this outing as looking like a "date," and obviously she wasn't ready for that. But as the kids chattered on and on about inconsequentials, the lines of her face eased. Finally she was smiling at all their banter.

It was nice, Ben realized, sitting there with the Maxwells and Jeremy. Ben tended to live too quiet a life, not getting out with friends as much as he should. So when the opportunity came along to enjoy human companionship, he appreciated it fully.

They ordered drinks, steaks, and then went up for the salad bar fixings. To his surprise, he found he liked watching everything Julia did. Her hands were slender and deft, and she seemed to take great pleasure in building her salad with fresh, healthful vegetables.

"Avoid the potato salad," she told him in a somewhat automatic tone. "It's full of mayonnaise—cholesterol, you know."

"Thanks for the tip." He followed along behind her, amused and touched by her concern.

"This is the no-fat salad dressing, right here."

Ben said, "Thanks, Mama."

She colored to a bright red shade. "Oh, I'm sorry, I'm being—I don't know, it's been so long since I've been anywhere with a man, I've forgotten how to act."

"You were being rather wifely," he said. "I think it's nice."

"Wifely? Oh God." She sounded as if she were in true anguish. "I shouldn't have come. I knew I should have stayed at home—"

"Julia please, relax." He ventured to place his large hand lightly on her shoulder, but removed it when she stiffened visibly. "I promise you, this is not a date. We're here to talk about the kids' wedding. That's all."

"Right." She took a deep breath and rubbed a forefinger under her eye briefly. "Forgive me. Sometimes I'm right on the edge and I get out of focus."

"I remember living through all that." Ben handed her a clear white handkerchief. "I spent years in active mourning—on the edge—myself. No one ever said it was the least bit easy, losing your life's partner."

Instead of helping, that statement seemed to send her straight past the aforementioned edge. Tears slid quietly down her cheeks, although she made herself look very busy with sliced mushrooms and carrot curls.

Wonderful. He wanted to kick himself.

"I'm sorry," he mumbled.

"No, no." She reached out for a helping of raw cauliflowerets. "I'm fine now. You just . . . somehow you validated my feelings, and that's a kindness."

He sighed. Maybe he hadn't bumbled the whole situation after all. He heaped his salad plate with broccoli bits, used the no-fat dressing she'd recommended, and walked back to the table feeling slightly better about everything.

He stared at Julia with the pale skin and wild black curls.

She was a beautiful woman. She was intelligent, loyal, sensitive, and he'd even seen great flashes of humor in her, when she wasn't trying so hard to be a proper lady in mourning.

Take it easy, old boy, he warned himself. *You haven't admired any woman since Lily.*

You haven't even wanted to date anyone, all these years . . .

So . . . why are you allowing yourself to obsess about Julia Maxwell, who's definitely not in the romance marketplace?

He tossed his salad with the low-cholesterol dressing and grinned over at his pal Cristy.

He had no answers to those questions.

When the salads had been demolished, Julia decided to take charge of the agenda.

"I think it's time to talk about something other than flowers and walkways," she said, pushing away her empty salad plate.

"What's that, Mom?"

"I spoke on the telephone to the rental company, the place where we'll be renting tables, canopies, tablecloths, and so on."

Cristy beamed. "Oh, aren't you an efficient little mother of the bride!"

"These items have to be ordered well in advance of the wedding, but before that we have to figure out just exactly what we'll need."

"A dance floor!" Cristy put in. "Can we rent one?"

"Yes, we can. But we have to come up with a number for the guest list—a ballpark figure—and then make up a complete sketch of our yard. We must figure out all the available space for a garden party—to the inch."

"I see what you mean," Jeremy said. "A plot plan. Where the tables go, where the food will be served from, where the DJ will set up—"

"Exactly."

"Hmmm." Cristy looked thoughtful. "And I thought all I had to do was sail along the garden path looking beautiful!"

"And have violin music playing 'Here Comes The Bride,' " Julia said with a smile. "But there's much more to it. So we'll have to work on a detailed plot plan when we get back home—"

The waiter arrived with four T-bones on sizzle platters, and all conversation came to a halt. Julia, who was not normally crazy about eating red meat, found she actually enjoyed the charcoal flavor of her steak.

Maybe it was because she wasn't eating alone, for a change. There was something to be said for a meal in a restaurant, with pleasant companions. Why had she been so resistant?

She stared for a moment at Ben. He seemed so confident, so thoroughly happy, slicing away at his lunch with a good, sharp steak knife. He truly was an impressive man, once you became accustomed to his large size. A nice, gentle man, too, she thought, and then decided to stop thinking about Ben.

She had a wedding extravaganza to produce. Those three might all be interested in the floral settings, but it was up to Julia to coordinate five million other details.

And she could do it. It would be a difficult task without Jay, but somehow she would make it all happen.

* * *

Back at home, sitting around Julia's dining room table, they did a quick guest list to come up with the ballpark figure. A quick call to Jeremy's mother, Michelle Crenshaw, firmed up the number of their guests to be considered.

Then they plotted out the backyard quite scientifically. They sketched in a dance floor and two long buffet tables, then used strategy in planning their round tables for guests.

"We should have a tent right there," Cristy said, pointing to the dance floor, "and another one over the food, I think. Then we'll be prepared for either hot weather or rain."

"God forbid," Julia said quickly. They didn't need rain. She'd done enough of these weddings to know how inclement weather could spoil even a normal, indoor wedding. It was unthinkable that their party might be under wet skies, with people slopping around in mud puddles in their best clothing.

Hadn't she seen an Alan Alda movie like that recently? *Betsy's Wedding,* wasn't it? Of course those people in the film had laughed and made the best of it but—

She made a mental note to hang a rosary on one of the hemlock trees. It was an old European custom designed to ward off rain for a bride's special day. Though Julia didn't think of herself as superstitious, she knew she'd do it anyway. Why on earth take a chance?

Ben was a lot of help in doing their plot plan, as he had a great knowledge of landscape design and brought a flair for mathematics into the picture as well.

Finally, after several hours, Cristy declared the project completed. "We've got it all," she said proudly.

"Yeah, on paper." Jeremy sounded slightly dismayed.

"Well, paper comes first, then reality." Cristy plunked a kiss on his forehead, then rumpled his hair. "Anybody for a sandwich or anything?"

"No," Julia said. "I'll never be hungry again after that wonderful steak."

"Nor I," Ben said, standing up and stretching his long frame. "I'll be on my way now, let you people do your family-type planning now."

That was considerate of him. Julia gave him ten extra points right there.

But not Cristy. "Hey, whaddaya mean? You're *family*, Ben. Why don't you spend the rest of the day—and evening with us? We could sit around, rent a movie, and make a vat of popcorn?"

"Sounds tempting," Ben said, "but I do have a class to teach Monday. Got to go over my lesson plan, like it or not."

"We'd take his course if we were at his college," Jeremy put in. "As it is we've taken every horticulture class possible up at Storrs."

"Someday we'll have a nursery of our own, you know." Cristy spoke with pride. "We'll find a way to make flowers profitable."

Dreamers, Julia thought, but with great fondness. It was easy to remember all the dreams she and Jay had started out with. They'd both wanted to be novelists in their spare time.

Needless to say, their dreams had drifted away in little puffs as everyday life caught up with them. They'd been glad just to own a home in this crazy world, and to be able the majority of the time to support their three daughters.

Just as with anyone else they'd had their share of financial disasters, so there were times when Julia was grateful to have secretarial skills to bring in extra income.

The creative writing had never happened for either of them, but they wouldn't have done anything differently.

"Hey, Ground Control to Mom." Cristy was calling to her and she'd been lost in her reverie. "Ben was just asking if he can get started this week, during the daytime, on some of the projects."

"Well—" She was surprised she'd tuned everything out like that. "Certainly. I won't be at home, though, Ben. I'll be at work."

"I know. I'll bring over most of my own equipment, but would you allow me in your garden shed, possibly, in case I forget tools?"

"Of course. I'll get you the key." She hurried to the kitchen, opened the cellar door, and lifted a small keyring from a plastic hook. Jay had put that hook there so they'd never lose the important keys.

Julia touched the hook tentatively, a wave of sentiment washing over her. It didn't seem right to give out Jay's keys to someone else. Especially to Ben.

And that made her frown. *Why*, especially to Ben? Was she admitting that she found Ben attractive?

She shook her head and slammed the cellar door. This business of being a widow was confusing. Nobody gives you any real guidelines for this hideous stage of your life. Just when you think you're doing pretty well . . . zap, something else comes along to throw you.

In this case it was a man, oversized and fuzzy like a teddy bear—and who needed *him?* Not me, she thought fiercely.

When Ben left, he noticed a small brown Ford parked down the street, just a few houses from Julia's property. Ordinarily he wouldn't have noticed it at all, but this afternoon something caught his eye. Whoever was in the car was hidden behind a newspaper.

Totally hidden. Even as Ben walked past the car, the newspaper somehow angled around in a way that blocked any view of the car's driver.

Odd, he thought. People were not usually secretive on this road. Why would someone be parked there, and reading—if the person were really reading—right within sight of Julia's house?

He stopped, curious, but he was already quite a distance beyond the car. The minute he stopped walking, the car's motor started up with a roar. The brown car zoomed up the street and was gone.

He'd never had any glimpse at all of the driver.

Very bizarre.

Eight

"I love to come to Grandma's house."

"Me, too. She has lotsa good puzzles and books!"

"An' oatmeal cookies. Squooshy ones."

Danielle and Emily, both three years old, were having this conversation sitting on the rug in Julia's living room. Their moms were visiting in the nearby dining room with Cristy, trying to convince her to have a church wedding. Julia was smiling, knowing they'd never succeed. She was enjoying the comments of her granddaughters.

Squooshy cookies—a compliment to treasure.

"St. Anthony's would be perfect for you," Bethany said in a quiet, reasonable tone of voice. "Father Hayes is great. You don't need to have a mass if you don't want. But just think about it."

"Will you people leave me alone?" Cristy snapped. "My mind is made up. God, nobody told you how to conduct YOUR weddings!"

"We only want to see you do things in good taste—like a normal bride," April said. She had her newborn son at her breast—Tommy Junior, also known as "little Fido."

The girls had continued the tradition of Jay's alphabet names, so Bethany's daughter was Danielle, April's daughter was Emily, and to Julia's horror, the baby'd been blessed with the nickname of "Fido." Julia thought it was a disgrace, but her three daughters seemed to find it hysterical.

"I hate having older sisters! You just want to put down my ideas," Cristy grumbled. "You've been doing it all my life."

Some things never changed. Julia experienced a sudden mental flashback to the tiny Cristy yelling at her older sisters—who were bigger, smarter, more wise to the world. Yet that peanut would always take them on at a moment's notice. She might have been the baby of the family but she wasn't going down without a fight.

"What kind of priest will marry you under the maple trees?" April asked. "Get real!"

"Father Hayes already said he'd be glad to perform the ceremony."

"Oh sure. And what kind of picnic food are you serving—hot dogs and sauerkraut? Come on, girl, be serious."

"Mom." Unexpectedly, Cristy turned to Julia for support, something she seldom did.

"Why don't you two drop it now?" Julia made her voice firm. "All our plans for a garden wedding are under way and no one needs your negative points of view."

"Yeah, and if you don't shut up," Cristy taunted, "I won't invite your little monsters to be my flower girls."

That hit the mark. Both April and Beth lit up like skyrockets. "You want them to be flower girls?" Beth said. "Why didn't you say so before? That's fabulous! They'll steal the whole show."

"I hardly think so," Cristy said coldly, with an admirable dose of self confidence. "This bride's going to look quite amazing too, you know."

"Sure you are," Beth said quickly. "But flower girls—?! Everyone loves to watch them."

"We ought to start thinking about dresses," April put in. "Let's do some preliminary sketches to see what you have in mind, Cristy. . . ."

Julia wandered into the living room. The tide had turned in favor of Cristy, so Julia needn't worry any longer. Jay's little

Punkin'head still knew how to do battle with the big guys and emerge triumphant.

"Did you girls hear the news?" she asked, sitting down with Emily and Danielle. They were struggling with a Big Bird puzzle.

"What news, Grandma?"

"Why don't you go and ask Aunt Cristy? She has some exciting news to tell you."

They tore off, leaving Julia alone with the puzzle. Absently she fitted a few pieces together.

Families were fascinating, she thought, gazing through the archway at all the females—and one tiny boy—of her immediate family. The interaction of so many different personalities had always excited her; family life was like having a three-act play in progress at all times.

She stared at them, fighting off sentimental tears. How wonderful it was when they were all here! The empty nest was highly overrated. She missed them all, missed having them under her roof as it had been just ten short years ago.

She shifted and made herself comfortable sitting there on the floor. She could hear Emily and Danielle whooping with happiness because they'd be flower girls in September.

"I want a yellow dress! I want red flowers!"

"No, I'm having the yellow dress, right, Aunt Cristy?!"

For a few seconds, Julia closed her eyes and felt a flutter of contentment.

"Grandma, Grandma!" Emily raced back and threw her arms around Julia's neck. "Aren't you happy? Aren't you glad we're going to be real flower girls?"

"I sure am, honey." Julia kissed the smooth little cheek. "It sounds like it's going to be a most beautiful wedding."

"When Jane wears her yellow raincoat," read Irmgard Krohler, "she likes to wear her black boots and carry a big, orange umbrella. . . ."

"You're doing great, Irmgard," Julia said warmly. They were seated in Irmgard's spotless, cozy kitchen as they'd been doing every Tuesday night for more than a year. Irmgard Krohler was Julia's first pupil in the Literacy Program.

"Only because you are such a good teacher, Missus Julia." Irmgard smiled shyly; she seldom said anything personal like that, and Julia could see that her round, ruddy face looked even redder all of a sudden.

An immigrant from postwar Germany, Irmgard was older than Julia but for some reason had never learned to read in any language because of the sporadic schooling she'd had. Now that Irmgard was a grandmother, she wanted to be able to read so she could make her grandchildren proud of her.

"You really are coming along very well," Julia said, and meant it. "I know you study constantly all week long."

"Yes. I will not waste your time, Missus Julia, and I will not disgrace myself by failing." There was a tough Germanic pride in the shy, sweet woman that would definitely see her through this whole project.

"So. I will read a more difficult book soon?"

Julia was pleased to hear that. "If you'd like to. We can go to the library together and find something that appeals to you."

"In children's library or adult's library?"

"I think whichever you decide, Irmgard." Julia's training had told her that if a student picked her own reading material she'd do infinitely better.

Irmgard went to her oven and carefully removed a steaming hot cake tin. "Apfelkuchen," she told Julia. "Apple cake with raisins. You would like some?"

"That sounds wonderful. I often wonder how you're such a terrific cook when you haven't been able to read recipes."

Now Irmgard really blushed with pleasure. "I learn from my mother and my ooma—the grandmother, you know. They did not read either, but they cooked for large crowds."

"They were caterers?"

"They ran a biergarten—a restaurant. And I have been cooking all my life, too, in private service in the U.S."

"Astounding. I admire you so much."

Irmgard waved the notion away. "No, no, nothing to admire about me. Working with food, that is what comes natural."

An idea came into Julia's head. "Have you ever worked at a wedding?"

"Ah, of course. Many, many times." Irmgard sensed there was a reason for the question. "Why, Missus Julia? You are having a wedding?"

"Yes, my daughter's, in September. We'll be looking for some women to help us serve the buffet. I wasn't sure where to begin to look."

Irmgard slapped her large hand down on the wooden table. "You look no more, Missus. Irmgard is strong and capable, and will serve gladly. I will find two or three friends, or my cousins, to help also."

Julia hesitated. "Are you certain? I didn't mean to obligate you in any way, Irmgard. . . ."

Irmgard shushed her. "It will be an honor.

Missus Julia, you come here every Tuesday, week after week, just to teach me to read. This is my life's ambition, to learn reading. I am so grateful I can never think how to thank you!"

"Oh, no, but I didn't want thanks—"

"Hush, please. I will make your daughter's wedding the best one ever. And I will not take no for the answer."

Julia nodded and felt an odd sense of comfort, knowing that Irmgard would bring her capable skills on Cristy's wedding day. She explained about the plans for the garden wedding, and Irmgard thought it sounded lovely.

"And I help you with flowers, too, Missus," she said. "Yes. In Germany my father was a nursery man, and I know much about planting."

"Well, that's very nice. . . . Thank you."

Things were falling into place in strange ways. Maybe she'd actually make it through this garden wedding and keep her sanity intact, after all.

Odd thing, though. When she arrived home that night, she thought she saw the same brown car she'd been noticing lately. It was parked across the street from her house—just parked and doing nothing—and then, as on other occasions, it pulled away as soon as she arrived.

It would take off quietly, however, and without any lights until it was way up the street. Julia had never seen the person driving because the car always managed to be in the dark under her neighbor's big old willow tree.

Awfully bizarre. But with all the things Julia had to coordinate this coming summer, a brown phantom car was probably the very least of her worries.

Nine

Wednesday was another dark, rainy day, but apparently a little thing like rain didn't deter Ben Wilson when he had his self-appointed gardening tasks to do.

Julia arrived home from work at four, tired and cranky, only to find Ben on her property once again. She stifled the impulse to let out a scream. Why did he have to show up so damned often? This afternoon she'd really looked forward to putting her feet up and doing nothing—a rarity for her, as she usually had someplace to go or someone to see.

There were two good novels she'd checked out of the public library, a Grisham and a Kellerman. She truly wanted to dive into them to enjoy a quiet evening at home. It had something to do with forgetting the pressures of the wedding just for once; she'd been devoting workdays to the school budget and all spare personal time to the Great Garden Wedding.

Wasn't a woman—even an M.O.B.—entitled to a break now and then?

"Hi, Julia," Ben called when she walked out, most reluctantly, to see what he was doing now in her backyard.

"Hello, Ben." She made an effort to smile. "Haven't you noticed it's raining?"

"Never stops me." He seemed to be fiddling with a large unpainted structure made of wood. "I fashioned this arch for Cristy," he began to say, and then he got so involved in setting up the huge thing that he forgot Julia was there.

"Can I help?" Obviously he did need a hand or two.

"Sure. Could you—if you could grab that end—" Together they yanked and hoisted until the heavy, unwieldy structure was vertical.

"Oh, I see what you're making," Julia said, suddenly enchanted. "That's stunning." It was more than just a wedding arch; it would be a permanent structure to hold vines or climbing roses.

"Thanks." He kept on adjusting, slamming the legs of the thing into Julia's soggy lawn, until he'd secured it firmly.

She inhaled a breath. "The arch will be beautiful."

"Well, it needs painting, of course, and

then we'll work on getting flower vines to cover it somewhat." He looked pleased that she admired his work so much.

The arch was at least twelve feet tall, and was graceful as well as ornamental, incorporating lattice work with sturdy curved beams. Ben had put a lot of thought into it, she realized, and also a great deal of work.

"I can't think of a more beautiful place for the saying of marriage vows." Julia looked up with awe. "Even though Cristy's sisters think she's crazy not to be using St. Anthony's Church."

"Do they really?" He looked truly surprised. "I can't imagine a more natural setting than out of doors, especially for outdoors people like those two."

"Yes." Julia nodded thoughtfully. "I agree with you. Jeremy and Cristy are quite special, almost like the flower children of the sixties. We'll be lucky if she doesn't show up barefoot for her wedding!"

He laughed and pushed away a film of rain from his eyes. "I just wanted to see this erected," he said. "I suppose I am crazy, doing things in the rain. But I tend to get over enthusiastic about something I've just created."

"I don't blame you. If I could create anything as wonderful as this, I'd be impatient to see it also."

He turned to look at her. "You have no hobbies, Julia?"

"You mean like arts and crafts? No, I'm ashamed to say I don't."

"But Cristy says you're involved in a great deal of volunteer work."

That blabbermouth daughter of hers again. "Yes, especially since my husband died. I volunteer sometimes at the library and I'm teaching literacy to a sweet German woman."

"Hey. Julia, that's really admirable."

"It's not the same as creating something." She reached out to touch the exquisite lattice work of the arbor. "Building something like this—that will last for years and years—now that's really contributing."

"Julia," he said firmly, "when your German lady learns to read, that skill will last for her whole lifetime."

She smiled. "Sure. But as for making something tangible—"

"Yes?"

"Oh, it's silly, but I've always had this one ambition."

He seemed to be waiting for her to continue. She didn't.

"What ambition, Julia?"

She laughed shortly. "To write a book. Isn't that crazy? Jay often challenged me to try it, and when he'd talk about it, I could sometimes visualize the end product."

Ben nodded. "You need to visualize the end product, to see the book on a shelf with *your* name on it. That's the only way we ever accomplish any of our life goals."

She smiled. "Even in gardening?"

"Absolutely in gardening. Do you honestly think any of us gardening types enjoy chopping away at earth when it's full of stones and clay? No, we have to picture that finished garden, sparkling under the sunshine with floral shapes, colors, and fragrances."

"So poetic," she said in a bright voice. "Well, you certainly have a good imagination if you visualize sunshine on a dark, wet day like this!"

He grinned. "They call me Mister I. Imagination at the college."

She laughed, and knew she was about to do something utterly stupid. And she didn't know how to stop herself. She spoke before she could retract the words.

"Would you like to come in from the rain, Ben? I could at least offer you a cup of hot coffee."

He watched her face for a full minute be-

fore answering. "I would like that," he finally
admitted.

Stupid? She was utterly moronic. But now
she was committed, and there was no way out.
She led the way inside.

"This is the apfelkuchen that my pupil
made." Julia sliced deftly into the cake Irmgard had insisted she take home.

"It looks incredible. So . . . tell me more
about this book you're going to write."

She felt a warmth in her cheeks. "I've
started half a dozen times but never completed anything. Evidently it's nothing but a
whim, or else I'd have done it years ago."

"Maybe not. Some people are late bloo-
mers." Seated at the kitchen table, he rested
his chin on his hands. "Some writers never
get going until they feel old enough to have
something worthwhile to say."

She stared at him. "You sound so knowl-
edgeable. Do you actually know any writers?"

"I do." He grinned boyishly. "You're lookin'
at one."

Stunned, Julia sat down in a kitchen chair.
"You—you're a writer?"

His hands went up as if in protest. "I've
done a number of gardening books."

"What do you mean you've *done* them? Are they published?"

He nodded. He was modest, she realized, which was very becoming in a big man who obviously had many enormous accomplishments.

"I'd love to see some of your books. Are they in bookstores now?"

"Sure, and in libraries. But I'll lend you a few copies if you'd like."

She was truly astounded. "How many are there?"

"Eight," he said simply.

Eight published books. And this was the fellow Bethany had labeled "that weird gardener guy." Why, none of them had had any idea! Or maybe Cristy knew, as she'd been over there to Ben's house often enough. She evidently knew all about the man but just never shared all the knowledge.

And why would she? Julia could recall herself complaining, especially in that first year after Jay died: "Why can't you stay home once in a while, Cristy? Why must you run down to that stranger's garden all the time . . . ?"

"He's not a stranger, he's my friend, and he's helping me through a shitty time," Cristy answered. "As for you, Mom, you're so full of grief you hardly pay attention to my pain."

"That's not at all true."

"It is true. You and April and Beth all stick together. He was my Dad too and I miss him like hell, and if I can get a few minutes of happiness by puttering in Ben Wilson's gardens then I plan to go for it . . ."

Remembering now, as she sat in her kitchen slicing apfelkuchen for Ben Wilson, Julia felt a wave of regret. But at the time she simply hadn't understood. She was seeing now that this was a good man, full of kindness and good will.

"I think I owe you an apology," she blurted out.

"For what?" He looked truly puzzled. "For getting the police after me? That was fun, if you must know the truth."

"Not that." She transferred a piece of cake to his plate. "I disliked you for a long time, and I'm quite ashamed of it."

He laughed it off. "No apologies needed. I'm aware I don't make a great impression. I look like an untidy old polar bear in rumpled up gardening clothes, most of the time." His grin made his face wider. "A widower like me doesn't even bother to iron his clothes most of the time."

"No, it wasn't about clothes or appearance.

I used to resent the time Cristy spent with you."

"Oh," he said softly. "Well, that's natural."

"Cristy always said you helped her a lot when her father died," Julia said. "She used to tell me I was no help at all."

"She was merely full of rage and pain." His eyes seemed compassionate. "You were there for her but she just . . . maybe she needed someone like me as a father substitute."

"I think so." Her voice was barely a whisper. "Anyway I did resent you because she liked you so much, and I was so lonely—"

"You don't have to explain, Julia." His green eyes were alight with rays of color from her Tiffany lamp. "Unless you want to . . . if it helps you to talk about that period of time."

She considered that. "No, I'll let it go for now. There are so many things more important right now with this crazy wedding coming up."

"Yes." He sipped at his coffee as if he savored the warmth. "I hope you know I'm willing to do anything to help out."

"That's kind of you." She couldn't think of what else to say. Her simple offer of coffee and cake had turned into so much more: confession time, apology time, even secret ambi-

tions revealed. Julia was extremely aware of
the man sitting there in her kitchen, aware
of him as a very large and very male entity.

She hadn't wanted this. She'd never intended to be anywhere close to any man for
many, many years. Loyalty to Jay, she strongly
felt, meant a strict period of not dating, not
even *thinking* of what men might be out there.

"What I'm trying to say," Ben went on, "is
I'd like to be considered a friend. Your friend,
Julia, not just Cristy's."

"I understand." She didn't, however, understand why she was having such a strong
reaction to his presence. She had trouble
keeping her gaze from him. She wanted to
stare at his eyes, so friendly and flecked with
shards of color, just as she wanted to watch
the way his sandy hair popped all around his
head now that his hat was off. And his face—
he didn't look at all like a polar bear, she
thought crazily. He looked more like one of
those big, capable mountain men in some romantic movie.

God, she was losing her marbles. All of
them.

She couldn't have said, afterwards, just how
she managed to get rid of him. She knew she

was "all shook up," as they used to say back in the fifties. She wanted the man out of her house, and somehow she accomplished it. Politely.

She couldn't as easily get him out of her mind, however.

After he'd gone off, thanking her for the coffee and cake, she leaned against the front door in gratitude, wondering why she was actually trembling.

She'd taken a few workshops on grieving and healing. The consensus of opinion had been that most widows miss love and intimacy most of all. The workshop leader stressed that widows could make many big mistakes if they allowed their loneliness to overcome their good, common sense. It annoyed her at the time, but of course there was much truth to it; she'd come to realize that through many long, dark, solitary nights.

Well yes, of course, but that didn't mean a woman of Julia's age should begin to weave fantasies around the first man to show up on the scene! Unthinkable. Unacceptable.

And yet it was beginning to happen. The last couple of nights, when she thought she was dreaming about Jay, she'd suddenly turned in her bed, half-awake, and realized that the man in the dream was bigger and fuzzier. Quieter and outdoorsy.

Not her husband. A large stranger with a beard. Someone with whom she had nothing in common . . .

Now, standing against the door, she realized she had to do something to counteract these alarming symptoms. Oh Julia, get a grip, she thought. Get a life!

That's when she decided to call her dearest friend Liz.

Ten

It took a while to get through to Athens; the overseas operator's English was not in top form.

"Yes, Greece," Julia kept saying. "Athens, you know, the big city in Greece. And the number again is—"

She waited, tapping her foot, while overseas lines tried repeatedly to make the right connection. If she'd calculated right, Liz would be at home right now. Liz's new husband was stationed there as some sort of army consultant, and Liz—Julia's longtime friend from college days—was, according to her many letters, simply enjoying the sunshine, sights, and shopping of ancient Greece.

"Hi, Liz?" Finally a voice had answered at the other end of the world. "Is that you?"

"Julia?" The throaty voice sounded delighted. "Julia, what are you doing, calling me? You're usually such a cheapskate!"

"I know, but I missed you today."

"Well hon, believe it or not, I was thinking about you too. I've been thinking that when you get here, we can take one whole day just for ourselves, if you can get rid of all those other people—"

"That's why I'm calling, Liz." Julia knew her voice sounded leaden. "We had to cancel our trip. Or postpone it, anyway."

"What? You're not coming this summer?"

"No. But the news isn't all bad. The reason I can't afford it this year is a happy one. Cristy is getting married in September to Jeremy. . . ."

"Oh, super-shit!" Obviously Liz was not a happy camper. "I was looking forward to seeing you. Your girls are so selfish, Julia, to expect you to drop everything in your life for them."

Julia bristled for a moment, as would any mother when her chicks are criticized. Then she excused Liz by remembering that Liz had never had kids and couldn't possibly understand.

"Cristy didn't expect it," she said, "I decided. I'm happy for Cristy and Jeremy. I want to give them a nice wedding, and they've opted to do it right here in our backyard."

"What? That sounds stupid. I'm not coming." Liz was only half-joking, Julia knew. She

probably wouldn't have planned to come even
if Cristy had hired the Trump Plaza.

"Let's not waste time moaning and groan-
ing," Julia said. "Tell me what's happening
in my wonderful Greece."

"Not a hell of a lot." Now Liz's voice
sounded leaden. "Tell you the truth, my marriage is literally falling apart here in the sunshine."

Julia was stunned. "You're kidding."

"Wish I were. This isn't working out for a
million reasons, Julia. Steve is probably a very
sweet guy, but I don't know how much longer
I can hold on. I think I was just waiting till
summer to see you, and then—"

"But you've only been married a year!"

"A year too long, apparently. Listen, I won't
discuss it right now, because it'd take too
long." Julia heard Liz take a deep intake of
breath. "I'm coming to Connecticut. I just
made up my mind. Make up a bed for me
and put on the coffeepot . . . or do you still
have that lovely bottle of Scotch?"

"You're coming *here?*" Julia knew a moment of total panic; she had so much to do
as it was: the wedding, the gardens, her
job. . . . "That would be great to see you,
Liz, but when? And for how long?"

"I'm not moving in with you forever, if that's what's scaring you."

"That wouldn't scare me. I'd love your company. We'd live here just like those Golden Girls on television."

"Sorry, I'm not ready to be some aging Golden Girl yet, Julesey. But I'm coming soon and I'll only stay a week or so. How would that be?"

A week or so with Liz could conceivably extend to months. Easily.

"Yes, great. As long as you realize I'm running around like a nut lining things up for Cristy's wedding."

"No problem. I'll help if I can. Otherwise I'll just pot around in your gardens and make myself useful that way."

A warning bell should have rung for Julia right then, but somehow she was too distracted to hear it. Fix up the guest room, she was thinking, and see if you can get a few days vacation time from work; Doubtful, during budget changes and preparation, but give it a try—

"I can't wait to see you, Liz. I'm sad about your marriage, but maybe we can talk it out and find some solution."

"You were always good at that," Liz admitted. "You've always been my Ann Landers."

"I'm glad. Well, let me know when your plane's arriving and I'll pick you up. Which airport?"

"Absolutely not! I'll take a limo and surprise you."

There was no arguing Liz out of that plan. Finally the two longtime friends said goodbye and rang off, though Julia felt more confused than ever.

Where were those two library books? She needed them now more than ever. There was nothing like escapist reading in times of crisis.

It was past ten that night when Ben and his beagle, Ivan the Terrible, were out walking in the dark. A spring fog was settling in after the rain. Curls of mist steamed up from the wet streets, evaporating in the occasional light of streetlamps.

Ben and Ivan loved their late-night walks. Their neighborhood was a quiet one, relatively safe, and Ben liked the anonymity of walking in darkness. He wasn't a peeper, not even remotely, but he enjoyed seeing lights framing the windows of each home, knowing that families lived there in what he hoped was harmony.

Somehow it made the solitude of his own life more bearable.

"What do you say, Ivan? Shall we walk one more block?"

There was an appreciable "woof" that had to mean yes. Ben continued on, knowing he wanted to pass Julia's house in any case. Her house was pretty much in darkness except for one light that might have been her living room. He guessed she was sitting there reading. Any woman who aspired to be a writer must also be an avid reader.

The thought of Julia sent his heartbeat soaring. Not that so very much had transpired today, but—there had been a few breakthroughs. She'd confessed her original antipathy toward him, for one thing, and admitting there was a problem was always a good beginning. She was obviously trying to overcome it now as she learned he was a perfectly respectable human being. Sounded like a major step.

Careful, man, he thought. This particular widow is not ready for any sort of new relationship. It's much too soon for her. You remember how it was after Lily. You simply can't rush the woman. It won't happen.

Those were the caveats of his brain. What his heart was telling him was another whole story. He thought of her standing there in the rain this afternoon, curly wet hair plastered to her face, that reluctant smile when she first greeted him, then that honest admiration when she looked up at the wedding arbor. . . .

His heart lurched and once again he told himself, *You can't do it, even if she should be attracted to you. No way.*

Ivan was letting out a low growling sound, his body poised and pointed toward Julia's house as if sensing something threatening.

"What's the matter, Ivan?" Ben asked, smiling with amusement. "Did you spot a big, bad raccoon?"

Ivan tensed even more stiffly. If this was a raccoon, Ivan was overreacting. Ben hadn't seen the mutt become so disturbed in a long while.

The fog was thick already along this part of Camelot Road, and the house mostly obscured, but suddenly Ben got a glimpse of something moving along the front borderline of Julia's property. Something tall, more like a person than an animal . . .

Whatever it was seemed to be dressed in black, because nothing discernible showed. It was more of an impression that a figure was loping along, attempting to avoid the growling dog and the man standing beside him.

"Hey, who is that?" Ben called out. "Who's walking there?"

Nothing answered except the sighing of the north wind. Ben was almost tempted to let Ivan go, but he had no idea what might happen if the beagle encountered someone truly unfriendly. The dog was straining at the leash as it was, still growling with a vengeance and acting ready to attack.

The mystery person disappeared totally, whether behind a bush or tree, Ben couldn't tell. He wasn't about to chase after a phantom at any rate. He did, however, swing decisively along Julia's driveway and straight to her front door.

She answered on the second ring. "Ben?" She looked astonished. "It's after ten—what's wrong? Is it Cristy?"

"No, no," he assured her. "But it might be important . . . Julia, can I speak to you for just a moment?"

"Well . . ." She was reluctant, no doubt because she wore some sort of lounging pajamas. And sure enough, her reading glasses were on and a fat, plastic-covered book, like the ones from the library, was in her hand.

"Sorry about the intrusion, but we were out walking." He spoke after she'd opened the door and he stepped inside. "Ivan and I do that often—this, incidentally, is Ivan the Terrible."

"Hello, Ivan," she said with uncertainty. "But what—?"

"I thought I saw someone sneaking down the side of your property, Julia, and whoever it was didn't answer when I called out to him. I just thought you'd want to know."

"My God." She paled slightly. "We've never had a problem in all the years we've lived here. Do you think it was—a burglar, or what?"

"I don't know." He stamped his feet on a thick rubber mat she had in her front hallway. "Even the dog was growling, so I know I wasn't imagining it. Is your house all secure?"

"Yes," she said. "I have one of those alarm systems. I'd have known if the—the person tried to break in. Jay insisted on getting the alarm system a few years ago, when he had to do some traveling for business."

"That's good." Ben found himself looking around, memorizing every inch of her living room. "Maybe it was harmless, but—but we did see something."

"I believe you." Julia seemed at a loss. "Should I call the police, do you think?"

He grinned, remembering the two cops coming at him with their weapons pointed.

"Not yet. How about if I take a look out back?" She nodded and found a flashlight for him.

They went out together, after Julia wrapped herself quickly in a raincoat and scarf. Ivan went between them, sniffing along suspiciously at everything.

The yard was quite a different world after dark, especially on a moonless, fog-shrouded night. While Ivan growled with disapproval, Ben and Julia made a quick search of the area.

"I don't see any footprints in the mud," Ben said. "Maybe he didn't even come back here."

"The shed looks fine," Julia said as they beamed the spotlight that way. "I had the door locked. It looks the same as it was."

"So maybe there was no one back here at all," Ben started to say and then stopped. The beam of the flashlight landed on the tall, unpainted wedding arbor he'd installed only today.

Someone had smashed it.

"My God," Ben said quietly.

Shocked, speechless, Julia put out her hand to touch the lattice work as if to convince herself it really had been damaged. It definitely was broken, and a splinter of wood speared into her hand, causing her to wince.

"Now you're hurt," Ben said, grabbing her hand.

"It's just a splinter. . . . Ben, who could have done this?"

He could only shake his head, which she could hardly discern in the foggy darkness. He muttered at last, "Someone who doesn't want to see Cristy and Jeremy get married."

"But that's crazy," she whispered. "There's no one like that."

He beamed the flashlight at the arbor for a closer inspection. The damage wasn't extensive, but someone had picked up a large rock and thrown it through the lattice, causing one large hole and a gaping mess that clearly spoke of malevolence.

"Do the kids have any enemies?" he asked gently. "Or do you?"

"Of course not. Nothing even remotely like this has ever happened before."

"I'm at a loss," Ben said. "I wish now I'd pursued the bastard, and maybe caught him with the help of the dog. But I'm not a cop . . ."

"You couldn't go tearing after someone. What if he had a gun?" She shuddered at the thought of such violence in her neighborhood.

"It might just have been a kid," Ben mused. "Someone looking for a prank."

She decided he was saying that mostly to alleviate her fears. He probably thought she was close to tears, though she considered herself to be basically a tough little lady.

"This is so vicious," she said. With the flashlight beam not far from her face, he must have seen her hair blowing in the wet wind. There was definite precipitation, and she knew her face was streaked by either rain or tears.

Then when she let out a small noise of frustration, they both knew she was crying.

"I know deliberate violence is hard to accept," he said. Before she could protest, his arms were around her.

"Someone sneaking around here . . . it makes me feel so—so violated," she blurted out. She pressed her face against his jacket, burying herself in the huge expanse of his chest. Ivan the Terrible gave a slight woof of complaint; evidently he didn't approve of seeing his master with a crying woman in his arms.

"There, there," Ben said soothingly. "I can fix the wedding arch, you know. It won't be hard at all."

She went on clinging to him, and she felt him tighten his grip around her shoulders.

There was something very comforting about a man this size, with arms as big as the whole state of Texas.

They stood there for an undetermined time, clinging tightly, two lonely persons temporarily united in the fog and the soft spring rain.

Eleven

Just when Julia decided she would pull out of Ben's arms, she did something totally the opposite. She reached up—as though she couldn't help herself—to touch his face. She'd never felt a beard before and had always thought they'd be extremely unpleasant.

"But it's so soft," she whispered, tracing her hand along his jawline with great fascination. "I guess I expected it to be scratchy."

She told herself she should be more disciplined than this. But there was something so classical, so frankly Grecian, about a beard. For a woman who'd been studying Greek art and architecture, the beard represented Socrates, Plato, Aristotle, Pericles—as well as Apollo, the sun god.

For his part, Ben stood very tall, unblinking, and completely still, as though he couldn't believe what she was doing. He didn't make a move toward her, nor did he relinquish the hold he still had after the friendly, comforting hug they'd just shared.

Temporary insanity, Julia thought, deciding that was the only definition for her present condition. She didn't want to leave the circle of his arms and she wouldn't stop touching his face. She found stroking the beard to be almost an erotic experience; even worse, she wasn't ashamed of herself for thinking that way.

"What kind of a nut am I?" she whispered aloud. "My daughter's wedding arch is in shambles, and I need to report the damage to the police department. . . ." She dismissed that. All she cared about was the warmth of Ben's nearness, the wonderful sensation of touching his face, and watching the twitch of a suppressed smile at the corners of his mouth.

"You're too tall to kiss," she said.

She managed somehow to stretch way up to brush her lips along one side of his mouth. If he was surprised, he didn't show it. She felt one of his hands in her hair, a gentle but firm gesture of possessiveness, and felt herself being slowly propelled closer toward him, into Ben's big, fuzzy space.

It was intoxicating to smell his clean hair, and that citrus-scented aftershave he used.

His skin felt cool against her forehead, but his mouth looked warm and inviting. Revelling in the madness of the moment, Julia pressed even closer until their mouths joined.

Up to now almost all the advancing had been done by her. But suddenly, with their mouths locked in a deliberate kiss, Ben's tongue became gently insistent, as if to test her intentions.

Will you truly kiss me, she thought he was asking silently, *or will you run away?*

She felt challenged. She responded to that challenge and met his tongue with hers boldly, as though sensuality were an inbred part of her DNA. She wasn't going to back away because—well, she had no idea why any of this was happening, but it felt so needed and so *normal,* after a very long deprivation. . . .

The kiss went on and on, while curls of fog closed in around them and a sweetness flowed all through Julia. The dog, Ivan, sniffed with alarm at their feet, barking in protest and trying to get in between them. Finally it was the antics of the canine that caused both of them to laugh—and the tender, challenging moment was shattered.

They pulled away with reluctance, their

laughter silenced, the specter of that white-hot kiss hovering between them.

"I shouldn't have done that," Julia said after a long interval in which nothing but the dripping of the trees could be heard. "But I won't apologize, either. I was grateful for your sympathy and help—"

"You needn't explain." His voice was low, almost sounding amused. "Now I know you're a woman of impulse."

Her eyes widened. A woman of impulse—was she?

"I doubt it. But totally aside from that—" She cleared her throat, trying for efficient and brisk. "I'd better report the vandalism to the police right now."

"Good idea," Ben said. In a shaft of pale light from the house she saw the golden gleam of his beard and had to fight the urge to touch it once again.

But—a woman of impulse? That hardly seemed to define her.

"Let's go inside then," she muttered, confused, "and I'll make that phone call. I'll put on a pot of coffee, too."

"Can I bring Ivan inside, too?"

"Oh, yes, sure. He seems like a civilized dog."

"He is." They started toward the house and

Ben gave a rueful laugh. "He doesn't do a thing for my love life, though."

"I noticed."

When the police had left, Ben slipped back into his jacket. It was past eleven, the rain had started up in full force, pattering against her windows. Julia was again herself—rational and calm.

"It'll be no problem to fix the arch," he told her. "But you might continue to think about any enemies, as the police officers suggested."

She shook her head. "I can't imagine any."

"I know, but maybe Cristy or Jeremy will think of someone. At any rate, you ought to let the kids know about the vandalism tonight."

"I will." Standing in her living room, she was extremely aware of Ben—the sheer bulk of his long bones and muscled torso beneath that jacket. She felt, to put it mildly, awkward. Was this what she'd heard called "the morning after" syndrome? Not that she'd done anything remotely like "morning after" activity—but still, a kiss was an intimate communication, one not easily dismissed from her memory.

And what about *his* memory? Oh, God.

"Goodnight, Ben, and thanks again," she said, trying to usher him toward the front door. "And good night to you, Ivan. It was lovely to meet you—"

Ben stopped her with a gentle hand on her shoulder. "You can't pretend it didn't happen, Julia," he said in a low voice.

"Look, let's not make more out of this than there was." She smiled brightly. "It was quite nice, of course, but . . ."

He shushed her by putting a finger on her lips. His touch made electrical shivers run hot and cold along her spine.

"But it did happen," Ben said, "and maybe, if you give it some thought, it tells you something about yourself."

"Don't bet on it," she said quickly, pulling way back out of his reach. She wasn't angry so much as befuddled, and she needed time alone to think things through.

"You don't have to run away from me." The lines of his face were relaxed, totally benign. "I'm harmless."

"Look, I know that. I just—don't know much about myself at this point, okay?"

He spread his large palms upward. "Whatever you say. I've never been a man in a hurry. Gardening teaches one to have infinite patience."

She laughed, a nervous sound that echoed through the arched doorways of her home. "Oh, you and your gardening wisdom! Don't I get enough of that with Cristy and Jeremy?"

"I'm sure you do." He laughed too. His eyes stayed locked on her as though he were memorizing her features. "Well, good night. And make sure your security alarms are all on."

"Yes." She walked him to the door, keeping several feet of safety space between them. That wasn't difficult because Ivan had a knack for pushing himself in the way. "Thanks again."

Ben stopped for a barely perceptible moment, staring down at her with big, innocent eyes that reflected sparkly green in the light of her contemporary lamps.

He's so big he's like a bull in a china shop, she thought inanely; he certainly looks too large for this house. But maybe that was only because this was Jay's house. Her heart bumped and lurched at the thought of Jay.

She expected him to say something more and then he didn't. He opened the front door. A whoosh of sweet, wet breeze came in through the hallway, cooling her face. Then, just as Ben stepped outside under her porch light, he turned once more to look at her.

"You surprised me," he said simply. The

tilt of his head and the laughter in his eyes conveyed he'd been most happily pleased with the surprise.

"G'night, Julia."

Twelve

"Hey! Turn the music down and let me in!" Cristy was yelling and banging on the door of Jeremy's room. Eventually the music dimmed and the door opened.

"My Momserina just called," Cristy said as she charged in. They lived in Collings, a coed dorm with men students on the bottom floor, then women on the second floor, then men again on floor three. This arrangement was done for the safety of the females as well as the hoped-for civilization of the college males. And it worked on both counts, for the most part.

"You look bummed." Jeremy was sprawled out on his lumpy bottom bunk bed, surrounded by textbooks and lecture notes. "What's the matter?"

"I am bummed." Cristy told him about the arch Ben had made, and then the bad news about tonight's trashing of it.

"God," he exclaimed, sitting up with real concern. "Who would go and do that?"

She shook her head and sat down beside him on the bed. She tried, as always, not to notice what a shambles the room was in. It went beyond sloppy—it was fast approaching Unfit for Human Habitation. Finally she couldn't help herself, she had to make a comment.

"I can't understand why the Board of Health hasn't raided you guys yet."

"Oh, very funny."

"Really. Someone needs to inspect these varieties of live green mold. It's purely scientific—look at all these unwashed cups and glasses! Not to mention the laundry."

"That mold is our ecosystem." Jeremy and his roommate, Kevin Deitrich, always had some intellectual excuse for the way they lived.

"I only hope one thing, Jer." She flicked her finger at a big, disgusting lump of dust on the bedframe. "After marriage—there had better be an attitude adjustment in the cleanliness department."

"Dream on." He grinned, incorrigible as always.

Rain was spiking against the windows of Collings Dorm. It would have been a perfect night ordinarily to cuddle up with some Van Morrison on the CD player, and enjoy the chill spring winds from the inside, looking out.

But not tonight; she was too upset.

"Someone's out to ruin our wedding," Cristy said firmly.

"Naaah. You have a prankster in your neighborhood."

"We don't. We never did. Jeremy, it happened right after our engagement photo appeared in the Stonewell Weekly Star."

"Jeez." He scratched his head, looking really cute with dark swirls of hair sticking out all over his head. "What are you saying?"

Cristy punched at a red throw pillow that had seen better days. As a matter of fact, it needed two or three cycles in a washing machine just to be relatively toxin-free again.

"Who would be the one person who's furious that we have a wedding planned?" she asked pointedly. "Who, Jer?" They both knew the answer, but it took Jeremy a while to articulate it.

"Mindy?"

Cristy nodded slowly. "Could be."

"But she's a nutcase," he said.

"I know it."

"If it's her, somebody's got to do something!"

"Tell me about it."

"We don't even know where she went when she dropped out of school. But if she lives anywhere near Stonewell—"

"Which is possible," Cristy said. "Anything is possible."

Kevin popped in just then, a cheerful and chubby senior who'd majored in electrical engineering and was going to be Jeremy's best man. "Hi, Cristy."

They told him their suspicions and he turned a few shades paler. "But Mindy's a loonberger," he said. "What're you going to do about it?"

"Try to find her," Jeremy said grimly.

"Try to stop her," added Cristy.

On Friday night, Julia was startled to open her door and see Jeremy, Kevin, and Cristy on her front steps. It was a surprise visit for the weekend.

"You might have let me know," she complained but with a large smile that let them know she was delighted to see them. She opened the door wider and motioned for them to enter.

"We brought sleeping bags," Jeremy said. "You don't even have to make up any beds for us."

"Don't be ridiculous," Julia said. "Of course you'll all have nice bedrooms to sleep in."

They traipsed into the front room. "We're here to help Ben get some of the garden beds ready," Cristy said. "There'll be a lot of digging and preparing the soil, even though the actual flowers won't be planted until May."

This is it, Julia thought with a stab of panic: The major renovation of the grounds. She'd been so firm all these years about keeping her property plain, practically maintenance free. She'd actually pitied women who were outside all the time, slaves to the weeding and watering that flowers need.

Now it was all reversing, and to her horror, she felt helpless to stop it. The only consolation she could offer herself was that she would put the house up for sale the minute the wedding ended. Let someone else deal with all that gardening work, she thought smugly.

"I'm glad to have you kids here. Are any of you hungry?" She knew exactly what the answer would be, with these three.

"Is the Pope Catholic?" Kevin asked, heading for the kitchen. He'd been there a number of times before, and knew right where to find snacks in Julia's refrigerator. "Your food beats dorm food any time, Mrs. Maxwell. Tonight we escaped from meatloaf parmigiana, yuk."

"Help yourself, Kevin. How about if I fix you some pasta with meat sauce?" Julia thought about a big, leftover hunk of apple cake made by Irmgard; luckily she'd thrown it into the freezer on a diet whim. Now she was glad she still had it.

She was about to follow Kevin into the kitchen when Cristy detained her in the living room.

"Wait a sec, Mom. We've been thinking a lot about the damage to the arch." Cristy hesitated for a moment. "We think we know who might have done it."

Julia felt her knees go weak. "You mean . . . someone who might have done it deliberately?"

"Possibly." Jeremy explained about Mindy Parsons. "There was this girl in our dorm last year who got obsessed with me, almost like a stalker. And honest, I never did anything to encourage her."

"He really didn't," Cristy said. "She's one of those really beautiful, big-haired girls who always get their own way, but she must be a total psycho, because if anyone says no to her—"

"Which I did." Jeremy's high cheekbones

deepened to a dark red shade. "I kept telling her I wasn't interested. I didn't even want to be *friends* after I found out what she was like."

"Mindy Parsons," Cristy explained. "The terror of our dorm. They called her the Brown Widow Spider because she wears brown all the time. Even her car was brown."

"But—a brown car?" Julia gasped. "I've been seeing a brown car hanging around the neighborhood. . . . Would this Mindy person be living around here?"

"Someone said she'd moved down this way, but no one knew where," Jeremy said. "We're gonna try to find her this weekend."

"Oh, God." Julia was stunned. Having an enemy seemed so totally foreign to her. She thought for a while, then said, "You know what? I'd rather believe this mischief was done at random, by an unknown kid. I choose to believe that it'll never happen again."

"I hope you're right," Jeremy said with doubt written all over his face. "We'd like to believe that, too, but we don't."

"You're a dreamer, Moms."

"Me?" Julia laughed. "You two want to go into horticulture, which sounds risky—and you call *me* a dreamer?"

"She's got a point there, Cristy."

"Yep, gotta admit that." The young couple

linked arms. "If we ever find career jobs it'll be a minor miracle, Mom."

Then they all went to find Kevin and to see if there were enough snacks to go around.

Saturday morning dawned bright and crisp, a cold day for late April. "And just perfect for starting gardens," Cristy declared as she and her friends devoured Julia's pancakes at the kitchen table.

"Ben should be here any minute," Jeremy said, peering out the kitchen window as if he expected to see Ben already hammering away at the broken arch.

Julia's heart skipped a tiny beat at the mention of Ben's name. To ignore her reaction, she scooped two more pancakes off the griddle and plunked them down on Kevin's plate.

"Thanks, Mrs. Maxwell." He reached for the maple syrup, the raspberry jelly, and the bowl of canned peaches.

"You're very welcome." She wished she had young people in her home all the time; it seemed so much like old times, when the three girls had still been here and Jay was the head of the household, full of laughter and jokes.

Stop feeling sorry for yourself, Julia.

Half an hour later, everyone was outside in the morning air, even Julia, watching as Ben fixed the broken pieces of latticework on the wedding arch.

"Hey, no lazing about," Ben told the kids with a grin. "You know where the new flower beds will be. Start digging!"

They did. Cristy had carefully planned where her wedding guests would sit, where she would walk "down the aisle," and where the largest collections of flowers should be planted. To that end, she and the boys began work with shovels, hoes, and pitchforks, turning over the earth.

"Another rock," Jeremy said, yanking a large one out of the earth. "These stones must be Connecticut's main crop!"

"We can use them all," Ben said, "when we pile up the retaining wall on the north end."

They seemed to know what they were doing, although Julia didn't understand much of it. She considered going inside to vacuum, do laundry, and dust her furniture—the easy, familiar activities of her life. Something, however, kept her out here. Maybe it was the excitement of these avid gardeners doing what they liked best, or maybe it was merely the pleasure of feeling the sun on her face after a long, miserable winter.

"You look pretty with the wind in your hair," Ben commented unexpectedly. He'd been digging but he looked up just as the fresh breeze caught her wild, dark curls and blew them all out of control.

She shivered and pulled her jacket close around her. It would be best to ignore statements like that. She had decided by now that the kiss the other night—enjoyable as it had been—was merely an aberration from her everyday normal behavior. Therefore, it didn't hold any importance, and she needn't be held accountable for it.

"You're doing a good job with that arch," she said. "It's going to look like new again."

"Hope so." He gave a piece of wood a quick sandpapering before attaching it. She watched as rays of the sun beamed on him, outlining those strong shoulders and arms against the budding green shrubs of April. Julia found herself fascinated by the skillful way he worked, when after all he was so oversized he ought to be clumsy.

"Now if only our prowler doesn't come back," Ben said.

"The kids told you their theory about that Mindy?"

"Yes." He nodded. "It sounds possible—even likely—but we'll hope for the best. Even if it was their Mindy, maybe she got her frustration all out in one shot."

"Sure. Let's hope that's the case." Julia wanted to believe the vandalism problem was history. She had so much else on her mind, she couldn't bear to deal with deliberate destruction.

Little by little she was pulling together the details of the wedding, but it was an enormous job. She doubted if Cristy had any idea of the minutiae involved in the catering, invitations, decorating, serving people, wedding cake, music arrangements, just to name a few items.

"Hello? Hello?" They heard a voice even as they heard the ring of the doorbell at the front door. Cristy ran through the house to answer it. She came back with Irmgard Krohler, Julia's literacy pupil.

"Hello, Missus Julia!" Irmgard was all smiles. She was in work clothes, jeans, and a heavy man's jacket, and her white hair was pulled back neatly. "I came by to surprise you! I wanted to see your land, for this outdoor wedding." Delighted, Julia introduced the German lady all around.

"Hey, glad to meet you at last, Mrs. Krohler," Cristy said heartily. "I've heard so much about you from Mom. She was right when she said you're a really neat lady, and a lot of fun!"

Irmgard looked terribly pleased, and shyly passed around a round tin she'd brought. It turned out to be homemade molasses cookies. The boys pounced on them gratefully, as if they hadn't eaten in a week, and Ben stopped to eat a few also.

"Mom says you might be helping us with the food at the wedding," Cristy went on to Irmgard.

"Yes, that I will, most definitely. And I came today because I want to help with flowers, too—" Irmgard noticed that flowerbed digging was under way even as they spoke, and she marched over to inspect a spot Kevin had been excavating near some big rocks.

"This will be perfect for rock-garden plants, yes?" Irmgard entered into an animated discussion with Ben about perennials and succulents. Julia did a mental shrug. Oh well, some people were into this garden stuff . . . and some were not. She couldn't help it if it bored her to tears.

"Cristy," Julia said, "while you're home, would you like to talk about what you'll be looking for in a wedding dress?"

"Not today, Mom." Cristy had returned to hauling good-sized rocks to make a retaining wall—at least that's what she called it—for one of the flowerbeds. "This is Build the Gardens day."

"Okay, okay. But just remember, if the dress should need to be ordered, this is the time to do it." Julia wandered around, feeling unneeded. Still, the sunshine and soft spring air felt good on her cheeks; she'd been indoors all week, of course, at the office. In the woods behind her property, she could see faint bits of green budding out, always the first official sign of spring for her. She puttered a little bit with the privet hedge Jay had grown on the property line, thinking of Jay as she snipped at ragged pieces.

The morning went quickly. She served sandwiches and coffee out on the patio for the crowd of workers. The crew now included Irmgard, who had rolled up her sleeves to work on a patch of soil that Cristy called "the future daylily mosaic."

In the afternoon they began constructing the bridal path, using the white stone they'd bought that day at Homestead Discount Depot. Irmgard was a great help, using her impressive strength to haul blocks and other supplies by wheelbarrow.

"This woman is a true treasure," Ben declared, grinning. Kevin was crazy about Irmgard also because, being of German descent himself, he enjoyed sharing little bits of the German language with her.

By the time dusk fell, some significant changes had been wrought. "I like what you did with the sundial," Julia said in surprise, coming out after finishing some household chores. The sundial had been placed in a special setting, almost a place of honor, and was gleaming like a piece of classical sculpture in the waning, reddish sun.

"It'll be surrounded by impatiens," Ben told her. "It'll be one of the most beautiful sights at the wedding."

"One among many," Cristy threw in.

"Sundials are great," Jeremy said. "You'll always know the time in Mrs. Maxwell's garden."

"That sounds rather like poetry," Julia said.

"Sounds like an old Beatles song to me!" said Kevin, leaning on a pitchfork.

"I know an appropriate quote that could apply to the sundial." Ben shaded his eyes and kept a steady gaze on Julia. *"What's old collapses, times change, and new life blossoms in the ruins.* That's from Johann von Schiller."

"Pretty," Cristy said. "Very poignant."

Julia stared back at the big man. He's trying to tell me that life goes on, she thought; that Jay is gone and a brand new relationship could possibly bloom if I were to let it.

But she turned quickly away, choosing to deny the underlying message in his quotation. She couldn't handle the idea that anything could ever be with Ben and herself. It was too soon, she'd already determined that. There would be no romance in her life for a very, very long time.

"So who's thinking about dinner?" called out Kevin.

"Nobody but you, Kevster." Jeremy threw a soft clump of earth at his roommate.

"I am," Ben admitted. "All this hard work makes people hungry."

"I've fixed a very large pot roast," Julia said. "It'll be done in about half an hour. You're all invited." She included both Irmgard and Ben in her invitation.

"No, no, I must get back home, Missus," Irmgard said. "My daughter comes to pick me up, but thank you."

"I'll be glad to stay," Ben said. "Pot roast sounds wonderful."

Why am I not surprised? she thought. But Ben staying was fine with her. She loved feeding people, and certainly Ben had earned a good meal here today.

Still, she knew she'd been right about one thing. The man would be a full-time fixture at the Maxwell house for the rest of the summer, if she wasn't careful.

Hmmmph. I told Cristy nothing is ever free, Julia thought, and marched back into the house.

Thirteen

Her pot roast dinner turned out very well, with perfect little red potatoes and finely cut carrot slivers all in a rich, mushroomy brown gravy. Kevin, Jeremy, and Ben went back for seconds and then thirds.

"You're a great cook, Mrs. Maxwell," Kevin kept saying.

"You just love to eat, Kev," Jeremy said, clucking his tongue.

"No, Mrs. Maxwell really is a great cook," Ben said in a voice firm enough to settle all arguments. "This is the best meal I've had in years."

"Thank you," Julia said.

"Tell me, have you started writing that book yet?" he asked, which of course got the kids into an uproar of asking "What book? what about? have you started?"

"No," Julia answered to all of them. "It's just an idea I've had—always—about writing. Something about family life, maybe, and about raising three distinctly different daughters."

"That should be a bestseller, Mom." Cristy's pretty dark eyebrows danced. "Don't forget, the youngest one is the uncontested beauty. And the brains of the family."

"Yeah, and the most humble," Kevin threw in.

Julia said, "I'll have to mention, though, that my youngest daughter put me through some sort of gardening hell."

"It can't be as bad as that," Ben said with surprise. "Or can it?"

Julia avoided looking right at him. She had decided never to think of the kiss. Still, she was having trouble being in the same room with Ben Wilson and not recalling, with terrifying detail, the kiss they'd shared that dark, foggy night. She was intensely aware of the man's large, solid presence and his quiet air of authority with the kids. Jay would have been joking and clowning with this group, but Ben—well, Ben was different. Even though he was a college professor, he was so much quieter than Jay had been.

You must never compare anyone to your late husband. That had been one of the Golden Rules she'd heard expressed at the Grief Workshop. She'd understood it very well at the time.

The rule's theory was obvious, because no two men were alike. But now, presented with a quite special man who was light years away from the partying personality of Jay Maxwell—

No. Such thoughts were too confusing to sort out. She had a sudden longing to clear out the room, be rid of everyone, and have her house all to herself again.

"I'll get the dessert," she said quickly, jumping up. "And then why don't you all think about getting some sleep? It was a very long, very hard-working day."

"You gotta be kidding!" Jeremy said. *"Sleep?"*

"We're going out to a late movie," Cristy said. "We're not tired."

"Young people never get tired," Ben said with a wry smile.

"Wanna come with us?" Kevin invited, looking at both Ben and Julia.

"No, thanks," she said immediately.

"Some other time," Ben said.

Dessert was also a big hit. She'd made an upside-down cake while they were out there gardening, and now she plopped whipped cream on top of the warmed slices. She didn't have any herself. Her stomach was slightly upset for some reason.

At the end of the meal, the young ones

carted all the dishes to the kitchen and made a production out of scraping, washing, and drying everything. They did it quickly because they didn't want to miss a minute of their movie.

"Okay—bye!" Cristy called out as they slipped into their jackets. "See you later, Mom. See you tomorrow, Big Ben."

Big Ben. Julia hadn't known Cristy called him that. There were probably many things she didn't know about her daughter's friendship with this landscape architect and college professor.

Julia and Ben were still sitting in the dining room over second cups of coffee. Suddenly the front door slammed closed and the house became silent.

"We have a lot to thank you for, Ben," she said with sincerity. "You're certainly working hard to whip our yard into shape for that wedding."

"You don't have to thank me. I love doing it." He kept his eyes down on his pale, delicate blue Lenox cup and saucer. The cup, she thought, looked dwarfed in his strong hands.

"It's kind of you, nevertheless." She looked down at her own chinaware, pretending that the pattern was fascinating.

"Julia—"

"Yes?" She looked up at him and was startled by the strong emotion she saw in those bright green eyes.

"I've been thinking about you."

"Why?" She stiffened. "Because I'm a woman of impulse?"

"Now please don't sound so frosty with me, Julia." He grinned pleasantly. "It seems to me that something happened between us the other night."

"Maybe so," she said slowly. "But there won't be a repeat performance."

"You don't really believe that," he said. "I know you don't."

"I know what I feel, Ben. How can I explain this?—I still feel *married*. I simply can't forget Jay that quickly."

He blinked. "No one's asking you to. My God, don't you think I still remember my Lily, every day that goes by?"

"Well, I—" She was flustered. She hadn't expected that.

"But do you recall that saying, the one I quoted out by the sundial? *Times change and new life blossoms in the ruins.*" He reached out to touch her hand, but she pulled it away.

"Look. Your wife has been gone more than five years, hasn't she?" Julia asked, and he nodded in assent. "But my Jay died two years ago. It's too soon for me, period."

He kept his gaze on her. "Nobody ever drew up a timetable, you know. Three years for this, five years for that—"

She stood up. "I'm not even ready for this discussion," she said coldly.

"You were ready for that kiss, though." Her cheeks went instantly warm. "You might want to rethink that self-imposed timetable, Julia."

"No, I don't intend to do that. But thanks for being here today, to help the kids, and— good night now."

He looked amused by her dismissal. "Such denial," he whispered. He rose, and somehow he moved close to her, so she could almost feel the warmth of his breath against her neck. He moved his forefinger very lightly along the side of her cheek, barely touching, yet leaving a trail of blazing hot sensations that seemed to rip all the way down to her toes.

How dare you touch me? she wanted to say, but she didn't. Her eyes closed for a second as she fought against the melting sweetness within her. In that second, Ben leaned over and placed a good-night kiss, as light as a butterfly's wing, on her cheek.

And then he was gone.

* * *

She was in for a sleepless night.

The grandfather clock ticked relentlessly while Julia sat on her ivory sectional couch, thumbing through old photo albums. She stared at pictures of Jay and herself, and allowed silent, unashamed tears to drip down her face.

"If you were here there'd be no question which one was the better man," she said to a picture of Jay—Jay as Father of the Bride—standing beside April at her wedding. He was smiling, an outgoing, confident man, always onstage, managing to say the exact right thing. She loved him. She loved him so very much. . . .

Enough. Her face wet, her eyes swollen, she slapped the photo album shut and placed it back on the shelf under the coffee table. This sort of weeping did no one any good.

Or maybe it did. You had to do your grieving, the workshop leader had explained, before you were ready to move on without making mistakes. She hated that expression, "move on." Where was she moving to? And what were these dire mistakes they assumed every widow was about to plunge into?

She'd just about gotten her face washed

with cold water, thus repairing the damage done by tears, when Cristy, Kevin, and Jeremy came home. They barrelled into the house, noisy and full of life, still talking about the movie they'd enjoyed.

"I love Jim Belushi," Cristy was saying. "Any film he's in is usually great."

"This was, anyway," Jeremy agreed. "Hi, Mrs. Maxwell, we're home. Did you have any prowlers tonight?"

"I hope not," she said. "I really don't think so, or I would have heard something."

The young people had to go out and look, aiming flashlights at everything in the dark backyard. Nothing had been bothered.

"Nope, all's clear," Cristy said when they came back in. "Not even a footprint that shouldn't be there."

"Good." Julia took a relieved breath. "Maybe this Mindy person wasn't the culprit after all."

"Maybe." Jeremy didn't sound convinced. "We started looking for her tonight. We haven't found any sign of her in the area phone books, but maybe she has no telephone."

"Of course she has no telephone listing," Kevin said, sounding impatient. "What is she gonna do, advertise that she's here in Stonewell just to do mischief?"

"We'll keep searching in different ways," Cristy said. "I was thinking about checking with the pharmacies in the area. Mindy's supposed to be on a certain medicine."

"Which she decides to ditch sometimes. That's when she really gets unreasonable." Kevin's voice sounded ominous, Julia thought.

"Let's not even think about her tonight," Julia suggested. "We've had a wonderful Saturday getting things ready for that wedding, and we'll do some more tomorrow before you have to go back to Storrs. It's been really fun having you here."

"I love your friend Irmgard, Momserina." Cristy frowned. "And where's Ben, anyway? I thought he might have stayed to keep you company tonight."

Julia blushed deeply. "No, why would he do that?" She turned away so Cristy couldn't see her face. "We hardly know each other."

"He's a nice man, y'know," Cristy said in a pointed way.

"I'm sure he is."

"So you don't have to push him away with a ten-foot pole!"

Julia turned to glare at her daughter, "You have no business talking to me like that, young lady."

Cristy mumbled, "I'm sorry," but she didn't

really seem sorry at all. She was grinning with mischief.

"Besides, I don't push him away. There's nothing going on, Cristy."

"If you say so." Cristy's face was a study in innocence.

"Look, would you like to go over the guest list and rental plans now?" Julia asked. "We could make cups of cocoa and stay up awhile."

"Nah," Cristy said. "It's way past midnight. I'm going to bed." She kissed her mother. "G'night."

All three of the young people trudged tiredly up the stairs. Only Julia felt wide-eyed and wide awake. She plunked into a living room chair with a library book and put her feet on a hassock.

"You might want to rethink that self-imposed timetable, Julia," she heard Ben saying to her in that calm voice "You were ready for that kiss. . . ."

Okay, yes I was, she thought belligerently. But just because I made one mistake—and that's all it really was, a mistake—does not mean I'll make another.

She made a valiant attempt to lose herself in a long, time-travel novel, a tale about a Scottish Highland lord and a feisty lady from another century. It was a romantic book but it did nothing to help her to sort out her own ragged emotions. The heroine, after all, was willing to forgo everything—even the basic modern conveniences of the twentieth century—because she loved the Scottish clan chief so deeply.

"I'll never love like that again," Julia whispered to herself in the deep silence of the night. "You lose someone and it hurts too much . . . no, I never want to be that vulnerable again."

Times change and new life blossoms in the ruins, she heard again, as though Ben had just finished saying it. Oh nuts. She couldn't even concentrate on the book. Might as well go upstairs.

Still wide awake, she went up to her bedroom. But instead of undressing, she sat down tentatively at the writing desk in the corner of her room. The electric typewriter sat there as it had for many years, covered carefully to keep dust from its keys and inner workings.

She uncovered it, turned it on so that it let forth a quiet hum, slid a piece of rough draft paper into it, and began to type. Maybe someday soon she'd have a word processor like the one at work, but in the meantime . . .

If she was going to be awake half the night,

she might as well experiment—and not with the wedding guest list, but with something she truly wanted to do.

"MY LITTLE WOMEN," she wrote in the center of the page, smiling. Really smiling. "A novel by Julia Ann Maxwell . . ."

Fourteen

"Julia, I heard somewhere you're giving a garden wedding for your Cristy!" Laurette Smith, also known as Mrs. Nosybody, caught up with Julia in the back of church right after Sunday mass. "I can't believe you're serious."

"Hi, Laurette. Yes, we are serious." Julia wasn't crazy about the opinionated Laurette, but had known her for years, ever since they worked in Religious Instruction classes together. "We expect to have it all worked out by September."

"You're brave but foolhardy, believe me." Laurette was fanning her overheated face with the Sunday church bulletin. "Too much stress, dear, doing it that way. You'll end up in a mental hospital!"

"I will not." Julia's annoyance level was beginning to hit the roof. "We don't always have to do everything the easy way, Laurette."

"But Julia! Think of what you're dealing

with. You have to have your home in perfect
order, let's face it, *every* ceiling, every wall,
every square inch of floor. And then the
yard—I can't even BEGIN to imagine how
much gardening you'll have to do this summer, when it's hot and miserable—"

"Don't worry about it," Julia said, moving
along as quickly as she could with the tide of
folks leaving the church. Because of the crowd,
she realized she couldn't get away from
Laurette, so she turned back, smiled and tried
to be pleasant. "We're getting everything under control, really."

"Take my advice and talk Cristy out of it,"
Laurette pushed on. "I've given four weddings now, and they were all h-e-l-l, to put it
mildly." Laurette glanced uneasily at the altar
when she spelled that naughty word. "But we
never tried to do anything as impractical as
an outdoor wedding!"

"That's the difference between us, then."
Julia decided to change the subject as long
as she was unable to escape. "How are your
children all doing? And their spouses?"

"Oh, they're well—" Laurette sputtered, evidently not liking to be diverted. "Julia, it's
positively *heathen*, a wedding not being in a
church! And have you thought of the possibil-

ity of rain? Or a heat wave? Or even a cold wave?"

"Of course we have. Actually, we expect it to be a very lovely event." *And you'll not be invited, you can be sure of that, dear,* she thought angrily.

Just then an avenue of escape opened up through the crowd. Seizing the opportunity, Julia ducked between several people and effected her getaway. Lord, what a pain some people could be! How, she wondered, could a woman possibly view the world with such negative eyes when she had just celebrated a holy mass?

Father Hayes, tall and graying, waved to Julia over the heads of the parishioners. She zoomed toward him.

"Hi, Julia. Good to see you. And please will you tell Cristy not to forget—she and Jeremy must come in for their pre-Cana sessions very soon."

"I'll tell her. Father, I have a question for you. Do you think there's anything heathen about having that wedding in our backyard?"

He laughed, a deep, rolling chuckle. "No, I don't. For a girl like Cristy it's going to be ideal. And God will certainly be present there. He'll be smiling down at that bride being married under the leafy trees planted by her father."

"Why—" Surprised and delighted, Julia fought back a wave of tears. "Thank you," she said. She reached out and clasped his hand. "I'm so grateful to you for saying that—and for agreeing to perform this wedding."

"I wouldn't miss this one for the world," Father Hayes said. "Are you kidding? I've been very lucky."

"Why?"

"The Lord usually sends me to the weddings that have the best eats—and you, Julia, are the finest cook in our parish!"

She found herself hurrying home . . . to be with Cristy and the boys, she told herself, though somewhere deep down she knew Ben would be in her backyard as well. Not that it meant anything, her desire to see him. Maybe she wanted to tell Ben she'd started her novel last night, and it had moved along rather smoothly. Or was there something more?

She pulled the car into Camelot Drive, waving to neighbors as she passed them. It was a bright, beautiful spring morning with soft clouds in a vivid blue sky. People were outside, looking over their property, tossing soft-balls, walking their dogs along the street.

As she pulled up near her house, she cal-culated what she'd serve the Garden Club for their lunch—leftover pot roast? She wasn't sure much was left, after Kevin and Ben's ex-tra helpings.

And then she saw the limousine arrive in her driveway. It was a long, powerful black Lincoln, the kind a movie star might travel in, with darkened windows and, no doubt, an interior bar with TV. She blinked, for a min-ute stymied. Then she grinned.

A Hollywood entrance—of course. Liz was here.

"Hello, everyone!" Liz stepped out the limo legs first, naturally, and they were spec-tacular legs, tanned and sleek in the best silk hose. Liz always looked twenty years younger than Julia, and that seemed even more true than ever, right now.

God, I could hate her, Julia thought, if I didn't like her so much.

The crowd from the backyard was gathering to see who was in the limo. Kevin and Jeremy gaped at Liz with bulging eyes as though they couldn't believe this was a contemporary of poor old Mrs. Maxwell. Cristy was beside herself with excitement, greeting Liz and introducing her to everyone else.

Ben stood quietly to the side, a shovel in his hands, a long smudge of dirt across his upper cheek. Farmer Jones personified, Julia thought with amusement. He certainly *doesn't* make good first impressions; luckily she knew how excellent he could look when he wasn't gardening.

"Ben, Jer, Kev, this is Liz Holworth, my Mom's oldest and dearest friend," Cristy was saying when Julia emerged from her car. She saw Ben offer a soil-covered hand for a shake, and Liz laughingly taking it. In a gorgeous hunter green suit, Liz didn't even look travel-stained or weary. She might have just stepped out of a star's dressing room.

Then Liz spotted Julia. "Oh, honey!" Liz flew across the paved driveway toward her friend. "It's so great to be back in the good old U.S. of A!"

They hugged, then Julia stood back to get a good look. "You're just fabulous, as always, Liz. What did you have done to your hair? It's wonderful."

"The latest Euro-cut, dear." Liz's sharply styled, sleek blond hair was set off by her astounding tan. Her face, always slender, now had a new slimness that accentuated the fine bones. Her sultry gray eyes were made up with such artistry she'd easily outshine every woman in Stonewell.

"Aunt Liz, how long can you stay?" Cristy asked, kissing Liz as the men hurried to help the limo driver with bags of luggage.

"Not sure yet." Liz took Cristy's face in both hands. "Look at you—a bride to be. Is this possible? I'm so thrilled for you, my Cristabelle."

"Oh, not that awful old nickname," Cristy protested, red in the face. "That's as bad as Punkin'head."

"You'll always be my Cristabelle. And this is my Julesey." Liz managed to grab both mother and daughter around the shoulders, one on either side of her. She squeezed them tight in a frenzy of bravado and love, and then burst out weeping.

At the first sign of tears, all the men scattered—fast. Even the limo driver who'd carried a trunk into the house, disappeared from sight for a while.

"What's wrong, Aunt Liz? Mom, why's she crying so hard?"

"I guess she's exhausted and overwhelmed," Julia said tactfully. "Liz, how about coming inside for a nice cup of tea?"

"Make it Scotch on the rocks," Liz said, still sobbing.

"You've got it." Cristy and Julia tried to push their guest toward the house. As it was they were providing a fascinating show for all the neighbors of Camelot Drive.

Finally they got Liz settled in the kitchen, paid off the limo driver, and Julia managed to find the bottle of DeWars White Label. Cristy provided ice cubes in a small glass and Liz did her own splashing. Generous pouring was more like it.

"Forgive me," Liz said after she'd taken one deep swallow. "I never intended to start blubbering like a baby. God."

"Don't worry about it," Julia soothed. "You came here to be coddled, remember? I'm your Ann Landers, remember?"

The men never did return; they could be seen outside, nervously digging with more vim, vigor, and vitality than ever before. A woman crying was one thing that could guarantee to keep males far away every time.

Cristy sat down with a glass of water for herself. "Do you want me to leave you guys alone, Aunt Liz?"

"No, no. I have no secrets from you." Another swallow of Scotch. "You're my dear Cristabelle." Liz was beginning to sound like an Academy Award actress giving the performance of a lifetime.

"I wasn't meant to be married, Julia," she announced with great melodrama, the gray eyes sparkling with tears, the cheeks streaked with mascara and liner. "I'm no good at it. I never should have attempted matrimony again."

Secretly Julia agreed with her, not even knowing the facts of this case. There had been two marriages before this one, both of them extreme disasters. But it didn't seem tactful at the moment to agree with Liz.

"We'll talk it all out, Liz," Julia said soothingly. "Would you like a facecloth? You're starting to look as though you were in a coal mine cave-in."

"Isn't she cute?" Liz turned to face Cristy and managed a weak smile. "Your mother knows how to make me feel better immediately. That's why I've always loved her—oh, God, Julia, what am I going to do? Get another divorce?"

"I don't know." Julia watched as Liz slugged down a swallow of Scotch that would have finished the Scottish chieftain. "Maybe we should—"

But, suddenly fortified by all that 80 proof, Liz lost interest in her matrimonial problems.

"Now . . . who did you say that wonderful man is, Cristy?" She leaped up and sashayed over to the kitchen window, peering out through the lace curtains.

"Which wonderful man?" Cristy grinned devilishly. "The one with the red jacket is the one I'm going to marry in a few months. The other young one is his roommate, Kevin."

Liz gave her a sharp look. "You know I'm talking about the older one, the great big darling one. The country gentleman."

"Now there's a description," Julia said dryly. "And I was thinking Ben would come off looking like Farmer Jones."

"Ben?" Liz was immediately entranced. "Great name, Ben. Look at the muscles on him . . . the buns aren't bad, either. He's not a spring chicken, I'll concede that, but he certainly is well preserved."

"He's a hard worker," Cristy said, looking amused by her Aunt Liz's frankness. "Ben is a genius with landscaping, and he's a college teacher as well as a book author."

"I love it," Liz declared.

"You love it? You're *married*," Julia declared, bristling with a tide of anger that was way out of proportion to Liz's teasing nonsense.

"Oh cool it, Jules, I'm only window shopping." Liz left the window and went back to her glass of Scotch. "A woman who feels abandoned can't help glancing in other directions."

"Abandoned?" Cristy looked horrified. "Steve Holworth abandoned you there in Athens?"

Liz inspected a long red fingernail. "No, not literally, but it's been a case of emotional abandonment all the same."

Julia had heard this before. Many times, in fact. She knew her friend had unreasonable expectations of marriage and—maybe because Liz was so beautiful and spoiled—she tended to brook no compromises.

"That's so sad," Cristy said. She'd been to Liz's wedding last year, a lavish affair in New York City, and was too young to remember the histrionics of Liz's earlier marriages.

"I don't feel like talking about it now." Liz pasted a bright smile on her face and perked herself up considerably. "How about if I get settled into my room, get changed into comfy clothes and give you people a hand outside? I adore gardening."

"Do you?" Cristy looked surprised. Julia was not.

I can read you like a book, Lizzie Tish, Julia thought rather jadedly. There's a good-looking man on the premises and your radar is telling you to go for it—as usual.

"Great idea," Julia said politely, standing up. "Let's go get your room ready—the green bedroom, don't you think, Cristy?"

"Sure. Aunt Liz, I'm just heartbroken about you and Steve."

"Put it out of your mind," Liz intoned, following behind Julia. "The only thing that matters now is your wedding, my sweet Cristabelle—and creating the most wonderful gardens to embellish it." Liz even managed to smile at that.

Julia shook her head. Maybe the booze will knock her out, she thought cheerfully. Then she'll sleep through it all.

But I certainly wouldn't count on it.

Fifteen

For a woman who lives alone, I certainly have a houseful of people right now, Julia thought as she slapped a floral bottom sheet on the bed in the green room. Liz had sailed off toward the bathroom, pleading she was desperately in need of a shower. Cristy had offered to help with bedmaking but then, when it came to the crunch, disappeared downstairs and out, where more interesting things were going on.

Julia wasn't sure why she was so angry, but angry was the word for it nevertheless. This had started out as a good day. Father Hayes said all those nice things, and she'd hurried home, knowing she had young people and Ben in her life today . . . and then, unexpectedly, Liz had showed up. Flirtatious, outrageous Liz.

Not caring in the least about the niceties of proper bedmaking, Julia finished up with top sheet, clean pillowcases and two warm blankets. There. Good enough for Liz.

She changed out of her church clothes quickly and hurried downstairs, disturbed by such uncharitable thoughts. Liz was her long-time friend; why was Julia annoyed at her?

She glanced at her kitchen, vaguely recalled that she was supposed to feed the Garden Club some lunch, and vetoed the plan. Instead, she slipped outside to be part of the Great and Venerable Restoration Process.

Immediately, sunshine and sweet, warm spring breezes drifted over her and improved her mood. She smiled at everyone, breathed in deeply, thought she smelled the beginning of lilac blossoms. Then she sidled over to where Ben was working.

"Hi," she said. "Can I help with something?"

"Sure." He turned to look at her with a large welcome on his countenance. "Looks like you've got a busy schedule—more than busy—all of a sudden."

"Oh, you mean with my house guest? Yes." She reached out to help Ben with the big bag of fertilizer he was pouring. He'd placed attractive rocks around the latest enclosed garden and now was filling behind the rocks with rich soil components.

Standing beside him, she felt tiny. He's a mile-high guy, she thought, the phrase jumping into her mind from some TV show she must have seen.

She touched the line of white, brown, and gray rocks. "This looks pretty. And you make it all look so easy."

He laughed and kept his green eyes on her for a full minute. "It is easy, after years of experience. Do I detect a woman who's becoming an aficionado of gardens after all?"

She felt her cheeks flaming. "Possibly. I suppose I ought to show some interest, since I'll be the owner of all this floral splendor."

"You already are the owner. And you're going to like it, Julia, once you see the big picture."

"The big picture, hmmm?" She nodded absently. "What kind of flowers will go into this section, for instance?"

"Zinnias and marigolds for the summer," he said. "Then if they've gone by before the wedding, we'll replace them with glorious hardy mums at the last minute."

She tried not to stare at the way his sandy-colored beard crinkled when he smiled. "I do know the names of all the flowers, of course," she admitted. "It was just that I never cared to grow any of my own."

"That's your prerogative."

"Is it? I feel as though I should be ashamed now for never planting anything ornamental."

"Julia, you have other talents." He sounded amazed that she'd even talk that way. "Look at that pot roast you fixed for us last night! Most of us can't cook to save our lives."

"I suppose so." She turned and looked him straight in the eyes. "Do you mean you? You can't cook?"

He chuckled. "When I don't eat out, I live on junk food—frozen stuff out of boxes, take-out Chinese, and deli cole slaw."

"But . . . I thought most men in the nineties liked cooking. Jay did. He was in his glory, whipping up fancy meals for our dinner parties."

"Not me," Ben said very quietly, and turned away so his face was hidden from her. "I'm not Jay."

She swallowed hard, realizing the significance of what he'd said—or hadn't said. (*The widow should never compare other men to her late husband.*)

"Of course not," she blurted out. She was thinking, *and I'm not Lily, am I?* But to get the conversation away from former spouses, she said, "I do have something to brag about this morning, however."

"You do?" He whirled back. The green

eyes were attentive as they danced in the sunlight.

"I began my book." She knew her voice
had taken on a note of triumph. "Wrote almost six pages last night."

Excited, he seized her two wrists and
squeezed them for half a second. "That's
splendid. I'm so glad to hear that."

She nodded. "It was fun. I couldn't sleep
anyway, so I thought I might as well give it
a stab."

"Terrific Julia. What's it about?"

My Little Women is the working title." He
was still holding her wrists lightly. She could
pull away, she knew, but she liked feeling con-
nected to him in this strange way. Possibly it
was because she knew Liz would be joining
them any moment.

"Maybe you'll let me read it," he said,
"when you're ready."

"I'd be honored if you read it and tell me
what you think. Er, don't we have more soil
mixing to do here?"

He laughed. "I'm holding on to you as
though I'm afraid you'll run away. That will
never do." Reluctantly he let go of her wrists.

"Never do," she said, and pulled back. But
she felt at ease with Ben now, not terrified
of the fact that he was a man—and an eligible

one, at that. Maybe that kiss on Wednesday night—inadvertent as it was—had changed her more than she'd realized.

She relaxed, and the day just kept getting more beautiful. The wispy clouds had floated off somewhere, so there was only a bright, cheerful sun blazing in the blue sky. From the woods behind Julia's property, birds took flight as though on schedule, some chirping loudly as they ascended and some just going quietly, with the flapping of wings as their only sound.

Ben and Julia puttered together, side by side, for a while. This isn't so terrible, Julia thought, taking a small garden spade and mixing the soil ingredients together as if she were mixing a cake. Ben was adding peat humus, cow manure, and lots of compost from his own private compost pile at home. Added to the poor clay soil of Julia's yard, this blend seemed to add up to a very rich garden soil.

"The results are quite impressive, Ben. There are tricks to every trade," she said with admiration.

"Of course. No professional would ever try to plant a garden unless the soil's worked over like this—big time."

"And you've got the kids doing the same thing, I see."

He nodded and kept on working.

"Hello, everyone!" The voice of Liz the Cheerful wafted through the backyard, bouncing off maple trees and trilling into the privacy hedges.

She's here, Julia thought, with something clenching up inside her belly. I'm angry with her, but she's my house guest and I have to be gracious.

"You look refreshed," Julia said, noting Liz's brightly colored costume, a vivid pink blouse, skin-tight pants with both pink and orange in great jungle scenes, and a fabulous pair of trendy leather sandals from the Greek Isles, no doubt.

"I'm dressed for gardening," Liz declared. "Ready and willing to work. . . . Hello again, Ben." She moved forward, her big gray eyes glued to him to emphasize that she was completely under his tutelage. "We met only briefly before, but I know a gardener when I see one. I am a kindred soul, believe me."

Julia heard a loud roaring in her ears. A kindred soul indeed! Liz may have tended a few gardens here and there, but she was hardly a horticulturist . . . and certainly not on the same level with Ben Wilson.

She watched as Ben greeted her old friend with his usual quiet politeness. "Glad you're here then, Liz," he said, smiling, that face lighting up with merriment. "Any friend of Julia's is a friend of mine, and all that."

Oh, Ben, you're so naive, Julia thought, walking off so no one would notice her face turning red with rage. She'd been enjoying the morning so much, working in the garden beside Ben—and now it was all ruined.

She forced herself to calm down before she went looking for a diversion. "How are you coming along, Cristy?" she asked, moving along toward her daughter.

"Good." Cristy looked up from the soil she was mixing. "Oh look, Aunt Liz is helping Ben now! Can you imagine her lifting manure bags when she's all dressed up like a princess?"

"Imagine," Julia repeated. "Well, I suppose I'll be relegated back to the kitchen now that we've had this royal visitation."

Cristy shot her mother a quick, puzzled look.

"I'll make some sandwiches for everyone," Julia mumbled.

"Yeah, that would be great, Mom."

Julia stalked off, resentful and confused.

She didn't want the man; she'd already decided that. She didn't want *any* man. So why was Liz's blatant flirting coming as such a shock?

* * *

"The Garden of Paradise is being constructed," Jeremy pronounced hours later, after he'd shored up a brand-new bankside slope with sleek wooden planks and ingenious pins. "This yard will be a veritable showplace."

"We'll call that one the Groom's Garden," Cristy said, giving her fiancé a warm hug. "It'll be awesome when we have all those showy annuals spilling over the wooden boards."

"Awesome," Ben repeated, grinning at the enthusiasm of the young. He winked at Julia and started gathering up his tools.

"Oh, Ben, you're not leaving already?" Liz asked with dismay.

"I am," Ben said. "These college students are taking off, going back to Storrs, and I have things to do at home."

"No!" Liz attached herself to Ben's arm. "Julia wouldn't hear of you leaving without a good, hot dinner meal, after all your slave labor here. Right, Julia?"

Julia didn't answer.

Ben did. "I'm sorry, Liz, but I can't stay. Besides, you ladies need a chance to talk. You must have hours of catching up to do."

Liz pouted but there wasn't a thing she

could do to change his mind. He'd devoted two full days to Julia's property, after all, and Julia knew he had preparations to make for his college classes for the coming week.

"Thanks again, Ben," Julia said. "And thanks to all of you—Jeremy, Kevin, everybody. It's amazing what you've accomplished here in just one weekend."

"It is pretty spectacular, isn't it?" Cristy agreed. "Now if only we had a gazebo . . . whoops. Only kidding, Mom!"

As volunteers usually do, they all took a walking tour, looking around and making an inventory before leaving. It was staggering, actually, what changes had taken place in the formerly plain, all-green yard.

The retainer stones gleamed in the sun, big and colorful, each one either pearly or jagged in its own way so as to provide a variety for the eye. Four such gardens had been carved out using the stones.

And then the Groom's Garden, as Cristy had dubbed it, was a fine piece of engineering that would hold up the bank and prevent erosion at the same time it made a cheery spot for flowers.

"This bridal path is going to be the hit of the whole wedding," Liz declared.

The new pathway with its graceful curves

had been well started; it would provide a spectacular passage across the carpet of grass on Cristy and Jeremy's wedding day. And there was the sundial, which looked terrific and artistic.

So even though not a flower had been planted yet—it was much too soon in the season, Ben assured them—there had been major structural changes. And Julia, who had believed she had no outdoor imagination, was beginning to be able to foresee how it would look in a month or so. The Big Picture, Ben had called it.

Autumn mums there, all scarlet and gold. Saucy zinnias spiking up from the rock gardens in pinks, reds, and yellows. Over there, red snapdragons, perhaps, and purple and blue delphiniums. She was surprised at how many names of flowers she knew, just from having lived a number of decades on this earth.

I do love flowers, she thought. I wonder why I was always so afraid of planting them?

"Well, we're heading back to school, so goodbye Aunt Liz," Cristy said. "And so long, Mom. Keep me posted, won't you?" She meant about the mysterious prowler, Julia knew. Or maybe she was concerned also about Liz's deteriorating marriage.

Everyone was kissing and calling out good-byes, but Ben managed to slip away without any kisses, somehow. Maybe he was less naive than she'd thought; after all, Julia wouldn't have been surprised to see Liz French-kissing him, truthfully.

They all went around to the front driveway. Ben waved and walked on down the street to his house, tools in hand. The college kids piled into their car with suitcases and sandwiches to go that Julia had fixed.

Then finally Julia and Liz were alone.

That evening, ensconced in her living room with the stereo playing a soft *Serenity* tape, Julia attempted to do her usual Ann Landers thing. Lord knew she'd been through it a million times before with Liz.

"Marriage takes compromise," she said to totally deaf ears. Liz was slathering scarlet nail polish on her toenails. "You could learn to give—just a little bit, Liz—and make this one work. Steve happens to be the best husband you've ever had."

"Impossible. He's impossible and so is the whole situation." Liz dabbed at a toe with a cotton ball. "He has no time for me, ever.

Does he expect me to exist forever in that god-awful ancient city? I'm lonely there."

"Liz, listen to me. Steve has a job to do over there, and it must be important. You could be understanding—"

"No." Liz stretched out full-length on Julia's sofa. She'd changed into lounging clothes, pure silk of course, and looked fresh as an American rosebud while Julia was still feeling rather grubby from her hours in the gardens.

"It was different with *your* marriage, Julia." Julia had heard this one before, too. "You married the one and only perfect guy on the planet."

"Oh, come on." Julia didn't care if her annoyance showed. "Jay was terrific but we had problems just like everyone else."

"So you two had troubles . . . but you compromised?" Now Liz was all ears.

"Well yes, we both compromised. That's my point. When you love someone you try to negotiate, not just give up."

"It's horrible over there in Athens," Liz muttered. "There's nothing to do and they all speak Greek. I'm sick of it."

Julia sighed deeply. "Of course they speak Greek. It's their native tongue. It's up to *you* to learn it. Why haven't you gotten out to an adult school to study Greek?"

"What, am I a kid? I'm too old for school."

"You're not too old for anything and you know it. God, Liz, I think you're the luckiest woman alive—to have a husband and a chance to be in Greece, which is my dearest ambition."

"Which is? The husband or Greece?"

"Greece, as you very well know." Julia found herself blushing slightly. "My whole life I've dreamed of seeing Athens and all the wonderful history of the Grecian empire."

"Well, you can have it," Liz pouted. "Take it. Go and keep house for Steve if you want."

Julia hesitated for a moment, then spoke her mind. "You're in your fifties now. Do you ever intend to grow up, Liz?"

Liz's eyes opened wide with surprise. "That sounds ominous. Are you about to start lecturing me? Because if so, I'll get another glass of Scotch—"

"You don't need any more Scotch. I'm trying to get through to you, Liz, but if you truly don't want the advice then I'll shut up."

"Really? Good."

"Really, but then there will be no more sympathy. You can cry your heart out and I'll be too busy to notice."

"My God. You're cruel, Jules."

"I'm tired of this neverending tale. You throw away good husbands like you throw away used Kleenex tissues. Is that the way you intend to live your whole life?"

Liz blinked, and appeared to think that over for a bit. "Maybe if I found the right man, it would be different. Maybe someone like that darling gardener man who was here today—"

"Stop right there." Anger surged up in Julia, causing her to see dark spots in front of her eyes. There was no stopping her now. "I've got some things to tell you, Liz, and this time you'd better listen up."

Sixteen

"This really sounds serious." For a change, Liz didn't mock Julia. She sat up, focused her eyes on her friend, and seemed to be listening with an open mind.

Julia perched beside her. "You say outrageous things like you need me for your Ann Landers—but you're acting very shallow lately, Liz, and it hurts me."

"I'm sorry." Liz's voice was tinged with sarcasm. "I never meant to ruin your Sunday. I thought you would understand how much I'm hurting because of a lousy marriage—"

"There's nothing lousy about your marriage at all," Julia said. "Come on, grow up and admit it. Steve loves you and you certainly loved him last year, when you had that gigantic, gaudy wedding."

"Why do you call it gaudy?"

"That's not the point right now. The point is, you did love Steve then. Now you're being childish. You simply want more attention than anyone can possibly give you."

Liz shrugged. "Even if that were true—I can admit that I do have feelings for Steve, in spite of it all—I don't feel like being in Athens, Greece."

"Well, that's your problem and I can't solve that one. But what I do want to solve is this— Liz, you are not to involve Ben Wilson in this marital farce of yours."

Liz's well-shaped eyebrows went up. "Excuse me, *farce?*"

"Exactly. He's a nice man, and rather a vulnerable one. His wife died a few years ago and he seems somewhat lonely, afraid to venture out too far."

"Well, maybe he needs an adventure then. Something real steamy, Julia."

Julia hesitated and then pointed a finger at Liz. "Ben Wilson is not ready for the likes of you, lady. He doesn't deserve to be trifled with by a married woman with a terrible track record."

Liz fell silent. She couldn't keep staring into Julia's accusatory look and so she looked down at the coffee table, her face slightly flushed.

"Do you understand what I'm saying?"

Julia demanded. She couldn't have projected more firmness if she wore a swastika.

"Fully." Liz nodded. She seemed to think things over, fully cognizant now of Julia's very real anger. Finally she found her voice. "I ought to apologize, Julia. I guess I have been rather manic since I got here—and you're right, I've been shallow."

Julia nodded and decided to let Liz do the talking.

Liz trailed a finger across the arm of the sofa. "I'm not saying my marriage is a perfect world, though. But for now, I'll try to be more considerate of you and your friend Ben."

"Thank you," Julia said very quietly.

"Don't be angry with me," Liz said, a tear sliding down her cheek. "Please? I didn't realize I was being such a creep."

"Well, you were, and I was pretty angry with you."

"I'd never want to hurt you, Julia, and you're so right about Ben . . . if I flirted with him it might mess up his whole life." Liz grinned to show she was exaggerating. "I'd probably go back to Steve eventually and poor Ben would never be able to get over me, never. . . ."

"Oh Liz, you're incorrigible. As always!"

They reached out and hugged, both laughing, sobbing and making noises of relief. "This is more like the Liz I expected," Julia said. "Now maybe we can settle down to talk about you and Steve."

"My house has been a total zoo," Julia said the next morning at work. "Selena, ever since Cristy got that idea of a garden wedding, there hasn't been a quiet moment."

"I know." Selena was feeding paper into the copy machine. "And now you have Liz staying with you, hmm?"

"I can manage that," Julia said optimistically. "I've already had a heart-to-heart talk with her, and she's realizing she can't step all over people. Meaning me—and Ben."

"What?" Selena's head snapped up at that. "She was putting the moves on your Ben?"

"He's not my Ben," Julia protested. "He's a friend who's been very kind."

"Julia, there's something going on here, I can tell. Are you honestly expecting me to believe there's not a shred of feeling between you and this Ben?"

Julia's heart skipped a little beat. "I didn't exactly say that. Listen, I have to get going on Mr. Drummond's requisitions."

"Right, change the subject." Selena smiled.

"You can't escape from me, you know. Sooner or later you'll end up telling me if something happened."

Julia dropped her voice very low. "Something did happen but it was only once. We sort of kissed."

Selena's reaction was instantaneous. She dropped the stack of papers she'd been copying! "That's a very big something," she said with a gulp.

"Oh, it depends on how you look at it. I see it as just—I was worried and confused after the vandalism, and he was so close I landed in his arms . . . that's all."

"That's all," Selena repeated, mischief in her eyes. "I won't give you the third degree about this, I promise. Your little secret is safe. But it sure sounds to me—"

"What?" Julia asked when Selena didn't finish.

"Sounds to me like there's a definite chemistry cooking with you two."

Julia made a clucking sound. "Chemistry. You make it sound like something in a soap opera. The kiss wasn't all that dramatic."

Wasn't it? Julia thought silently as she turned on her computer. She remembered his lips on hers, gentle and firm, his tongue challenging and questioning. Unexpectedly she felt an odd, melting sweetness flowing through her, telling her that "chemistry" was not an inappropriate description after all.

She shook her head trying to clear it of sensuous, unwanted cobwebs.

"I'd like you to come for dinner one night this week," she said to Selena. "I want you to meet Liz."

"Sure, that sounds like great fun. Will I get to meet Mister Chemistry, too?"

"No," Julia said firmly and began to type up the requisitions.

When Julia arrived home that afternoon, Liz was nowhere to be found. No note, nothing. Julia wandered around the house looking for clues, finding none. With suspicion gnawing at her, she changed into her relaxation clothes, jeans and a sweater.

Where the devil did the woman go? Annoyed, she looked to see if Liz's handbag was in her room. It was. Didn't that mean Liz was somewhere nearby, then? In the neighborhood, probably? Julia stood rooted, clenching and unclenching her fists.

She'd gone down to Ben's house.

Her pulse racing double time, Julia charged outside and started walking down the street toward Ben's. She'd never been there, never even seen it. His home was hidden behind privacy evergreens and a large natural clump of rock, so even when she took her frequent walks she'd never been able to figure out what sort of home he had.

She raced up his driveway, hopping mad. She'd better prepare herself for the worst. Even though Liz had promised last night not to involve Ben in her schemes . . . Julia probably shouldn't be surprised if she found them in bed together. Liz had acted in a totally irresponsible way like that many a time before.

Damn her anyway. I ought to kick her out on the street, she was thinking as she stabbed at Ben's doorbell. His home, she now saw, was a giant, ultra-modern log home that looked masculine and rugged. Not a woman's type of home at all, she thought. Had his wife Lily ever lived here?

She hit the doorbell again, hearing it ring inside the big home. Was it possible they were involved in a clinch?

The door opened. Ben, his face visibly brightening with surprise, pulled the door open wider for her.

"Julia. This is a treat. Would you like to

come in, or are you merely collecting for the Kidney Foundation?"

"I'm not collecting for anything," she said crossly. "I'm looking for my houseguest. Tell her I'm out here, please, and I've had about enough of her shenanigans."

Ben frowned. "Do you mean Liz? She's not here."

"But—" Julia tried not to sputter. "I was sure she'd come down here. You mean you haven't seen her?"

"Not at all. But I did see what looked like a rental car at your house sometime this afternoon."

"What? That's crazy. She has no car."

"I saw one in your driveway, Julia."

"Well . . . she couldn't have left. She didn't even pack, and no woman goes anywhere without her purse."

"Are you worried about her?"

"No, truthfully I'm furious with her. She might have written a note."

Ben stood in his doorway with patience.

"Forgive me, I didn't mean to involve you in this, Ben."

He craned his neck to look up the street. "Actually, there's that car up there now. See?— the blue one in your driveway."

Julia turned and looked up the street. She

saw the strange car also. "What is she up to? That car wasn't there a few minutes ago! May I call her on your phone?"

He nodded and she went in, through a very large living room and into an attached kitchen. She dialed home. Liz answered.

"Hello, Liz? It's Julia. What's going on?"

"Oh hi," came a dreamy voice, purring with contentment. "I had a surprise today, Julia. Guess who's here?"

"Hmmm. Let me take a wild guess. Could it possibly be Steve?"

"Yes, it certainly is. At first I thought you called him, Julia, but he says no. He missed me and was worried about our marriage—so he came after me, all the way from Greece. We just came back from a short ride."

I'll bet when she left Athens, she scooted out on Steve without a note, too, Julia thought, shaking her head.

"Sounds like you're working things out, then," Julia said hopefully. "Are you?"

"I believe we might. We're going to sit here and talk seriously for a while, Julia. Could you—would you feel like staying away for an hour or so?"

Hard to believe the nerve of the woman. But Julia agreed because she was delighted the newlyweds were communicating, at least.

She put down the receiver, shaking her head and clucking her tongue.

"Everything okay?" Ben asked.

"Yes, fine, except she doesn't want me to come home for an hour, if you can imagine. She's working things out with her husband."

"That's good news, then." Very gently he brushed a stray curl away from Julia's forehead. Then he backed off and smiled. "Will you stay here for that hour, then? I'll put on some coffee."

"Well, I don't seem to have much choice." She smiled and took a moment to look around at her surroundings. "Your home is lovely, Ben. I'm surprised it's so bright and light inside, when everything is made of pine logs."

"Thanks. I'll show you the whole place if you'd like."

She hesitated a moment or so.

"The tour includes my greenhouse. You'll love it."

"If I were a greenhouse sort of person," she teased, smiling.

"Even if you're not . . . no one can resist the magical world of gardens under glass, and all that steamy warmth even on a cold April day. What do you say?"

She laughed at his eagerness to show off his domain. She had no objections, certainly.

She had to hang out somewhere, obviously, in this time of exile while Liz and Steve conferred.

"Okay, why not? That's very kind of you, Ben. I'll take that coffee, too."

Seventeen

"I'll say it again," Julia remarked when the house tour was completed. "This is a really nice house, Ben."

She meant it. But she saw absolutely no feminine touches anywhere, and wondered for a second time whether Lily Wilson had ever lived there.

"Thanks for the compliment," Ben said. "I think of it as my bachelor's quarters, hence all the mooseheads and beer mugs." He was grinning shyly as he spoke.

"Your house is in perfect taste. You have no mooseheads," she countered.

"I don't?" He grinned. "I'll have to remedy that."

They headed back to the kitchen—another log-walled room full of light and space—where the coffepot was gurgling.

"Are you game for a coffeeklatsch outdoors?" he asked. "I know it's cool out there, but I'd love for you to see my gardens."

"Of course." Julia helped him set up a tray with the coffee paraphernalia and found she was actually looking forward to the garden tour. Now that was strange, for her—Julia Maxwell, caring about someone's gardens?

They stepped out back through a sliding glass door, onto a deck partially covered with an arbor and thick, twisting wisteria vines. Instantly Julia knew she'd been transported to a real "garden of paradise."

Though it was early spring and very little was in bloom except April flowers, Ben's garden seemed fragrant already. There was the musky scent of earth and loam, and some sort of floral scents, thick and perfuming the very air all around his house.

And visually—she couldn't believe how, in a yard similar to her own, every available inch had been transformed into specialty gardens.

"That's my rose garden over there." Ben pointed to a vast area filled with green, waxy rose plants, with a tidy mulch over the soil. "This is my Japanese garden; you'll note the many rocks I've put in, the way the Japanese do."

"I'm astounded," Julia said. "It's overwhelming."

"Thanks."

She couldn't begin to take it all in at once.

There were little bridges and waterways, fountains and statues, fences, trysting benches, walkways, and vine-covered arbors. But way beyond all these store-bought features were the plants themselves. Thousands of perennials, glossy green and full of health, were shooting up, out of the dark brown earth with a will of their own.

"Over there's the Italian Renaissance garden," Ben said, pointing to a section with statuary, columns and a running brook. "But I won't do the whole run-down, Julia. I know you're not truly a horticulture person."

She turned to face him. "I can certainly appreciate this," she said with honesty. "You've worked miracles here."

"Well—" He looked embarrassed. "Thank you. Let's sit and have that coffee. I'm sure we can talk about something else besides gardens."

Under a spreading maple tree was a round glass patio table, and it was there they sat to drink their coffee. As dazzled as Julia was by the splendor around her, still she felt at ease here on Ben's sunny patio. Somehow in these past few weeks she'd come to think of him as a friend, despite the fiasco of the kiss.

"Ben, I've never asked you any questions about yourself," Julia said. "Which seems unfair, since you seem to know all about me from Cristy the Motormouth.''

"Okay." He smiled. "You want to ask—what?"

"I'm curious about something. This house—you call it a bachelor's place—did your wife live here?"

"No." He shook his head and pulled a bill-fold of photos out of a back pocket. "Here's the house where Lily and I lived." He showed her a picture of a small, ordinary Cape with a white picket fence and wisteria climbing over the sturdy front gate.

"Nice," she said. "Was it around here?"

"Next town over. Broomfield." He shuffled through more photos. "Here's a picture of Lily."

She reached out carefully and took the small snapshot. It was slightly blurry, but showed a slender, laughing young woman wearing a bright-red blouse and a full, red print skirt. She was beautiful—high cheekbones, a full mouth, large dark eyes.

"She was very beautiful."

"Yes."

She gave back the picture. "You felt the need to move out of the other house after she died?"

He nodded. "I did. I stayed a few years but

it always felt sort of haunted. That sounds stupid, but I think you know what I mean."

Julia nodded. "Of course I do. My house feels extremely haunted. I expect to see Jay every time I turn a corner . . . and worse, sometimes I think I do see him."

"Exactly." Ben put the photos back in his billfold.

"Nobody knows," Julia began in a soft voice. "Nobody can ever imagine, unless they've gone through it—" She stopped because words seemed to fail her.

"I agree with you," he said. "If you want to talk about it, I'll be glad to listen. Otherwise—"

"Otherwise what?"

He grinned, the smile splitting his beard. "Otherwise there are other, less morbid, things to discuss."

She wasn't sure exactly what he meant. But upon thinking it over, she decided she didn't want to talk about Jay, or the agony of losing him, right now. She'd done a great deal of reminiscing and crying on Saturday night, just before Liz arrived. She didn't relish the idea of going through that again so soon.

"It's almost twilight, and the air is sweet," Julia said with a smile. "Maybe we should just enjoy the moment and not try to solve any problems."

"Fine. That's up to you." He sipped his coffee. "Let me ask you this: why did you expect to find your friend Liz here at my house?"

She laughed. "Well, Liz is quite a flirt, as you may have noticed."

"As a matter of fact I did notice."

"How could you not? Anyway, she kept talking about having a fling with you and I know her well enough to believe she'd do it."

"A fling with me? And you thought I'd go along with that?" He was frowning. "Your friend is married, isn't she?"

"Well—yes, she is. But she can be very persuasive."

"Not with me she couldn't," he said. "I don't touch another man's wife—ever."

"Oh. I don't know all that much about you, after all . . . but Liz is a very beautiful woman."

The lines of his face locked into a cold, hard remoteness. "You don't think too much of me, Julia, if you imagine I'd be lured into a—a fling, as you call it—with a troubled woman who ran away from her husband."

Julia felt her heart racing. "I apologize, I was wrong, I can see that now. But I really didn't know what sort of person you were."

He pushed his chair back, looking troubled. "Will you please tell me . . . how can I establish my good character with you?" His tone was light, but there was clearly something quite serious in those deep green eyes all of a sudden. "What does a man have to do, Julia, to be considered honorable in your estimation?"

"Don't be silly, Ben, I didn't mean to insult you."

"But you did. I feel I need to vindicate myself." He stood up and paced around the patio, stopping sometimes to tuck a stray piece of wisteria vine into the overhead arbor. "Would it help to know that my brother and sister have always called me Dudley Do-Right?"

She laughed. "Is that a compliment?"

"No, from them it's an insult," he said. "To me it's a compliment. They say I'm the only guy they know who doesn't cheat on his taxes."

"Very commendable." She squirmed uncomfortably. "I never cheat on my taxes, either."

His face lit up. "There, you see? We do have something in common. Something most significant."

She just stared at him. It was the sort of remark that could have flustered Julia enough so she'd jump up and make an excuse to go straight home. Fortunately, however, Ben had the sense to stop the discussion cold right there.

"Oh, I'd like to bore you with one more gardening thing," he said, waving to her to follow him across the garden. "There's a birdbath down that path that Cristy is crazy about—the one with all the bunnies on the rim. I'm thinking of giving it to them for a wedding present."

"What a sweet idea."

She did follow behind him. It was easy to be enthusiastic about his garden—every bit of his garden. She saw nothing but perfection, with every inch manicured as if five hundred professional gardeners worked there each day.

She realized she was enjoying this late afternoon visit at Ben's house, despite the fact that it had been forced on her by Liz and Steve. She strolled along his paths and found herself touching things at times, whether rose plants, vines, or small statues.

She was grateful, too, that Ben had stopped the discussion about what they had in common. It seemed he was always trying to win her approval, paving the way for an intimacy that she was totally unwilling to accept.

All right, Dudley Do-Right, she thought. If you're really as honorable as you claim, let's just make sure this friendship goes no further than friendship.

She reached out to touch the smooth, waxy stem of a rose bush, even knowing there were thorns somewhere on the thing.

A few minutes later, Ben's doorbell rang. He went to answer it and into the house came the latest guests. Ben called to Julia to join them in the big living room.

There were Liz and her Steve, arms intertwined, a loving, reunited look in the eyes of both. "Hi, Julia," Liz said, marching in, unabashedly curious to see Ben's log home. She introduced the two men and they shook hands.

Julia kissed Steve warmly. He was tall, blond, and slightly balding. "I'm so glad you came, Steve," she said. You'll never know how glad, she was secretly thinking, but she focused on the joy of seeing her friends' marriage patched up once more.

"This was an expensive way to find out she needed more of my attention," Steve said, smiling ruefully. "We could have worked things out over there in Athens, but no, not my Liz."

"Liz always does everything the dramatic

way,'' Julia finished for him. They smiled with mutual understanding.

Steve hugged his wife. "Well, I love her and that's the main thing. She says she loves me. What else do we need?"

What else indeed, Julia thought. She had no idea what it would take to satisfy Liz Holworth, but—if Steve thought he'd found all the answers on this trip, then more power to him.

"We want to celebrate," Liz said with a flourish. "Will you two be our guests tonight? We plan to eat the best lobster dinner to be found in North America."

"Please say yes," Steve coaxed.

Ben threw a questioning glance over to Julia. Her stomach did a minor somersault for a moment, and then she took control of her emotions. What was dinner, after all? Nothing. She and Ben had eaten several dinners together already.

"This is a most happy occasion," Julia said. "I would never say no to a joyful celebration."

"Nor I," said Ben, looking pleased and boyish.

"Great!" Steve grinned triumphantly. "Let's all get into our best clothes and we'll meet in half an hour."

Liz rushed over to give Julia an emotional,

tear-filled embrace. "You're my best friend, Julia," she choked out. "Don't ever give up on me, even when I behave terribly. I don't know what I'd ever do without you."

Eighteen

Leave it to Steve Holworth to find the most romantic restaurant in all Connecticut. Romance was not what Julia personally needed, of course, but she knew it suited the trance that held both Steve and Liz enthralled. The four of them stepped out of Steve's rental Ford as the keys were handed over to a young parking attendant.

The Colonial Inn, dating back to the eighteenth century, was a big old wayfarer's inn made of graystone and fieldstone. It sat firmly on the shore of Lake Waramaug, towering far above the other restaurants in the vicinity.

"How did you know about this place?" Julia asked Steve. "You've never lived in Connecticut, have you?"

"Not exactly." He smiled. "I grew up in New York, as you know, but one summer my folks rented a cottage up here on Lake Waramaug." He tilted his head to look at the big Inn. "I used to think that if I ever got old enough and rich enough, I'd come back here some time, right to this Inn, for a celebration."

"And you made it, dearest," Liz said, purring and nuzzling her nose into his tweed coat. "Not that you're old, I don't mean, but certainly you're rich enough now to enjoy your childhood dream."

"Yes." Steve gave Liz a warm, affectionate pat on her shoulder, a quiet and husbandly gesture. Something about that little act made Julia's eyes mist over. How very long it had been since she'd been patted tenderly like that by her husband, Jay. . . .

Don't think about that.

Trying to blink away the tears, she turned and spoke to Ben. "They have some famous gardens here, did you know that?"

"No," he said with interest. "I hadn't ever heard of it."

Julia said, "I believe they're rose gardens, so they would be in bloom—when? in June?"

"Possibly, or maybe even all summer long. I'd like very much to see the roses when they come into season."

The four walked up wide fieldstone steps toward the entrance. Isn't this peachy? A double date. She hadn't been on a double date since—well, since college, when she and Liz often dated as a duo; that was so the boys wouldn't try to get too fresh with them.

Inside, they surrendered their coats and were led into the big, round Glass Room, seated at a table by tall windows that overlooked the lake. Vivid scarlet cloths on each table were enhanced by sparkling silverware and cut glass goblets.

"Isn't this wonderful?" Liz said. "Now honestly, isn't this better even than the trip you were planning to Athens, Julia?"

"Er, no," Julia said honestly. "Actually I wanted that trip."

Ben was studying her with interest. "I hadn't realized you were planning a trip to Europe."

She sighed. "I was. I had the brochures and the two weeks' vacation this summer, and I was all set to see glorious ancient Greece."

"And then Cristy's wedding plans stopped you?"

She nodded, but smiled faintly because she'd vowed, a while back, to be the quintessential good sport about the turn of events.

"Well, you're just a good Mommy," Liz said. To Julia it sounded extremely patronizing.

"That's not what you said on the telephone," Julia reminded her. "You told me my girls were horribly selfish."

"Me?" Liz laughed airily. "What do I know? I have no children."

Julia picked up her menu. They all spent some time studying the selections, and finally made their choices—lobster for all. Just as the waitress finished taking their orders, a small band began playing both pop and soft classical music in the far corner of the Glass Room.

"I'll ask them to play our song," Steve said, nibbling at Liz's ear. He rose and ambled over to the band.

"And what is your song, Liz?" asked Ben.

" 'Fascination,' " she said in a droll voice. "It was playing the first time Steve and I danced together."

Within minutes, the strains of "Fascination" lilted through the Glass Room. Liz rose, melted into Steve's arms and they danced away looking like Romeo and Juliet.

"Nice to see a happy ending there," Ben said quietly.

"Yes. If only it *is* the ending." Julia sighed. "If I know Liz, she'll leave him every six months from now on, just to get this sort of special treatment."

Ben frowned, looking horrified. "That would be terrible. How can they ever hope to build a solid marriage like that?"

"They won't," Julia said, and then realized

how cold she must sound. "Oh, don't listen
to me. I must be getting cynical in my old
age. Maybe they'll live happily forever after."

Ben's soft green gaze was on her fully.
"Would you like to dance? I'm not Fred Astaire
by any means, but if you'll take a chance, I'm
game."

She should have said no. She should have
said she wasn't much of a dancer herself, and
besides didn't enjoy it.

Something. Anything.

But instead she acted upon impulse, and
wasn't that exactly what Ben had said she
was—A woman of impulse?

Oh, God.

Too late. She was already standing up, smiling tentatively, lulled into a relaxed mood by
the musical strains of "Fascination." Ben stood
up, a mammoth man impeccably dressed tonight in a crisp brown suit. His shirt was
cream-colored linen and his tie a slender one
with mixed brown hues. His sandy hair, freshly
washed, sparked with electricity and a glow
from the overhead chandeliers.

A wonderful looking man, if you liked men
with thick beards like the old Greek Gods . . .

She couldn't allow herself to think that way.
Just one dance, and then she'd plead a head-

ache. It was easy to have a headache with Liz around anyway; the woman exhausted her.

"You ladies must have a long and very strong friendship," Ben commented, almost as though he'd been reading her mind.

"We do," Julia said, fitting neatly into the circle of Ben's massive arms. Her head came up to his tie, and this somehow made her feel smaller. She didn't like that feeling. Jay had been exactly her height, so there had been an equality between them in many ways.

The odd thing though, was that she'd never felt quite as protected with Jay as she did right now.

The music was soft and soothing, the dance floor a shining platform of rich oak planks. The mirrored chandelier threw an odd pattern of light across Ben's face, first illuminating his intelligent green eyes, then spotlighting the fuzzy sandy beard.

I need to be careful, she thought, stiffening her spine. I'm getting too interested in how he looks. It's possible that my hormones are trying to take over, here. I won't allow it.

"I have treasured friends like that myself," Ben said, his eyes still on Liz. "Two very special ones, that is, although there are other buddies from along life's way who are also good guys."

She couldn't help but be interested. "Who are these two friends that are so special?"

"Hank Chaffee is one, and Killer Carlyle is the other. I know—Killer. His name is a weird one. Both guys are from my Bronx neighborhood and both are living on Long Island now."

"You—you're from the Bronx?" She was astounded. "But I am, too! Where exactly are you from?"

They exchanged street names and proximity to El trains as well as the public school numbers and the local parish. It turned out they'd been far from each other, but still it seemed like a strange coincidence to Julia.

"And I can't believe your friend's name is Killer," she said, laughing.

"Yep, Killer Carlyle, the toughest guy at P.S. 68. Of course his real name is Henry, but nobody better dare call him that."

"Of course not." She realized they were dancing with enough skill to be graceful, if not totally polished like Liz and Steve. Enclosed in his arms with the music swirling around them, Julia felt almost consumed by the bulk of Ben's body, though he wasn't the least bit fat. He was big because his long bones were sleek with muscle and strength.

Snap out of it, Julia.

Ben made no attempt to be anything but

friendly. One could only call him a perfect gentleman. He was talking away in a cheerful tone about the crowd of guys with whom he'd gone to grammar school and high school in the Bronx. He was perfectly happy.

No, it was Julia who had the problem.

She found she had to resist putting her face against his chest, as she would automatically have rested it against Jay's cheek. The temptation was strong. Without a doubt, she had overactive hormones that were trying to betray her. It wasn't fair.

She would be glad when "Fascination" was over.

Driving home was even worse.

Now they were in the backseat of the rental car, as Steve drove through the warm, sweet spring night. Above in the sky there were not only bright star pinpricks, but a glowing half moon as well.

To Julia, being in the backseat felt *exactly* like college and the old double dates with Liz. Except that the man close beside her was no college sophomore. He was big and powerful and soft spoken, a fully mature, gentle giant.

Ben seemed relaxed, totally at ease as he carried on a conversation with the Holworths and didn't even attempt to hold Julia's hand. That was good. That helped.

Still, their arms and shoulders were touching in a companionable way. Julia decided to ignore her racing hormones, if that was her problem, and keep the conversational ball rolling. At times she wondered if she was talking too loud or too swiftly.

Once Liz turned around in a questioning way. "What's with you tonight, Julia? You sound like Chatty Cathy!"

"Didn't mean to bore you, Liz. Why don't you talk? Tell us more about Athens . . ."

Then Julia fell silent and let the others carry the conversation. Either way she was sadly aware that she was out on "a date" long before she was ready for one.

If she could have relived this entire day, she'd never have walked down to Ben's house searching for the errant Liz. Never. Look where it had landed her—sitting in the backseat with Benjamin Wilson. Damn it.

But Ben continued to be a gentleman, and all in all, it turned out she had nothing to worry about. She reflected that in a perverse way it still felt like those college dates; back then, whenever the boy didn't make a pass, she was partly relieved . . . and at the same time, slightly disappointed.

"Tell us about your books, Ben," Liz said as they drove along. "Julia said you're an author? Of gardening books?"

He did speak of his work, not in a boasting way but merely to answer Liz and Steve's questions. He was extremely modest.

"You did promise I could borrow a few of them," Julia reminded him. He nodded. When they reached Camelot Road, Ben asked to be taken home first so he could get the books.

They waited in the driveway while he went inside.

"Anything going on there, Julesey?" Liz asked pointedly.

"I have no idea what you mean."

"Yeah you do. Backseat kind of stuff. You and this guy Ben—maybe he's not just some friend of Cristy's after all, hmmm?"

"Wrong." Julia didn't feel like discussing it. She sniffed and sat up straighter, realizing she'd been tense and on edge all the way home from the Inn.

"He's a sweet man," Liz said.

"I'm aware of that."

"The way you two were avoiding each other," Liz said shrewdly, "makes me positive you've already kissed."

"*Liz!*" Steve sounded slightly shocked.

"Well, I've known Julia almost all her life. Whenever she'd kissed a guy, she always had that telltale look in her eyes."

"Sssssh. Here he comes now," Julia said, seeing Ben's front door opening. He emerged with Ivan trotting along at his side and a stack of hardcover books in his arms.

"We need to have another little talk, you and me." Liz chuckled; obviously she was highly amused by her deductions. "Guess it's going to be little old me who plays Ann Landers this time, bub."

Nineteen

Always shrewd, Julia worked at evading Liz who wanted to have that little talk about Ben and kisses and Ann Landers advice.

It wasn't difficult. Liz was completely enthralled by her very attentive and affectionate Steve, albeit temporarily, so she readily forgot all about Julia's imagined love life. That night the two lovebirds went off to sleep (*sleep?*) in the green guest bedroom, while Julia breathed a sigh of relief. She really hadn't wanted to discuss Ben or her own love life.

The next day Steve and Liz were scheduled to take off, with plans to visit families in Rochester, N.Y. Then it would be back overseas, to Athens ultimately but first to romantic spots in Italy.

"For a prolonged honeymoon," Liz said, sipping early morning coffee in Julia's sunny kitchen. The two women had a few minutes to themselves while Steve was upstairs showering. "And yes, Julia, I promise I'll even do something about learning to speak Greek after we get back to our everyday life in Athens."

"Wonderful." Julia plunked boxes of cold cereal on the table. "You'll have to make do with this stuff, I'm afraid, unless you want to cook. I have no time; I've got to get going to work."

"Raisin Bran will be fine. You've done more than enough for us, Julia. I will forever be grateful."

Julia stared down into her own coffee mug. "Glad to be of help, if I was. I didn't do anything."

"You lectured me. You scolded me." Liz gave her dazzling smile. "And for once, I listened—that whole bit about compromise in matrimony. You're a wise lady, my friend, and I respect you because you made such a wonderful success of your own marriage."

"Thank you. I hope you did take the advice to heart," Julia said. "Steve is a truly good man and you could have a happy life together if you behave like a grownup."

"And what about you?" Liz leaned forward to stare at Julia. "When do you come out of mourning, hmmm?"

"Some things take time, Liz."

"Isn't it about time to throw away the black mourning clothes—"

"I don't wear black clothing!"

"Symbolically you do, sweetie. When will you get ready to notice that something extremely special is right at your doorstep?"

Julia turned away. "You don't know what you're talking about."

"Yes I do. I've seen the way Ben looks at you—and by the way, why didn't you tell me you had a thing going with the adorable garden man?"

"Because I don't."

"Julia, I must apologize now for all that flirting I did, but I had no idea you two were an item."

"Nobody is an item! Only Cristy and Jeremy, and that's all I'm thinking about this summer. Their wedding."

"Don't try to pull the wool over these eyes." Liz helped herself to another steaming cup of coffee. "I know you, pal."

Julia looked out the window; she was doing that more and more now that her yard was being transformed. She'd never realized she craved outdoor beauty, but she was quite aesthetic after all. The renovation was well under way—the paths, the rock retaining walls, the gleaming sundial and the gardens of rich earth ready to be planted.

"Just out of curiosity," Liz pushed on,

"was last night the first time you two danced?"

"Yes."

"You looked mighty sweet together. He's very different from Jay, of course, but maybe that's all to the good."

"Liz, no. I'm not at all ready for any sort of involvement."

"But he *has* kissed you, hasn't he? I wasn't wrong about that."

Julia didn't answer her. She slipped into her navy blue suit jacket, getting ready for work. "I'll miss you, Liz, but I hope you have a great visit in Rochester. Say hello to Steve's sister for me."

"Julia." Liz put a hand on her friend's shoulder. "Don't be closed minded about this. Sometimes a fantastic opportunity comes along before a person is ready—but that doesn't mean it still isn't a very good thing."

"Such words of wisdom," Julia said, pulling out her lipstick case to craft her lips with Perfectly Peach. "You've been divorced twice, Liz, but you've never been a widow."

"Hey, that doesn't mean I can't understand what you're going through. I can—well, a teeny bit, anyway."

"You can't. You simply can't." Julia snapped

her lipstick closed. "And now if you'll excuse me, I have to get going to the office."

"I need to say goodbye to you! We're leaving right after you do." Tears welled up in Liz's eyes. "Oh Julia, thanks again, really . . . and do try to come to Greece soon."

"As soon as I can," Julia promised. "The minute I sell the house, I'll have the money for Greece."

"We look forward to that, honey. And maybe by then you'll be traveling with Ben Wilson, who knows?"

"Are you insane?!" Julia felt a surge of unreasonable annoyance. It simply wasn't cute or funny any more, this teasing of Liz's. "I'll be traveling with Selena, you know that. And if you don't stop irritating me, I'll travel right past your house in Athens and never even stop in to visit."

"Don't do that." Liz kissed her friend fondly on the cheek. "You go to work and I'll stop tormenting you." Liz managed to raise one eyebrow devilishly. "But you must admit—the man looks like a veritable powerhouse."

"Liz."

"I know, you're not interested in love, sex, or a dalliance with anyone. Dalliance? Now

there's a word that means nothing. Honey,
you do deny your sexuality."

"Bye. I'm leaving now. Have a good life."

"Bye, Julia. Don't forget this one thing, because it's worth a consideration . . ."

"What?"

"He's a *powerhouse.*"

Julia slammed the door behind her, but it
was a few hours before she could forget Liz's
words.

Jay Maxwell's grave, high on a hill in St.
John's Catholic cemetery, was a place she
liked to visit. She would have gone every
day—and did, back in the beginning—except
that the Grief Workshop had advised against
it. "Try to cut down to once a week, and then
once a month," they had suggested. Julia, always looking for a way to lessen the pain, had
complied.

That afternoon, however, she went after
work. She was the only visitor in the whole
forlorn area, and it seemed lonely. A north
wind, blowing and tossing leafless, skeletal
trees, gave the place a strange sort of anima-
tion. Silence didn't dominate the long stretch
of cemetery plots today; the howling of the
wind had taken over.

Julia placed a small bouquet, three white roses tied with a plain silver ribbon, near Jay's headstone. She had intended to talk aloud to him, as she always did, but this afternoon the words wouldn't come.

How, she wondered, could she explain away all these odd incidents with Ben? She was thrown constantly into contact with the man, couldn't help but find him likable, and yet—

And yet there seemed to be something more growing. It was something Julia didn't want but that kept mushrooming out of control, until she would prefer to avoid Ben Wilson altogether.

She didn't say these things at Jay's gravesite. She knelt instead, yanked out a stray tuft of crabgrass, and patted the earth in a familiar, absent way.

"Everything's fine," she whispered, finding her voice at last. "Spring has arrived, and we're doing okay, all of us. The wedding's going to be good, I think, and—" She stopped, wanting to mention Liz's visit, the subsequent reunion with Steve, the book Julia had started to write, the postponed trip to Greece, and April's fast-growing new baby boy.

Once again the words didn't flow, but just being there with Jay reinforced her feelings that she was his wife, totally not receptive to someone like Ben Wilson. The wind whipped at her hair, slashing at her skirt until she had to push it down. The sky looked blackish gray to the west where it should have been a benign sunset. Julia shivered and decided to leave.

Across the vast sea of graves she spotted another visitor, someone etched against the dark sky like a motionless piece of statuary.

What disturbed Julia was the way the person appeared to be watching her, totally unmoving, totally unapologetic for staring. It was eerie. Well, the only way to solve this one was to start walking toward the person to ask what the problem was.

Julia hiked as swiftly as she could in that direction. The lone figure stood still for quite some time, then suddenly whisked behind a copse of sturdy oaks—and was gone.

Completely gone.

Julia blinked. The person could have gone off into the woods that bordered the graveyard—must have done so, in fact, because there appeared to be no one in St. John's Cemetery now.

Too many loonies running around in this world, she thought, without any real concern. It wasn't until she was back in her car, gunning the motor, that she remembered the

Mindy person who had Cristy and Jeremy so concerned.

Could it have been?

No, that would be stretching things way too far.

Back at home, she found a large spray of flowers waiting on her doorstep. She carried them inside, thinking that Liz had become more thoughtful in her mature years. When had Liz ever sent thank-you flowers to her hostess before?

But these were odd flowers if they were from a florist. Julia frowned as she put them on her dining room table and slipped out of her coat. She wanted to look at them carefully because she suspected they weren't from Liz after all. They weren't wrapped in florist's crinkly paper and had none of the fancy trappings of florist gifts.

They'd been tucked with professionalism into a thick white urn that might have come straight from Greece. It was no cheapie container, but one embossed with Greek symbols that made Julia think of Athens and the Acropolis.

A Grecian urn?

The more she studied her gift, the more

she was convinced these fresh cutting flowers came from someone's personal greenhouse, not a commercial florist. The small white card, when she found it, verified that.

"For Julia: Thanks for a lovely evening," he had written in a strong, bold hand with black ink. "Hope for an encore. Ben."

She touched the flowers with awe. He had grown these and cut them and delivered them just for her.

Dahlias, zinnias, columbine, China asters, and snapdragon . . . a rainbow of colors, tastefully arranged around sprigs of fern and other green things that she couldn't even name. What a remarkable floral piece!

Ben had that wonderful greenhouse where everything smelled so earthy and natural even though it was, in reality, an unnatural atmosphere created just for growing plants.

I do love cut flowers, she thought.

They were perfuming the air of her dining room already, and the gleaming colors dazzled under the chandelier lighting. The whole room looked richer, somehow, as though part of some very pampered household.

Flowers mean love, Julia.

She stepped back as if her hand had been scorched by the floral arrangement. But not in this case, she corrected. Ben had had a

lovely evening and he hoped for an encore—
but that had nothing to do with love, neces-
sarily. Ben was a lonely man, that was all.

But why was Ben doing all this?

Kisses that turned her knees into strained
pablum, and flowers to thank her for going
to dinner . . .

She didn't want such complications. Not
now.

"Sometimes a fantastic opportunity comes
along before a person is ready," Liz had told
Julia this morning.

". . . but that doesn't mean it still isn't a
very good thing . . ."

I'm sorry, Julia thought stubbornly, turning
off the light in the dining room and walking
away from the flowers.

I'm sorry but there will be no encore, Mr.
Chemistry.

A figure in brown clothing was standing
outside, hidden behind a hemlock tree in the
Maxwells' backyard. The person watched as
Julia Maxwell put the flowers on her dining
room table, studied them for a few minutes,
then backed away.

A minute later the light was turned off.

Twenty

"It's not too soon to be planning the bridal shower," April said, strolling across Julia's backyard with her baby boy and little daughter Emily. She tilted her head to study the wooden wedding arch. "You know, this thing is really cool. Is that Ben Wilson guy a carpenter, too?"

"No," Julia said. "He's a retired landscape architect who gardens and also seems to have learned how to make a great many things with his hands."

"Neat." April bounced her baby on a hip and stepped back, looking at the whole yard. "They've done a lot of work here already. It's starting to look so different."

May had arrived, fresh and sweet and warm. Birds chirped in the tall sugar maples overhead, enchanting all of them, Emily, Julia, April, and the baby, as they toured the gardens on Saturday morning. Darkly purple lilacs cascaded on the two prolific bushes Jay had planted years ago. The grass of the back lawn had dried out since the spring rains, and looked sharply green, like a new shamrock.

"I know, I can't get over how much they've accomplished here. . . . May I hold little Tommy?" Julia put arms out for the baby and April surrendered "Fido" gladly. A grandmothering instinct took over, so that Julia cuddled the small bundle of boy with a fierce possessiveness. April, meanwhile, wandered around and inspected the white stones on the lawn, not secured yet but ready to be installed as part of the bride's path.

"Bethany's coming over soon," April said. "We thought we'd start talking about Cristy's shower."

"I love showers, Grandma," Emily declared, her round face alight with excitement. "We're going to have a surprise shower for Aunt Cristy!"

"And that means we keep it a secret," Julia admonished her. "Do you know how to keep a secret, Em?"

"Yep." But Emily didn't elaborate, and Julia knew full well that the three year old would blab whatever she knew the minute she spotted Aunt Cristy. Luckily the bride in question wasn't expected home from college for some time—not until after graduation day.

"So Mom," April said, "you really think this wedding will be acceptable?"

Julia started with surprise. "Acceptable? By what standards? We're not out to impress the country club set, if that's what you mean."

"No, but—will it have some class?"

"Definitely. I have no qualms at all." Julia was exaggerating somewhat, but she felt you had to put a positive face on things. "Father Hayes is all for it, so there's no problem with church regulations. And the rental company's been very helpful to me with tasteful planning."

"So we're talking about a really elegant setting?"

"It won't be tacky, if that's what you think. It'll be in good taste but also somewhat informal, a fun day . . . you have to remember Cristy is different from you and Bethany."

"Hi ho, who's talking about me?" Voices erupted from the area of the gate as it opened with a big thud. In marched the O'Donnell girls, Bethany and little Danielle, both smiling. Bethany was carrying a coffeecake.

My little women, Julia thought with unabashed sentimentality; she was reminded happily of the seven more pages she'd written this week—late at night, whenever she couldn't drop off to sleep—on her fledgling novel.

"What a gorgeous day," Bethany said as the two girl cousins hurtled themselves at each other like small rocket missiles. They collided, laughing, shrieking, and hugging. They hadn't seen each other in a couple of days, probably.

"And look at this yard!" Bethany walked around with a critical eye. "Things sure are changing. Not bad. They should have put a small stone staircase right here, though, to break up this slope. Didn't they think of that?"

"They're way ahead of you," Julia said, rocking the baby in her arms. "They already decided it's next on the agenda."

"I feel ashamed of myself," April said. "We ought to come and help next time they have a work day."

"Me, too." An avid gardener herself, Bethany fingered the thick, dark, loamy earth that filled the new garden spaces. "Mmm, nice mixture. The flowers they plant will be incredible, Mom."

"Good."

They all sat on the redwood chairs that April had hauled up from the basement and placed on the patio. With the warm sun dappling through the tree leaves, it felt like the first official day of the coming summer season. Even the little girls wanted to be seated around the patio table with the grownups.

"Now," April said, producing a steno pad and pencil. "The shower. When and where?"

"Not in a garden, I should think," Bethany remarked. "That would take away from the wedding itself."

"Mmmmm. How about having it at my house?" April loved to entertain and was talented at organizing, cooking, and serving. Julia often marveled that a daughter of hers would be so adept as a hostess.

It was that firstborn trait, of course, that made April an overachiever. Julia believed firmly in the qualities of birth order: Bethany, the middle child, had always been the designated peacemaker, while Cristy was the prototypical "baby" of the family—truculently mature one minute, frustratingly immature the next.

"Mom, do you have the wedding guest list made up yet?" Bethany asked.

Julia nuzzled close to the baby's downy-soft face. "No, but we have a basic outline. We haven't even gotten together with Jeremy's family yet to celebrate this engagement. I guess that comes right after their graduation."

"So," April concluded, looking quite annoyed, "without a wedding list, we can't do much to finalize this shower."

"Lighten up," Bethany said. "There's time."

"There's not time! You have to plan these things many months in advance. God, I can't believe the wedding itself is only four months off and things are so tentative!"

Little Tom (Julia would never think of him as Fido) scrunched up his nose, sneezed and let out a deep baby sigh. She hugged him closer, delighted with him, oblivious to everything else that was happening. She still couldn't believe there was an actual boy-child in her family, after all the girls she'd raised. She liked to think of the little guy as an extension of his grandfather, and therefore imagined his eyes and brow were exactly like Jay's.

"Hey, Mom, how was your visit with Aunt Liz?" April asked.

"Short."

"Why'd she have to take off so quickly? We wanted a chance to see her. Steve, too."

"They reconciled," Julia said, "and had to go off on their extended honeymoon, according to Liz." She shrugged and grinned. "What more can I tell you?"

"That Aunt Liz is a bird. She did call me, anyway, to say goodbye." April cut slices of cake for the little girls. "She says you all went out to the Colonial Inn for a celebration dinner."

"All of who?" asked Bethany.

"Liz and Steve," April said carefully, "and Mom and that Ben Wilson."

A thousand eyes seemed suddenly to be focused on Grandma Julia Maxwell. Even the children looked fascinated.

"Grandma has a boyfriend?" Emily asked.

"No, grandmas don't have boyfriends!" Danielle told her.

"So what's going on, Mom?" Bethany's eyes were wide with surprise. "Something we should know about?"

"No." Julia busied herself swaddling the baby tighter in his blankets. "I wonder if Tommy's cold?"

"Fido's all right as he is," April said. "Let him get a little fresh air . . . We can't help being curious, you know."

"Well, curiosity killed the cat." When flustered, Julia often resorted to quotations from her mother.

"That sounds like a Nana Francie expression," April teased.

"What cat?" Danielle was distraught. "What killed a cat? What happened to the cat?"

"Don't be stupid," Emily shot at her cousin. "Not a real cat! Just a cartoon cat on TV!"

"Don't say stupid," Danielle scolded right back. "It's not polite, you big dope."

"Girls, stop it." April's big brown eyes stayed right on Julia, studying her mother like a bug under a microscope. "Eat your cake and then go play."

"Mom, you've been out with this man several times now," Bethany remarked.

"Only twice," Julia said. "Neither time was by my choice. Cristy roped me in once and Liz the second time."

"You don't have to apologize to us," April said.

"I'm not apologizing to anyone. I'm trying to clear up the misconception that—well, that—"

"That we think you're dating?"

"Yes. I am absolutely not dating."

Bethany put out a hand and touched her mother on the shoulder. "Would it be so terribly wrong if you were?"

Julia sputtered, holding tighter to her grandson as if afraid someone were trying to run off with him. "I don't believe this interrogation. Girls, is this the real reason you came here today?"

"Mom, we've been worried about you," April said gently. "You've been lonely, and in a lot of pain since Daddy died."

"That's the natural way of things," Julia said with dignity. "You girls have felt the same sorrow, too."

"Yes, but you're so alone, Mom. We sort of think that Daddy wouldn't want you to stay alone forever."

"I don't even want to discuss this topic." Julia's face was flaming, her mind flashing the unwanted memories of Ben's late-night kiss and her treacherous bodily responses to him. She could hear his quiet voice saying, "You can pretend it didn't happen, but it did . . . what does that tell you about yourself?"

"You're allowed to date, you know," April said.

"They say it's a tribute and a compliment to her deceased spouse," Bethany said, "when a woman is willing to consider marriage again."

"You sound like a textbook. Is this what you learned as a psych major?" Julia glowered at her middle daughter.

"Sure," Bethany said with a grin.

"You girls have the wrong ideas. Now you've got me considering marriage, no less. What'll be next, a double wedding in September with Cristy and Jeremy?"

Both her daughters chuckled. "We don't mean to drive you crazy, Mom," April began.

"Sure you do." Julia grinned widely now. "You've been driving me crazy since the very day you were born, April Jean. And you, too, Bethany Marie."

"You want to spank them, Grandma?" asked Danielle with excitement. "You can do it!"

Little Tom Jr. woke up with a howl. "Fido wants his nummy nums," Emily said very solemnly. "That means my Mommy has to feed him in her chest."

"You mean BREAST, you silly!" Danielle wasn't to be outdone by her cousin's knowledge of infant nourishment.

"Girls, knock it off." April reached out for her infant son and reluctantly Julia handed him over.

"I think I'll just take a little walk." Julia stood up, restless now that she'd been relieved of the baby. "I wonder if there are any little girls anywhere who want to walk, too?"

"Grandma, come with me," Danielle said, pulling on Julia's hand. "I wanna show you where you should put a sandbox!"

"Yeah, a sandbox," Emily echoed. "And a swing set and a nice pool, too, okay, Grandma?"

Julia trotted along with the little girls, glad to put a temporary distance between herself and her daughters. *My interfering little women,* she thought. She found it rather funny the way they tried to boss her. Thankfully, with the discussion of a possible sandbox and play-ground, the topic of Julia's possible social life came to a close.

They mean well, I'm sure, but—I'll be darned if I'll take advice from anyone who calls her newborn child "Fido."

Twenty-one

"Help. I need a day in the city."

"Julia . . . you must be a mind reader." Selena, at the other end of the telephone line, sounded joyous. "I've been thinking about Manhattan, too. Shall we go for it?"

"Yes. Let's catch the first train and then try to get tickets for some really great Broadway matinee."

"We need some civilization."

"Lord, yes. We can walk in the spring sunshine and pretend we're city people—"

"—Instead of country bumpkins. You're on," Selena said. "Meet me at the Brewster train station in an hour."

"How about half an hour?"

"Even better."

As she tore out to her car, Julia reflected that she hadn't seen Ben since the dinner at the Colonial Inn. She'd called and thanked him for the flowers, of course, but he hadn't been around lately. It seemed odd because he was usually there puttering away in her back-yard several times a week.

He must be busy, she thought, and locked up her house with a lighthearted feeling. "Hey, give my regards to Broadway," she warbled in her joyful but awful singing voice. She was psyched for New York. If she couldn't have Athens and Delphi, at least she could go for The Big Apple once in a while.

Selena, looking sharp in blue pants and a sweater with a floral applique collage of spring colors, was waiting by the diner in Brewster. Julia herself wore a gold silk blouse with comfortable black slacks and huge gold earrings. They both sported Nikes so they could walk the city streets to their heart's content.

Their train came rumbling into town only minutes after they got to the platform. They boarded and settled comfortably in big old coach seats.

"What a great idea," Selena said. "Everybody needs a city fix once in a while."

"I'm so glad you could do this on a minute's notice."

"No problem, Julia. What else have I got to do? My hand washables?"

"We don't get out enough lately." Julia checked her face in a pocket compact, decided she looked passable, and relaxed.

"You can say that again. But I thought you were overloaded with things going on at your house."

"Overloaded, yes, but none of it is for me, if you know what I mean. Cristy shows up with her gang to renovate the yard, and the girls come over to plan the shower, and Ben's there running the flower show . . . but I feel like the fifth wheel."

"Didn't you say you helped Ben with some gardening last weekend? And you said you didn't hate it totally?"

"Mmmm, yes. Well, and then yesterday April and Beth ganged up on me, tried to find out all about my social life with Ben. . . . I needed a major break." She managed a rueful grin, knowing Selena would understand. And not pry.

"I'd say you're lucky to have such a concerned bunch. I wish some of my kids would care that much. They're all too busy making tons of money."

Julia gave some thought to what Selena said and decided she might be right; it was preferable to have daughters who rallied around and cared. Most of the time.

She stared out at the landscape speeding by—budding green trees, shining silver lakes, small New York towns with church steeples and railway depots. The train clackety-clacked in a safe, familiar rumble, and Julia loved the knowledge that they'd shortly be in the greatest metropolis in the world.

As soon as they pulled into Grand Central Station, Julia felt she was "home." She'd grown up here, her roots were here, and a person never stopped being a city enthusiast. The possibilities of Manhattan were endless; it was exhilarating just being far from Connecticut's hills, rivers, and bumpy old country roads.

They headed first for Forty-seventh Street, to wait in the long outdoor line for theater tickets. Luck was with them; they were able to get two for the matinee performance of a newly staged Neil Simon classic.

"That gives us the whole morning free," Selena said. "New York City, look out! Here come two very merry widows!"

They checked out toys at F.A.O. Schwartz, buying small, easy-to-carry gifts for the grandchildren. They browsed at the Museum of Modern Art, ambled through Tavern on the Green just to enjoy its elegance, and ate super-expensive chocolate truffles at a candy shoppe.

After the play, they popped into St. Patrick's, each to light a candle. In a quiet pew, Julia knelt, bowed her head, praying first for Jay and then for all her family.

Leaving, she said, "This cathedral makes my heart feel truly peaceful."

"I know what you mean." Selena grinned and blessed herself with holy water. "After all the ramming around we did today, there's something soothing to the soul when you take a minute at St. Patty's. . . . So Julia, you haven't said much yet about that big ole bear."

"What?"

"You remember—Mister Chemistry, the big old bear? You said the gardener guy was big and fuzzy like an old bear? And last I knew, your friend Liz was hitting on him, never mind the fact that she's married, and you were pretty upset with her."

They strolled along busy streets, heading toward the theater district.

"That problem was solved when Steve showed up . . . but no, I was only upset because I didn't want Liz to play her stupid games with poor Ben."

"Poor Ben?"

Julia grimaced. "By that I mean—I explained to her the guy is probably vulnerable, and not used to the kind of nonsense she can dish out."

"He might surprise you."

"He might." Julia peered into the window of a bookshop. "I don't really care about his personal life."

"Have you read any of his books yet?"

Julia nodded. "Yes, I've been thumbing through them in the evenings. Hey, do you want to see whether this bookstore carries them?"

They went in, found the gardening section, and sure enough, there were four of Ben's books.

"Wow," Selena said. "They're published by a reputable firm."

"Exciting, isn't it? He doesn't do the photographs, but he plans and writes everything else. It's all quite impressive."

"He sounds like a peach of a man," Selena said.

"I think he probably is." Julia left the bookstore and Selena followed. They stood out on the sidewalk, breathing in deeply. "Oh, don't you *love* the smells of New York? I don't care if it's polluted or crime ridden, this is still the best city on the planet."

Selena nodded agreeably. The sun was sinking in the west and tall buildings threw long shadows across the path they were traversing. The people around them were out strolling, walking their dogs or running in sweat togs—a typical Sunday in Manhattan.

"I conclude you don't want to talk about the big ole bear," Selena said after a while.

"There's nothing to talk about. He's sweet but I'm not ready for romancing." Julia reached out to touch a baby leaf budding out on a small white birch. "It's nice when spring comes to the city, isn't it?"

"You say you're not ready," Selena persisted, "but it sounds like you've already done some dating."

"Oh please. Et tu, Selena? My girls raked me over the coals yesterday about this—I'm not interested. Is that plain enough?"

"Sure." Selena sounded remorseful. "Sorry about that, pal."

They arrived back in Brewster long after dark and still had to drive home to Connecticut. But it had been well worth it, Julia thought, cruising along on Interstate 84. She'd really needed a break from all the wedding frenzy, and today's trip to the city had filled the bill.

When she pulled into her driveway at home,

she noticed right away that the backyard gate was open, swinging on its hinges. Unusual. Maybe Ben had been here working on the path.

She turned off the car's headlights. Her property was thrown into total darkness; she hadn't left the front lights on earlier today. Ordinarily Julia didn't mind darkness, but this particular night was full of shadows and soft noises, with shrubs that swayed in the wind and swished against other branches.

Something wasn't right, but she wasn't about to examine it at such a late hour. She clutched her key and ran to the front door, unlocking it swiftly. Once inside, she switched on lights quickly.

The phone rang, making her heart jump. Who calls up at this hour? But she answered it.

"Julia, I'm sorry to call so late." Ben sounded rather grim. "I spotted your car lights so I knew you'd just gotten in."

"But—what's wrong?"

"The prowler struck your yard again," he told her. "I've already reported it to the police, Julia, but I wanted you to be aware of it. It must have been last night. They messed up our gardens, pulled away the rocks we had so carefully set in—"

"I can't believe it," she whispered, sinking into a chair as she spoke.

"I notified Cristy and Jeremy, too," Ben went on. "They're stepping up their efforts to find that Mindy Parsons they were talking about. Apparently the girl dropped out of school and left her home, too. Even her parents claim they don't know where she's living."

"That sounds rather bizarre."

"Yes. Listen, we can fix all the damage she did—or whoever did it—but Julia, are you sure you feel safe there? Alone in your house, I mean?"

Startled, she said, "Of course I do. I told you about the security system Jay installed. I'm not worried."

"You could have Ivan the Terrible to keep you company if you wanted," he said. "You could even have me if—never mind, scratch that. I know you're not about to allow a man to sleep in your home."

She laughed. "There's no need, Ben, but thank you just the same. I'm not a scaredy-cat sort of person. Hey, I just spent the whole day roaming around New York City. If a person can survive that, she can certainly handle whatever Connecticut has to offer."

His turn to laugh. "You've got a point

there. Well, call me if you do have any problems, Julia."

"I will."

"How's your novel coming along?"

"Slowly, but it's toddling, sort of like a baby taking its first steps. I plan to keep at it."

"Hey, great. I'm glad."

"And thanks for letting me read your books. I'm enjoying them."

"Terrific. If they can appeal to a non-gardener, I must be doing something right." He said a quick goodbye then and hung up.

Julia stood there holding the telephone, feeling slightly bereft once the connection was broken.

Not that she was nervous about the prowler. It wasn't that. It was simply that she'd been discussing books with Ben and it felt cozy—as though he were an old friend like Liz or Selena. Why had he hung up so soon when they might have talked longer?

She shivered briefly, thinking of the vandalism that had been done to her property. She hoped Cristy would locate that disturbed girl soon, if Mindy was indeed the perpetrator.

Sometimes you just can't win, she thought, heading toward the bathroom for a shower. You manage to get a wonderful day away from everything, you taste all the excitement of the big city, and then you come home to the same old creepin' crud.

Only worse.

Twenty-two

In the morning before work, she checked the backyard, and was shocked at the violence that had been done. The big wooden wedding arch hadn't been hit this time, luckily, but tiles on the bride's path had been overturned and smashed by an angry hand.

Beyond that the gardens, as Ben had said, were stomped, ripped and scattered. Even though no plants had been put in yet, the soil itself had generated a major mixing production—and now the soil was flung all throughout the grassy lawn.

She was stunned, and at the same time tears began sliding down her cheeks. That someone could be so full of hate that he or she could do this amount of damage . . . it was sad and frightening.

Julia touched a jagged, broken piece of the bridal path and a moment of despair washed over her. Would they ever be able to pull off this garden wedding? Or would some force of evil be triumphant in the long run?

Shivering, she hurried back into the house. I'm going to find that Mindy Parsons, she thought. If she exists and if she lives somewhere around here, there must be a paper trail of some sort . . . and I'll find her!

That same morning, Cristy tapped out the telephone number of Mrs. Ruth Parsons of New Haven. The phone was picked up on the second ring.

"Mrs. Parsons, it's me again—Cristy Maxwell. Do you remember talking to me before about Mindy?"

"Of course I do." The woman was wary but not unfriendly. "I still have nothing to tell you about my daughter."

"You *can't* tell me," Cristy demanded, "or you won't tell me? Because I've got to know where she is, Mrs. Parsons."

"I understand that. I'd like to know her whereabouts myself, Cristy. She's my little girl and she's not well—" The hoarse voice broke off with a sob.

"Mrs. Parsons, I'm sorry to keep pestering you. Can you think of anyplace she might have gone? To a relative, maybe, to hide out?"

"She has an aunt in Stonewell but—no, if she'd gone there my sister would have told me."

"Stonewell? That's my home town, the exact town we're concerned about!"

There was a hesitation. "Mindy always did like it there. They have that big manmade Candlewood lake and she loves to swim."

"I know. I grew up there. Mrs. Parsons, please, does she have money?"

"Actually, yes. She took the whole amount that was supposed to pay for her tuition this semester, cashed it, and must be living on it."

"Great. So she may not even need a job." Cristy rapped her fingers against her dorm room desk. "What about—does she have a car?"

"Why, yes. She has that brown Ford her father bought her for her high school graduation. She'll never be parted from that car." The woman's voice broke with anguish. "But I don't know why she won't keep in touch with us, her own parents."

"May I ask one more question? The last time you saw her—did she mention anything about Jeremy Crenshaw?"

"The boy from her dorm, yes. She said she was hurt because he'd led her on, so she thought he cared for her—"

"But that wasn't true. Not at all. He never encouraged her at all."

A deep sigh could be heard coming over the line. "I'm sure it wasn't true. She often made up crushes like that, even in high school."

Cristy extracted the name of the aunt in Stonewell, a Mrs. Temple. She certainly had to be checked out, too.

"It's extremely important for us to locate Mindy," Cristy said. "Will you get in touch if you find out anything?"

"Yes, dear, I will. And you'll call me if you find her? We'd like to get help for her."

"Yes," Cristy said. "We'll keep in close contact with you."

When Julia's work phone rang, she thought it would be a secretary from another school who was supposed to get back to her on a curriculum matter. Instead, it was Ben Wilson.

"Good morning," he said.

"Is it? I went out and looked at that mess in my yard."

"I know; it's really awful. Listen, Julia, I called to tell you I'm thinking of putting the wedding arch back in my garage, if it's all right with you."

"Good idea. At least it'll be safe from—whoever our visitor is."

"We were lucky he or she didn't get at the arch this time. As for the rest, we can fix all that. But Julia, we have to start planning for a way to safeguard your property."

"What are you thinking of?"

"There are electronic devices we might invest in—"

"My money is limited right now, Ben." When she spoke his name, she noticed Selena's head pop up in great interest.

"Well, how about a dog? We could get you a mature mutt, one who's old enough to be a watchdog."

She groaned. "I really don't want a dog. Besides, I plan to sell my house later this year and move to a condo."

"Oh. I see what you mean. We'll have to keep thinking about this. We can't have that vandal ruining everything for Cristy's wedding."

"No," Julia said very softly.

"Okay if I come by later this afternoon?" he asked, sounding hopeful. "So we can talk?"

"Well, yes . . ." Since when had he asked permission? Usually he just showed up at the garden gate.

"Listen," she said impulsively. "My friend Selena, from work, is coming over for dinner tonight." As Julia said that, Selena almost fell off her chair. "I thought I'd roast a few pieces of chicken, nothing special—Would you like to join us?"

He sounded surprised enough to fall off his chair, too. "I'd love to, if it's not an important night for girl talk."

Julia laughed. "It's not. Selena and I did all our gabbing yesterday. So come over about sixish, Ben."

When she'd hung up, Selena pounced. "Excuse me? This is the very first I heard of any dinner invitation, Julia. What's going on?"

"No big deal. I want you to meet Ben and see the things going on in the yard and—I feel like having a tiny dinner party. I'm tired of being alone. Okay?"

"You sure it's not because you need a chaperone with Mister Chemistry?"

"Positive."

"Okay," Selena said, shrugging and grinning. "So I'll be there. Chicken, hmmm?"

The chicken was Julia's best orange-glaze recipe, the squash was baked just right, and the home-baked biscuits came out of the oven soft and flaky. She found she was enjoying her little impromptu dinner party—with soft music on the stereo, the table set flawlessly in her dining room, white candles flickering, white wine flowing along with the conversation.

And a spectacular vase of greenhouse flowers hand-delivered by Ben—carnations, daisies, tulips, and daffodils. Julia placed it as the centerpiece on her table.

"Thank you," she said, marveling at the talent he had for growing and arranging the blooms.

"So this is the poor guy you tried to have arrested," Selena said as soon as she'd been introduced to Ben. "He does look real shady, I must say. Must be all that facial hair!"

Ben laughed heartily. "I only wear the beard because it makes me look like a college professor. You think it gives me that criminal element?"

"Nah, it's kinda cute," Selena said.

Selena and Ben hit it off very well. Of course, Julia thought—both were avid gardeners. There was always a ready topic of discussion when one could mention compost, mulch, peat moss, and Miracle-Gro.

Meanwhile Julia bustled around, serving her dinner proudly, listening as her two friends chatted with great ease.

What a nice contrast to having Liz there with Ben!

"This meal is so good, Julia," Selena said, reaching for a fourth biscuit. "How do you put all this together after working an entire day?" She turned to Ben. "I'm lucky if I put a frozen Budget Gourmet in the microwave."

"Me, too."

"Cooking is easy," Julia said. "It's that puttering around outdoors that would drive me crazy."

"Oh no." Selena was ready for a debate. "There's nothing more relaxing than working out in the sunshine, mucking around in the dirt. . . ."

"You know that expression about being nearer God's heart in a garden," Ben said, "than anywhere else?"

"Oh ho," Selena said. "If it's quotes you want! My grandmother used to say, 'A man of words and not of deeds, is like a garden full of weeds!' "

All three of them laughed. "Perfect, Selena," Ben said. "I only hope that's not me you're describing."

"That remains to be seen, doesn't it?"

"Ben is a man of words, of course, being a writer . . . but his deeds have been remarkable, too." Julia hoped she wasn't blushing.

"We saw your books in a store in Manhattan," Selena said.

"Which reminds me, Ben." Julia buttered another biscuit for herself. "Do you have another gardening book in progress, or are you looking for a new topic?"

"I'm in the process of looking, actually."

"I wonder whether anyone's ever done a how-to book about a garden wedding?" Julia lifted her eyebrows. "I mean, like in our case, turning an ugly duckling yard into a beautiful swan?"

He stared at her without moving a facial muscle. "That's an incredible idea, Julia."

"Sounds great to me!" Selena seemed to be enjoying the conversation much. "Wouldn't you need lots of photos?"

"Yes, of course . . ." Ben's voice trailed off. He was faintly smiling, lost already in some reverie they could only guess at. "It's not too late to begin photographing Julia's property. . . . You *did* mean, didn't you, that we could illustrate with your yard?"

"Well, sure . . . I suppose so. Sure, why not?" She grinned. "Do you think your publishers will go for it?"

"We'll find out," Ben said happily. He raised his wine, looking at her across the rim of the

Wish You Were Here?

You can be, every month, with Zebra
Historical Romance Novels.

TREAT YOURSELF TO 4 FREE BOOKS.

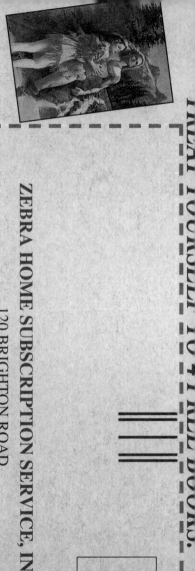

AFFIX
STAMP
HERE

ZEBRA HOME SUBSCRIPTION SERVICE, INC.

120 BRIGHTON ROAD

P.O. BOX 5214

CLIFTON, NEW JERSEY 07015-5214

||...|.||..||.|.|.|.||.|.|.|.|.||.|..||.|.|.|.||..||..|

crystal goblet. "Here's to a great idea, and thank you."

"You're welcome," Julia said, pleased. She raised her wine glass, too, as did Selena.

"To inspirations—and the meeting of great minds," said Selena. Her round face was filled with mischief. "Why, there's almost a *chemistry* to it all."

Beneath the table, Julia poked her.

Selena insisted on washing all the dishes while Ben dried and put away. They had a pleasant time of it, all working leisurely in Julia's spacious kitchen.

"We still haven't discussed how we're going to foil the vandal," Ben said as he dried a saucepan. "You won't consider electronic safeguards for the backyard?"

"I might have to," Julia said. "But isn't there some cheaper way? And less drastic?"

"I know." Selena turned her head from the kitchen sink to stare at both of them. "What about Rent a Dog?"

"What? There is no such thing."

"Then start your own! I just made that up, but maybe you could borrow Ben's dog once in a while. He's a good watchdog, isn't he?"

"Yes." Ben nodded. "I've been thinking that

myself . . . use my Ivan as a detective. Anytime, Julia. Ivan would be most honored to be called in on the case."

"Maybe that's what I'll try then," she said thoughtfully. "But in the meantime, I'm going to find that girl."

"What?" demanded both Ben and Selena in unison.

"The girl, Mindy Parsons. If she's here in Stonewell, I'm going to find her."

"That sounds dangerous, Julia." Frowning, Selena pulled her hands out of the sudsy water and dried them on a towel.

"It won't be dangerous. I'm just going to do some detective work . . . not chasing after the poor sick girl."

"The poor sick girl could be highly vicious," Ben said. When he was worried, his eyes turned a wonderful dark green color like the early morning shimmer on Candlewood Lake.

"I'll be careful," Julia said. "I promise I'll never go near her. I'll just inquire, that's all."

"Julia, please, call one of us if you get any leads," Selena said in a gruff voice. "Promise?"

"Yes, of course."

The subject was forgotten, she thought, by the time her guests announced they had to be going home. She went for their coats and walked them to the front door.

"Thanks for the great dinner," Selena said, charging out the door with no fanfare. "See you tomorrow!"

"Good night," she and Ben called out, both surprised at the rapid way Selena disappeared.

Instead of leaving, Ben firmly closed the door behind Selena. He was in his coat but seemed in no hurry to go. The two of them were crammed together in her little entryway hall, the space between them quite limited. Julia tried to back away without making a big deal out of her action.

"Stay here, Julia," he entreated softly.

"No. Go home."

His face looked very solemn. "I need to be sure you won't go chasing after that girl."

"I told you I won't. I only said I would find her."

"Julia." Ben reached out his long arms slowly, questioningly, as if to give her a chance to consider. She stood mesmerized, unwilling to escape even though she felt she should resist. He folded her into his arms as easily as a giant bear would scoop in a pot of honey.

"I don't want to do this."

"I think you do." His mouth grazed along the side of her cheek; her heart raced and a sensual flutter made its way through her insides.

"I'd like you to leave, Ben," she managed to say.

"I will." Very gently, as though in slow motion, he tilted her chin up toward him. She was an inch away from that beard and some erratic thing was thumping away in her throat.

"Tell me you don't want one kiss, Julia."

"I don't," she began, "want . . ." Her words were silenced by the soft pressure of his mouth closing over hers. The fuzziness of the beard enveloped her, surrounded her so completely she was drowning, lost in it—and again she was reminded of ancient, classical Greeks, the heroes of her Grecian dreams.

Their tongues met. She thought how very different this kiss was from any she'd ever shared with Jay—was it because of the all-pervasive beard? Ben's mouth was sweet, warm, fluid in its movements as he angled closer, probed deeper into her own.

She truly wanted to stay lost in that kiss forever—and yet her common sense insisted that she pull away. She gave him no explanation, either, just stepped backward into her living room, putting space between them.

"Pure denial, Julia," he said in his soft, musical way.

She didn't answer. She rubbed her arms, chilled to the bone. Already she felt cold and alone, yearning to melt back into that embrace where warmth would always be part of their togetherness.

Ben smiled. "I told you once, I'm a very patient man." He pulled his coat around his throat and opened the door. "Good night."

Without another gesture, he was gone.

Twenty-three

You had to give the man credit. He knew how to kiss a woman and make her crazy. . . .

That night, Julia's dreams were of love, the love of a man whose face she could never quite see. She knew though, if he turned toward her in the light she'd see Ben's familiar face with those lake-green eyes and the smile in the soft beard . . .

But truthfully, kisses from Ben were the least of her worries right now. She was concentrating on other priorities—namely the wedding and the finding of Mindy Parsons.

The following afternoon Julia drove toward the north end of town, to the address Cristy had given her. She came to the country road—Sullivan Lane—and searched among the tract homes, large raised ranches, for number fifteen. Finally she found it—a ranch like all the others except for embellishments with antique brick. She stepped out of her car and went to ring the doorbell.

A woman peered out, then opened the door.

"Good afternoon, I'm Julia Maxwell. Are you Mrs. Temple?"

"Yes." She was a short, plump woman with bright blue eyes.

"I need to talk to you about your niece, Mindy Parsons."

Luckily Mindy's aunt was friendly and willing to talk. They sat together in the L-shaped living room; Julia declined the offer of coffee or tea.

"My sister told me people were looking for Mindy," Laurie Temple said, twisting nervously at a child's cloth doll. "I believe she's here in Stonewell, but that's only a hunch, truthfully."

Julia leaned forward eagerly. "Why do you think that? And where do you think she might be?"

"Mindy came to see me just once, back in January when she dropped out of UConn. Said she was planning to settle here."

"Did she stay with you?"

"No, she said she had a girlfriend named Christine, or maybe Cristy. I assumed they were going to be roommates somewhere in Stonewell."

Julia felt an icicle making its way along her spine. *"Cristy?* Are you sure?"

"Fairly sure. Anyway, I never saw her again, but—"

"What?"

The woman squirmed with discomfort. "Sometimes I feel as though she's around. You know, watching me. Or even slipping into my house, somehow, when I'm not here. . . . It's eerie and I can't prove it, but that's how I feel."

The girl on the cemetery hill, Julia thought with a cold horror—watching, waiting, just standing there in the dim twilight, then slipping silently into the darkened woods.

Julia explained to Mrs. Temple exactly what had been happening at her house, and why Mindy was the chief suspect.

"You mean because Mindy had a crush on this boy Jeremy?" Mrs. Temple looked angry. "That's why you think she'd try to ruin everything for their wedding?"

Julia nodded. "What do you think? Is she capable of something like this?"

Mrs. Temple hesitated slightly. "Oh, I'm afraid so. I'm afraid she has a terrible temper and some very sneaky ways. I frankly think she should be in a hospital where she could get treatment—I believe she could get well eventually."

They continued to talk, and Julia became

convinced the aunt really had no clear idea of Mindy's whereabouts.

"You'll notify us if you hear from her? Or see her?" Julia asked, handing over her name and phone number.

"Sure. But she won't let us see her. You or me." Mrs. Temple bit her lower lip with concern. "She'll make sure she sees *us*, though. You can bet on that."

Julia spent the following morning at the Stonewell Town Hall. There were a number of places where a resident, even a new resident, might be listed, and she tried them all. The tax rolls, for one; if the girl owned a car—the brown Ford her father had given her—she'd eventually come up on the motor vehicle tax rolls that were issued from the Connecticut DMV. But no, there was no Mindy Parsons listed in the tax assessor's office.

She tried the town clerk's office—nothing there, she found, among fishing licenses, dog licenses, or marriage licenses. Didn't hurt to try, however. The registrar's office: No Mindy Parsons had enrolled as a voter in Stonewell, either, so there went that hope.

I thought I was so smart, Julia thought, clunking dismally down the stone steps of the old brick town hall. Thought I knew right where to find someone. Well, the average someone, anyway.

This Mindy would be findable somehow, but it wasn't going to be as simple as Julia had believed.

She looked up and, with a start, realized a vivid spring day had bloomed, with sweet breezes and racing white clouds. May at last had turned beautifully warm, the sun coaxing bulb flowers—tulips and daffodils—up from the earth and readying blossoms on crabapple, dogwood, and cherry trees.

Julia decided to do something she hadn't done in all the years she'd worked at school—take a day off. For no reason, other than that it was spring and she was in need of a small break.

"You're a woman of impulse," she could hear a tiny voice whispering to her, but she ignored it. She really was not.

She made her call to the office from a telephone right on the village green near the bandstand. Then she stood there, trying to think of every way that she might track down a girl like Mindy Parsons.

Rentals, she thought; the girl has to have a place to live so she must have rented an apartment somewhere.

She traipsed from office to office, talking to real estate people and rental agents. No one had heard of Mindy Parsons, nor did they recall a single girl, young, intense, thin, and wearing all brown.

Then Julia tried the drugstores, because Kevin had said Mindy was supposed to take a certain medication. Drugstores, however, weren't about to give out the names of their customers for obvious reasons of confidentiality.

Julia ran out of steam at noontime and drove home, thinking about a cool shower and putting her feet up to read a book.

But of course, she should have known. Ben's pickup truck was in her driveway. He was at work in her backyard as usual, no doubt.

I'm not obligated to spend time with the man, she thought. She hurried into her house and upstairs. But when she looked out her bedroom window, she saw not only Ben but someone else—a young man with some pretty impressive photographic equipment.

"Hi, what's going on?" she called out, throwing open the window.

"Good news!" Ben looked euphoric. "My editor likes the *Garden for a Wedding* idea,

Julia. He sent Bryce out here to get a few preliminary pictures."

She stared down. "That is good news for you." She smiled, positive she could see the flickering, friendly green of Ben's eyes even from this distance. His thick hair glistened in the May sunshine, and with his impressive height he actually made a better-looking specimen than Bryce, the photographer, who seemed to be in his twenties.

Stop it, Julia!

She changed clothes, slipping into slacks and a shirt, went downstairs and out in spite of all her vows to stay away from Benjamin Wilson.

"So glad to meet you, Mrs. Maxwell," the young man said, shaking her hand as Ben introduced him as Bryce Cameron. "This sounds like an exciting project."

"It has been eventful," she admitted. "Are you taking what they call the 'BEFORE' pictures now?"

"Exactly," Ben said. He had straightened up after the vandalism, so things were relatively back to normal. "We're especially shooting all the plain spots on your property, Julia, places we haven't begun to renovate yet."

The plain places. "This is embarrassing, in a way," she said to Ben. "What will you tell your readers? That you found this weird or lazy woman who had never planted even one geranium in her whole life?"

Ben shook his head. "Of course not. We'll say we met a homeowner who was an indoor person—a great cook, a superb mother, a model housekeeper, and a successful secretary in the school system."

She scoffed at that. "You're trying to make me sound respectable, Ben, but the fact remains I've been a total dud at Gardening 101."

"Don't worry about it," Ben said. "We are who we are."

"The readers will enjoy this garden transformation so much." Bryce had adjusted his tripod and was focusing quietly on Julia. "Would you mind just one shot, Mrs. Maxwell?"

"Oh, no, I—"

"Would you rather not?" Ben stepped in between Julia and the camera. "You look fine, but if you say no, it's no."

She lifted her head and leveled a sharp look at the man who'd kissed her against her will last night. "If I say no, it's no?" Her voice was steady, heavy with significance. "Is that what you just said?"

He colored, then grinned sheepishly. "Touché. You got me that time."

"Well?" asked Bryce from behind his tripod. "What about the picture?"

Julia laughed. "Why not? Go ahead." She was still laughing as Bryce clicked the camera once, twice, three times.

"I can just see the caption," Julia grumbled. "PICTURED HERE: The uninspired homeowner who didn't have even one flower planted for her daughter's wedding."

Ben was standing beside her, signaling Bryce to shoot a picture of them together. Without fanfare, Ben's arm took possession of her shoulder and she was drawn imperceptibly closer to him. There was something warm, protective, about the way he accomplished this; but Julia felt enmeshed in a male conspiracy out of her control. She didn't struggle against it, yet felt deep down that they had no business taking her photo.

Most confusing.

Birds darted about the trees with tremendous noise. Mellow sunshine sliced through the pale green lacework of newly budded maple and oak branches. Julia's yard, private as it was because of Jay's thick hedges, seemed a quiet haven on this springtime day.

She knew by now that her bit of real estate was filled with promise. Ben had made that promise: to fill the entire area with floral beauty so Cristy could be married in a garden setting. He certainly hadn't planned to do it for a new gardening book; he wasn't that sort of self-serving man.

She was delighted, nevertheless, that he would receive literary compensation for all his hours of labor here.

"This might turn out to be your best book yet, Mr. Wilson." Bryce was clicking away as he made slow circles around Julia and Ben. "Going to use one of these for your jacket photo?"

Julia stiffened. "Absolutely not. The book jacket should contain a photo of Ben alone."

"We'll see."

The arm around her shoulders pressed a little tighter, demonstrating a strong conviction that dismayed her. Before she could pull away, she felt a feather-light kiss at the top of her head just where her curls were tumbling in the breeze. Ben's swift kiss affected her, giving her a split second of light-headedness along with an increased heartbeat.

"There! That should make a great jacket photo," Ben said in great amusement. "Everybody likes to see the author with a pretty lady."

"That's ridiculous, Ben," she began.

"You look noticeably happier this time, Mr.

Wilson," Bryce commented and winked knowingly.

It *was* some kind of gigantic male conspiracy, she thought, it really was. She yanked herself away.

"Don't you dare use my photo without my permission," she said, keeping her tone light but her meaning quite clear.

"You're the boss," Ben said quietly.

"I'm going inside." She marched off, barely mumbling, "Nice to have met you, Bryce."

Twenty-four

Fullblown spring, almost a pre-summer, seemed to be with them after that. Outside Julia's sliding glass doors, many shades of green showed themselves—in the curly oak leaves, the pale sugar maple leaves, the enamel-green of the privet hedge.

Jay's lilacs burst open in a riot of color and perfume and had a surprising effect on Julia. She found herself cutting them, arranging them in vases around the house, poking her nose often into their rich scent. Odd, but all these years she'd tended to ignore them, she couldn't imagine why. She felt disappointment when the lilacs withered as the month of May marched rapidly on.

But lilac and green weren't the only colors to be seen through her glass sliders. Ben showed up day after day, each time with some new flowering plant from his greenhouse to set into the soil.

Zinnias, marigolds, pansies, alyssum, snapdragons, and impatiens arrived in small peat pots; Ben had started them himself from seeds, and they were sturdy little plants that already bore the beginnings of blossoms.

"Sweets for the sweet," he joked once, pushing his flower-laden wheelbarrow through her gate.

"That sounds pretty corny," she told him with a smile.

"Oh, I am corny." He grinned as he lifted out a nasturtium plant. "Cornyness is a trait of us Dudley Do-Rights."

She rather looked forward to each day's offering. Ben would carefully put the plants into the prepared soil, his large hands astoundingly gentle with the small nurslings and within days pert flowers opened their faces to the sunshine.

The best part of these May days was Ben hadn't made any recent overtures; the photographing in the garden was the very last time he'd touched her.

He was so busy, both planting her gardens and cultivating the many beds on his own property, he didn't once even mention her "total denial," "woman of impulse," or any of that seductive nonsense.

They were platonic friends, now, it seemed. And *I'm grateful for it,* she told herself.

Julia was busy beyond belief, too. Besides the usual everyday bustle at school, she had the wedding, with lists upon lists to refer to: the guest list, the rental list, the DJ list she was compiling, the numerous catering places and bakeries. Once in a while she stole a few hours to work on her novel but that was moving along slowly.

Jeremy's parents in Stamford, the Crenshaws, called to invite Julia to dinner as an official recognition of the couple's engagement. She hadn't yet met them, but they sounded nice. They decided to make it the week after the UConn graduation.

"And don't forget, I have two tickets to my graduation ceremony," Cristy told Julia over the telephone. "You get one of them, Momserina."

"I should hope so! And who else will you invite—April or Bethany?"

"Neither. They're not all that interested."

"Neither? But they're your sisters."

"Mom, I've already invited someone. Ben Wilson. He accepted and it's all set. Would you like to drive up with him that morning?"

"Well . . ." Julia was surprised. "Let me give that some thought. In the meantime, what have you found out about Mindy?"

"Not much more, really. Well—we did get

something from Kellie, her former roommate. . . ."

"Which is?"

"She says Mindy is obsessed with grave-
yards. Loves them. Isn't that creepy? Visits
them, walks around, makes a hobby out of it,
so to speak."

"My God." Julia recalled again the tall,
dark figure watching her from the hill in St.
John's Cemetery. "Maybe that's how we can
catch her, Cristy." She told the story about
that day.

Cristy let out a long, low whistle. "Keep an
eye out for her then, Moms . . . but call the
cops if you spot her. No detective work on
your own!"

"I'm not trying to be Nancy Drew," Julia
said with great dignity, though actually she
was, in her own way. She was desperate to
find Mindy in spite of the fact the phantom
vandal hadn't struck again—yet.

In her spare time, Julia continued to stop
off at town halls in neighboring towns, checking resident and taxpayer lists. Nothing had
yet turned up, but she kept trying. They had
to find Mindy Parsons before she flaked out
again.

It would be unthinkable if their lovely
yard—Cristy's wedding gardens—were to be

destroyed now, just when they were beginning to bloom under the bright, warm sunlight.

Julia and Irmgard had visited the public library several times now. It was becoming a ritual they both enjoyed.

"I think it's time for a mystery," Irmgard would say sometimes; but in May, she said, "I could go for a romance now, Missus Julia." At that, her jolly round face crinkled with delight, the soft blue eyes dancing with devilment. They headed over to new fiction paperbacks to search for something juicy enough to satisfy the slightly risqué taste of the sixty-year-old grandmother.

"This makes reading more fun," Irmgard insisted, clutching several hot romance novels to her chest.

"They're not too difficult for you?" Julia asked. "Because you could start with young adult romances."

"I find a way, always." Irmgard proudly displayed her very own library card to the person at the checkout desk. "Even if I have to use dictionary to look up words like—pulsating? throbbing? plundering?"

"Oh dear Lord," Julia groaned, grinning but wondering what she had started here.

"You're making that up, Irmgard! And what was wrong with Dick and Jane, anyway?"

"Too easy, too boring." Irmgard scooped up her pile of books. "Do you borrow books today, Missus Julia?"

"I can't." She sighed. "I miss reading but I'm so busy right now I can't even breathe. The wedding, my job, the gardens—"

"Weddings make much work." Irmgard held open the library door and they stepped outside into a soft spring rain. "But will be a lovely wedding, you'll see."

Julia smiled wearily. "Thanks, Irmgard."

"And how is *your* romance, hmm, Missus Julia?"

Julia almost toppled over. "What are you talking about?"

Irmgard looked supremely wise as she picked her way across a puddle in the middle of the library plaza. "I see the way the man looks at you, that Ben Wilson."

"But that's ridiculous. He's nothing but a friend of my daughter's. Well, he's been a friend to me, too, but nothing more than that."

Irmgard wagged a finger. "I know much about romance, Missus Julia, even if I don't know how to read all these years. I can see if man is very much in love with woman."

"No, no, no." Julia was adamant. "That's not the case at all."

"Mister Ben, he looks at you with soft eyes. Eyes of love, nice green eyes like leaves on this forsythia bush. I was watching."

Julia sighed and plunged through a puddle herself, not caring if her shoes got wet. "Love, soft eyes, pulsating, throbbing—I don't think you ought to be reading any more of these romance books, Irmgard!"

"Nobody can stop me now. And you—you should try reading one or two. Maybe you learn how to appreciate a good man."

Julia threw a scornful glance toward her pupil. "I know all about a good man; I was married to one. I'm still in the process of letting go."

"You are educated lady, Missus Julia." Irmgard stopped walking, placed a hand tentatively on Julia's arm, and looked up into Julia's face. "You finish college, I never even learn to read. But—I know some things about life."

"Well, of course you do, but *surprise*—so do I."

"Old German saying, very full of wisdom," Irmgard said in a most serious tone. " 'Good man is hard to find.' My grandmother tell me this many years ago in Munich."

Julia stared for a moment. "You little faker,

you. That's from some old song, and not an old German saying at all!"

Irmgard grinned wickedly. "So? Is still a good saying. When God sends you someone most special—that's like a miracle—you should say *thank you*. Not, *no thank you.*"

Julia couldn't speak for a moment; then she said in an even tone, "Do you seriously think God sent Ben Wilson to me, Irmgard?"

She saw the gleam of a grin again. "Gott in Himmel sends us what we need, very often. He sent you to teach me reading, yes? And now—he sends to you a good and sexy man."

"You sound like Doctor Ruth."

"So you should maybe listen to me, in that case."

"I can't believe we're standing here in the rain discussing this nonsense. Let's get to your house and have our reading lesson."

The topic was dropped and the two women walked side by side toward Irmgard's home.

But in her dreams that night, Julia again saw the tall man whose face was hidden from her . . . and she kept hearing a German-accented voice advising her, "You should say thank you, not no thank you. . . ."

Twenty-five

Afterward, she thought about how she might have refused to travel with Ben to the graduation. She might have exerted her own power of refusal; she didn't have to be swept away always by Cristy's well organized plans. But somehow when the Big Day at the end of May arrived, she went along with everyone's idea of what was convenient.

Therefore, Ben would drive by for Julia and they'd head for UConn together. It would have been great to go in his big maroon Lincoln which was—as Cristy pointed out—an unusually comfortable vehicle for travel. But Ben decided to take his pickup truck because there would be a huge pile of Cristy's dorm room possessions to transport.

Ben appeared at her door very early that Saturday morning because they'd decided to leave before six A.M. They took off without so much as a cup of coffee, then stopped right away at the Dunkin' Donuts in Stonewell.

"You look very nice," Ben said as he carried two steaming paper cups of coffee to the car.

"Thanks. So do you." She was wearing a new flowered dress with a lacy scoop neckline and full skirt. He was spiffed out in a classic suit of dusty blue-grey. He looked truly special, like that "miracle" Irmgard had mentioned: tall, sparkly clean, smiling, and well dressed. But maybe it was only because Julia was accustomed to seeing him in gardening clothes.

He settled back into the driver's seat and said, "Is this awkward for you, Julia?"

"What do you mean? Drinking coffee in the car? No."

"I mean traveling with me. Being coerced into it, in fact, by your exuberant daughter."

"No problem." She thought carefully before she continued. "I'm okay with this trip, although you're right, I was railroaded into it. Cristy never seems to take no for an answer."

"She's a pistol, all right." He grinned with fondness and sipped his coffee. "But maybe this trip today is a good chance for us to talk. Maybe we can lay down some ground rules."

"What?" Startled, she had to hold tight to her Dunkin' Donuts cardboard cup to keep it from sloshing over.

"Ground rules." Ben faced her straight on,

his eyes soft with sincerity. "I've had the impression you didn't want me coming close, Julia. So I've been on my very best behavior lately, in case you haven't noticed."

She couldn't help it; she laughed out loud.

"Oh Lord, yes, I have noticed. I wondered what was happening. . . . I simply thanked my lucky stars, that's all."

Freudian choice of words? She heard Irmgard's voice again in the back of her head, scolding: "You should say *thank you* to God, Missus Julia—not, *no, thank you!*"

"You thanked your lucky stars, did you?" His smile was wide and appreciative.

"Yes." She raised her chin with dignity. "It's been very pleasant, being friends."

He was quiet for a few minutes, then said, "Guess we better get going again or we'll miss that graduation. . . ." He turned the key. "Anyway, that's what I meant by ground rules. If you, Mrs. Maxwell, want to remain merely friends—no hugging, no kissing, no anything—then I intend to honor your wishes."

She was touched. "Thank you, Ben."

He accelerated the motor and headed out for the highway once again. "So does that take some of the tension out of our trip?"

"Of course." She tried not to stare at him as he drove, though she noted he was a superb driver with a quiet, calm confidence. Jay had been jumpy at the wheel, always looking to pass other cars, often quick to yell if another driver did something the least bit ornery. As sweet a man as Jay was, he transformed into Mr. Hyde on the highway.

"I have a question for you, Ben," she said.

"Sure."

She stared out at the scenery whizzing by: the city of Waterbury, crowded and slightly smoggy in the early morning light. "How long after your wife died—after you lost Lily— did you begin dating again?"

His brows went up as he kept his eyes on the road. "Interesting question. You probably won't believe my answer."

"Why? Try me."

"The answer is never. I never did begin."

"But—she died so many years ago."

"Six years ago. What can I say? I didn't feel like getting into that singles scene. I do meet plenty of single women at the college, all ages, but I've kept a low profile socially."

"But you—but that's so lonely for you."

"I told you you wouldn't believe me."

"I believe it if you say so, but—well, with me, you—"

You're always trying to kiss me, she was thinking.

He turned briefly to look at her. His eyes seemed to reflect the leafy green of weeping willow trees they were passing along I-84.

"What? I act as though I'm fond of you?"

"Exactly. I mean, what's going on? If you don't date, then are you doing some preliminary practice work on your neighbor?"

He laughed at her. "Julia, you can't seriously mean that. Is that what you think of me?"

She shrugged. "I don't know what to think of you."

He didn't answer right away. "Isn't it possible I've been attracted to you, and that's all there is to it?"

"That seems unlikely. I'm not exactly Farrah Fawcett and I've never even been all that pleasant to you, Ben. First I had you arrested, practically, and then I harbored a resentment toward you for a long while—"

He was shaking his head firmly. "Can I tell you precisely why I'm attracted to you?"

"Well . . . I don't know why we're on this topic anyway. I thought we had those ground rules we just started."

"You wondered about my love life and I've told you, honestly. Now I want to say this: I like my neighbor lady because I've observed a very brave, cheery, and hard-working woman who is completely selfless—"

"I am not!"

"Selfless? Yes, you are—remember Greece?"

Her face colored. "Well, Greece, sure—but any mother in the world would have postponed her trip for a daughter's wedding."

"Maybe not, Julia."

"Oh, yes. I think so. We mothers are all like that. Listen, I have one more question, even if it means changing the subject."

"Okay."

"Why do you really wear the beard?"

Now it was his turn to look startled as well as amused. "I have no idea," he said. "Should there be some deep, dark significance to the beard?"

"I only wondered, that's all."

"Hmmm, let's see. Seemed easier than shaving all the time. Made me look more like a college professor, I would suppose. And—"

"Yes?"

"Maybe I thought it would appeal to a certain type of woman." The corners of his mouth were twitching with irony. "When I was ready to go looking for her, that is."

Oh, God.

Her mind flashed her a memory of that rainy, foggy night in her garden, when she'd stroked the beard in utter fascination. He'd been aware of how mesmerized she was; now he was alluding to that incident that led to their first kiss. . . .

Her face must be a bright scarlet. She turned away from Ben, staring straight out the side window, trying to gain some composure.

"I think I'm going to stop asking questions," she said, shaking her head. "I'm finding I don't like the answers."

Ben laughed heartily. Julia forced herself to sit back and breathe deeply in an effort to relax. It was going to be a long ride to Storrs.

The strains of "Pomp and Circumstance" always made Julia cry—always. Ever since the girls were toddlers graduating from their little nursery schools, she found herself with tears rolling down her cheeks at the very first note of the graduation march.

Today was no exception. The hundreds of graduates trekked into the field house, slowly and proudly. They looked scholarly but at the same time they looked rather lumpish in their gowns and those foolish caps. The music swelled, repeating over and over, and Julia marveled at the thought of Jay's little Punkin'head being now a college graduate. . . .

She was sobbing. Her last little girl, her

sweet, plump baby who'd been virtually her shadow years ago, after the other girls went off to grade school . . . feisty, tiny Cristy Lynn, now a grown, educated woman who knew her own mind and loved her man with intensity, enough to take a vow of marriage . . .

She pulled out tissues by the handful, dabbing at her face, trying to appear normal in case anyone looked her way. And in fact, Ben was looking at her and seemed quite concerned.

"Are you all right?" he asked. "I've never seen you cry before."

"So much for your brave neighbor lady," she said crisply.

"Of course you're brave." He produced a clean white handkerchief and offered it. "You happen to be sentimental, too. I'm only just learning all these things about you."

She kept on weeping as long as the music played. Once the graduates had all filed in and taken their seats, the music stopped and Julia regained her composure. She dabbed her face with the linen handkerchief and managed a smile.

"I could have given you a hug for comfort," he said with a devilish grin. "But I restrained myself. Ground rules, you know."

"Duly noted."

"By the way . . . do you cry like this often?" he whispered as they sat down.

She craned her neck to get a good look at her daughter's graduation. "Only when the moon is full," she said.

Spring on the UConn campus was incomparable. Because it had originated as an agricultural college, everywhere you looked there were brightly blossoming fruit trees, billowing shrubs, and tidy flower beds. Birds chirped and darted from tree to tree, making as much noise as the students. The lawns shimmered an emerald green, with a velvety texture to the grass that sparkled under the sunshine.

The kids of Cristy's dorm had organized a graduation picnic for families and guests. Tables were set up, food laid out in typical college-kid confusion, but it was a bittersweet, poignant event for the brand new graduates.

"Our last meal together," Cristy said to some of the girls from her dorm floor. "Whenever we have reunions after this, we'll be old farts, employed and settled."

"Old and *married*, some of us," teased her roommate Sara.

"Hey, here are some more lawn chairs,"

Jeremy yelled, arriving with an armful of plastic-weave chairs. It was all very haphazard and spontaneous.

One of the boys said, "Here, Cristy, I got these chairs for your mother and father."

Julia blinked. She hadn't expected that; but of course, there she was, standing beside Ben, looking very much as though she belonged with him. What else would the kids think?

Music blared from someone's portable radio and a beer keg was tapped. "We're not even seniors any more," Kevin called out. "We're alumni and we can have a beer keg whenever we want."

The sun shone high in the sky. Sitting in the shade of a linden tree, sipping beer from a plastic cup, Julia reflected for a moment on how unexpectedly happy she felt. After the sadness of the past two years, it was good to be alive and extra wonderful to see your child graduate from college.

Ben had been unusually quiet as he sat in a plastic chair not far from her, also enjoying a beer.

"Does being on campus ever make you feel like a kid again?" she asked with a big smile.

He shook his head. "Nah. I always feel like a professor, old and conservative, no matter what."

She studied him. "So what *would* make you feel like a kid again? Just to satisfy my curiosity?"

"A kid again?" He considered that. "Well, maybe going skinny-dipping. In the broad daylight. Yeah, that might do it."

"At least you're honest."

He shrugged. "Most of the time I feel a long way from being a new graduate like these kids. But when I dive into the lake, or untie a boat from a dock—now that makes me feel young."

"Really? A boat . . . do you have a boat, Ben?"

"No." He downed his beer. "It's one of my dreams, though. I'm planning to spring for one eventually—a good-sized one, like my friend Killer has."

"A cabin cruiser?"

Ben nodded. "Something I can live on for weeks at a time, if I want to. Of course I don't know who'd take care of all my flowerbeds if I went off adventuring, but—"

"But it's nice to have a dream," she finished. "Like my trip to Greece." She sighed and Ben smiled. They were like an old married couple, she thought with sudden horror, sitting there talking about dreams.

"This is crazy," she said, jumping up.

"Maybe it's the novelist in me, but I want to move around and talk to lots of people. Want to come?"

"You go ahead," Ben said lazily. "I'm having a good time just sitting here watching these crazy graduates."

So she left him there.

Forget about it. She wasn't about to become an old lady sitting in a chair at a college picnic!

Twenty-six

"Where did I ever get all this useless crap?" Cristy grumbled, carrying load after load down the dorm stairs toward Ben's truck. She'd tried to pack before graduation, but dismantling a college girl's dorm room was nevertheless a Herculean task. All of them—Cristy, Jeremy, Ben, Julia, and Kevin—were involved in transporting Cristy's things to the truck, and still it was taking forever.

"For one thing," Jeremy said, "you happen to have the biggest teddy bear collection on the planet. I mean, is that *normal?*" He was heading down the many flights of dorm stairs with parts of her stereo system balanced on his shoulders.

"Better to have teddy bears," Cristy shot back at him, "than a room like yours, full of green mold. Yukkkk."

"Well, we're almost done," Julia said, hefting a pair of suitcases. She was thinking this was the very last time; there would be no more dorms, no more daughters to deposit at—or pick up from—UConn. She felt nostalgic enough to start crying again, so she moved as fast as she could down the staircase.

"Hi, Mrs. Maxwell." On the stair landing, one of the girls called out to her. She vaguely remembered meeting the girl at the dorm's graduation picnic a few hours earlier.

"Hi there! Is it Heather?"

"Yes, what a good memory. Listen, I heard somewhere you've been looking for Mindy Parsons . . . did you see her before?"

Julia stopped dead in her tracks. "No. Are you saying she was here today?"

"Yes. I saw her outside the dorm a while ago."

Julia wanted to howl with frustration. "Well, we didn't see her, Heather. Was she with anyone?"

"Mmmm, no, she was alone. She was probably staring at Jeremy, as usual. Creepy, isn't it, the way she has that crush on him?"

"Yes." Julia wondered if they could find Mindy if they went looking right now. Then, because it was already late afternoon, she rejected the idea. The campus was enormous and what were the chances that Mindy was still around?

Even so, she began asking all the departing

college kids, as she crossed paths with them, if they'd seen Mindy lately. No one had.

"What do you think, Ben?" She caught up with him trying valiantly to pack the truck. "Should we be trying to look around for her—or maybe for her car?"

"Can't be done today, I'm afraid," he said. "With a load like this, we'll be lucky to make it back to Stonewell."

Julia nodded. "I really should have brought my car as well."

"I'm glad you didn't. I enjoyed being with you for our drive up here." Was she going to blush again?

Ben began to whistle some merry tune—it sounded like "Getting to Know You"—and looking, she thought, like a very triumphant polar bear who believes he's already caught the salmon.

It was wonderful having Cristy back home again. Julia constantly missed the hustle and bustle of family life, so when any one of her daughters was back in the house she was euphoric. Now there was someone to cook for, someone to talk to and share jokes with, someone to watch VCR movies with . . . everyday life became sociable once more.

In reality, however, Cristy was a busy bride-to-be and was on the go like a whirling dervish. That first week she was home was a virtual circus: making room for her dorm junk, getting her and her teddy bears settled into her room, sitting down with her to write out the final guest list so firm wedding plans could be made.

Together she and Julia visited the Party Rental Palace. Cristy wandered around with stars in her eyes, examining wedding tents and canopies—pure white, gold or yellow striped?—and an amazing selection of tablecloths for the round tables they were ordering. Cristy finally settled on a color scheme of maroon and white—shimmering white china, deep maroon tablecloths, and all-white linens for the buffet tables. Her plan was to offset each table with maroon and white mums in crystal containers.

"That sounds lovely," Julia said, proud of her daughter's brisk decisions and excellent taste. Neither April nor Bethany would be able to criticize this outdoor wedding, not after such care was taken to do things correctly.

They ordered a few more items, such as coffeepots and punch bowls, and then signed their contract with the rental people.

"And now," Cristy declared, "I want to treat my mother to lunch." They drove to The Salad

Plate in Stonewell, talking about gigantic diet salads.

"Fewer calories," Cristy said after she ordered, "now that we have to start worrying about formal dresses for both of us."

"Fine with me." Julia sipped her glass of water and again felt a great admiration for this girl-child she had raised. Here was a complete human being—tall, pretty, long-haired, full of spunk and spirit. She'd been educated, thank God, and now was engaged to someone terrific—what more could a mother ask? Looking down at her place setting, Julia smiled fondly.

"You've been looking happier lately, Momserina. Sometimes I even catch you smiling all to yourself. Is it getting easier—to be without Daddy, I mean?"

Julia nodded yes, not really sure if she meant it but because people needed to hear her say it was getting easier.

"And how are you getting along with Big Ben?" Cristy pressed on. "At times you two look like a real solid couple."

"We're not a couple at all," Julia said. "I'm getting tired of telling everyone that Ben and I are just friends. Period. End of story."

Cristy grinned. "Can't blame people for trying, Moms. He is awfully cute, though, isn't he?"

"He's ursine," Julia said.

"Huh?"

"And he's hirsute."

"Mom, is this a vocabulary quiz? I was an Aggie major, remember? I didn't learn those words."

Julia laughed. "I just meant he's bearlike and he's hairy, as in bearded. Don't you think he's very much like a big bear?"

"Oh, sure. That's what's so special about him. And besides the way he looks, Ben almost seems to hibernate there in his home. He's alone too much, I think—seldom getting out except to garden or teach classes."

"Seems to me he gets out often," Julia said. "He's always marching into our backyard."

"Well, that's because he's helping me and because—" Cristy stopped mid-sentence. Julia ignored her; she had a feeling she didn't want to hear the rest.

But Cristy continued with the rest anyway. "Because he seems to be crazy about you, Mom. Haven't you noticed?"

None of your business, kid.

"The only thing I've noticed, Cristy Lynn, is that we have lots more planning to do for this wedding of yours. Have you thought any more about what the bridesmaids will wear?"

Their salads arrived just then with tall glasses of iced tea.

"We'll go shopping next week with Mrs. Fud and Mrs. Dud—also known as April and Beth," Cristy said. "And Renee—you know my friend Renee's going to be my bridesmaid, too? But meanwhile, why are you changing the subject when I ask about Ben?"

"Because I'm entitled to my privacy."

"Hmmm." Cristy looked impressed even though thwarted. "Fair enough, Mom. You are entitled."

When they left the restaurant they walked around the town—Stonewell's long Main Street that enclosed its New England village green—for about half an hour, peering into shop windows and enjoying the warm spring day. Finally they decided they'd wasted enough time and went back to the car.

"Oh, no, did we get a ticket?" Julia saw a piece of paper clipped to her windshield wiper, where none of the other cars in the lot had similar notices.

Cristy yanked the paper from the wiper. She paled as she read it, and Julia rushed to look over her shoulder.

"I KNOW YOU'RE HOME NOW," it said in thick crayon lettering. It was printed like a child's message. "I KNOW HOW TO FIX YOU."

That was all. No signature.

"We don't need a signature," Cristy said, her shock turning to visible anger. "That Mindy—she's letting us know she watches us, no matter what. She thinks she can scare me!" She looked around furiously, as if she expected to see the girl in question lurking somewhere nearby.

Julia, truthfully, felt the same way, as though not far from them would be the figure of Mindy Parsons, watching to see their reaction to the note. It was an eerie, paranoid experience but then that's what they were all fast becoming—paranoid.

"The hell with her," Cristy declared, making as if to rip up the paper.

"No, don't," Julia said. "Keep that. It's evidence to show the police, especially if anything more should happen."

"Yeah. We need evidence." Cristy jammed the note into her pocket. "We'll catch her, don't worry about that."

Julia thought of the malicious damage that had been done twice in her yard, and felt an involuntary little shudder. Their pleasant day together had been tainted all of a sudden, invaded by the presence of evil and possible madness.

"We will get her," Julia vowed. "Because as of tonight we're going to *Rent a Dog.*"

"What?"

"Ivan the Terrible. He'll be on the case from now on. Ben said he could sleep at our house any time."

Cristy grinned. "I love that silly old mutt! Great news. I believe he'll do a fabulous job as watchdog."

"I hope so," Julia whispered, thinking of all the flowering plants in their gardens—and that threat, "I KNOW HOW TO FIX YOU."

Twenty-seven

"Ben, can we ask a great favor?" Julia telephoned him as soon as they returned home. "We're having another problem with Mindy. . . . Can we take you up on your offer to borrow Ivan overnight?"

She heard an intake of breath, as if in surprise. "I can hardly believe this; I was just about to call to ask if Ivan could stay with you."

"Why? Are you going away?"

"Yes. My friend out in Long Island—remember when I told you about Killer?—is sick."

"I'm sorry. I hope it's not serious?"

"It might be. I suppose they're not sure. I'm driving out this afternoon, might stay over a day or two. I didn't know whether to contact the kennel, or check with you ladies."

"Check with us ladies, definitely. We'll take Ivan gladly." She told him about the unsigned note on her car. "It sounds as though Mindy is gearing up for something, and we'd be very grateful to have the dog."

"Have no fear," Ben said as if trying for a light tone. "Wonder Dog is here. . . . I'll bring him around in about an hour, if that's agreeable."

"Wonderful."

Ivan arrived with his paraphernalia: leash, water bowl, food bowl, bag of food, two over-sized chew bones. He marched in like some kind of beagle royalty, as if he were checking into the Ritz Carlton, and made himself comfortable near the dining room sliding doors.

"Just where we want him," Cristy said with delight. "He'll keep watch on the backyard and be sure to spot Mindy if she shows up." She plunked down beside the large beagle and petted him on the head.

Julia thought Ben looked worried about his friend Killer. There was a tension about his eyes and mouth that she'd never seen before, and he kept running nervous fingers through his hair.

"I hope your buddy will be all right," Julia said softly.

"Thanks." The fingers chopped at his beard, now, something he never did. "I'm not sure what to expect. Haven't seen him in over a year and now—it has to be under these circumstances."

"We'll say a prayer," Julia promised. "Even Cristy." She walked to the front door with Ben. "And please drive carefully in that crazy Long Island traffic."

"You're doing that wifely thing again," he said, grinning as he started out the door. "I really like it."

"Don't you start," she warned. "Remember those ground rules?"

"I remember." His tone was amused.

She watched as he made his way to his car and took off. That wifely thing! She was trying to be a good friend to him—and that was the interpretation he gave it.

You think you really are Mister Chemistry, she thought. Well, I have news for you . . . this chemistry set has fizzled out.

Just before dusk, Julia and Cristy strolled around looking at the newest gardens, with Ivan the Terrible following behind on the Sniff Patrol.

"Our land is starting to look beautiful," Cristy said with an excited squeal in her voice. "Did you know Ben and Jeremy are planning to put stone steps right there in that bank?? I think that'll be so cool."

Julia nodded, dipping her nose down to a garden full of lily of the valley. They were tiny bell-shaped flowers, she noted, but their scent was powerful on the evening breeze. *Lily*, she mused; that was his wife's name, Lily. How fitting for a man who loves gardening . . .

"Ben has many great pictures of our yard already," Cristy said, pulling a weed from among the marigolds around the sundial. "Can you imagine this whole thing going into a book—my wedding? Wonder what my fuddy-duddy sisters will think of that?"

"They'll be happy for you." Julia wandered over to look at something Ben had planted in a large Grecian urn. "What is this thing, Cristy?"

"He calls it a topiary wreath. . . . It's just ivy planted in the pot, trained on a wire circle. Elegant, isn't it?"

"He does amazing work."

"You've seen his gardens, Mom?"

"Yes. Beautiful." She touched several peat baskets that hung from the branches of the big old oak tree. "Look at this, he put red geraniums in here. This ought to be flowering all summer long."

Cristy was quiet for a while, walking around on the springy carpet of grass and watching Ivan as he staked out his territory.

"Ben has some terrific photos of you, Mom, standing here in the gardens . . . and some of you two together."

"That's nice." Julia didn't know what else to say.

Cristy smoothed some lumps of earth around one of her antique rose bushes. "I wonder if Mindy's planning anything more," she said, her voice turning to steel. "Just when we're getting our land so perfect, we sure don't need her showing up."

Julia said, "What if we took turns sleeping in the dining room? We could roll that small folding bed in there and then we'd be close if Ivan started to bark at an intruder."

"Great idea, Mom. Let's do it. I'll be first."

"Fine with me. As long as you remember to call the police, and do NOT step outside to chase that lunatic girl."

"Yes, sure." Cristy looked pleased that a plan of action had been formulated. She bent down, pulled a few weeds in the impatiens bed and looked up at Julia. "So tell me, when is my surprise bridal shower going to be?"

Julia laughed. "What makes you think any-body would give a shower for *you*?"

"Come on, come on, might as well give me the date." Cristy's grin was wide and impish. "And while you're at it, let them all know I want plenty of see-through lingerie. I'm not ready to be Betty Crocker, with the pots and pans."

"I'm shocked." Julia tried to keep a straight face. "I can still remember the exact words of advice given to me before my wedding—"

"Was it about sex?"

"No. This was my grandmother we're talking about! She told me: When a young lady thinks about marriage she should decide to be the best wife, cook, and homemaker possible."

"Yeah, yeah, maybe in your day, Mom. Not in the nineties."

Julia had been teasing but now she voiced her real opinion. "I'm not all that sure things have changed so much. You'll still need to learn to cook, Cristy, whether it's the nineties or not."

"Are you kidding? Even my two Nanas are more liberated than you. You sound like some bride from the fifties, Mom! Get with the program."

"Excuse me, but I *am* a bride from the fifties, remember? And I've always been glad my women relatives taught me to cook."

"Well, Mom." Cristy stood up and brushed dirt from her hands. "What if you become a bride in the nineties? What then?"

Julia let out a little gasp. "What are you talking about? I have no intention whatso-ever—" She found herself sputtering, unable to finish.

"It could happen," Cristy said more gently. "And if we threw a bridal shower for you, we'd buy you sexy lingerie instead of Tupperware. Let's face it, Mom, everything *has* changed."

"You will not," Julia said with great dignity, "be throwing a bridal shower for me. Not in the nineties and not even in the new mil-lenium. Now I'm going indoors."

"Going to polish up your Tupperware, Mom?"

She ignored that and marched off. Ivan trotted along beside her, contented to be their visitor.

"Let's just hope Mister Ivan stays alert through the night," Julia said, sliding open her glass doors. "Maybe with him we can end this reign of terror . . . soon."

Counting sheep wasn't working. At two A.M., weary of trying to force sleep, Julia arose and slipped into a cotton robe. She'd sit at the typewriter for a while, and maybe she could use the insomnia to good advantage.

"What's the secret to your writing that best-seller, Ms. Maxwell?" She could hear Phil Donahue asking her that on his afternoon talk show.

"Couldn't sleep, Phil, that's all," she'd answer modestly. She imagined herself in a wonderful Liz Claiborne suit, her face made up to perfection, her hair swept into something infinitely more sophisticated than the usual black curls.

"Why, Phil," she'd say, "almost anyone can write a novel if only she suffers from major insomnia. . . ."

She chuckled and went to turn on the desk lamp. But her hand froze where it was. She heard some kind of noise from downstairs.

Ivan was growling, an ominous low rumble that came from deep inside him where dogs seem to recognize the existence of pure evil. Scared for Cristy, Julia raced through the nighttime gloom, down the stairs and into the dark dining room.

"Ssssh," she heard Cristy whisper, though she didn't know whether the girl spoke to the dog or the mother.

"Is someone out there, Cristy?" Julia moved

in the dark with hands outstretched, batting at dining room furniture like a blind person. She stood beside Cristy finally, squinting to peer out into the blackness of their yard.

"Yeah, I think she's there," Cristy said quietly. "Mindy. Why don't you call the police, Mom—and hurry!"

Julia tapped out the phone number that she had committed to memory by now. Cristy kept a close vigil by the door, finally deciding she'd waited long enough.

"I'm not gonna let her wreck our gardens." She flung open the sliders and Ivan, roaring like a gigantic German shepherd, went flying out into the dark night.

Twenty-eight

"You shouldn't have done that," Julia said even as Cristy peered out the open doors. "What if she's carrying a weapon? She might hurt Ivan."

"I think he can take care of himself," Cristy said bravely. "I hope so anyway."

"The police will be here shortly. You should have left it up to them. . . ."

Together the two women kept vigil, hearing a lot of loud doggy noise out there. The darkness was too total to see what was happening—did their prowler deliberately choose moonless nights for her forays?—but the sounds were frightening.

Ivan seemed to be circling around and around, barking wildly as if confronted with something very real and menacing. But then Ivan would probably bark that way at a small garden mole, too, Julia thought.

Impatient, Cristy snapped on the outside light which illuminated only the patio area.

Nothing could be seen, not even the madly circling dog.

"I feel like going out there." Cristy's words sent a dagger of fear through Julia.

"No, don't even think that. Let's just wait—"

Ivan's barking seemed to be getting farther away. Julia guessed he was over in the area of the gate now; was he following because the intruder was taking off in a big hurry?

"She's gone, Mom." Cristy sounded bitter. "I could run out front and try to catch her, you know." But Julia was relieved to note Cristy didn't follow through with her heroic suggestion. They hurried to the front door, looking out but seeing nothing. They couldn't even hear Ivan any more.

"Great, now we've lost Ben's dog."

"He'll be back." Julia peered through the storm door, saw headlights slicing through the dark night.

"Here comes the police car," Cristy said. "Better late than never. I doubt if they'll be able to do a damn thing."

And she was right. By the time the police officers patroled the property, there was no sign of anyone. Ivan, however, showed up, prancing and snuffling, looking very proud of himself.

"You did just great, Ivan," Cristy told him, fetching one of his dog biscuits for a reward. "You chased off that creep anyway. You saved the day."

Julia went out with the police to check the backyard. Sure enough, a large shovel was found; it hadn't been there at dusk when Julia and Cristy strolled the grounds.

"This person came prepared to do damage, Mrs. Maxwell," the officer said. "I'll take the shovel into the station, keep it for evidence. If we ever catch this person we'll be able to build a case."

If we ever catch this person . . . Julia shivered. She herself had vowed to find Mindy and up to now had failed. Someone had to stop the girl before any real damage, or even bodily harm, was done.

When the inspection was completed and the report written up, the police left. Cristy yawned widely.

"Why don't you go back up to your own bed, honey? I'm not at all tired and I'll take the next watch."

"Thanks, Mom. She probably won't come back tonight anyway." Cristy trudged up the stairs like a zombie.

Wide awake.

Julia wondered if she'd stay up the whole night, angry and charged with adrenaline. She paced the floor for a while, aware that Ivan was looking at her as though she had a few screws loose.

"Don't judge me, Ivan. My life is extremely stressful right now." Julia glowered at the silent beagle. His big eyes were soft and moist as he studied her.

"We're trying to do a wedding, we're being attacked by the creature from hell, and my whole life is topsy turvy." She peered out the glass doors, saw nothing out there, then sat down on the folding bed.

"Yeah. Topsy turvy, with flower gardens and bridal showers and—I admit it—even a few very hot kisses from your incorrigible master . . ."

Julia grinned. "But don't tell him I said that, of course."

Smiling, she decided she felt better for having complained to Ivan about her life.

"You want to know the saddest thing of all?" She kicked off her bedroom slippers and wiggled her toes. "All I ever wanted, Ivan, was my trip to Greece."

That said, she was ready to give sleep a try. Oddly enough when she forced herself to stretch out on the foldaway cot, and put her head down on the cool, soft pillow, she dozed off.

Ben called the next day to say he'd be staying in Long Island for the rest of the week.

"Killer's not doing well at all," he said in a deep, weary voice. Reading between the lines, Julia deduced Killer was suffering from something serious.

"I'm sorry to hear that, Ben."

"I like being here with him; we get in a game of chess or do crossword puzzles, or just talk about old times in the old neighborhood. Hank comes by when he can, too."

"Of course you should stay," Julia said, feeling tears sting her eyelids for this man Killer she'd never even met. "We'll take care of watering your plants, Ben, and don't worry about Ivan. He's the super-hero of Camelot Road."

She told him about the prowler and Ivan's subsequent chase.

"I guess he's earning his keep, then," Ben said, "but I am worried about you and Cristy being there alone. Couldn't Jeremy stay with you for a few nights?"

"I don't know. We can ask him. Meanwhile, we're still praying for your friend, Ben." She felt a flush of warmth in her face; was she being "wifely" again? She'd have to be more than careful in this friendship.

"Thanks, Julia. Hope to see you in a few days."

That weekend was the engagement dinner with Jeremy's parents, Michelle and Bud Crenshaw. Julia and Cristy dressed up more than usual and took off for Stamford, both feeling a bit nervous about the in-law dynamics.

"It's not the same without your dad," Julia said as Cristy drove, speeding, down Route Seven. "He'd have handled this occasion so perfectly. He was always the life of every party."

"I miss him, too . . . but you have a good personality, too, Mom," Cristy told her. "Diplomacy, intelligence, good humor. People always like you a lot."

"Well." Julia looked down at her hands, nervously knotting themselves together in her lap. "Thanks, but I'm just saying, this engagement dinner would be so much better with Jay here."

"Yeah," Cristy agreed, her voice suddenly husky, saddened. Julia knew it was time to talk of something else, so she mentioned the farm they were passing and how it looked deserted, ready to be annihilated, like so many other rural spots in this part of Connecticut. Condos would be built there, probably, or another shopping plaza nobody needed.

"When Ben called, he suggested we ought to ask Jeremy to come to the house," Julia said. "For our safety."

"He can't, Mom, he'll be job hunting. You know we both plan to look for some kind of nursery jobs until we have enough money to buy our own florist shop or nursery."

"I guess we're on our own, then, as far as getting rid of Mindy."

"We'll get her. Next time she shows up we'll be staked out there at the dining room door and we'll do things differently."

"What do you mean?" Julia felt a flutter of fear.

"Don't worry, we'll figure out something safe. Now let's see, is this the turnoff to Stamford over here—?"

Eventually they found the Crenshaws' house, one of those fine old stone houses near the water. They were greeted with affection, and right away Julia's feelings of apprehension fell by the wayside. She felt entirely comfortable with both Michelle and Bud. Jeremy was the oldest of five; their family of youngsters were lively and well-behaved.

The Crenshaws and their guests enjoyed a superb meal out on a screened porch, with brisk, salty breezes that seemed to come straight off Long Island Sound.

"Let's have a toast," Bud Crenshaw said, raising his wine goblet. "We're delighted about this marriage—and this is to toast the couple's total happiness."

They raised their glasses. "Oh, Bud, that wasn't a romantic toast!" Michelle scolded him gently, and added her own tribute. "Here's to a sweet girl, dear Cristy, who will be a wonderful influence on Jeremy, and here's to dear Jeremy, who—oh, dear, am I allowed to boast about my own firstborn boy?"

They all laughed at her consternation. "Well, I will boast," she said, grinning. "Jeremy is a fine young man even if he would rather be a flowergrower than a stock broker! There. Oh Lord, I suppose I ended up insulting you, Jeremy . . . ?"

Laughter rocked the table. Julia felt she should present a toast also. She raised her glass. "Jay and I always wished for a son but we had three daughters. Now with Jeremy added to the family, I'm fortunate to have three sons-in-law. Jeremy's a very special man.

"Here's to a long life for these two love-birds," she said with vigor. "And let's pray we have a sunny day in September for this garden wedding of the century."

"Amen." They all sipped at their wine.

"We hear you're continuing to have trouble from the prowler," Bud said, his voice sobering as he leveled a gaze at Julia. He was a fine-looking man, dark haired and dark eyed like his son, only with more muscle than the junior version.

"Mindy the prowler, yes," Julia said. "We feel as though we're under siege all the time. We're even living with a watchdog named Ivan the Terrible."

"Oh, dear," Michelle said. "I wonder if we should change all the plans, and have the wedding here in our yard? We're right on the water, so it would be beautiful."

A silence followed. Cristy looked stunned. "Oh, no, we have so much already under way! We've been working for months—"

"Well, but perhaps we could foil that Mindy that way." Michelle was perfectly serious about her plan. "She might not dare come here with all these males around to stop her."

Julia was surprised to feel a stab of disappointment; if the wedding were not to be in her yard, all Ben's efforts would be in vain. It was unthinkable.

And besides, she'd come to look forward to the wedding. She hadn't known it until just this moment, but there it was. She actually, was excited about the prospect of the garden wedding.

"We'll leave the plans the way they are, for now," Julia said firmly. "But I wish someone—Jeremy?—could tell us more about Mindy Parsons, to help us to find her."

Jeremy turned beet-red, his hands going up in helplessness. "Honestly, I hardly know the girl. She used to trail around after me, but I was always straight with her. I told her that I was going with Cristy, and finally I used to tell her to leave me alone."

"He did, Mom, truly," Cristy confirmed. "And he was always polite to her, though it wasn't easy. But she had this enormous crush on Jeremy so she wouldn't accept reality."

"I believe you," Julia said, "but we need more information. Someone said she liked cemeteries. Do you think—?" A light suddenly went on in Julia's brain. "I wonder if she lives *near* the cemetery? Oh my God, that could be it. . . ."

She told them about the day in the cemetery and how the slim, dark figure had disappeared into the woods. "But there was no car around, at least none I could see . . . so it's possible she had walked there, was just hanging out when she spotted me."

"There're plenty of big old homes around there," Cristy said, "where a person might rent a couple of rooms. Yeah, Mom, you might have stumbled on a good idea."

"Well, it's all rather scary," Michelle said. "And I wish we didn't have anything bad to mar this happy occasion. Now how about if I bring out a happy engagement cake?" She bustled off toward the kitchen.

"Is she serious?" Jeremy asked. "A happy engagement cake?"

"Better be quiet," his father said, laughing. "Next she'll even have us all singing *Happy Engagement to You.*"

"Oh my God," Jeremy moaned. His face was red with embarrassment, but the twinkle in his dark eyes showed he was pleased. He'd never admit it, of course, but anyone could see he was a sentimental young man. His mother's unconditional love had given him a priceless source of self-esteem.

He's a good person, Julia thought. If she could do that toast over again, she'd say, "Here's to a marriage that might just be perfect. . . ."

A perfect one. If only we can manage to pull off their wedding day.

The person in brown clothes made a sound like a groan, and fingered a pearl-handled knife.

The dog's presence had been unexpected.

The blade gleamed under the artificial lighting, ready to take care of anything else that got in the way.

Twenty-nine

The weekend was peaceful—no Mindy, anyway—but the big surprise arrived on Monday afternoon. Julia had just returned home from work when she heard a delivery truck pulling into her driveway. She raced to the window.

"Lumber? Nobody ordered lumber."

She slipped into shoes and ran out to stop the delivery.

"No, we got the right house, ma'am," the truck driver told her. "Here's the order here, see? 134 Camelot."

"But we didn't order anything," Julia insisted. "What on earth is this for?"

"The guy said he was building a gazebo." The driver shrugged. "This here's one of those kits for building a gazebo."

"But what guy? Who signed that order?" She looked but was not surprised, at that point, to see the name Ben Wilson in his firm handwriting. "Oh, Lord," she said wearily. "What next?"

When Ben called from Long Island later that day he confirmed that he was indeed going to build a gazebo for Cristy, since she'd wanted one so much for her wedding day. "I hope you don't object, Julia," he said with concern. "If you do, we can cancel the whole thing."

"No, it's a lovely idea. . . . It's only that I plan to sell this house later, Ben. Will the gazebo be something that could be moved— possibly to your yard?"

"Could be. Listen, I'm coming home tonight because Killer seems a little improved. He told me he's sick of seeing me hang around the hospital."

"That sounds like he's greatly improved then. I hope so." Her mind had leaped ahead a million miles—she was envisioning the gazebo, tall and proud, gently rounded, crafted of polished oak or redwood. It would gleam in the sunlight, surrounded by a profusion of flowers and ferns; it would be the perfect centerpiece for the wedding. They could use it for dancing or it might hold the D.J., or—

"Julia, are you still there?"

"Sorry. I was daydreaming about the gazebo. I have a premonition it's going to be lovely."

"I'm glad, then," he said softly. "I'd never

want to go ahead and do a project you didn't
approve of."

"Cristy will be so excited. This is truly generous and thoughtful, Ben."

"Well . . ." He sounded at a loss for words.
"I'll see you later, then."

She was totally unprepared for her reaction,
when he did arrive at their front door that
night. Glad to see him, yes, but so much more
than that, an attraction that staggered her in
its intensity.

"Hi, ladies." Just outside the front door,
he pretended he was tipping a hat. "Where's
my silly mutt?"

Julia stood rooted to the spot, her heart
pounding quite unreasonably, as Cristy
opened the door to admit Ben. He filled the
doorway with his massive frame, but he also
seemed to fill the house instantly with a presence—something that had been missing a
very long time.

Was it simply a male factor? Julia tried to
tell herself that's all it was. Clearly, though,
Ben brought other qualities unique only to
him—a calmness, a solidity, a most willing and
capable friend sort of presence.

She watched, smiling, as Ivan hurtled himself toward his beloved master, and saw Ben's large face light up with great affection.

"Hey, old boy! Hey there, Wonder Dog . . . how'd you like being here with these two gorgeous women, hmmm?"

Julia swallowed. You weren't supposed to compare him to Jay. But if you did, you knew you were looking at a different man altogether—a quiet man, a man who probably never cared if he went to a party, or gave a party, or even had guests in his home. A man who, by his own admission, hadn't bothered to start dating again after his wife died.

A loner? And yet he had friends of long standing, and he wasn't at all the shy sort. He was a college professor, for Pete's sake. Articulate, personable, and certainly a man who gave the appearance of extraordinary middle-aged vitality . . .

Enough of that. Liz had labeled him a "powerhouse," but Liz had meant it in a lewd way. Julia didn't want to entertain such thoughts.

"I'm so glad to see you, Ben," Cristy said with a loud squeal. "A gazebo! When I got home today there was all that wood—and Mom told me what it's for and that you ordered it." She went hurtling toward him too, in very much the same way as Ivan, and hugged him until it looked as though she would strangle him.

"Thank you, thank you, thank you!" Cristy said.

"You're welcome, though nothing's built yet." His eyes rose above the demonstrative Cristy who was hugging his large frame. His gaze seared across the room toward Julia. She thought she saw a question mark there in those moss-green depths—like, *Did you miss me?*—but she was incapable of telling him just how much she did miss him.

"You've certainly made this bride-to-be happy," Julia said with a smile.

"Good." He extricated himself from Cristy's hugs. "Now tell me the latest about our prowler."

They sat down in the kitchen with a pot of coffee and talked, Cristy giving him the details of the other night. They discussed Julia's hunch that maybe Mindy lived somewhere near the cemetery in town.

"That's definitely worth checking out," Ben said. "And I'm going to do it myself—starting tomorrow."

"How?" Cristy asked.

"I'll go from door to door, explain that I'm looking for a certain young lady. Most of all, I can be on the lookout for that brown

Ford . . . and I hope people will be willing to answer my questions."

"They will, because you look like an upright citizen," Cristy said.

"Dudley Do-Right," Julia added. "But unlike your siblings, I mean it as a compliment, Ben."

"Thanks." He sipped his coffee, looking deep in thought about his forthcoming detective work. "Meanwhile, why don't you two make frequent trips to the cemetery—but please, go together. Even take Ivan with you. You might spot her again and get an idea where she disappears to."

"We'll do it," Cristy said. "It's not my favorite place to go, but I'll sacrifice for the greater cause."

"So . . . we all have our assignments." Ben stood up and looked out the kitchen window. "Think I'll walk around and take a look at the wedding gardens . . . and this week, ladies, I promise I'll start working on the gazebo."

"Great." Cristy said. "Can we keep Ivan for a few more nights, Ben?"

"Of course." He nodded with no hesitation. "I brought a flashlight, Julia," he said quietly. "So I can take inventory of all the flowers. Will you take a walk with me?"

"Uh . . ." She couldn't think of a quick excuse. I have to wash my hair, I have to call my stockbroker, I have to consult the Psychic Network. . . . It would all be extremely lame.

"All right," she said and was sure she saw Cristy rolling her eyes in surprise.

Ivan trooped along with them, delighted to be with his master again after a number of days apart.

It was a soft, balmy night. When they stepped outside, cool air traced along Julia's cheek as a breeze lifted her hair. She felt reluctant to go walking with Ben—Mister Chemistry, as Selena called him—therefore, all the whispering night sounds seemed exaggerated. The rich, earthy scents of the garden seemed overly sensual, an affront to her inbred common sense.

"Look at that, we even have a slight moon," Ben said in his quiet way. They walked side by side, not touching. She wondered why she didn't bolt; she could still say she needed to wash her hair, for God's sake. She was insane if she allowed herself to stroll in the pale moonlight with this man. . . .

"Why are we out here?" she asked curiously.

"Because . . . I wanted to tell you I missed

you." His voice was disembodied. They strolled in a patch of total darkness, under the tall elm tree that blocked out the moonshadows. From the darkness she heard the man's voice speaking, telling her frankly that he'd missed her. She panicked.

"We had ground rules and you're breaking them," she said, turning sharply on her heel to go back inside.

"Julia." His calm tone stopped her. "Our rules were about touching. Am I touching you?"

"No, but—"

"Look, I know you don't want to hear mushy sentiments from me. Sorry if I sound like a Valentine's day card—"

"You do."

"That's because I really did miss you." She heard him sigh. "Things were pretty bad with my friend Killer. He slept a lot in the hospital, and I sat there in the waiting room thinking about a certain pretty lady back here in Stonewell."

"I'm sorry about your friend." Her chin was raised high and her whole body taut; she was alert to any suspicious moves he might make.

"Thank you. Relax, Julia, and let's just enjoy the walk. That's what gardens are for, you know."

"I suppose they are, at that. . . ."

Well, I'm only staying only because I feel sorry for you, she thought sullenly. Because your friend is sick and you seem upset about that situation . . .

They walked in a friendly silence, their feet crunching in the dewy grass. Ivan led the way, sniffing, inspecting, growling at bits of dandelion, even attacking a stray acorn. It was tough work but somebody had to do it.

Moonlight illuminated the garden beds Ben had created, throwing a shimmer against the retaining rocks. Cristy's rose garden was beginning to fill out, too. When he beamed the flashlight at the area, there was a sheen on each green leaf among the plants.

"So . . . what are you doing next weekend?" Ben asked.

"Well, it's going to be a busy one. April, Bethany, and Renee are giving the bridal shower on Saturday night. I'll have a houseful of overnight guests, including my mother and my mother-in-law, who both come from out of state."

"Ah. The traditional women's ritual, the bride's shower." She looked up and saw he was smiling widely. "Did you know men always wonder what sort of secret things go on at a bridal shower?"

She chuckled. "I suppose they do. Just as we wonder what obscenities go on at the stag party."

"Which, by the way, I hope they'll include me in, when they set one up for Jeremy," Ben said. "Is Kevin to be the best man?"

"Yes. I know he has tentative plans to hold some kind of bachelor get-together, and I know he'll put you on his guest list."

They continued walking, a silence between them. "It's a very exciting time, isn't it?" Ben said. "Since I have no children, I've never been through this as you have."

"Lord, yes. Weddings are total chaos for months ahead of time, especially for the bride and her mother."

"Have you thought of how uneventful things are going to be—afterward?"

She smiled. "No, but I suppose you're right. After all this commotion, my life will return to deadly dull. I always keep busy, though. I have my job, my book to write, and I'll start saving right away for Greece. . . ."

"I've never been to Greece either," he said casually.

"I hope that's not a hint. You know I'll be traveling with Selena and some other women, Ben."

"Are you always this defensive? No, it wasn't

a hint. . . . I only meant to say, it's always been a dream of mine as well. I just never mentioned it before because I thought you might not believe me."

"Well, it does seem too coincidental."

"Greece is the one country in the world I've longed to see. But Lily didn't want to leave the U.S. She felt there was so much to see right here."

"Why . . ." Julia was astounded. "That's exactly how Jay felt. I'd get so furious with him because he'd laugh at my dreams. Why would you want to look at a bunch of old ruins?, he said."

"I think I'd sell my soul to see Crete and Mykonos," Ben said. "And Athens—the Acropolis, the Royal Palace, the Panathenian Stadium . . ."

"You'll get there someday." Julia spoke fervently. What she really meant was: *I'll get there some day,* and she was trying to convince herself of it. "When you want something so terribly much, it has to come true. Eventually."

A cloud must have shifted just then, because full moonlight slanted into her garden and highlighted Ben—his impressive height, his fuzzy and pleasant face, his wide shoulders. She stared for a moment, realizing her emotions were affected by lunar stimulation, the magic of moonbeams. It wasn't possible she could really be attracted to Ben, not as strongly as she was feeling right this minute.

Thank God for the ground rules that kept him from making any romantic moves.

"I've got to get inside now," she said hastily. "Uh, thank you for everything."

"For what?"

"Oh, for lending us the dog, and for thinking of the gazebo, and all these flowers everywhere—"

"You sound so flustered, Julia. Are you afraid of me?"

"Absolutely not. Good night now." She moved away from him before she could be tempted to touch that beard—because she knew full well where that would lead.

"Sweet dreams," he called out.

And she did dream. She slept soundly and in her dreams there was a tall bearded man who didn't say much but was always by her side. She came to rely on him completely, so that when a prowler slipped into her yard and he was in mortal danger, she was terrified. . . .

"I can't lose you now," she cried out, but he disappeared into the darkness . . . headed toward the cemetery after the girl prowler.

Julia had the feeling she'd never see him again. The dream turned into a raging nightmare because Mindy had made the tall man disappear just when Julia was beginning to appreciate him. . . .

Thirty

"So . . . how are you getting Cristy here?" each woman asked as she entered April's house. Somehow that was always the standard question: people wanted to know if the bride was to be surprised by the shower, or not.

Balloons bounced off the ceilings and fresh, satiny roses burst from tall vases all around April's L-shaped living room. A giant white umbrella, beribboned and lace-trimmed, dangled near the bride's chair to symbolize the showering of good wishes.

There were to be some forty or more guests—family, neighbors, longtime friends of Julia's, Cristy's many girlfriends from UConn, and some newer friends like Irmgard and Selena.

"What we did was, we asked Cristy to stop by for lunch," April said to each inquiry about getting the bride there. She shrugged. "It's almost impossible to surprise my sister, so—she probably has it all figured out."

"Cristy is a shrewdie," Bethany announced. She continually placed gifts in an enormous pile near the chair of honor. The wrappings were impressive—white, gold, silver paper gleaming with umbrellas and wedding lilies; huge bows of satin that complemented the ribbons around each gift; there were even costly, gleaming silk flowers that adorned the tops of many packages.

Renee, Cristy's best friend, passed out glasses of punch to the ladies. Renee was one of those naturally beautiful girls—much like a fragile woodland doe, with large eyes and a cloud of soft brown hair to her waist.

Guests kept filing in, and Julia worked hard to remember each name and keep the introductions flowing smoothly. Jeremy had a large family, so Michelle Crenshaw made sure everyone met the women from her side of the contingent. Many of the women brought their young daughters, which made the day even more exciting for Danielle and Emily. Those two girls were beside themselves as it was.

"We're the FLOWER GIRLS," Emily told everyone who walked in the door. "Me and my cousin Danielle—we get to carry flower baskets for Aunt Cristy's wedding!"

"No, let me tell," Danielle said with a pout. "Guess what? We're the FLOWER GIRLS!"

"That's a very important job," the women would tell them, and the girls swelled with even more importance.

Both grandmothers were there. Julia's mother, Nana Francie O'Shea, had been driven in from northern New Jersey where she lived in a senior complex. Jay's mother was Nana Carolyn Maxwell, a spunky, tiny lady who'd been a nurse and still worked three days a week as a hospital volunteer in the Bronx.

These grandmothers were great friends, both alert and believing themselves to be thoroughly modern in their thinking. They tended to huddle together, whispering remarks like, "Isn't Julia looking fine? She seems to be coming along all right," and, "She'll never be totally free of grief, but she's trying so hard, you can see that. . . ." Their whispers were embarrassingly loud, though, because they both were hard of hearing.

Before half an hour had elapsed, Julia began to feel exhausted. So many names to introduce, so many glasses of punch to hand out, and all those lovely young girls who looked sassy, sexy, energetic. Julia wondered if she was coming down with a virus or just feeling weary in the confusion of this gigantic party.

Or—even more likely—was she apprehensive about the one special, unexpected package she'd carried here today?

After another half hour of waiting, finally someone spotted Cristy coming up the walk. Cristy came alone, her head held very high, the long brown hair swinging out behind her. Julia watched her from the front window, struck with the thought that Cristy ought to find an old-fashioned sort of wedding dress, if possible. The girl often seemed anachronistic, as though she'd stepped from a tapestry . . . like a medieval princess who had landed in the wrong century.

Cristy tapped on front door, something she ordinarily wouldn't do; usually she'd stick her head in and say "Hey, anybody home!!??" Today she was on her best behavior, no doubt having guessed what was going on.

April went to open the door and the crowd yelled out "Surprise!" all in unison. Emily and Danielle flung themselves at their aunt, hugging her before she even came in the door.

"This means it's a *SHOWER!*" Emily yelled.

"No, let me tell her! This is a *BRIDE SHOWER!!!*"

Cristy was beaming. Her smile was genuine and warm as she scanned the roomful of women who'd traveled so far for her prebridal party. "Hey, you guys, this is beautiful." Her voice suddenly became thick with emotion.

"But are you surprised???" many of the women asked eagerly. Cristy just shrugged in a mysterious way.

"Hey, Nana Francie!" she called out. "And Nana Carolyn! God, this is so wonderful—" The truth was, she hadn't been at all surprised by the shower, Julia could see, but now tears were welling up in Cristy's eyes. The real unexpected surprise for the bride came in realizing that so many good people cared enough to be here—and to amass that big pile of gifts just for her.

"I'm not going to cry," Cristy vowed bravely, making her way around the room to exchange kisses and hugs. "I swear I won't." But she kept wiping her eyes after each embrace.

"Of course you're not, my darling," said her Nana Francie, squeezing her cheeks with great love. "Look at you, all grown up and ready to be a wife!"

"I'll teach you to cook, my sweetie pie," Nana Carolyn offered. "Just say the word and the lessons will begin."

Cristy grinned. "That sounds wonderful, Nana."

"Well, I'll teach you to bake!" Nana Francie hastened to say. She looked outraged and huffy. Julia suppressed a smile; quite obviously, the grandmothers were as much in competition as the two little flower girls.

Fortified with punch, Cristy finally plunked down in the bride's decorated chair. Emily and Danielle had worked on it, covering it with ribbons, pink balloons, silk roses and bows in their own special style.

"Shall we open gifts first?" Bethany asked, "And eat a little later?"

Everyone agreed to that. Julia sat back to watch the long procedure of unwrapping gifts, oohing and aaahing over every item, passing it around so each guest could see the towel monograms or cheese board. Ironically, she noted that the gifts tended to be kitchen items, and not the filmy lingerie that Cristy had asked for.

Finally most of the gift pile had been demolished. Bethany was making a paper-plate hat out of ribbons and Renee was writing down the names of the gift donors. The flower girls had their noses into everything, exclaiming about each present as if it were the finest of royal crown jewels.

"Here's a gift with no card on it," April said, handing the mysterious package over to her sister. Julia tensed; maybe she really was getting sick. She felt a wave of slight dizziness, and felt her heart pounding quite out of control.

"A gift with no card," Cristy called out, holding it up. "Anybody want to claim this one?" No one did. Julia decided not to say anything yet.

"Open it anyway," they advised. Cristy tore at the wrapping paper carefully, uncovering a square box of creamy white cardboard.

"A Macy's box," the bride said. "Now does anybody recognize—?"

She fell silent as she slipped the cover off. Inside, wrapped in soft tissue paper but still visible, was a spectacular Lladro ceramic figurine.

Cristy turned white as the tissue paper in her hands.

"But . . . this is from my Daddy," she said in a whisper. She turned to look at Julia with suddenly red eyes. "Only, how can it be?"

"What is she talking about?" Nana Francie demanded.

"I don't understand either," Nana Carolyn yelled. "What does she mean, a gift from her Daddy?"

Julia stood up, knowing it was now time to explain. "Jay bought one of these figurines for each of the older girls for their weddings." She was trying desperately to keep her voice from cracking. "A different figurine for each, according to her personality. The other two loved their gifts so much that he—"

She had to stop. A lump as big as Alaska was blocking her windpipe.

Someone put a steadying hand on her shoulder. It was her dear friend Selena, and she was grateful for the show of support.

"So Daddy bought one for me?" asked Cristy in a quivering voice "A long time ago?"

"Two years ago." Julia nodded. "Just before he died, he saw this one that looked like—like his little Punkin'head, he told me. So he bought it and wrapped it, knowing you'd be getting married someday."

"Oh my God," someone whispered, sniffling.

"There ought to be a card inside somewhere," Julia said. "I remember he wrote one. . . ."

Cristy, blinded by tears, delved into the box. First she pulled out the figurine. It was an exquisite wheelbarrow filled to the brim with a profusion of colorful flowers and pushed by a little girl who did resemble the young Cristy Lynn.

The entire room fell silent. The figurine was beautiful, but even more, it was shockingly appropriate for a girl like Cristy who'd majored in horticulture and opted for a garden wedding. Jay hadn't known the type of wedding Cristy would choose, of course, but his instinct had been exactly right.

There wasn't a dry eye anywhere.

Oh God, I knew this would happen, Julia thought, pulling a small Kleenex pack out of her skirt pocket. Every face in the room had tears sliding down, tissues were being passed around, and here and there a small sob could be heard.

"Here's the card—and it's in my Daddy's handwriting." Cristy's voice was hoarse, scratchy. "Should I read it out loud?"

"Only if you want to," someone told her.

She read it silently, and swallowed. Then she said, "It is kind of private, but—oh here, Beth, you read it for me. I can't." Cristy handed the small gift card over to her sister and reached out for tissues.

Bethany read: "For my Cristy Lynn—the last but never, ever the least. . . . I wish you happiness on your wedding day and for your whole lovely, flower-filled life. Love, your Daddy."

Eventually the roomful of women stopped crying.

"Buffet time," called out April, hoping to break the spell. The guests clustered around April's buffet table, where trays of specialty foods awaited. As for the decor, it was flowers—roses on the plates, roses on the napkins, and morning glories on the paper cups.

"So perfect for a garden wedding," Nana Francie said, still sniffling a bit but trying to be cheery for Nana Carolyn's sake. "You all right now, Carolyn dear?"

"Trying to be, Francie," answered Nana Carolyn. "Somehow I knew my Jay would be here today in spirit—but I never expected anything like that, I can tell you."

The wheelbarrow figurine had been placed on the buffet table as a special centerpiece, because everyone wanted a closer look at it. The piece glimmered, coming to life in the glow of light from April's chandelier, so that each flower appeared to be real and the little girl almost live enough to speak.

Julia had recovered. She had no choice, she figured, because she needed to be helpful to

April in serving a buffet dinner to all these people. Her head was aching a bit now but that was from all the crying. She smiled and continued to make small talk with a procession of well-wishing ladies.

Her cousin Adrienne pulled her aside. "So Julia, are you *really* going through with this—the garden wedding idea?"

"Of course we are," Julia said. "It's all planned."

Adrienne shook her head. "Insanity, if you ask me."

"We don't think so," Julia answered without missing a beat. "We're proud of our yard, which is looking very festive already, and we're quite looking forward to a big, old-fashioned wedding."

"Well, I wish you luck," Adrienne sniffed, "but I still think it's a bad idea. After all . . ." Luckily she was interrupted by one of the girls from Cristy's UConn dorm.

"Have you found that Mindy Parsons yet, Mrs. Maxwell?" Marta asked. "I heard about all that trouble she caused."

"No, Marta. We've been searching all spring and summer, but nothing has turned up yet." Julia stared at the girl. "Do you have any helpful ideas for us?"

"Well, maybe . . ." The girl hesitated. "This

could be totally a long shot, but . . . if Mindy were renting a room around here, she might be inclined to pick out a brown house."

Julia blinked. "Are you serious?"

"Mmm-hmm, yes. She loves cemeteries and she loves the color brown, to the point that she was always choosing brown everything. I mean, if that helps at all—"

"It might," Julia said.

"In fact, sometimes people called her the Brown Widow Spider. Sounds cruel, but she was so creepy. . . ."

"Thank you, Marta. Every little bit helps."

The two grandmothers had filled their plates and were ready to be seated.

"April's an excellent cook," Nana Carolyn commented, studying the array of food on the buffet table.

"Thank God I was there to teach her the fundamentals of the kitchen," Nana Francie said rather smugly.

"*You?*" Nana's eyebrows went up in surprise. "I worked with April all through her teenage years. Who do you think taught her to make this potato salad? And this kind of cole slaw?"

Julia watched them and grinned. Some things never changed. It was reassuring, in these unpredictable times, to be able to count on that.

***

"There's another brown house," Cristy said, pointing.

"I think I checked that one last time." Ben Wilson stood still, however, staring at the tall, gothic brown house in question. "I remember the owner told me he had no renter, but—"

"But what?"

Ben frowned. "We'll just ask him once more. Coming with me?"

"Sure."

The pair made their way through the iron gate that was part of a long iron fence. They went up the walk toward the front door of the place.

Immediately a man popped open the door. A small, balding, excited looking man, he seemed to recognize Ben at once.

"What do you want?" he asked.

"We're looking for a girl," Ben said carefully. "We think she might be living here."

"No. No girl. Nobody here!"

"Look, we're not trying to make trouble, Mr.—?"

"Petrini. I told you before, I have no renter on my property."

Ben nodded. So he had been to this house previously. He'd thought so, but then there were so many homes around here, in the cemetery area, and he was starting to lose count.

"What about that brown barn of yours, Mr. Petrini?" Ben thought he'd make one more stab. "That would be a perfect place for you to build an apartment. Did you?"

"No!" The old man was beginning to look incensed. "I don't like to have renters. Why do you keep coming to bother me?"

Ben stared at the rattletrap old barn. It was a mess, he had to admit. But was it possible? Could there be a small apartment somewhere inside there?

Cristy handed Mr. Petrini a small piece of paper. "This is my phone number, Mr. Petrini. If you ever see a girl named Mindy Parsons around here, will you call me?"

"Never heard of her. Now you get out of here before I call the police."

"Take it easy, we're going." Ben backed down the stairs, his hands out in a gesture of surrender.

"And don't come back here again!"

Ben and Cristy let themselves out by the rusty old gate.

"I don't know, Cristy, there's something about that barn—"

Cristy stared at it. "I don't think so, Ben.

Even if the guy does have an apartment in there, it's definitely not the kind of place Mindy would rent."

"Why not?"

"She's a princess, that's why."

"A princess?"

"Of course. Mama and Papa's only little girl. A true spoiled kid . . . no, she's weird and she likes cemeteries, but—a barn? Nah. I think she'd want a place with more class than *that.*"

Ben tried to shrug but he found himself staring, still, at the old barn that sat way back on Petrini's property.

"You might be right, but I sure have a hunch, Cristy. . . . look, she could even park her car in there. Out of sight, so we'd never find it."

"Believe me, Ben." Cristy sighed, weary because they'd been searching an entire afternoon. "Trust me. There's no Mindy in that place."

The figure in the dark brown clothes moved away from the window, smiling.

Thirty-one

The month of June slipped by quickly, fragrant with the unexpected scent of American Beauty roses. Cristy had gone wild with rosebushes, planting them in a sunlit terrace garden and also near the spot where they would later re-erect the wedding arch.

They still hadn't found Mindy even after checking every house near the cemetery, and every brown house in Stonewell. But Mindy hadn't attacked again, either, so they wondered whether she might have moved on.

"Maybe the dog incident scared her off," Cristy said to Julia and Ben with great optimism. Eventually they began to feel safe again, and sent Ivan back home to Ben. They even stopped taking turns at sleeping nights in the dining room.

Throughout June, mother and daughter shopped until they dropped—continually, at least, until The Wedding Dress was found and purchased. To Julia's delight, it was a gown that reflected Cristy's personality. Its skirt was full, a creamy silk that would whirl whenever the bride whirled. The intricately beaded bodice, detailed by thin panels of Alencon lace—ice-cream white—looked as though it had been crafted by a body of nuns in a seventeenth-century lace shop.

On her head, Cristy would wear a ring of petite silk roses braided with strands of small pearls, and a long veil, also of Alencon lace. It was exquisite, perfect for this misplaced child of the Renaissance.

"And now we have to find the right dress for you, Momserina," Cristy said, but they weren't having luck. Julia didn't like anything she saw in local shops. People began saying, "But it's almost July! Don't tell me you haven't got your *dress* yet, Julia?"

I'll find something eventually, she thought. She was sick of shopping and weary of the constant confusion around her house. Yes, she loved having Cristy home, but their property was a continual botanical garden in progress.

And then there was Ben with the ongoing gazebo construction.

He was always there, it seemed. Sometimes Jeremy and Kevin would show up to help him, and sometimes the two sons-in-law, April's Tom and Bethany's Daniel. They'd hammer and hold boards and construct away like guys on *Tool Time* . . . but a good portion of the time Ben worked alone out there.

So of course the Maxwells felt obligated to invite him to dinner. Well, at least Julia felt obligated; Cristy invited simply because she loved Ben's company. Not that he always said yes. He had his pride, evidently, and often would go home, Julia suspected, to another of his Hungry Man frozen TV dinners . . . just to avoid being a pest.

For the Fourth of July, Cristy took off with Jeremy and a bunch of other UConn grads for Cape Cod. Julia found the sudden quiet of the house unnerving, and telephoned April.

"Anybody feel like having a picnic?"

"Oh, Mom, I'm sorry but we're going out to Tom's family's cottage at Lake George. Bethany and her gang are, too. Want to come?"

"No, no." Julia had her pride also. "I think I'll catch up on some chores I need to do around the house."

"Mom, no, you should have some fun on the Fourth. Go somewhere to watch fireworks. . . . Get drunk. . . . Go swimming nude if nothing else. . . ."

"Yeah, right," Julia said, laughing. "That's

all I need to do is take up nude swimming!"
It made her recall, though, what Ben had said
at the graduation party: that skinnydipping
would be the one activity that would make
him feel like a kid again.

Well, never mind that.

Julia was stubborn. She decided she actually looked forward to a day all to herself.
She wouldn't even call to see what Selena was
up to; after her chores, she'd bask in solitude,
enjoying the sun right in her own yard, re-
reading her favorite Mary Stewart mystery
novel, the one set in Greece.

That afternoon she had just settled into a
lawn chair, with feet up and a big smile on
her face, when the garden gate swung open
with a creaky sound from the hinges—and
there stood Ben.

"I'm sorry. I thought no one would be
home today, Julia." He turned as if to leave.

"Wait. What's up?" She pulled the sunglasses away from her eyes and squinted at
him across the yard.

"I thought I'd work on the gazebo rails today. But not if you're here relaxing."

"Ben, please. Do whatever you had planned.
Just ignore me."

But that didn't work, either. He concen-
trated on his construction work, but she was

keenly aware of him even though he did absolutely no talking to her. Finally she put
down her book and went over to give him a
hand. His work went much better after that.

By four o'clock they'd had enough. The sun
was beastly hot, there wasn't a bit of a breeze
anywhere, and they both were drenched in perspiration.

"That's it for the day," Ben said. "Why
don't we go for a cool swim?"

"Where?"

"Candlewood Lake. Don't you ever go
there?"

"No. At least, not since the girls were little
and had their swimming lessons . . . why,
that sounds really good right now!"

"Let's do it, then," Ben said.

"But wait . . . you do mean with bathing
suits, don't you?"

He laughed until his eyes were dripping
tears. "You think I'd suggest taking you skinnydipping?"

"No, not really, but—"

"You, a proper grandmother type lady who
works for the Board of Education? My God."

She grinned with him. "I didn't know I was
considered *that* proper," she said with just a
tinge of regret.

Ben went home for his bathing suit while

she ran upstairs for hers. The house was hot
and airless; Julia's hair felt matted with perspiration, her face covered with a sticky sheen.
She couldn't wait to jump in that lake.

Beeep. Ben's car was out in the driveway.
Candlewood Lake, only ten minutes away, was
a manmade body of water, a marvel of engineering to Julia. Sometime in the '30's, engi-
neers had somehow dammed up two rivers
and flooded the floor of the valley. The re-
sult was a long, gleaming blue lake that
stretched for miles, from little Sherman in
the north to the city of Danbury. Ben drove
to the Stonewell beach, a public park, where
he purchased a season sticker from the man
at the gatehouse.

The beach was crowded on this holiday, but
they managed to park, and within minutes
they were floating in cool, calm lake water,
far from gazebos and other wedding chores.

"Wonderful idea," Julia said, thoroughly
soaked and loving the coolness of her skin as
she sliced through the water. It was pure bliss.

The sun was just starting to head down in
the western sky, with tinges of crimson, pink
and purple slicing in among the clouds. Instead of staying where the hordes of beach-
goers were, they swam well beyond the town
park. Finally they settled in a quiet, rocky,

fern-filled cove far from the noise and splashing of the public beach.

"I could stay here all day and night," Ben said, his voice weary but his spirit sounding renewed. They did stay for hours, never leaving the water. Finally, when the sun truly disappeared over the mountain ridges, they swam to the shore and toweled off.

"I feel like a new person," Julia said. She couldn't believe how cool her skin was now.

"Could you go for a good spaghetti supper right now?" Ben peered like a hopeful boy over the top of his Disney World towel. "Or do the ground rules dictate that I'm not allowed to invite you out to dinner?"

"Ground rules . . ." She hesitated only a moment. "Don't be silly, Ben. Friends can go out to dinner . . . and yes, I'm hungry enough to eat six spaghetti suppers."

He smiled, his teeth gleaming white inside the sparkly wet beard. Darkness was falling fast now under the trees. Ben was staring at her, and she felt the full weight of his gaze.

"What's wrong?" she demanded. "Do I have a piece of seaweed in my hair?"

"No." He spoke softly. "I was just thinking that we've come a long way, Julia. You actually said yes to my dinner invitation."

She sighed. "That's only because I'm *hungry*, mister. Don't get any strange ideas."

His big hands went up in defense. Grinning, he said, "I wouldn't think of getting strange ideas."

When they left the Villa Milano, the sky over Stonewell was already alive with fireworks. The insistent popping and booming brought back strong memories; Julia could remember dozens of evenings watching fireworks with Jay and the children.

"I love 'em, don't you?" Ben asked, pointing to the sky.

"Yes."

"So what do you say? Instead of watching them alone, why don't you come to my house? We'll have a great view of them from my back deck."

She considered. The idea of going home alone to her own house didn't seem appealing now, after the pleasant companionship of the day. "Okay, I'd like that," she said with honesty.

Once settled on Ben's deck, the sky stretched out before them, bursting with multicolored rockets—white, blue, pink, green—and the loud noise of explosions overhead. In between demonstrations, Ben's darkened gardens buzzed with friendly insects. The night was velvety soft, rich with flowery aromas.

"It's very lovely here," Julia said. "Thank you for inviting me." She was content to sit back in the deck chair, feet up, feeling cool and well-fed and peaceful.

But Ben was quiet, petting his dog absently as he watched the turmoil in the sky. Sometimes Julia wondered what he was thinking, but she had no clue.

At one point he asked if she'd like a drink of anything.

"Mmmmm, maybe just water," she said. "But I'll get it."

"No, I will. I need to check my answering machine."

"You sound worried."

He shrugged. "Something's been nagging at me. I feel uneasy."

"Any special reason?"

"I guess I'm thinking of Killer. . . . Excuse me for a minute." He went inside, moving silently for such a large man.

Julia closed her eyes for a minute, reliving the happy hours at Candlewood Lake. What a perfectly beautiful day it turned out to be, she thought. From start to finish—from the gazebo to the lake to the Italian restaurant to this moment—it had been everything a Fourth of July should be.

No swimming nude, as April had suggested, but that had never been an option anyway. She smiled and wiggled her toes inside her sandals.

The door opened and Ben stood there, totally filling the doorway. She turned with concern because he was so silent. She could see on his face, from the kitchen light, that he had been stricken with bad news.

"Ben . . . what is it?" She leaped out of her chair but he stood there, unmoving, saying nothing. "Ben?"

Lines of grief were etched around his eyes. Finally he opened his mouth to tell her, though the words came out raspy, like some stranger she'd never before met.

"Killer died this afternoon. That was his sister who left the message to let me know."

Thirty-two

"I know how much it hurts, Ben, oh, I do know. . . ."

She was holding him tightly, trying to soothe with words while he moaned very softly, a large human animal in pain. Above them the night sky exploded again and again with huge spheres of bright light, while on the ground a gentle summer wind was whooshing in from the northern end of his property.

They stood together on the deck, because he wouldn't sit down when she begged him to, and she kept rocking him in her arms the way she used to comfort the children when they were little.

Not easy in this case, because there was nothing little about Ben. It felt strange to be touching him; he was powerfully made, with large, strong bones and taut muscles.

"You must be glad you spent that time with him," she whispered. He was shivering, and she made her hands busy, gently rubbing at his arms as though he'd been bruised. "You had your chance to say goodbye, didn't you? You played Scrabble and did crossword puzzles in the hospital. . . ."

Unashamed tears streamed down his cheeks. "I can't believe I was swimming all afternoon," he said. "Swimming while my best friend was dying."

"Oh hush, Ben, you didn't *know*. Please don't berate yourself for anything like that . . . please, dear, won't you sit down now, so we can talk reasonably?"

At last he allowed himself to be eased down on the bench he'd built along the deck's rails. Julia sat beside him, still massaging his arms as though she could scour some of the grief away. She wanted to get him through the initial shock, which was always the worst part, she felt. Once he had settled down—the fact of death being accepted—then she believed he'd snap back, at least almost to his usual Ben self.

"No, it wasn't a real goodbye," he said, still sounding dazed. "The way we left it, he'd be getting better and we'd go out fishing on his boat sometime in August—" His voice broke, and this time he covered his face with his hands. Wisely Julia didn't try to interfere.

She sat silent while he wept, a ragged sort

of crying that many men won't allow of themselves, but the sort that Julia happened to think was beneficial. His large shoulders heaved, their strength diminished by a slumping over and the desolate air that had overtaken him.

This went on for what seemed like a long time. Maybe it was no more than five minutes; Julia didn't know. She held tightly to Ben, one hand on his back, the other on his knee, just because she felt she ought to maintain some physical contact.

"Maybe you should say a word or two to Ivan," she suggested gently. "The poor dog is going crazy."

Ivan was right there with them, of course, whimpering in confusion, unable to figure out what was wrong with his master. Once in a while he'd jump up, trying to knock some sense into Ben and garner attention for himself.

"Good boy, Ivan," Ben said in a hoarse voice. "Good old fella . . ." And then finally the long silence broke, and Ben began to talk, which was a good sign. It was what Julia had been hoping for.

"You know . . . we all grew up in that same neighborhood—Hank, Killer, and me." His voice was ragged but he kept the words coming. "Our mothers were friends, so they'd sit and talk on the stoops while their little boys played, in good weather. . . ."

On and on he went, memories spilling out of him like cold milk from a pitcher. He recalled the good times and the get-in-trouble times, the growing-up rites of passage, the separation of their lives as the boys each grew older, went to college, left the Bronx and married.

"But we always kept in touch, you know?" She could see a strange glow in his eyes as a bright green rocket went off; they were reddened and sad, so totally unlike the cheery Ben she was used to seeing. "A lot of men don't keep in touch, but we—all three of us, we made sure we had our reunions—and it was always great."

"You're very fortunate, then," she said softly. "Many people live a whole lifetime without friendships like that."

He bent over as if a sudden pain had sliced through his midsection. "I thought nothing could be worse than losing your spouse," he said in a ragged voice. "Nothing *is* worse—but at the same time, when your contemporary— the little boy you used to play marbles with—"

He wound down then, silent and grieving, wrapped up inside of himself where no one could possibly reach him.

If she couldn't touch his soul, she could touch his exterior, at least. She reached out for his hands, holding them tightly, then tracing her own fingertips against the flesh of his knuckles, finger bones, and wrists, so he'd know he wasn't alone. She couldn't think of anything else to do. There were no right words to say . . . there was simply no antidote to this sort of wrenching loss. Julia knew that so well.

The fireworks finale suddenly began, a display that seemed obscene right now in its garish, loud, overhappy energy. She said, "For the rest of my life, whenever I see a fireworks finale, I'll remember this sad time on your deck, Ben."

There was a silence in which he seemed to be fighting to gain control of himself.

"Look what I'm putting you through. . . . Thank you for this, Julia." All of a sudden, his head raised high once again, his voice was almost back to normal.

"Oh please, I haven't done anything at all. I only wish I knew a few magic words—"

"You've helped me a great deal." His eyes were locked on her, and she felt self-conscious, suddenly, because of the way she'd been caressing his hands. Should she pull them away now?

"Well, a lot of good people helped me,"

she said in a low voice, "two years ago when I lost the person dearest to me in the whole universe." She patted his hands again. "It's what we do for each other in the bad times."

Now they sat silent for a while.

When the fireworks ceased, his garden became dark once again. They were surrounded by plants and ferns with deep green, glossy leaves that rustled in the quiet night. Ivan let out a happy yip, satisfied that things were getting back to an even keel, possibly, but he never left his post. He was glued to Ben's knee with enormous loyalty, just as Julia was still clutching Ben's hands.

"We need other human beings at times like this." Ben spoke with a calmness that she knew was only an eye in the center of the storm; in a while he'd be restless again, or raging against whatever disease had taken his friend away.

"We always need other human beings," she corrected. "We only think we can go it alone. Can't be done, I'm afraid."

For some reason she felt a sudden stinging behind her eyelids. Was she about to give in to crying now, as well? This didn't seem an appropriate time to air out her own personal sorrows.

Ben's big hands moved slightly, angling so

that now he was holding tightly to her fingers and wrists. The pressure felt strange to her, but pleasant.

"I've become too much of a hermit lately," Ben admitted. "I can see now I was getting in a lonely sort of rut."

"But you teach at the college, and you seem to have some friends."

"I was much too solitary," he said. "Until Cristy started coming around a couple of summers ago, and then Jeremy, and I was so grateful to be with young people, kids who were full of hope for the future. . . ."

"Cristy was hurting for the loss of her father."

He considered that. "Yes, but she wasn't letting it destroy her." He grimaced slightly in remembrance. "She wanted to take up a whole new hobby, an interest in flowers and plants, just to keep her mind occupied."

"She certainly did love coming to visit you."

"I guess that's when she changed her major, huh—and decided to specialize in horticulture?"

"Yes. Kids can be resilient." Julia cleared her throat. "I'd have been better off if I came down here with her, to visit you. This lovely setting might have done me some good, too."

He stared. "Do you really mean that?"

"Sure. I might have taken up gardening then, and who knows, I might have done less weeping." She smiled. "Selena always says she handed me hundreds of Kleenexes at work."

"You had to do your weeping, Julia. . . . hey, wait a minute. Are you saying you have an interest in gardening now?"

Her mouth formed an O. "I *did* say that, in a way, didn't I? If it's true, I've never admitted it before . . . you know, I find myself looking out my back windows continually now."

"To enjoy the flowers?"

"Absolutely. And I take little walks out back all the time, just to see what might need watering, but mostly to breathe in those wonderful flower scents. . . ."

"Is that so?" He put a hand to her forehead as if testing for fever. "Oh oh, you've got it bad, Mrs. Maxwell."

She laughed. She knew it was healthy to be able to crack tiny jokes after a serious bout of mourning.

"Well, if I've got the gardening bug, good or bad, it's all because of you, Ben. You and your wheelbarrow coming into my yard that day—"

"When you tried to have me arrested and thrown into handcuffs?" Now a half smile lit his face. "We have been having an interesting spring and summer, haven't we?"

She nodded in agreement without speaking. Her hands were still intertwined with his as if it were the most natural thing in the world.

"I have something to ask," he said.

"What?"

He hesitated for a second or two, then went on. "Please think about this for a little while, Julia, and please don't think I'm taking advantage of the situation. . . ."

"What, Ben?"

"Will you consider staying here with me tonight?"

Julia stiffened instantly. She swallowed hard and stood up, pulling her hands from his as she backed away.

"The Lord knows I'm not some shocked little virgin," she blurted out. "But I'm—surprised, to say the least!"

"I'm sorry if I've offended you," he said very softly, "but you must know I didn't mean anything sexual. Julia, please . . . I don't want to be alone tonight."

She ran her tongue over her lips. "I can certainly understand that. I know it's very difficult when you get sudden bad news. . . ."

Sitting there in the dark, quiet garden, Ben's large face was half hidden by shadows—but what she could see of it looked like a pleading young boy. The little boy from the Bronx, she thought in a crazy, sentimental moment. All alone because his mother's not watching from the stoop any more. So cute and uncertain—and right now, so in need of a friend to help him make it through the night.

"Of course I'll stay," she said. Even as the words came out, she wondered if she'd slipped a major gear. Spend the night here with this man who—let's face it, Julia!—this man who had such a strong and sensual effect on her?

She squared her shoulders. She was an adult; they both were, for that matter, and there simply was no problem about staying the night. It was nothing sexual, he'd said so himself.

And she had no one waiting for her. Cristy would be gone until Saturday. There wasn't a soul to worry about Julia or wonder where she was.

Unless her mother or her mother-in-law were to call to say happy Fourth of July. But she'd deal with that some other time.

Right now Ben needed her. "I'm going to make a pot of coffee," she said in her best bustling, efficient voice. "Or would you rather something stronger, like a drink?"

His bloodshot eyes looked up at her. "Coffee sounds like heaven right now. Maybe it'll help this migraine headache that's moving in on me."

"I didn't know you were subject to migraines."

"Only when under extreme stress . . . don't worry, coffee will probably calm it down."

So there, she thought, hurrying to his kitchen to search for coffee and a paper filter. He has a headache and he's not about to go breaking the ground rules, obviously.

But what was that expression about reaffirming life in the midst of death—that rationale why so many people make love after hearing news of someone's sudden death?

Oh, grow up, Julia, she scoffed, and measured out the scoops of coffee. Nobody's thinking about making love. Nobody.

Except maybe you.

Thirty-three

She couldn't shake the feeling, however, that staying here was a big mistake. They sat down to their cups of coffee, the kitchen darkened so no light would bother Ben's headache. She sensed he still wanted to talk, especially about his friend Killer, so she tried to draw him out.

"Who was the first of you three pals to be married, Ben?"

"Killer was always first at everything." Ben smiled in a rueful way. "First to be divorced, too. His marriages never lasted. He had no kids either."

Ben looked at her, seeming to be sensitive to her silence. "Are you wondering why Lily and I never had children, Julia?"

"Why would I be wondering that? Well, I suppose I have been curious at times, but it's none of my business."

"Maybe it is." He looked down at a spoon, moved it around on the table, finally stopped fiddling with it. "Lily was never in good

health. She had the very severe diabetes one
is born with. She took good care of herself
but still—that's what killed her in the end, at
too young an age."

"I'm sorry."

He sighed. "Thank you. Anyway, we decided right from our wedding day that a preg-
nancy would be out of the question. And we
were right; she couldn't have carried or delivered a child."

Julia experienced a "weltschmerz", as her
maternal German grandmother used to call
it—a pang of regret for someone else. "You'd
have made a terrific father."

"Thank you. I'm crazy about kids, and I'm
glad I'm a teacher these days. It helps."

"You've been so kind to Cristy and
Jeremy . . . almost as though they're your
own."

He klunked the spoon against his mug.
"Well, they're not my own. She's *your* daughter, and Jay Maxwell's, and I do know the
difference." His voice sounded weary, deep
and flat and resigned.

*Christy loves you almost as much as she loved
her Dad*, Julia wanted to say . . . but couldn't.
That would sound contrived and pitying, even
though it was quite true.

He buried his forehead in his hands. "Sorry

if I'm grumpy. This headache . . . I'd better take two aspirins and get to sleep."

"Good idea."

"I don't know where to put you," he said in confusion. "I should make up a bed in the spare room—"

"You'll do no such thing! You have a headache, so go and lie down. I'll find whatever I need and fix my own bed. Really."

"The couch opens up in here, too," he muttered. "And the towels are in the downstairs bathroom closet—"

"Stop worrying. I'll be awake for a while after all this coffee, so if you need me, give a yell."

He looked at her with bleary, bloodshot eyes. "You're sounding wifely again."

"Stop it, wise guy. I'm trying to be a friend."

Ben's house was quiet in a different way than her own house could be quiet. She had a number of ticking clocks at home, but here there seemed to be none. He did have a medium-sized fish tank, however, with its gurgling sound of filtering water. She watched this for a time. It was oddly restful, watching the golden and silvery fish glide in their mindless circles, and listening to the water bubbling.

Otherwise the house was silent, and she walked around restlessly, wondering what she was doing here. He'd said he needed her but now he was sound asleep.

Oh well, it wouldn't kill her to do a favor . . . and when he woke up he'd need a friend once again.

She searched for photos of Lily and found a number of them. But she was stunned because she spotted a picture that hadn't been on Ben's wall the first time she visited here—a photo of herself!

She went over to the wall between two of his vast windows to verify what she was looking at; and sure enough, it was a gold-framed nine by twelve color study of Ben and herself . . . taken that day in the garden behind her house. The day his photographer, Bryce, had been snapping official pictures for the book.

She gaped at it, not knowing what to think. Why, they looked like a couple, not like friends. Ben stood a head taller than Julia, and he'd moved in close, protectively, his arm wrapped securely around her. The expression on his face was—well, to her it looked like a man who would do anything on earth to protect this very cherished woman.

She could only stare. What did it mean? Was

he more fond of her than she could possibly imagine? According to the sweet, bearded face in that photo, he was . . . and yet he knew full well she was nowhere ready to love or be loved.

He knew that.

She shook the thoughts away. Now was not the time to try solving the problems of the universe . . . there must be other diversions here in this bachelor-boy log home, so she'd look for one that would be simple to concentrate on.

She examined the oak bookcases that covered three walls of Ben's living room. If she'd expected to see all gardening books, she was mistaken. He had novels, classics, school texts, and plenty of how-to books on everything from auto repair to carpentry to plumbing.

And he hadn't been kidding about Greece: he owned more books on classical Greece than she'd ever seen before. Evidently Greece really *was* his lifelong dream, just as it was hers. She'd never been quite sure he told the truth about that.

Julia sat down with six books on Greek history. She lost herself in the fine, glossy pages, picturing herself over there next year, going from the Acropolis Museum to the Temple of Apollo to the Temple of Zeus. . . . It was a blissful reverie.

A clock somewhere struck midnight. So he did have clocks. They just weren't the ticking sort.

Still wide awake, she stood up and stretched. She supposed she ought to think about fixing a bed for herself.

Just then Ben trundled out of his room, which was directly down the hall, the first door from the living room. He was wrapped in a huge white terrycloth robe.

"What a robe. You look like the biggest vanilla ice cream cone in the world." She was joking out of nervousness. "Are you feeling any better?"

He nodded. "Much better, thanks." He shuffled toward the kitchen, not quite awake yet. "Headache's gone and I feel hungry."

She followed him. "Go easy on your stomach, Ben. A bowl of cereal might be the best thing."

"Cereal? Ugh." He obeyed, however, reaching up for a box of Cheerios. "Want some?" Julia shook her head.

He poured some into a thick brown bowl, drowned them in milk, and munched for a while. "That was no migraine anyway, because thank God it's gone. Maybe it was a sun headache, or just tension from hearing about Killer."

"I'm glad it's gone." She sat opposite him at the table, watching as a pale light gleamed across his strong facial features. As he began to wake up, he looked more like the Ben she knew so well—confident and capable, but quiet and modest. A very nice man . . . with a very sexy beard . . .

Her fingers itched to touch it.

Stop it, Julia.

"Thanks for being here," he said. "I had no right to ask such a favor of you, but I'm glad you stayed."

"No problem. I seem to be a night owl lately . . . well, since Jay died, anyway. I spend hours prowling around so it's nice to be with another human being, for once."

He smiled. She wondered why the whole room lit up when he did that. He cleared his throat before he spoke.

"You and your husband . . . did you have a perfect marriage?"

"About as perfect as can be. Truly."

"My marriage was, too." He sighed. "Well, no sense raking all that over the coals, is there?"

"Nope." She heard a few firecrackers going

off somewhere in the distance. "We're supposed to be grateful that we were given a gem of a marriage," she said, quoting from the grief workshop.

"Yes, that is the positive way to think. I've got something more recent to grieve about, with Killer passing away. I'll be driving to Long Island tomorrow night for the wake."

"Would you like some company? I could go along if it would make things easier."

He smiled at her, rose, took his empty cereal bowl to the sink. "Thanks, Julia. I appreciate your offer but I'd rather not put you through that."

"Why not?" Her chin went up. "I'm a strong person."

"Oh, I know that. But each funeral is a reminder of your own loss, you know? I don't think you're ready for that."

She stood and walked over to look out the glass sliding doors. Outside the gardens were hidden in mist, and silent, and the night moonless.

"You don't know what another person's readiness is, Ben. Everyone is different in the way they handle grief."

She stared out, seeing clouds scudding across the black sky and a few visible stars sprinkled across the vast universe. She shivered slightly, rubbing her arms.

"I wish now I had worn a sweater," she said. But of course she'd never dreamed she'd be spending the night anywhere other than her own house.

"Are you cold?" His voice was close behind her, so near that his breath felt warm against her hair. "Of course you are . . . I'll get you one of my sweaters, though it'll be huge."

"That would be nice, thank you." She expected him to pull away, to go off to find the promised sweater. But he didn't move.

Julia shivered again, not entirely from the cool air in the kitchen. She kept her eyes glued to the back doors, staring mindlessly at the tops of oak and maple trees that were swaying slightly in the night wind.

"Don't get all tense, Julia." His voice was so soft it was almost a whisper. "I won't touch you if you don't want me to."

"I know." Her breath caught in her throat. Here was her chance; all she had to do was say "Leave me alone." Her fingers gripped the frame of the door in front of her, and her lips refused to move.

A long silence stretched out. The man stood behind her, waiting, tall and powerful.

"Tell me to go away."

No, don't go away, she thought. She never said the words to chase him off. Then ultimately she turned, quite slowly but of her own volition, and made the imperceptible movement that slid her smoothly into his waiting arms.

And it felt so right.

Bunches of white terrycloth closed in all around her. His arms held her firmly, his face moved in closer so the vast stretch of beard was silky against her cheek . . . and a quicksilver sweetness ran through her body.

"We do have those ground rules," Ben said, his voice almost a moan as she followed her impulse and traced a forefinger along the rim of his ear.

"No ground rules tonight," Julia whispered.

He leveled a look at her. "This isn't about *pity,* is it? Because I won't have that—you staying in my arms because my friend died. Especially if you're not ready to be with a man, Julia."

The warmth continued to spread through her, gentle and sure as an embrace. "It's not about pity," she said simply. "And . . . I'm doing this whether I'm ready or not, it seems."

Still, she snuggled closer, burying herself in yards and yards of great-smelling terrycloth. Beneath the robe there was the scent of his skin, crisp and hirsute and boasting of male chromosomes. Their mouths came together, flooding all her senses, knocking away inhibitions, guilt, doubt, fear.

Ben had kissed her before and left her shaking—but always she'd been in a state of denial. Tonight she was ready to move beyond denial, though she had no idea why.

Their mouths pulling slightly apart for a moment, she spoke in a clear, surprised voice. "When I buried Jay I thought I'd never, ever do this again."

There was a small silence.

In the stillness of his house the fishtanks glubbed peacefully, and outside the door there were more popping fireworks. But the man holding her waited a full minute before he kissed her, just a light grazing over her eyelid. When he spoke, his voice was low and controlled.

"I don't want to hear about Jay right now."

As their kisses deepened, Julia recalled Irmgard's comical—and wise—advice: "When God sends you a miracle, you should say *thanks,* not *no thanks!*"

Okay, Irmgard . . .

She placed both hands against his chest, trying to feel the thump of his heart beneath the terrycloth. Couldn't be done. So she went one step further and opened his robe, sliding her small hands against that massive wall of rib and muscle. He breathed in very sharply and didn't move.

There was so much hair across this chest! She had forgotten all about that, even though they'd been swimming this afternoon. Her fingers wove playfully in the thick, golden tangle, realizing she was touching the bear-like chest for the very first time. The sensation was every bit as erotic as touching his beard.

"Maybe we both need a little miracle at this point," she said carefully. "Maybe this will be it."

The miracle was that they ever made it into the bedroom at all. Both shy, both feeling awkward, they continued to kiss but neither made the first move toward a serious walk down the hall.

Finally Ben spoke. "If you're totally sure, Julia . . ."

"I am. I am sure." Her heart pounded and her body temperature had risen to feverish. Still, she had never been less sure in her life.

"Then we can certainly get comfortable."

He clasped her hand and led the way to his bedroom. She felt an instant of hollow panic and stopped, seeing his large bed in the vast, rather masculine room. The room was darkened because he'd been sleeping, but she could see it was tidy, filled with large pieces of solid oak furniture and decorated with many green plants, some hanging and others arranged on the bureaus and window sills.

A man's bedroom. She swallowed hard. They both knew this was more than the literal threshold, it was the point of final decision on her part. She teetered there on that edge for a frightened moment.

"So?"

A sigh of surrender. "I can't resist a man with a beard," she whispered helplessly.

He laughed, a deep, humorous sound. Now they stepped over that threshold, and very slowly he turned Julia to him, kissing her with a mouth that was warm and inviting. The sweetness ran through her body like quicksilver.

At some point she pulled away and undid the belt of his robe, opening it slowly, studying what she saw inside all that terrycloth. A large and powerful man—"a powerhouse," Liz had called him, and now Julia had to agree.

Large, but not fat in the least . . . a cold shiver ran down the length of her spine.

Julia, are you sure you can do this?

Gently, he turned her around and helped her to unzip her dress. He slid his large hands beneath the fabric to ease it carefully off her shoulders.

He was so gentle; was that a trait of very large men?

Her dress dropped to the floor; Ben picked it up with his customary tidiness and draped it across a chair. She slipped out of her sandals and stood there in her slip, glad she'd chosen the one of ivory silk trimmed with brown lace.

"Come here," he said. He sat, causing the mattress to go way down with his weight. He patted the bed and said again, "Come here." She did.

His mouth covered hers, sweet and warm and possessive. She slid both arms around his neck, tracing the large bones and hard muscles that made his shoulders so massive.

Well, if I'm going to do this, might as well jump right in, she thought. One swift motion removed the robe from his frame.

Together, forgetting shyness now, they finished removing Julia's underclothes. Then they slowly angled downward, falling together

companionably until they landed in comfort
on the bed.

"You know, Ben," she said lightly, "this all
started because you promised me a sweater."

"You won't be needing it."

You weren't supposed to compare, she reminded herself over and over again. But it
was impossible not to remember certain fac-
tors—that Jay had been no taller than herself,
with small bones, thin limbs and a lean, almost gaunt face.

This man Ben was so *large* . . . she shivered. Even just lying face to face, Julia felt
like a Thumbelina who had no business being with this Apollo, the oversized Grecian
sun god. Now that they were undressed she
couldn't help staring, finding his body wonderful—but at the same time, it was the body
of a stranger.

I was married almost thirty-five years; how
am I supposed to turn off those memories?

But when Ben's mouth closed over hers she
was able—quite able!—to forget the past and
her familiar marriage bed. There was that
wiry, rough hair on his broad chest, something so new to her that she gasped, catching

her breath sharply the first time the sensitive tips of her breasts nuzzled against him.

"Oh, my God," she whispered. Jay had had no chest hair, which was fine, but now this sort of friction was incredible, quite indescribable; a melting sweetness flowed through her bones in an alarming way. You mustn't compare but everything is so very very different. . . .

"I knew you would be beautiful, Julia." His hands were gently cupping her breasts where she was swollen and tender.

"Gallant of you to say that," she mumbled by way of contradicting him; she intended to remind him this was a postmenopausal body that had seen better days . . . but, as if he knew, he silenced her with one finger across her mouth.

"Ssssh. You're beautiful, I said."

His own mouth moved lightly across one of her aching nipples and then the other, and she found herself arching in a primitive sort of agony.

Breathless, she blurted out, "I haven't done this in such a long time, you know. . . ."

"Sssh. I haven't done it in much longer than that."

She was shocked. He couldn't mean that he never—?

"Never in all these years?" she asked. "In

the six years since your wife died? You can't be serious."

"I am serious, and we're not talking about our spouses, remember?"

"Yes . . . I do remember, actually. . . ."

Then she stopped thinking altogether, because here was the awaited miracle. . . . Her body was unbelievably moist and eager for him; his body was quite visibly ready for hers.

"How would you feel about doing this immediately?" she whispered. She felt embarrassed but the time seemed so *right*.

"Now?" he asked softly.

"Oh, yes."

He had a wonderful grin. "I would be more than agreeable."

But oh, God . . . deeper and deeper and deeper . . . no, Julia, you can't do any comparing, you can't because nothing has *ever* compared to this . . . this man is an Apollo, this man is a lover who might come along only once in any woman's lifetime, nothing on God's earth has ever reached to this depth. . . .

She thought she was moaning but she was screaming. She made herself stop that. She watched the fine sheen of perspiration on his forehead and smiled. She loved the sensation of feeling submerged—drowned—in the pas-

sion light of his sweet green eyes. She knew
if she were to die right now she'd die a happy
woman.

Her release came only seconds before Ben's.
When it came it was astounding, overwhelming. It seemed to wash away months of sadness,
weeks of weeping, days of wrenching grief. She
clutched so tightly at Ben's back she was afraid
she'd tear his skin . . . but there were no com-
plaints forthcoming.

They stayed together a long time afterward,
both smiling with surprise, both playful with
their kisses and stroking.

She didn't say the things that were on her
mind.

But in her heart she knew she had dropped
all comparisons . . . and she had loved this
man truly and purely during the act of love.

Hours later, after a long sleep, Julia awoke
in the strange, high-ceilinged bedroom. The
bedsheets smelled of lovemaking, which made
her dive under the blanket with a brightly
pink face.

Ben was asleep, snoring ever so quietly beside her. She turned to watch him; there was
enough dim light to see his dark eyelashes,

the strong line of his nose, the flyaway sandy hair that made him look boyish.

Okay, let's think about this.

She was quelling a stab of panic.

Until tonight I was a respectable widow, going through the stages of mourning one by one, with lots of help from the Grief Workshop, not making mistakes because I'm a sensible, intelligent, strong woman.

And now I've blown it all with one night of hot, sensual loving. So? And what comes next after *this?*

Her eyes were wide and she felt a lurch in her stomach. No one would ever understand. Even *she* didn't understand.

She sighed deeply. Maybe a change of attitude was needed. She squared her shoulders and framed a new thought: "Oh, cool it, you prude. We're not talking about life and death here. Good grief."

Somewhere in the house she heard the gurgling of the tropical fish tank, the only sound in an otherwise dark, silent haven. Ben made a funny little snorting sound in his sleep and moved closer to her, his hand reaching out to touch her arm.

She grinned wickedly. Her body felt very, very different. She had to admit she felt a peaceful, contented glow all over. Whatever he'd done, and whatever the emotional cost in the long run, surely it was well worth it. She slid back down to snuggle against Ben. Yes, well worth it.

Thirty-four

"Happy Fifth of July," Ben said when the sunlight poured into his log-walled bedroom. "I hope you're not going to hate me today."

She blinked awake and the first thing she saw were his eyes—large, concerned, dark green with worry. He was leaning toward her but keeping a distance as if respecting her space.

"Hate you?" Julia wanted to put his mind at rest but she'd been wondering the same thing herself: What was to come next? And why—she smiled—why in the name of Apollo had this happened?

She put her fingers into his beard, stroking lightly as if it were her talisman. "I might hate myself, Ben, when I have time to think about it . . . but hate you? No. You never meant for all this to take place."

He grinned. "I didn't plan it, you're right, but I must confess I've always thought about being with you. Ever since the first day I rolled that wheelbarrow into your yard."

"Really?" Her finger moved along the wide, sensuous lines of his mouth. "You rather knocked my socks off, too," she admitted. "But . . ." She sat up, frowning slightly. "I can't make a habit of this."

He watched her closely, his face unreadable. "You can't make a habit out of this . . . why?"

"It's hard to explain." She stared at the walls, masterfully decorated with pictures of plant specimens, both photos and watercolors. They brightened up what would otherwise have been a rather dark bedroom.

Ben kissed her bare shoulder, causing her to shiver. "Want to try?"

"No, I don't think so. Not right now. Can we—" She pulled away, trying to be casual about it. "I probably need some time to think, Ben. Maybe I shouldn't have led you on when I'm not at all ready for a relationship."

Deadpan, he said, "You didn't lead me on. You made love with me, Julia, and quite actively, I might add."

"Well, that's what I mean." She spoke rapidly. "The stages of grief, Ben, are very important. I've studied up on this. We may do crazy things—widows, I mean—along the way, but we still have to take the stages one at a time. Otherwise we'll end up making huge mistakes."

"Mistakes?" He looked thunderstruck. The frown on his face caused her stomach to lurch. "What are you talking about—stages? Who made up the blueprint? And who says you have to follow it?"

"Look," she said reasonably. "I'm in an early stage. I haven't even taken off my wedding ring yet, Ben."

"I'm damn well aware of that."

"So . . . what does that tell you? Maybe I'm slow, but I'm not ready yet to close out my long marriage to Jay. I'm trying and I'm working at it as fast as I can, but—"

To her utter disgrace, she began crying. Large, salty tears rolled down her cheeks, dropping on the crisp percale sheets.

"I'm sorry," she blubbered, continuing to weep and dab her eyes with the sheet. Ben did not put his arms around her, she noticed. It would have been a perfect time for a snuggle and a bit of comforting, but instead he pulled a few inches away from her, merely watching.

Finally he spoke, but each word was like a lead weight.

"I can't tell you how to proceed with your widowhood," he said. "I barely know how I got through my own situation, and even today I wonder if I handled anything right. Probably not."

"But at least you now have the advantage," she said, "of all those years. A slightly faraway perspective, so to speak."

He nodded. "Yes, there's that."

"So you won't sit in judgment of me, if I seem to have a problem with this, Ben?"

"I'd never sit in judgment of you." Still he didn't touch her, but he was regarding her with obvious puzzlement, she thought.

"We can take things slowly, then?" she pressed.

"Yes, of course."

She felt a vast sense of relief. They could go back to being platonic friends, if necessary, until she could get her emotions about Jay sorted out. Yes, that did seem the best course of action for now.

"You're a sweet man," she said. "And to be honest, you're a sexy man and I wish— well, never mind what I wish. I'd like to go home now so I can regroup."

"Sure." It was as though a dark cloud passed over his face. "You probably want to light a candle to Jay."

She was so startled she stared at him. "What—?"

Ben stood up and strode briskly for the bathroom. "I'm going to take a shower. I don't feel like talking any more."

And he left her, still wrapped in the sheets that she'd dampened with her foolish tears. She sat there and cried some more, a rush of sadness washing over her. She had no idea why.

Who ever knew men could be so *touchy*, she thought later that day as she ran the vacuum over her downstairs carpets. Well, he simply has to accept the facts. I made one big mistake last night but I can't keep doing it.

She decided she was too busy to regret anything. She glanced down at Jay's wedding ring once, felt a guilt pang, then looked quickly at the big pile of engraved wedding invitations that were stacked in boxes in her dining room.

If nothing else she had to start addressing envelopes. But before she did even that, there were rooms to clean out and plans to be made for accommodating all the out-of-town guests during Cristy's wedding weekend. . . .

No time to think. And so she immersed

herself in the millions of trivial chores she did all the time as well as the much bigger ones that needed care once in a while.

. . . while her body betrayed her by remembering.

At intervals she'd get a sudden, unexpected flashback to last night and her knees would positively turn to mush. Her pulse would hammer; she'd feel a weakness from head to toe that had nothing to do with the warm July day or the bustle of her life.

It didn't seem fair. But she became proficient eventually in pushing away the sensual memories and longings, reminding herself she was a grandmother and very busy mother of the bride.

I can do this, she thought. I can forget for a while about a large man whose mouth is sweet and full, and whose beard drove me to new heights of ecstasy, and whose—

Oh, God. She felt her face flaming scarlet.

Time to take another cold shower, Julia, she thought with great sternness.

She turned back into "Grandma" the very next Sunday when the children came to visit for the day—Emily, Danielle, and baby Tommy. Their parents had a fireman's picnic to attend, adults only, and Julia was thrilled to have a chance with her little people.

Especially now. Especially now when she needed to occupy her mind and body.

"Look at us, Grandma," Emily yelled. "We're going to stick our feet in the pool!" Julia joined them out on the back lawn where they'd been filling up a tiny wading pool she bought last summer for just such occasions.

"No, let me do it," Danielle whined. "Grandma, she never lets me do anything."

"Why don't you be good little girls? Cousins are supposed to love each other." Julia had the baby in her arms and was smiling with delight. She couldn't imagine anything she'd rather be doing than babysitting with her three babies.

Even waking up in Ben's arms . . . but that wasn't to be thought about.

"Your face is all red, Grandma. Do you have a sunburn?"

"Yes, a little bit. I swam in the lake the other day."

It had been four days since she left Ben's house that morning, and she hadn't seen him since. She knew he'd gone off to Long Island, though, for the wake and funeral. He left a note in her mailbox that said he'd hired a neighborhood boy to feed the fish and take care of Ivan. He also mentioned that if she and Cristy wanted Ivan with them, they only needed to tell the boy about it.

"We don't need Ivan any more," Cristy had said when she returned from the Cape. "Thank God, Mindy hasn't struck in a long time."

The sun was hot today, and Julia blessed the coolness of the shade from her maple and oak trees. Her granddaughters, pert and plump in their ruffly bathing suits, stepped gingerly into the pool water. But they contrasted. Emily was a fish; she leaped immediately and splashed down as if in the briny surf. Danielle, more of a worrier, stood there and hesitated.

Soon they were squabbling again, and as Julia separated them, she suddenly wondered how she could manage the logistics of going inside to warm a bottle for little Tom. She'd have to drag the girls out of the pool; she certainly couldn't leave them there alone, even for a moment.

This mothering stuff was harder than she'd remembered!

She heard a knock-knock in the vicinity of the wooden gate. Had April or Bethany come home ahead of time?

But it was Ben who strolled into the yard, tall and wonderful looking . . . well dressed in slacks and a bright white shirt. Her heart accelerated.

"Hi, Mister Ben!" the girls yelled out fondly. They knew him from the many gardening and gazebo-building sessions this summer. "Watch us! We can swim. . . ."

"Hi," Ben said back. His smile was there, but not full of mirth as usual. "Hello, Julia."

"Welcome home," she said. She had to force the words through a giant lump in her throat; she was dazzled at seeing him so unexpectedly. His powerful frame seemed to dwarf her entire backyard, but maybe that was because she was sitting down with the baby. She wished she could give him a light kiss of hello, but that would really precipitate questions from the peanut gallery.

He took a seat in one of the chairs near her. "How are you doing?" he asked.

"Good. Ben, how are *you*? Was the funeral awful for you?"

He nodded, looking tired and rather beat. She could tell he wasn't going to talk about it right now, that maybe he needed a break from the sorrow of the past few days.

"And who are these lovely ladies?" he

asked as the wet and wild tiny girls gathered nearby to stare at him. "Can these possibly be the famous flower girls?"

"Yes!" the little ones screeched with excitement.

"You ought to meet them formally," Julia said, playing along with the gag. "This is Miss Emily Tanner and this is Miss Danielle O'Donnell."

"And the baby is my brother Fido," Emily said.

"No! I want to tell! The baby's my cousin!"

She watched as Ben handled the girls with great skill. Before they could continue arguing, he had them walking around the property with him as he pointed out plants and wildflowers.

"Thanks, Ben. I have to run inside for a minute."

This gave Julia the needed opportunity to fix the baby's formula, heat it, and settle back out on the patio to feed him.

Grandparenting is much sweeter when there's a grandfather sort of person around, she thought. In all fairness, Ben would make a fantastic grandfather, if a woman were to give him half a chance. All in her own good time, that is.

He stayed the day and she was grateful to

have him. Before the sun had set, he'd rigged up two little wooden swings for the girls and hung them from a thick branch of the maple tree.

"I love Mr. Ben," Emily said fervently.

"I love him more! More and more than her!"

Sometimes I wonder if I love him too, Julia thought, trying not to stare at the big, competent man who was making himself so useful around her house.

She kept her face nuzzled down to little Tom as he glugged through his next bottle. The sun had set by now, the yard was blessedly cool, and she planned to carry out a nice cold picnic supper for all of them.

It was pleasant, being outdoors like this, especially when you suddenly had a yard that teemed with rich perennials, hybrid roses, old-fashioned beds of hollyhocks and poppies . . . and of course the bursting rainbow colors of the annuals that tumbled from behind rocks everywhere.

She wondered. Maybe she'd miss this place when she sold it and moved into the condo. Maybe she'd even miss *gardening,* for Pete's sakes.

But about loving Ben . . . how was a

woman to know? It was complicated right now.

Well, she certainly had missed him these past four days. She had to admit that.

Thirty-five

Making coffee the next morning, Julia glanced out the small kitchen window above her sink—and realized the children's swings were no longer on the maple branch.

Her heart plummeted. Where were the two swings?

She threw open the kitchen door and ran out back, barefoot and still in her nightgown but not caring. She took a quick inventory. The swings had been cut down, the ropes sawed with something jagged, like a knife. Zinnias, impatiens plants, and marigolds had been brutally torn out of the earth and flung to the four winds.

Dirt and disorder were everywhere. Even the children's wading pool had been slashed; heartbreaking pieces of pink and blue plastic floated in a sad puddle of water. Emily and Danielle would cry their eyes out if they saw this.

She's still around. She still hates us. Mindy in-

tends to destroy everything we try to do for Cristy's wedding. . . .

Biting her lip to keep from crying out, Julia went in to telephone the police. Cristy came down the stairs as she was doing so, heard the conversation and raced outside herself to inspect the damage. When she returned, Julia had just put down the phone. Cristy exploded with pure rage at the unseen Mindy Parsons.

"I'll kill her! I'll find her and I'll kill her!"

"Don't say that, please," Julia asked. "There won't be any killing, honey. We'll let the law handle this." She was frightened at the redness and rigid, set lines of her daughter's face.

"The law? The law sucks! Our garden is ruined. Jeez, at least she missed the rose bushes this time . . . but on her next trip she'll probably bring gloves so she can yank them out. I'll kill her, Mom!"

And this was even more disturbing to Julia than the damage in their yard: this Cristy who was raving about revenge and killing. After all, Julia had worked overtime to raise three decent girls who would have compassion for a sick person. . . .

The morning was total chaos. Julia called in to work, explaining she'd be late. No problem. July was a quiet month anyway for the staff at the elementary school.

Ben must have spotted the police car from his house, because he was knocking at the front door within half an hour. He found both Julia and Cristy sitting slumped at the kitchen table, dejected and miserable.

"All right, that's it," he said as soon as he knew the extent of the damage. "I had a slight hunch last time about that girl—not even a clue, but just a detective's intuition—and I'm ashamed to say I didn't follow it through."

"You did? What sort of hunch?" Julia asked.

"There were two clues: a big brown house, and a lying landlord. And I should have checked closer."

"What do you mean?" Cristy jumped up with excitement. "That big brown house near the cemetery? The one where you and I talked to that Mr. Petrini?"

"Exactly. Who wants to come with me?" Ben's eyes had hardened like cold steel and Julia felt an icy-cold trickle make its way along her spine. He was a big man who certainly wasn't inclined to violence, she'd bet her life on that. But when he was righteously angry, you maybe didn't want to get in his way.

"We'll both go with you," Julia said. She and Cristy rushed upstairs to finish dressing, then joined Ben in his truck.

The hunt was on.

Ben drove to High Road, the street just past the cemetery.

"But you've already checked every house around here, haven't you?" Julia asked.

"Yeah, and I talked to the owner in every case. But that brown one right there—" He pointed to the tall, gothic style home—a very New England structure—with the iron fence around all the property. "I suspect somebody's been living in their barn."

"But didn't you ask them?" Julia said.

"Of course I asked the owners." Ben pulled the car alongside the gateway of the iron fence. "He either lied to me, or they weren't aware of it. . . . there's the barn back there."

They stared. The old barn, brown and weatherbeaten, sat slightly tilted, forlorn in the early morning shadows. It didn't look occupied in the least. In fact, it wasn't a pleasant sight, somehow . . . and the two women couldn't help wondering whether Ben had slipped his trolley.

"I have a plan," Ben said. They jumped from the truck and went through the iron gate without asking anyone's permission.

"Look at this!" Ben pointed to fresh tire tracks that led to the closed barn doors. Someone had very recently driven a car into the barn, probably in the morning dew.

"That doesn't mean much," Cristy said. "The owner might keep his own car there."

"We'll see. . . . Now let's each watch a different entrance," Ben said. He must have been formulating his plan as he drove to High Road.

"You two wait out here and I'll go in that barn door." Ben's face looked grim. "If anything happens, call for help fast."

"It's dangerous, Ben," Julia protested, but one look at his determined face told her he wouldn't be dissuaded.

"If she's in there, I'll find her," Ben said in firm, measured tones.

"Hey! Get outta here! Get off my property!" They heard an angry voice and saw the small, bald man charging out of the main brown house. He looked outraged to see people stealing toward his barn.

"Sorry, Mr. Petrini. I'm going in this time,"

Ben told him. "You lied to me when you said you had no tenant."

"What—are you people crazy?" The short balding guy frowned and shook a fist at them. "I can't have renters here. I'm not zoned for an apartment."

"I believe you've got an illegal renter," Ben said quietly. "And if you want to get me off your property, you'll have to call the police. Because I'm going to find her."

To Julia, Ben whispered, "Talk to him, Julia, while I proceed. Try to explain what happened at your house. Maybe he'll tell you the truth."

Ben strode quickly toward the barn. He was certainly big enough that the owner wouldn't attempt to stop him physically. Julia noted that Ben went very silently to the side door and opened it with care.

And that's when Julia decided she didn't want him going in there alone.

"Cristy honey, *you* talk to the property owner," she directed Cristy. "I have to make sure Ben's all right." She followed right behind as he entered the vast cavern of the barn.

Right away she noticed the place smelled like hay, rotted old wood and animal manure—but it also had an odd, lived-in scent that could only come from humans.

He's right, Julia thought. There is an apartment here somewhere.

And besides . . . there in the dimness of the old building was the brown Ford, the one they had seen hanging around Camelot Road before any of the vandalism occurred. And probably it was the same one described by Mindy's aunt as being a gift from Mindy's father. Julia felt a shock to see it there, yet Ben didn't look at all surprised.

"Should've checked this out weeks ago," he mumbled, sounding angry with himself. "I suspected that Petrini guy was covering up something."

They looked for anything that might be considered a place to live. Finally, toward the back of the barn, they saw a fairly new interior door built into a wall.

"There it is. That old rascal built a small apartment back here." Ben moved forward quietly and Julia followed along behind him.

"Do you think Mindy would be sleeping?" Julia whispered.

"Very possibly. If she roamed the town all night long, she'd be pretty tired by now."

At that moment, the door swung open. A pretty but glittery-eyed girl stepped out, dressed all in brown—brown slacks, shoes and a brown turtleneck sweater—an odd selection for July.

Julia stared. Mindy was as thin as they had all said. Her heart-shaped face was topped by an enormous volume of bushy, healthy brown hair; she might have been any normal coed from any college.

But Julia knew that this girl was no longer a college coed. They were having their first good look at Mindy Parsons, the so-called Brown Widow Spider who'd been making their lives a living hell.

"Who are you? What do you want here?" Mindy demanded. She was cool. In fact, she was actually icy and amused, as if she knew they couldn't do a thing to her. It dawned on Julia that they had absolutely no evidence on the girl.

"You know who we are, Mindy." Ben spoke softly, firmly, and kept moving toward her. "You've been keeping an eye on us for a long time now."

"I have no idea who you are." She had a way of looking down her nose at them. "You will get away from my apartment now. Immediately or I'll have you arrested."

"I'd like that." Ben smiled. "Go on, give

the police a call, Mindy. We can solve this thing right now."

The girl smiled as though she were enjoying the challenge. Julia was amazed at the sheer bravado of the girl.

This is not going to be easy, she thought. We didn't catch her in the act, so how will we ever, ever prove she was the person who entered our backyard?

"Your hands look rather scratched, Mindy," Ben said. "Hard work, pulling up all those flowers?"

"I have no idea what you're blathering about."

"I'll bet there's still some soil under your fingernails, too, soil that will match the soil in Mrs. Maxwell's gardens. We'll have the police lab check that out."

"You're fantasizing," Mindy said with a cold, almost sweet, undisturbed smile. Julia's heart sank because she could see that in truth Mindy's hands were spotlessly clean.

Julia and Ben were the ones who were in trouble. They had barged in here, trespassers with slander on their lips, and they had no case against this girl.

The barn door swung open, and Cristy came charging in. "Mr. Petrini called the cops! He wants to have all three of us put in jail." Cristy stopped short when she saw Mindy across the long expanse of the barn.

Julia was afraid Cristy would lose her temper. But Cristy knew how to play it cool, too, fortunately.

"Hi there, Mindela," she said in a soft, lulling voice. Julia found it chilling to listen to her.

Now Cristy moved forward like a cat, slowly and carefully, talking as she came. "You look mighty fine, all dressed up in your brown outfit . . . almost like the Brown Widow Spider of Collings Dorm."

Now this was something different. Cristy was a new catalyst to the situation, and Mindy's amused look disappeared. Her eyes narrowed. A dark flush creeped up from the turtleneck collar, tinging her face with a shade that might also have been brown.

You almost could imagine she *was* a poisonous spider.

Cristy kept advancing. Ben, meanwhile, was doing the same, but quite silently. They all knew that her appearance could be the element to set Mindy off in some way.

"Guess you never expected to meet up with me face to face, did you?" Cristy gave a lopsided, innocent smile. "You thought you could do everything behind my back. Like you could come in and wreck my mom's yard but never get caught." She paused to smile brightly.

"You're crazy," Mindy said. Her amusement as well as her brittle cool was long gone.

"But you know what, Mindela?" Cristy kept pressing. "You can't stop Jeremy from loving me." She spoke clearly, tauntingly, and Julia knew the bait was being thrown out.

"Jeremy told me he loves *me,*" Mindy said after a hesitation. "He doesn't want to hurt you, but he has no intention of going through with that wedding."

"I don't think so. And you know it's not true, too . . ."

The barn door crashed open just then, to Julia's vast relief. Three police officers stood there, hands on guns. They would be witnesses now.

At the sight of the police, Mindy's face darkened even further. The girl changed right before their eyes from the calm, cool victim of trespass—to the bundle of rage everyone considered her.

"I could tear you apart," Mindy said, eyes wide with hatred, lunging at Cristy. "I've got tools! I can not only ruin your sappy wedding but I can rip that head right off your shoulders. Then we'll see how Jeremy feels about you!"

Julia shuddered while Ben rushed in to get between the two girls. The police officers pushed their way in, getting to the shrieking Mindy right after Ben did.

She continued to scream and kick as Ben held her tightly. The police took over, brandished guns, and still had a difficult time calming her down.

A woman spurned, Julia thought sadly.

"Mindy, stop fighting," Cristy said suddenly, her voice compassionate. "Settle down. Your parents want to get treatment for you . . . so maybe, you know, maybe you can go back and finish college eventually. . . ."

Mindy took a breather from her struggling, and glared at Cristy suspiciously.

"I mean it, Mindela," Cristy said like a friend. "Even though you did a lot of stuff to hurt us, I'd like to see you get well. So why don't you calm down now?"

Julia's heart swelled with pride. In spite of it all, her daughter did have a streak of generosity. She knew Cristy meant every word she was saying.

Maybe after all, I did raise three decent and caring girls.

"Why not wait outside now, Cristy," Ben suggested. "Your mother, too—"

Both Julia and Cristy did go outdoors then,

leaving the troubled girl to the authorities. Mindy wasn't fighting as hard any longer, and Julia felt sure they'd have her in custody soon.

Mr. Petrini was out there in his front yard, wringing his hands and looking worried. "I'm sorry I lied to Mr. Wilson. I didn't want the police to see my apartment. . . . I was afraid of the zoning commission."

"We understand," Julia said.

"I didn't know she was a crazy person!" he howled.

"It's okay, Mr. Petrini," Cristy said soothingly. She drew in a long, deep breath; her cheeks were stained with a fresh, hopeful pink color. "I personally think everything's going to be okay from now on."

Hours later they were able to relax and draw a deep breath as they discussed their morning adventure. They were sorry for Mindy, of course; it had been sad to see her so deteriorated.

"But she really will receive treatment now," Julia said, "and that never would have happened if she'd continued to hide in that barn."

Mindy's parents had been called by the po-

lice, of course, and they'd hurried to Stonewell to make arrangements for hospitalization
of their daughter.

"What a mixed-up girl she is," Julia said,
pouring coffee for people in her backyard.
Jeremy and Kevin came up from Stamford as
soon as they heard about the wrecked gardens
and Mindy's capture. April and Bethany had
both rushed over, with the kids in tow, when
they heard the news on the police scanner.

Ben, quiet as always, was sitting with his
coffee, making plans already for immediate
reconstruction of the gardens.

"Be nice if we had more people," he said
hopefully.

"I've already called more people." Cristy
winked with great confidence. After that,
Julia's yard kept filling up with volunteers
who wanted to help. Selena took a vacation
day, Irmgard showed up, and Cristy's bridesmaid Renee arrived an hour later. Michelle
Crenshaw, looking cute in gardening overalls,
popped in unexpectedly, as did Father Hayes,
of all people. He wanted to lend a hand, too.

It was a beautiful breezy day, not too warm,
and everyone had come prepared to work
with Ben. In the early afternoon, even Tom
and Dan, Julia's sons-in-law, would arrive
from their jobs.

I should be thrilled with the way things turned out, Julia thought. So why am I feeling unsettled? Her mind, oddly, kept thinking just one thing: "I could have been in Greece now."

These were, actually, the two weeks she would have chosen as vacation time . . . for Greece. Instead she was saving her vacation time for sometime after September, when maybe she'd treat her mother to a little girls-only trip to Saratoga, New York.

"Here are the goodies we picked up," Bethany announced, opening a large box of mini donuts for the crowd. "Wanna make another pot of coffee, Mom?"

"Sure." Julia went inside. Thank God Mindy is now out of the picture, she thought. We're having an exciting summer here, I must admit. I ought to be grateful beyond words.

She sighed. Was it so wrong of her to yearn still for those weeks on the continent? Greece would have been educational, stimulating, memorable . . . and away from it all.

Through her window, she stared at the crowd in her backyard. Family and friends . . . such good people. So much energy all packed together, ready to fix up the torn wedding gardens.

Julia would take the rest of the day off—

might as well, now—and while everyone gardened, she'd probably take charge of the baby, Emily, and Danielle. She wouldn't be with Ben, but she'd make herself more than useful.

And that was great. She loved being with her grandchildren.

She sighed again and started fixing coffee for the multitudes.

What was the problem with her now? Was she tired? Overextended? Was she a little bit wedding-ed out?

All of the above. If she had the money she'd run away right now—right this very instant, truthfully—and head for Athens.

Leave the rest of them to worry about the wedding.

I need a vacation, she thought. Desperately.

Thirty-six

But of course a vacation was out of the question. The matter of money aside, Julia was not a woman to shirk her responsibilities, and Cristy's wedding definitely fell into the category of her responsibility.

So she plugged onward. Hot July faded away into even hotter August as they addressed the invitations in the air-conditioned living room. "Write them super carefully!" said Cristy. "They have to look classy, almost like calligraphy."

Fine with me, thought Julia, slowing down and making each envelope a work of art. Then there was the endless shopping: gowns for the girls, headpieces, shoes, even special trips to lingerie shops for slips and other appropriate foundation garments.

Numerous sessions with the rental people. Sit-down meetings with the caterers, a local place called Michael's Deli that would be catering all the food. A contract meeting with the D.J., who brought along a guy who'd be taking videos. A contract also with a Porta-potty company—not a romantic item but certainly a necessity with so large a guest list!

They canvassed nearby towns for the bakery with the exact right wedding cake—until Ellie, a wonderful, talented niece of Jay's, offered to make one.

"That cake's going to be gorgeous," Cristy said with great joy. "My cousin Ellie's the most creative baker I've ever met. . . . We're starting to be in good shape now, Mom. I think we've covered most everything."

"I keep feeling we've forgotten things," Julia said.

"That's because you're the MOB and you're supposed to feel worried. It's your job."

"A photographer!" Julia said in panic. "What about someone to do formal portraits?"

"Got it covered," Cristy said. "There's nothing formal about my wedding, Momserina, so I'm having the photographer who's doing pictures for Ben's book."

"Bryce? Oh. That sounds all right." She knew he did good work, because she'd seen the formal photograph of Ben and herself on his living room wall.

"So stop your worrying, Mom. Really we're

coming along great . . . that is, if you'd get serious and buy your MOB dress."

Julia kept putting off that particular trip, but finally one weekend in August she forced herself to go shopping in New Haven. For moral support she invited Selena, Irmgard, and Cristy—and right away was lucky enough to find a soft, full-skirted turquoise dress that suited her perfectly.

"Okay now. Mission accomplished," Julia said to her entourage. "How about if we all sit and relax with a frozen yogurt?" They found and entered a frozen yogurt shop, each dreaming of large sundaes. "And I thank you all for coming to help out. I do hate shopping."

"Julia, this was fun," Selena told her. "I'm getting in practice for someday when I become a mother of the bride."

"I'm happy if I can do favor for you, Missus Julia." Irmgard picked up the frozen yogurt menu with great pride. "So. Anyone want to hear me read?" Her eyes shimmered as she picked out the words she knew. "Special today—chocolate! Strawberry with . . . sprinkles?"

"That's fabulous, Irmgard." Cristy gave the older woman a genuine hug. Irmgard had become a real friend to the entire family this summer. She popped in at the strangest times, always to work in the gardens and add some touch of her own to the planting. She and her two cousins couldn't wait to help with serving the wedding buffet.

"Julia, we haven't been hearing much about Ben Wilson lately," Selena observed when they'd been served their yogurt delights. "What's happening with him?"

"Did you hear his good news?" Cristy was excited. "When his friend Killer died, of course Ben was heartbroken. And then last week, when they read Killer's will . . . it turned out he left his big, fancy-schmancy cabin cruiser to Ben!"

"My God," Selena said, turning to stare at Julia. "A boat! You never said a word about that. How exciting for him."

Julia nodded. "It's been a real pickup for Ben. He admired his friend so much . . . and felt lost without him. Well, he was really honored to receive Killer's boat. He's bringing it across the Sound this weekend, I think."

"You *think*?" Selena picked up on that. "You don't keep in touch with him now?"

Julia's face flamed. In truth, she hadn't seen much of Ben lately.

"He finished building the gazebo, you know," she explained, "with the help of all the family . . . and since the gardens are totally fixed up now, it's been Cristy's job to keep them watered. . . ."

Selena waved a hand to shush her. "I'm not talking about the *work* Ben does for you, Jules—though Lord knows it's been more than most human beings would do! I mean, what about your budding romance? And don't tell us there was none!"

Julia didn't answer. In the silence that followed she thought about how few times she and Ben had been alone since the Fourth of July. Almost never. She wasn't quite sure who was responsible for that.

She never made the attempt to talk to him, and he evidently had enough sensitivity to see that she was confused. He'd made no overtures either, in all these weeks. She did think his absence was rather bizarre—considering their intimacy—but she kept telling herself both of them were busy.

Finally she said, "Ben's writing a new book, you know. He received a contract to do that special book, *Gardens For Weddings*. It's going to be a triumph for him."

"Mmmm-hmmm" Selena wasn't satisfied with that for an answer to her question. "So what else? You two never get together any more?"

"Well . . . no." Julia frowned, realizing just how very long it had been. Four or five weeks . . . was she deliberately making herself so busy she never gave Ben a single thought?

Cristy patted Julia's hand. "My mom seems to think she's supposed to put her entire life on hold lately, just because she's the mother of the bride. I wish you ladies would tell her she's being ridiculous."

"Are you saying I act like a martyr, Cristy?" Julia smiled but spoke in her most frosty tone.

"If the shoe fits, Mom. . . . You never take even a minute's rest lately and—I don't know, you *have* been ignoring Ben even when he's around. I've noticed that, too."

Julia tried to laugh off the criticisms. "Irmgard, you're the only one who's not picking on me tonight. These two think there's nothing else in life more important than romance. Is this a conspiracy?"

Irmgard gave one of her tough, stubborn smiles. "Missus Julia, you remember what I told you at the library, about miracles? In the spring?"

"Yes, I do, but—"

"I still say so, Missus." Irmgard leaned forward, her blue eyes sparkling with energy. "You learn how to say *thanks, God,* and you will find a very happy life with this man Ben Wilson, who loves you."

Julia shook her head, stunned at being outvoted. "Three against one here. Some friends you turned out to be."

Selena placed a hand over Julia's. "We *are* your friends, Jules. And that's why we'd really like to see you get on with your life."

"Get on with—I hate that expression!" Julia spooned up some of her frozen yogurt and then plopped it back down into the bowl.

"Hate it or not," Cristy said gently. "What your friends are trying to say, Mom, is that— maybe Dad would have wanted you to make some changes by now."

"What changes? What are you people talking about?!"

"Maybe you could take your wedding ring off," Cristy said, though it pained her to say the words, you could see. "Just put it in the jewelry box, you know? See how that feels . . . so that maybe new things could develop."

"You three have no idea of what I'm going through," Julia started to say, but Selena and Irmgard stopped her.

"We're both widows," Selena said firmly. "So, yes, we do have an idea."

"We love you, Missus Julia." Irmgard's features were softened by empathy. "We just don't want you to wait forever. We Germans have an expression, *We grow too soon old and too late smart!*"

"Hey, that's neat, Irmgard," Cristy said.

They all laughed, Julia along with them. "Okay, okay," she said. "You've worn me down. I'll give the man a call—strictly as a good friend, though, to see how he's doing. Okay? Will that make everybody happy?"

The three heads bobbed up and down, their grins widening.

Yes, they were obviously happy.

"Hello, Ben?" she said into the telephone later that night. "I called to wish you good luck with your new boat."

"Why, Julia." He sounded surprised and pleased. "How nice to hear from you. Yes, can you imagine? Killer wanted me to have his boat, the Bronx Bombshell."

"What a name! But I do remember that having a boat was one of the major aspirations you mentioned a while ago."

"Yes, that and a trip to Greece," he said.

"I am glad for you . . . about the boat."

He was quiet for a moment. "How are things with you? I know how busy you must be."

"We have been," she said, "but it's quieting down a little. Cristy keeps saying we have everything all set. But there are only three weeks to go and—it's getting scary."

"It's going to be beautiful, Julia."

"Thanks to you, Ben. The gazebo is breathtaking and the gardens are—well, just beyond words. I never thought I'd see such a colorful sight right out in my backyard!"

"Glad you're enjoying it."

"I am. I never knew I was a garden sort of person, but—I run out there the first thing every morning. I sip my morning coffee out on the patio now, and just stare at all those flowers. And in the evening when I get home from work, I race out there again to see what needs watering. I must be addicted."

"Great."

There was silence again. Julia had the feeling she was supposed to take the ball and run with it, but she wasn't sure just how or why.

"Ben . . . I kind of miss seeing you," she blurted out before she could stop herself.

"And I miss you, Julia," he said. "Very much."

"Well, we were supposed to remain friends, remember?"

"I remember. And we are friends."

She wanted to bite her lip in frustration. "Friends get together once in a while, don't they?" She spoke somewhat sharply. "How about coming over for dinner some night?"

"That sounds nice but I'm tied up this week."

It was her turn to grow quiet. Finally she said, "I guess you're saying you don't want to see me."

"I never said that. I don't mean that at all."

"Ben, I know a brushoff when I hear one. Even from a friend."

"You're wrong. Tell me something—are you still wearing that wide, bright-gold wedding band?"

"Why—yes—" She looked down at her left hand. "Of course I am. Why would you ask?"

She heard a long, deep sigh from his end. "Ah, Julia, you figure it out. No living man can compete with a ghost."

"A ghost . . . ?" She stood rooted while the room seemed to be spinning all around her, the wallpaper wavering like water. Now it became totally clear to her, the true reason Ben had been staying away.

"But Ben, you knew. You understood I had to proceed at these grieving things according to my own time schedule."

"I do know and I do understand. I simply

can't be part of that particular struggle of yours. Not any more."

"But—"

"Good night, Julia," he said and put the phone down.

Thirty-seven

At last something had jolted her—big time.

Within minutes, Julia was out walking in the dark, striding briskly and forcing herself, for the first time, to think.

Really think.

Rain was threatening but for the moment the skies were merely clouded, a curious mixture of black and gray layers, the air heavy with humidity. She walked around and around her neighborhood—up hills, down hills, across streets she'd been familiar with for many, many years. Yet tonight everything looked different.

Tonight she had decisions to make. She felt alone, because in the long run, there was no one to help her make them. Her family and friends could give their advice, but they couldn't possibly pinpoint life-altering choices for her.

She walked, enjoying the coolness, and imagining that each house she passed was beaming a message toward her. Happy families, loving young couples, blended families, unhappy and dysfunctional families . . . all sorts of situations existed among her neighbors, and odd communications seemed to come charging at her from staring at the homes.

Either that or she was ready for the funny farm.

Tonight she had to think, and evaluate, and do some remembering. . . .

"Promise me," Jay *is saying at different times, at least five or six times during their marriage.* "Promise me that when I die, you'll get out and meet other men."

"Absolutely not," she answers, horrified. She always answers him that same way.

"I'd like to know you'll get married again, Julia, if the chance comes along."

"I won't."

"For you to love again, that would be a testimony to me . . . it would mean you were happy with our marriage."

"I certainly am happy with our marriage, but I won't marry someone else," she continues to insist. *"I will never want another man. . . ."*

And she had meant it. That's what confused her so much: she had meant it at the time, and yet . . . after two years of unspeakable loneliness, she had plunged herself gladly into the arms of a very sweet, very large man in a white terrycloth robe.

How could she make any sense out of this?

She plodded along now on the almost-rainy August night, passing beneath dark trees that were heavy with green summer leaves. The exercise was doing her some good; she began to feel awake all over, alert to the task at hand.

Okay. She would admit right now—she'd been a martyr lately to Cristy's wedding. It had been her way of not dealing with Ben. Or her feelings.

But dear Lord! She had *slept* with the man, reveling in it, making fantastic love out of some primitive need that belatedly shocked her.

Julia Maxwell wasn't a person to take love-making lightly. She had never in her life been with anyone but Jay.

So. What did that tell her?

She stopped for a moment by a neighbor's mailbox, thinking she felt raindrops. She couldn't be quite sure. But she looked at the homes of her neighborhood, the lights twinkling far back from the road, the people inside each home oblivious to her presence.

So. *Think now, Julia.*

If it's a fact that you don't take lovemaking lightly, then you must go one step further and admit something else. What?

She turned her face upward; yes, here came cooling raindrops that pattered lightly first on the top of her head, then felt wonderful against her heated face.

What did she have to admit?

She took in a sharp breath. Then she said in a low voice, "I have to admit . . . that no matter how hard I tried not to, I seem to love Ben Wilson."

The words, spoken aloud, stunned her.

And then again, they shouldn't. She must have known all along how she felt. She was merely trying to be loyal to Jay, who—when she became really honest about it—had always begged her to date others after his death.

To love again. To marry again.

"I do love you, Jay," she whispered fiercely. "I do."

But it was *time*, just as they'd said in the Grief Workshop she would know when it was time. Time to let go, once and for all, of the old ties . . .

Standing there under Mrs. Bellflower's weeping willow tree, Julia slipped off her wedding ring.

No big ceremony, no long speeches to Jay. She held the ring out at arm's length, and watched it gleaming in the dark night, the thick gold band slick with rain. She almost never took it off. She'd worn it constantly for almost thirty-five years.

"I'll always love you, Jay," she said simply.

Then the ring went into the pocket of her skirt. The ring finger of her left hand felt bare; it hadn't been without a ring since her wedding day, all those years ago.

She felt bereft in one way, but at the same time, she could hear Jay's voice saying to her: "Promise me you'll give yourself a chance, Julia. . . ."

"I didn't promise then, but I can make the effort now," she whispered with quiet, peaceful tears sliding down her cheeks. The soft summer rain was quickening, splashing against parched lawns, pattering on tree limbs and leaves. It felt absolutely wonderful.

Julia began to walk again—not ambling along, but striding with a definite destination this time.

She chuckled. Something Irmgard had said today in her thick German accent suddenly tickled her fancy.

Oh, Irmgard, she thought with great affection. You always come up with the darndest sayings to help me along in my times of crisis.

Ve grow too soon oldt und too late schmart.

We sure do.

She continued her walk in the rain, heading straight for Ben's house. If his lights were out, she'd go home. But if he seemed to be still awake . . .

The roads were slick with raindrops and the streetlamps gave off a peculiar gleam, surrounded by luminous aureoles in the mist. She marched along Ben's driveway, eager to see if his lights were on. They were.

She knocked on his door. Rain was pelting her now and she knew she looked a sight, more like a drowned kitten than a reasonable human being.

"Julia," he said when he opened the door. "Come in. It's pouring out there!"

"Feels wonderful and cool, actually," she said. "But now I'm dripping all over your hallway rug."

"Who cares?" His face showed he was astonished to see her. "Please come on. I'll get you a towel for your hair."

"No, wait." She put a hand on his arm. "Can we talk?"

"Of course."

"I've got something to say and I need to do it while I have the courage."

His big face looked quite serious. "You don't need courage to speak to me."

"Yeah, I do." Her grin was automatic but mirthless. "That remark you made about the ghost earlier tonight . . ."

"Yes?" He was standing still suddenly, such a large presence in his front hall, his face devoid of any expression.

"Well, you were right. I was holding on to a ghost. I apologize, Ben, and . . ." She held out her left hand to show him.

"Tonight I removed my ring. So no matter what happens—maybe it's too late for you and me, Ben, but I just wanted to explain. I believe I'm ready to move forward."

At first he said nothing, but she could see the shimmers of light that sparkled, with a diamond brilliance, in his green eyes. Happy lights. A surprised glitter, but joyful and tender.

"I'm not sure what to say."

"Well, how can there be words to cover this?" Julia said, looking down at her hand, noticing the whiteness of the finger where the band had been. "It's a bittersweet thing to do, you know, taking a wedding ring off."

"I *do* know." He blinked. "I was still wear-

ing mine when I first started working on your
garden in April."

Now it was her turn to look amazed. "I
didn't know that! I never noticed it."

"No, I'm sure you didn't, but it's the truth.
I slipped it off sometime in May."

Aware that her mouth was hanging open,
she clamped it shut with her fist. "But why
didn't I realize that, Ben?"

"You were trying not to notice me at all,
if you recall." He held his arms out, inviting
her to move in closer.

She did, with no hesitation whatsoever. Immediately she felt herself enveloped by Ben's
presence, dwarfed by his large, solid body,
wrapped in the clean, wonderful scent of him
that made her go weak all over.

Even the ambiance of his house closed in
around her to remind her—not that she'd ever
forgotten—of their magical Fourth of July
night. She heard the watery glub-glub of the
fish tanks and the slapping of Ivan's tail
against a doorjamb. Ivan apparently accepted
her now, even when she was folded into the
master's powerful arms.

She stared at the log walls, breathed in the
familiar scent of his home, and remembered
sharply the hours of sweet, intense pleasure
they'd shared that night.

His chest was a solid wall to lean her head against.

"Ben, I'm sorry it's taken me so long."

"Don't apologize. I told you I'd never be judgmental of anything you do."

"But you—that statement about the ghost—"

He brushed his lips against her forehead; she felt a shudder of warmth right down to her knees.

"I wasn't judging. I only meant I couldn't compete with the ghost of Jay . . . but you had every right to hold on to him, for as long as it would take, until you could feel free."

She thought about that. "The ring may be off but I'm still not positive where I am, Ben . . . you understand?"

He nodded. "I think so. I'll try not to talk about love yet."

Her heart accelerated to an alarming rate. Love . . . he wanted to talk about love?

He pulled her closer and spoke in a low, uncontrolled voice, his mouth against the curly tangle of her hair: "I can't help it. I do love you, Julia."

She didn't answer because the words had sounded so strangled it was possible to have misunderstood.

She decided to pretend he'd never spoken at all.

"This is terrible of me," she said, "but I wish I could spend the night here with you. Cristy's at home, though, and how would I explain it to her?"

"Doesn't sound terrible to me." He laughed softly. "You'd certainly have to phone to tell her where you are, or she'll call out the National Guard."

"You're not kidding."

"She's going to understand, you know. Completely."

"Do you think so? Nobody at all in my family knows about—you know, about the last time, the—"

"—the Fourth of July," he said. She felt his lips on hers, gentle and firm, and her heart quickened.

"I have a suggestion," Ben said. "Make that phone call to Cristy soon, will you?"

It was easy enough to tell Cristy not to worry, that Julia was talking things over with Ben, at his house.

"I don't know what time I'll be back, so don't wait up for me. Please."

Cristy sounded amused and did seem to comprehend quite well. "Stay as long as you need to, Momserina. I'm off to bed myself."

And now the whole night was free, and it belonged to both of them. Julia knew she was fortunate to be in Ben's arms—exactly where her nighttime dreams had been taking her all these past weeks.

This time they weren't shy with each other. They were already lovers; they were familiar with each other's bodies and, quite simply, they were grateful to be together, and intimate, once more.

"I wondered if I'd ever hold you again," Ben said as they welcomed each other with a slow, joyful hug on his bed.

"I wondered the same thing." She kissed his shoulder and then lower, where his chest was covered with thick hair. She'd almost forgotten what a large frame he had, and she rejoiced in such a powerful torso. Apollo the Sun God, she had thought him.

"I can hear that great big heart beating in there," she said, smiling.

"Then maybe you can hear this, too, Julia." With a large hand, he brushed dark, still-wet curls gently away from her face, and spoke into her ear.

"I love you and I have to say so." Now he placed a finger over her mouth, so she couldn't protest or argue with him.

"Sssshush. I love you."

* * *

"The place looks great, Mrs. Maxwell."

"Thanks, Bryce. We've had a lot of good help here lately."

It was two days later and Bryce was taking photos again of the Maxwell backyard. He managed to show up just about every week, to shoot plenty of pictures for Ben's newest book.

"So you really had some nut tearing up the yard, hmm?" He aimed his lens at the new flowers, the mums and impatiens plants that Ben had put in as replacements.

"We did," Julia said. "She was just a young girl, Bryce."

Because Cristy was out job-hunting, Julia was watering the plants as Bryce took pictures. Dusk would be arriving soon, so it was a nice cool time for outdoor chores. Bryce had told her he needed a few late-afternoon shots just for a different shadow viewpoint.

"Well anyway, Mr. Wilson says you caught the nut—I mean, the girl. You must be relieved."

"Yes." Julia didn't feel much like talking, although she liked Bryce well enough. She was wishing everything were over—the wedding, the book on gardens for weddings, the big brunch she was giving the day after the wedding—all of it.

She grinned. Every once in a while she became tired. Maybe she should take her vacation in late September or October, even if she did nothing more than sleep for two whole weeks.

She certainly could use the rest.

"One more shot of that gazebo," Bryce muttered to himself. "Mr. Wilson did a great job with that, didn't he?"

"He sure did." She sighed.

What was she going to do about Ben Wilson? She'd never told him how much she loved him. But she knew in her heart that she did love him . . .

In a different way. Not at all like the comfortable love that a long marriage provides— no, this was more like skyrockets and jingle bells, all that silly stuff that goes along with what they call "romance."

Ooooops. She realized she was drowning a garden full of daylilies and yanked the hose from that spot.

I love him. He says he loves me.

So what am I holding back for?

She knew the answer to that one.

Her mother-in-law, Carolyn Maxwell, above all, but also all the Maxwells she had come to love as her very own family.

Of course they'd want to see Julia happy, and they'd probably accept a man in her life eventually.

But now? Much too soon.

Jay's relatives would be outraged, and his mother would simply be stricken as if by the plague. Carolyn would be heartbroken to see someone with Julia, someone taking Jay's place.

So really . . . all the ghosts haven't been conquered after all. Sometimes there are other people's ghosts to consider, too.

"Hey! Here comes your daughter, Mrs. Maxwell."

Cristy came bounding out from the kitchen, still all dressed up in her jobhunting clothes.

"We got it, Momserina!"

"You got a job?" Julia felt a shiver of excitement. "You and Jeremy both?"

"Yep!" Cristy paraded around the yard, grinning with joy. "Hi, Bryce. Can you believe it, Mom? Jeremy and I both—it's a gardening job at that Malden Estate park in New Milford. Where they have those beautiful gardens!"

"That's wonderful. Congratulations," Julia said.

"And . . . not only are we the two chief groundskeepers . . . we get a fabulous cottage to live in!"

"Cristy . . . that sounds perfect."

"It is! We're so excited. . . . Bryce, will you snap a picture of Jeremy and me, when he comes out?"

"Of course."

"I want to remember this moment forever," Cristy said. "I want a picture of us—both all dressed up in power suits—oh God, what a wonderful day!"

Julia watched her dancing with pure happiness. How nice to be young, she thought, and have no complications in the way of your love.

No sorrow, no baggage, no ghosts to ruin things.

Oh, stop it, Julia.

Every problem will be solved . . . in time.

Just be patient and in a year or two, maybe you and Ben will know where you stand.

Just stop your internal whining, Julia.

Julia had no premonition when she picked up the telephone later that evening. "Hello? This is Mindy," said a small voice.

Julia froze. "Mindy Parsons?"

"You probably don't want to hear from me, Mrs. Maxwell, but it's important that I—" The girl stopped to take a deep breath. "My coun-

selor here at the hospital says it's necessary—
for our healing—to apologize to those we may
have harmed."

"I imagine it is important." Julia's heart
went out to the young girl who sounded so
frightened. She signaled to Cristy to get on
the line as well, and Cristy dashed toward the
phone in the front hall.

"I really am sorry," Mindy managed to
blurt out. Julia had the feeling the counselor
was standing right beside the girl for moral
support. "I did terrible things to your gardens."

"You weren't well, Mindy," Julia said. "So
you're in the hospital now? How are things
going for you?"

"Better. They tell me I'll make a full recovery if I take my medication faithfully.
Maybe I'll be able to go back to UConn."

"That's great news, Mindy!" Cristy spoke
into the phone for the first time. "We're all
rootin' for you!"

An awkward silence followed. Then,
"Thanks. That means a lot, coming from
you, Cristy. And—I wish you a happy wedding day, really. Tell Jeremy, too, for me."

"I will." Another silence. "Take care and
get yourself well, you hear?"

"Thank you for the apology, Mindy," Julia

added. "It was brave of you and it truly does help, even on this end."

"Good," said the tiny voice, and there was a click and the line went dead.

"Can you believe it?" Cristy asked, her face pale as she ambled slowly back into the kitchen. "Guess miracles really do happen."

Julia smiled. "Sure they do. Now if only we get the miracle of good weather on your wedding day—"

"We will, Moms." Cristy managed to look positive. "Because we have Daddy up there—and he'll put in a perfect September order for the Day of the Punkin'head."

Thirty-eight

"Thanks for driving us here, Cristy! We'll see you back in Connecticut tonight," Julia called out.

On Saturday morning, Ben and Julia were on Long Island standing on the deck of "Bronx Bombshell." The inboard cabin cruiser Killer had bought—when he made a small fortune on a computer program—was a beauty, with its dazzling white fiberglass hull and the gleaming, well-appointed cabin.

"Now it belongs to you, Ben," Julia said, touching the rich walnut wood that graced a cabin window. The crisp denim curtains that hung in each window were cute, she thought. "What a big responsibility."

"Yes," he said tersely.

They'd had Cristy drive them to the marina in Long Island so they could sail the Bombshell across the Sound to Connecticut. Now Cristy was waving goodbye as her little car pulled out of the marina parking lot. She wanted to get back quickly to talk to her D.J. about some last minute changes—or so she'd said. Julia strongly suspected Cristy wanted to leave Ben and Julia alone for this shakedown cruise.

"So . . . you really know how to drive this thing?" Julia asked with apprehension. The boat seemed huge to her, one of those gleaming new vessels with polished chrome and brass fittings. "Look at this—the motor alone resembles the Queen Elizabeth! It's pretty scary."

"I don't scare easily." Ben was wearing nautical clothes, which tickled her greatly: he wore dark blue sailor pants, a striped nautical shirt, a cap right out of "PT 109." He looked sturdy and competent, and she wished she didn't care for him so much already. She'd never tell him so, of course, because she wasn't ready to say so just yet. But he was lovable.

On the cockpit bench, he had spread out charts that showed the waterways from Long Island to their harbor in Connecticut.

"I do know the rules of the road, so to speak," he told her. "I've been studying hard about bell buoys, lighted buoys, nun buoys . . . but it's all book learning. So, just in case, let's wear our life jackets on this maiden voyage."

"I'll agree to that." She slipped into her bulky life preserver without reservation.

The day was hot, the air seemed clear and briny, the sky a cloudless China blue. Ben showed her which ropes to cast off, he started his engine, and they pulled away from the dock with great bravado.

"Wish Killer could be here to teach me the ropes," Ben said, taking his place at the captain's wheel. "I'll take power squadron courses the first chance I get, but it would have been great with my best friend teaching."

"I wish he was here, too," Julia said. "I'd like to have known him. But just think, he wanted you to own this fine boat because he knew you'd be the one to appreciate it."

"You got that right." Ben squinted in the sunlight, slipped on sunglasses under the visor of his cap. "Well, we follow those particular buoys until we're out of the harbor, I know that much. . . ."

Together they studied the buoys in the channel, sailing carefully across water that gleamed with late August sunlight. After a while they were way out there, far from the flat green shoreline of Long Island, yet still a long way from Connecticut's busy shores.

It was exhilarating to feel the fresh wind battering at their faces as they navigated.

"I've never been out on the sound like this, except on a ferry," Julia said, watching the wide swath of the boat's wake. It swirled upward, catching the light, bubbling and frothing as it curled over. "This is so peaceful, and at the same time it's wild and untamed—you know?"

"The sound is untamed. When I was a kid my folks had a boat out of Pelham, so I've always known I loved the sound."

"When you were a kid . . ." She watched him navigating the wheel with his inbred male confidence. "Some day I want to know all about you, Ben. In time will you tell me stories about when you were a kid?"

He grinned. "Not much to tell. I was pretty quiet even then, except when I was out hell-raising with Killer and Hank. Of course it was always the two of them who started all the trouble."

"Oh sure, tell that one to the marines," she scoffed.

"No, really. I told you I was Dudley Do-Right. You'll have to meet my sister and brothers and they'll convince you."

"Saint Benjamin, hmmm?" She snuggled up against his back and just stayed there, soaking in the warmth of his body. "I believe you, Dudley."

When they were out in the middle of nowhere, he cut the engine. "Game for a swim?" He had an anchor in hand, ready to throw it over if she said yes.

"Of course. This is the hottest August on record, isn't it?" They anchored, set out a ladder, and peeled off their clothes to the bathing suits underneath.

Julia dove in first. She was astounded at the saltiness of the water; she absolutely loved it. "Look, you barely have to paddle to stay up. The salt practically keeps you afloat."

Ben jumped in, his face relaxing visibly when the cool water closed over his head. The waters of the sound were deep and dark blue-green but somehow there was nothing frightening about them.

"I can't get over it, this is like going to heaven," he said. Then, in a serious voice, he added, "The trouble is—Killer really did go to heaven."

"It's sad, but . . . you can accept his gift, Ben," she said slowly, solemnly. "And in time you can learn to let him go."

"That's the hardest part."

"I know. I've had to struggle with that same problem myself, this whole summer."

"Since you met me, you mean?" His eyes sparkled green-gold in the bright glare of sun.

"Yes." She was reluctant to admit that.

"Maybe we've both come a long way in a few months, Julia."

"It seems so." She floated over to him, kissing him lightly on his mouth. "And all because of Cristy and her plans for a wedding in a garden."

"Speaking of gardens." His hand slid around to close on the back of her neck. He was grinning. "You know what? I've grown a lot of flowers in my lifetime. But this summer, my Julia's the one that has bloomed the very brightest."

"What a lovely, poetic thing to say." She splashed him unmercifully. "Sweet and absolutely goofy! You're such a total cornball."

They continued to splash playfully for a while. Then they went back to wet, salty kisses as they floated atop the fathomless waters of Long Island Sound.

What with kisses and sunshine and the gleam of a white fiberglass boat, it turned out to be one of those perfect days that shimmer on in a person's memory for as long as they might live. They were alone in an aqueous world, miles from the turmoil of Cristy's wedding frenzy. Their only responsibility was to each other and to Killer Carlyle's boat.

Frankly, Julia thought, it was one of the most wonderful days she could ever remember.

When they finally arrived in the new home inlet, they motored to the marina dock where Ben had rented a slip. They tied the boat off tightly and gave her a good washing down with fresh water from a dockside hose.

Eventually done, they stood on the narrow wooden dock just staring at the big cabin cruiser. They had made it. They'd crossed the sound—rank amateurs but true enthusiasts. Ben's eyes, in a newly suntanned face, shone like a little kid's.

"I wonder if I'll ever get used to her."

"Sure you will, Ben. Good luck with her . . . you deserved to get your life's dream."

He surprised her by turning slowly and kissing her. "You deserve to get your dream, too, Julia. I'm talking about Greece."

She smiled. "Don't worry. Someday I'll get there."

He had his arms full of boating equipment but his gaze stayed on Julia. "I mean soon. I mean—how about this fall, after Cristy's wedding is over."

She frowned. "What are you talking about? I'm not going anywhere this fall, except to work every day." She pulled back a few inches and the dock swayed to and fro. It was an unsettling sort of motion.

"Julia . . ." He put down pails, ropes, fenders, and a tool kit. Gently, he took her face in his hands. "If you'd marry me in October or November, we could go to Greece for our honeymoon."

She heard herself gasp. "You've got to be joking," she said quietly. "You're getting way ahead of things. Ben, there's no way I would ever—"

He shushed her again, his hand closing firmly over her mouth. "Don't say no right now. You think about it. I love you and I'd really like a wedding . . . that can't be too hard to grasp, can it?"

"Mmmmm-phhh!" She couldn't say a word with his hand right there over her lips. She blinked against the glare of the late afternoon sun in the west.

There was boyish mischief in his sea-green eyes. "I realize you have to think for a long time, because you're a little slow about making big-time decisions, Julia."

"MMMMMMMMMMMPPPH!" Now she was getting angry.

"But I love you anyway, for all your indecisiveness." His grin was lopsided and cocky;

he was enjoying this tremendously. "What a way to propose, huh? Standing on a dock at sunset . . . I'm sorry, it's not very romantic."

"Aaaaargh!" She managed to yank herself away. "That's a terrible thing to do! Propose marriage and hold a girl's mouth closed so she can't say a damn thing!"

She squinted and looked up at him, her big fuzzy bear all covered with salt and sunburn, his eyes looking greener from the day in the sun. Her heart wanted simply to leap out of her body and race to him.

But he was right, she was slow in making the really big decisions. Cautious. Which any widow rightfully should be.

"I don't know," she said, trying hard to sound crabby. "This really will need a lot of thought. A wedding would not be in my blueprint for a very long time."

He grinned. "You think, then," he said amiably. He bent to retrieve all the gear he had dropped. "And you let me know when you've come to a decision. Meanwhile I'm going home for a nice freshwater shower."

She followed along behind him, more dazed than she would ever let him see.

Had she really just received a marriage proposal?

And had he dangled a trip to Greece, of all places on earth, before her?

Oh my God, she thought, swallowing over a very large lump that had settled in her throat. This is getting serious.

She was more befuddled than ever before.

Marriage right away? Impossible.

There were so many dear relations of Jay's who would be heartbroken if she were to rush into a new marriage.

Especially Carolyn, Jay's elderly mother.

No. What Ben proposed simply wasn't an option at this time.

Thirty-nine

"Happy the bride the sun shines on, Cristy."

"Thanks," Cristy said. "I ought to be nice and happy, in that case."

"You'll be happy in any case, sweetheart," her mother said.

Julia went to the living room window and opened the Venetian blinds to let in a cheerful stream of sunlight. It was getting close to noon, which would be the magic hour of the wedding ceremony.

"Will you help me with this headpiece, Selena," Cristy begged. "Because my bridesmaids, who are supposed to be my helpers, are all worried about themselves."

Selena hurried forward. "Of course I will, sugarplum. And where's your Mom heading off to now?"

"Worrying as usual, and checking everything outside for the five millionth time . . . let's go in here." Cristy grinned and ducked with Selena into her bedroom, to hide from her noisy, excited sisters and nieces.

The sun indeed was shining for Cristy and Jeremy. A bright September day had dawned, chilly and crisp but relentlessly sunny. Julia, walking around outside alone, was enchanted with the perfect weather. She congratulated herself for putting out those two chains of rosary beads the night before; they hung even now on two of the hemlock trees at the side of her property.

People would probably think she was certifiably nuts when they saw the rosary beads. Well, too bad. You had to indulge in superstition just a tiny bit when it came to weddings—otherwise why would anyone bother with something old, new, borrowed and blue?

"Hello, Missus Julia," called out a familiar German voice, loud and happy. There was the trusty Irmgard, the first to arrive. She was wearing sturdy, practical clothes for kitchen work, and was accompanied by two other ladies. "This is my cousin Katrina and my cousin Anna," she introduced.

"Hi. I'm so thrilled to see you here." Julia rushed to shake their hands. "This sets my mind at rest, you can't imagine. . . . The caterer will be delivering the food soon but we certainly needed someone to oversee it."

"Have no fear," cousin Anna told her, slipping into an apron that covered the whole front of her dress.

"Looks beautiful, Missus," Irmgard said with stars in her eyes. The tents had been erected yesterday—white and gold canopies, sharply clean, the flaps moving just slightly in the breeze.

For the buffet, long tables were set up and draped in crisp maroon linen tablecloths. On one them, as a centerpiece, Cristy had placed the gleaming wheelbarrow figurine that Jay had bought. It looked perfect there.

Throughout their lawn, the round guest tables had been appointed with glittering white cloths and maroon napkins. On each table sat a fat and sassy pot of maroon mums.

Best of all, though, were the flower gardens, visible from almost every location in the yard. Thanks to Ben, Cristy had a bounteous crop of blossoms—mostly chrysanthemums at this time of year, but there were also a few roses, pink and white geraniums, crimson and yellow zinnias, and white impatiens.

The begonias were healthy and the dahlias simply sparkled with fresh blossoms. Because of Ben's artistry there were tall stalks of rich, wonderful greenery that added to the decor.

"Looks like the Garden of Paradise," said Irmgard's cousin Katrina. "It's very beautiful."

"Thank you. My daughter wanted to be married under that maple, the tree her father had planted," Julia said, her voice cracking a bit with emotion. "Well, there it is—" She pointed to the maple that shaded the spot where Cristy's wedding arch stood.

The arch itself, now painted an ivory white, had been decorated in soft tulle with wide satin ribbons, and was surrounded by a wealth of cut flowers in large, colorful sprays. Rich vines had already covered a good portion of the arch with glossy leaves and trumpet-shaped flowers.

"And that gazebo!" Anna looked delighted with the big structure. "You will have the music coming from that?"

"Yes, the D.J . . . he's here somewhere, too." Dazed, Julia took one last look around and decided to surrender. It was almost time to get herself dressed and she was still worrying about last minute touches.

"You go get your pretty new dress on," Irmgard told her. "I will watch for the food, the cake, the priest, the D.J., the photographer—and say hello to guests and—what else?"

Julia felt tears stinging her eyelids, and she

hugged her friend gratefully. "That's it, you've covered it all. Thank you so much."

"She thanks me?" Irmgard said in a husky voice to her companions. "She's the one who teaches me! Now I'm reading big fat books for the first time, all because of this lady."

Julia couldn't help the tears that trickled down her cheeks.

"Now I'll ruin my whole face before the wedding, Irmgard! I'll look like a puffed up balloon if you keep saying sentimental things."

"No, you'll be pretty no matter what," Katrina assured her.

Irmgard gave her a warm, reassuring hug. "You had many problems this year, Missus, getting this wedding ready. So if you cry now, in the home stretch . . . it is understandable."

Julia nodded. She was thinking about friendships, which added so much to occasions like this. And she thought about Jay, which was inevitable: how he would have loved to be here to give away his youngest daughter and host this unusual, festive outdoor party.

"Thanks for the hug, Irmgard. I really needed that."

She thought she heard car doors slamming out front. That meant either that guests were arriving or that more of the wedding necessities were being delivered. Irmgard had promised to take care of whatever came along, so . . .

Time to get inside, lady, she told herself, dabbing at her cheeks with a tissue and scooting in the kitchen door.

"Hi, Mrs. Maxwell!" Renee looked worried because the MOB was still in grungy work clothes. "You'd better start getting dressed!"

Bridesmaids seemed to be everywhere. Cristy's girlfriends from college were running around the house in various stages of undress, while April and Bethany were busy running after their daughters to get them ready for the big flower girl caper.

It was a crazy house, all right. Julia fled to her bedroom and closed the door for a minute of quiet. It didn't even last a full minute because there was a knock on the door.

"It's me, sweetie," said Selena, knocking again, then walking on in. "Can I help?"

Julia sank on her bed, her face dripping with tears again. "Yes, you can help me get *through* this, Selena. How do I dispel the sad feelings about Jay so I can concentrate on my Cristy?"

Selena sat beside her, looking sober. Her round, freckled face was somehow comforting to look at in a crisis.

"I don't have all the answers, sweetie. But I can tell you this—you do not have time to feel sad! You've got a big, major party shaping up out there—and guess what? You're the hostess, lady."

"Oh, God." Her heart fluttering, Julia tried to take a long, deep breath. "I'm not usually such a crybaby."

"What? You're telling the wrong person, remember? Me who handed you all those Kleenexes at the office?" Selena made her voice firm and stern. "Pull yourself together, Jules. This will be the happiest day of your daughter's life!"

"Unless I ruin it." Julia dabbed away the tears, nodding. "Okay, thanks for scolding me. Now I'll shape up."

"I know you will." Selena sounded pleased. "We'll get you into that gorgeous turquoise dress and apply makeup to those puffy eyes—"

"Oh, no, puffy eyes?"

"Weddings make everyone cry." Selena went to the closet for the dress. "Come on, start girdling up, woman! Get out the eighteen-hour thing and the control top pantyhose, or whatever it takes!"

Julia laughed. "You're a pip, Selena. Thanks so much."

"Who, by the way, is giving away the bride? The big old bear?"

"You mean Ben? No, although Cristy asked him. He declined because he thought it should be one of her relatives. She argued like crazy with him, but he won in the end. It's going to be Daniel, Bethany's husband."

"That's nice. But I don't get it. What's Ben afraid of?"

"Afraid of?" Julia stared at her friend. "Ben doesn't want to step on any toes because . . . well, he thinks people in my family might resent him already. Especially Jay's family."

"Because you two are going together?"

Julia nodded and went to work on her pile of new underwear for the wedding. "Can you help me with this new necklace, hon? I bought it last week but forgot to take the tag off. . . ."

Selena helped. "That big old bear wants to marry you, doesn't he?"

"Yes, but—" Julia hesitated. "It's out of the question."

"Why?"

"Because he wants to plan something soon and that's ridiculous. He's rushing everything all out of proportion. You know my mother-in-law. Carolyn would be devastated! Any mother would."

"Well, I have just one thing to say." Selena

tried to close the clasp on Julia's new necklace. "If you were twenty years old, Jules, that would be one thing. But y' know—once they've sent you your AARP membership card, you can't count on how much time you've got left."

Julia laughed out loud. "I suppose that's true in a sense, but—"

"No, really. Think about it. Suppose you put off this wedding for a few years . . . and then what? One of you gets too sick—God forbid, but it *happens*. Then you can't even go on a decent honeymoon—where are you gonna go, some old folks' spa?"

A small silence. "I don't think that's any rationale to go rushing into marriage, either. . . ." Julia stared at herself in the big square mirror above her dresser. "Oh, Selena, do you know what he wants to do for a honeymoon?"

"Don't tell me. Not . . . Greece?"

Julia nodded.

"Oh my God. Grab him, Jules! For a honeymoon like that I'd marry anyone . . . even Peewee Herman!"

Julia sputtered helplessly with laughter. "You are so *terrible*, Selena."

"I know. Hurry up now and get dressed."

* * *

"Grandma, look at me!"

"No, Grandma, look at me! My dress is prettier than hers."

Emily and Danielle danced around Julia the instant she emerged from her room.

"You look very beautiful, Grandma! Are you getting married, too?"

"No, honey."

"You're silly, Emily," Danielle sniffed. "Grandmas don't get married. Ever!"

Julia smiled. Maybe they did and maybe they didn't.

But she hadn't a moment to think about it now. She pushed forward through the throng of bridesmaids and flower girls, headed for the back door. In the kitchen she was brought up short by the incredible cake that was being assembled, layer by layer, by her niece.

"Ellie . . . that's the most gorgeous cake I've ever seen!"

"Thanks, Aunt Julia." Ellie was working with tall white support columns, very much like the columns of Tara Plantation.

"We knew you'd do a great job," Julia said. "But . . . it's so perfect. All those roses . . . and how do you actually put each candy pearl on the icing like that?" Suddenly Julia was afraid she'd cry again, and that would ruin her careful makeup.

"Oh, it's just amazing. How can we ever thank you, Ellie?"

Ellie's pretty face was aglow with smiles. "You just did."

What was truly shocking was that the back-yard had filled up with people in the short time Julia was in her room dressing. This was a crowd scene. The noise escalated by the minute as friends and relatives greeted each other, hugged, exclaimed over the flowers and decor for Cristy's wedding.

Under the buffet canopy, a great deal of food had been delivered by Michael's Deli. It smelled heavenly and was being tended by Irmgard and her two aides . . . nothing to worry about there.

The two young D.J.s were setting up their electronic equipment in the gazebo—speakers, mikes, stereo sound systems. In no time they were playing soft strains from Mozart as back-ground music. Perfect.

Everything seemed to be running smoothly. Yet Julia still had to take a deep breath before walking directly into the chaos. She felt alone, maybe that was the problem. Had Jay been here, they'd have been facing everything to-gether. Side by side.

As soon as she stepped off her patio, the cool September air made her feel infinitely better. She looked upward, again appreciating the fine day. Wispy clouds were racing along in the pale blue sky, looking more like autumn than late summer.

"We certainly have good weather," she heard her mother say.

Nana Francie and Nana Carolyn, dressed in their best satin and sequins, were standing over the buffet table. Their noses were slightly crinkled as if they wondered who on earth had cooked all this *food*. Certainly no one had asked their advice!

"Do you suppose the potato salad will keep all day long?" Nana Carolyn asked.

"I don't," the other Nana said. Neither one of them realized they were shouting.

"After all, it might warm up later, and then what?! Mayonnaise can be so tricky."

"I think it will be fine if they refrigerate it right away," Nana Francie said. "But I can't understand why Julia would order that lasagna from a caterer! Good heavens, both of us are such good cooks. Why, we could so easily have . . ."

Julia moved quickly away from the Nanas. She was thinking she'd let them cook to their heart's content tomorrow morning at the after-wedding brunch.

She began greeting her guests, forcing herself to come up with a bright, sincere smile—and then, all of a sudden, she was enjoying the occasion. It was wonderful to entertain relatives and friends she hadn't seen in a very long time.

Compliments kept pouring in. She gave credit where credit was due: "Cristy and Jeremy and our friend Ben did most of the gardening. . . . Isn't it astounding? Whoever thought any daughter of mine would have such a green thumb."

She sailed through the crowd loving every minute. Yes, she would have liked Jay there to help and be at her side—but she was handling it alone somehow, the best way she knew how.

Finally it was time for everyone to take their seats. They'd set up white, wooden chairs in front of the wedding arch, leaving an aisle in the middle for the bride's path.

Sitting in front, her mother beside her and Carolyn just beyond her, Julia thought only belatedly of Ben. He might have liked to sit there with them in the front row . . . but it was too late for that. People were already in their places.

Soft music heralded the beginning of the wedding procession. Julia craned her neck looking for Ben, and finally spotted him way in the back. He was keeping an eye on the display of flowers along the path for the bride.

Dear Ben. He was always, always doing something kind for Cristy.

Julia sighed, determined not to think about anything but today's wedding. The brides-maids—Renee, April, and Beth—began walking in through the far gate, smiling, resplendent in their flowered dresses and bright white flat shoes.

Then came the flower girls, and that was quite a sight. Emily and Danielle were chubby little attendants in soft pink dresses, squealing with giggles as they walked. Their baskets were full of rosebuds for show and rose petals to throw.

The girls had been rehearsed to walk side by side but they kept pushing, each frowning intently, each trying to get ahead of the other. The guests were being pelted with rose petals and, for the most part, were trying very hard not to laugh at the little girls.

Father Hayes stood under the maple tree, near the arch, with Jeremy and his grooms-men, waiting. The boys looked stunning—youthful, energetic, enthused—and just elegant in their black tuxedos.

At that point the music swelled louder, and then through the gate came Cristy Lynn . . . and Julia's heartbeat simply soared.

Tall, proud, regal as a medieval princess, Cristy smiled with confidence and happiness. She walked slowly, sailing along on the arm of her brother-in-law—though she had con-fided to Julia that she'd carry her own secret with her along that path: she would envision her daddy walking along with her. He would be the one giving her away, Cristy had said fervently.

Julia swallowed hard at the thought. Yes, she could almost see Jay gliding along beside his Punkin'head . . . in spirit, anyway.

Cristy Lynn had chosen the right dress for this garden setting. Her neckline was low, but the beads and thin panels of Alencon lace simply gleamed under the sunlight. Cristy's long dark hair was swinging free, set off by the ring of silk roses and her long lace veil.

"You look simply radiant, my daughter," Julia whispered to herself. "At times you've been the goofiest or the most contrary of the three . . . but today you're a lovely bride who's shockingly all grown up.

"And your daddy *is* walking along with you, just as proud as I am, honey. . . ."

"What did you say, Julia?" her mother asked in a very loud voice. "Are you talking to me? I can hardly hear, with all that music!"

"Ssssh," Julia said, smiling, squeezing her mother's hand.

Forty

Father Hayes performed a poignant wedding ceremony. Julia surprised herself by not crying, but she saw Selena sniffling, Irmgard weeping into a large linen handkerchief, and Nana Carolyn sobbing softly. Even April and Bethany had silent tears rolling down their cheeks.

Why? They must all have been thinking about the bride's father who—they thought—could not be there. Cristy and Julia knew better.

The wedding party stood directly under the maple trees Jay had planted, a leafy green canopy that sheltered them all from the noontime sun. Whimsically, the tree seemed to have been placed exactly in the right location as though Jay had somehow known, twenty years ago, that Cristy would one day need that maple as her wedding tree.

Julia shivered ever so slightly, feeling a large lump in the back of her throat, but she kept her face serene and calm.

The wedding arch was right behind the priest, with white ribbons fluttering in the breeze, the satiny roses bobbing their heads as if in approval. Beyond that the gazebo soared toward the sky, rich in its redwood tones and amazing angles. Its peaked roof provided shade now for the musicians, and later for the dancers. Vivid red and gold mums burgeoning among feathery ferns made the gazebo a focal point of the entire wedding.

And Ben Wilson had built all that.

I wish Ben were sitting here with me, Julia thought, surprised at how intensely she wished it. With a slight pang of guilt she thought, he proposed marriage to me and I've never given him any answer. Of course the answer has to be no, at least for now, but I haven't told him so. . . .

Cristy and Jeremy spoke their vows and were united in holy matrimony by Father Hayes, who smiled broadly. He was enjoying this garden setting immensely, everyone could tell. He gave a jolly sermon that spoke of bountiful nature and the joy of the outdoors for family gatherings. Luckily, he kept it short.

When the bride and groom finally kissed, the triumphant wedding recessional march burst forth. People threw symbolic rice and birdseed that had been provided earlier by the flower girls.

Cristy and Jeremy clasped hands and ran happily through the barrage of well-wishers and rice. Somehow Cristy managed to grab Julia's hand in the middle of this newlywed retreat.

"Come on with us, it's time for the receiving line." The young bride looked into Julia's face with great earnestness. "And just in case I didn't say this before—thank you for everything, Mom."

"You're . . . you're welcome, Cristy." And now Julia did unexpectedly find herself crying just a tiny bit.

The next few hours flew by in a blur. The logistics of feeding some 180 hungry guests were enough to keep any hostess hopping. Julia was grateful for the help of her friends—and there were many of them who pitched in unexpectedly. Even Father Hayes, surprisingly, at one point was seen carrying trays of coffee across the patio to the two Nanas.

It was that kind of an informal gathering.

As for Ben, Julia was having an impossible time connecting with him. She'd see him from across the patio, or on the other side of the tent, but someone would always grab her for conversation, so she couldn't even call to Ben. He appeared to be working away, helping Irmgard's group, and watching the festivities with a contented smile on his face. Once in a while he'd make an amiable remark to whoever was standing nearby.

We're not being fair to Ben, Julia kept thinking; he did so much to make this the perfect garden wedding! He should be in a place of honor but instead he's just . . . nobody, an observer, someone standing off to the side because he's not family.

She didn't know where Ben was during the buffet line because she had absolutely no time to go searching for him. There was always somebody asking for a large fork, a big serving spoon, a potholder, mustard, butter, or some other specialty that she had to go to find in her kitchen.

"How's that potato salad taste to you?" Nana Carolyn yelled out loud when Julia sat at their table for a stolen moment. "Is that mayonnaise going bad, do you think, Julia?"

"No, Mom, it's fine," Julia said, though she

was only guessing; she'd had no time to eat anything.

"I have to admit the lasagna's all right," Nana Francie said grudgingly. "That was a good caterer you picked, Julia."

"Thanks, Mom. I'm glad you approve." Julia was twisting, straining her neck to look for the big man with the beard. He was terribly important to her, and maybe she hadn't ever quite realized just how much until right now.

"Ben!" she called out, spotting him over at the head table with Kevin and Jeremy. He turned, saw her, and smiled.

The moment stood out with sharp clarity: Ben looking almost like part of her family, Ben with shafts of sunlight filtering through the green leaves across his sweet, fuzzy face. After a few minutes he made his way through the crush of the tables toward her. She felt a sudden joyous lurch in her stomach.

And now what? she thought; I'm sitting here with my mother and mother-in-law. Do I honestly think they want to meet someone I'm dating? Not to mention sleeping with . . .

Get real, Julia.

Ben stood before the ladies, tall and handsome in his best blue suit and a neat, conservative blue tie. His smile looked like a very nervous one to Julia.

"Hi," she said, feeling a rush of color in her face. "I was hoping to see you before this. . . . Ben, you're the one who made everything so wonderful and you've been hanging out all alone. . . ."

"I'm doing fine," he said quietly.

Introductions, she knew, were in order. The two Nanas were staring at Ben as if Saddam Hussein had suddenly materialized.

Julia said, "This is my friend—Cristy's friend—our neighbor—" She was stammering and blushing, so she let that go. "I want you both to meet Ben Wilson, who made the gazebo and the wedding arch. He also fixed all the flower gardens—"

"Oh, my!" The two Nanas looked instantly enchanted.

"Ben, this is Carolyn Maxwell, my mother-in-law, and Francie O'Shea, my mother."

Both the Nanas fluttered their arms out to shake hands with this new, wonderful person.

"My gracious, you did wonders with all those flowers!" Nana Carolyn looked quite impressed. "And that gazebo! So old-fashioned and decorative . . ."

"What a talented man," Nana Francie said. "Isn't it nice to know a man who's handy around the house?"

"It's a pleasure to meet you ladies," he said

when he was finally to get a word in edgewise. Ben was shy; he was no smooth politician, as Jay had been. Ben was simply a man who was tense because—as he'd said—he loved Julia and wanted to marry her.

And these people represented her family.

"So you built the gazebo yourself." Nana Carolyn smiled. "I imagine those are very, very difficult to construct."

"Yes, ma'am." He looked so young and scared that Julia almost wanted to burst out laughing. He might have been sixteen and trying to impress his date's mother before the junior prom.

She had no idea how the Nanas would accept him if they knew the extent of Julia's involvement with him. However, that wasn't her problem at the moment. She had an entire wedding to get through.

"Sit with us, Ben," she pleaded. The soft green eyes looked pleased, again like a youngster, and he took a seat beside her with no further fanfare.

"CEL-E-BRA-TION!!!!"

Music was blasting from the gazebo and a few young guests, finished with their meal, were up there dancing already. The outdoor scene was very Middle Ages, like some pagan festival of long ago. Julia loved it.

"Your party's a great success," Ben told her. "I've heard nothing but compliments."

"Thanks very much to you, Ben. And is your photographer getting all the shots you'll need for the book?"

"Definitely. Bryce is busy." At that, the Nanas perked up and wanted to know, *what book?* They squealed with excitement at the idea of their granddaughter Cristy being in a real, published garden book.

Wait till their friends heard about this! Ben as a garden-book author went up quite a few notches in their estimation, Julia noted with amusement.

Now, the traditional ceremonies took place. In his toast, the best man, Kevin, raised his champagne glass and wished the couple a long and happy life.

Renee didn't want to make a speech, but April and Beth, complete hams like their father, each had to give a toast.

April went first. Standing, accepting the microphone from the D.J., she spoke clearly.

"Daddy would have said, *Here's to the little Punkin'head!*" She smiled affectionately at the newlywed couple but her eyes glittered with tears. "He'd have loved this day, and loved

Jeremy, and we can only hope he's watching it all from his box seat in heaven. . . ."

Suddenly devastated, she sat down quickly, dabbing at her eyes with a Kleenex.

Then Bethany rose. Her glass was held high and mischief in her eyes. "Cristy Lynn is my little sister, and sometimes she was a pain in the you-know-what. But through it all, we always knew she was one of the great Maxwell sisters—so that made her all right."

"Thanks for nothing!" Cristy howled, drawing laughter from the crowd. The little sister was always the scrapper.

"Wait, I'm not finished!" Bethany grinned. "We thought this whole garden wedding was just another of Cristy's nutty ideas . . . but thanks to Mom and a lot of good people—especially Ben Wilson—you pulled it off, Cristy and Jeremy. It's *beautiful*. Mazel tov."

The guests went wild, clapping, cheering, calling out messages of good luck. Imagine girls giving wedding toasts these days, Julia thought proudly . . . I absolutely love the idea. *My Little Women*. This traditional ceremony might become another chapter in the book.

She turned, caught Ben's eyes on her, and she smiled, feeling a warmth all through her body. The girls' toast had been an unforgettable moment. It was nice to share it with someone special.

The bride and groom danced in the gazebo to their special song, the music from *Robin Hood*, "Everything I Do." Guests gathered around, watching them with affection, clapping whenever they kissed. The video guy was on hand at all times, getting candid action shots, and Bryce was there as well with his camera.

Jeremy danced with his mother, which was sweet and touching, but Cristy would allow no one to stand in for her father. There would be no "Daddy's Little Girl" played at this wedding.

Cristy and Jeremy cut the cake and fed each other with none of that smashing of icing into faces—thank the Lord. Julia was proud of them and she knew Michelle and Bud Crenshaw were, too.

Afternoon was advancing so that shadows became elongated by some of the trees. The backyard cooled off and guests were even more inclined to dance in the nice, shaded gazebo.

All the good old wedding reception tunes were played—"Alley Cat," "Beer Barrel Polka," "the Hokey Pokey"—and some new ones including "The Electric Slide" and the South Seas number, "Hot Hot Hot," a favorite of the bride. Finally a few slow songs began to be featured.

"Will you dance with me, Ben?" Julia asked after going in search of Ben and finding him helping Irmgard and her crew to clear the buffet table.

"Sure," he said but kept working. His sense of responsibility never stopped; he'd help for as long as the women needed a hand.

"Just one, please, Ben?"

He must have caught the urgency in her tone, because he excused himself and went with Julia to the gazebo.

"What's wrong?"

She fitted into his arms and they began to dance to a slow number. "Nothing's wrong exactly . . . I just wanted so much to see you and talk to you for one little bit of this day."

He grinned. "That's flattering. Does this mean you've come to some sort of decision?"

"Decision—you mean about us? Oh no, I haven't had a second to think about it."

"Be truthful." He pulled her close and whispered in her ear. "I'll bet you've done a lot of thinking about us."

She felt her face turning bright red. Of course she had.

"You owe me an answer, Julia."

"I know that."

"I asked you to marry me in October."

"Oh, Ben, it's not so simple! I would have a very difficult time." She felt lightheaded for a second as they whirled around the crowded gazebo. "I mean, Nana Carolyn would be heartbroken. You met her. You can imagine how she'd feel if I were to get married so soon, only two years after Jay . . ."

"She'd have to face it, that's all," he said. "She seems to be a resilient little lady."

"Oh, but not about her son's widow—"

He was quiet for a while. "You're afraid, Julia, to let anyone in your family know about us."

Something in her cringed. "Yes. Yes, of course I am. Well, I mean the girls know, at least some of it, but—not the Nanas . . ."

"That's a hangup you'll have to deal with."

She nodded her head and they danced quietly. The euphoria she'd been feeling had vanished. She felt a sick thunk in her heart.

"The important thing is, do you love me, Julia?" The words hung there between them, stark and unadorned. "Because you've never said so."

That was true, she had never said so, not directly to Ben. She'd admitted it to herself a few times, but that was certainly the coward's way.

She searched for words. "Today is a difficult time for me," she blurted out.

"It is, I understand." She knew he did understand. It seemed as though every single wedding guest was looking at the two of them, wondering. Julia's face felt as crimson as the mums on the round tables.

"Can I talk to you tonight?" he asked.

"I'll have a houseful of guests." She bit her lip. "There are at least ten people staying overnight, and in the morning I'm throwing that big brunch for everyone—you included, of course."

Ben stopped dancing. "Just try, all right? Try to sneak away after everyone's settled in bed."

"I doubt if I can—"

"We'll talk for just a few minutes. I'll be out here by the gazebo. It doesn't matter how late."

"But why does it have to be *tonight*?" she started to ask.

She was speaking to empty air, because Ben was already on his way down the gazebo steps.

"I want to get back to help Irmgard," he called out, smiling as he left. "Don't forget— tonight."

Forty-one

The wedding reception lasted until dusk, and even then a large number of people stayed on. The evening was cool, friends were eager to help fold up the many rented chairs and tables, and pick up the general debris. After the Maxwell yard had been restored to almost normal, there were at least three dozen folks sitting around drinking coffee and munching leftover food and wedding cake.

The wedding was considered officially ended when Cristy announced she was leaving. She came downstairs in her "going away" clothes—which consisted of comfortable jeans and a blouse; Cristy always was different and less formal than any of the other girls. She and Jeremy would be boarding a plane in the morning bound for St. Thomas, but tonight they were going no farther than the local Marriott Hotel.

Cristy looked around at the crowd gathered

in her mother's dining room to say goodbye—all her wedding party, her new in-laws, her cousins, her college friends, and Julia's many friends.

"Oh nuts, I'm not going anywhere yet!" she declared. She plunked down her suitcase. "Somebody tell Jeremy this party is too good to leave. We're staying a while."

"Young people are different nowadays," Nana Francie announced loudly. "Why, Cristy, in the old days, brides simply couldn't wait to sneak away with their brand new husbands!"

"No kidding, Nana?" Cristy winked at her friend, Renee. "Why were those brides so eager, do you suppose?"

"Well—" Nana Francie sputtered, unable to answer for a moment. "They were in love! They wanted to start their married life!"

"You don't mean . . ." Cristy was being devilish now, putting an arm around her small Nana. "You don't mean to tell me those brides in those days were anxious to have . . . S-E-X???!"

"Oh!!! You're a rascal, Cristy Lynn," Nana Francie said, her face red. She began laughing. "You truly are a naughty girl to tease your grandmother that way!"

"So I guess what you're saying is, they *did*

have such a thing as S-E-X in those olden times," April put in, adding to the teasing.

"Well, I'll tell you something," Nana Francie said, wagging a finger. "Marriages lasted a whole lifetime in those olden times. And maybe that was because nobody put the cart before the horse!"

"The cart before the horse?" Cristy repeated, deadpan.

At that bizarre, old-fashioned expression, the entire party broke up, the young people especially rocking with laughter. Meanwhile the two Nanas—even though they were laughing, too—managed to maintain expressions that were quite huffy.

"And in the old days the brides knew how to *cook,* which was the proper way," Nana Carolyn said. "But this is the nineties, so everybody eats those Big Macs. I suppose we have to bow to all the new ways."

"You really mean that, Nana?" Suddenly sounding serious, Cristy zoomed in and took hold of her grandmother's two little hands. "You really do see some merit to the modern ways?"

Nana Carolyn frowned ferociously. "I didn't say there was merit! I said we have to bow to the new ways, like it or not. Hmmmph."

Cristy took time to phrase her words carefully. "What about other changes closer to home? What if certain things within our family were changing also, Nana?"

The elderly lady frowned. "What are you referring to, Cristy Lynn?"

"I'm talking about my mother." Cristy landed a light, reassuring kiss on Nana's cheek. "What if my mother were to meet a man who cared for her? How would you feel about that, Nana?"

The silence was as thick as a winter fog.

It seemed as though Nana Carolyn understood perfectly well, but she looked as if she were struck dumb. Her face went paper white and she tried to pull back from Cristy. Cristy held tight and wouldn't let her.

"I'm the bride today," Cristy whispered to her grandmother. "You could grant me this one wish, if you love me, and listen to what I'm saying."

Julia, standing in the doorway, felt her pulse hammering. God almighty, she couldn't believe Cristy was doing this.

As for the many others in the crowd, they began to disperse to other rooms, quietly and discreetly, sensing that a private conversation was underway all of a sudden. Even the other

Nana wandered off toward the kitchen. Only April and Bethany stood their ground, because they were part of the situation.

"Nana, this could be important." Cristy's pretty face seemed to be pleading that her words receive a careful hearing. "My mother needs to find a new life someday . . . but she would never want you to be hurt."

"Uh . . ." Nana Carolyn tried to swallow but failed. Then she somehow got control of herself—"pulling themselves up by the bootstraps," the women of that generation often called it. She closed her eyes for a brief moment, tugged at the pearls at her throat and nodded her head to show Cristy she comprehended.

There was only family in the room now. Nana Carolyn patted Cristy's hand, then turned to address her daughter-in-law. Julia's stomach was doing somersaults; she simply wasn't up for any sort of confrontation tonight. And she'd never want to see Carolyn hurt.

Once again Carolyn pulled on the expensive pearls. Her pale blue eyes were watery but most lucid.

"Julia . . . you think I didn't notice that the wedding ring was off?" Carolyn said slowly. "I noticed."

"Oh, Mom, I don't know what—" Julia began.

"And you think I didn't see you dancing with the big man with that fuzzy beard? The man who makes gazebos and plants gardens?" Carolyn eyes sparkled with tears but she was trying to smile bravely.

"I noticed, my darling," she said firmly, holding out a hand toward Julia. "And I said—good for my Julia, *good,* if she has a chance to love again."

"You did?"

"Oh my God," someone said; it might have been Bethany.

Blinded by tears, Julia moved toward the little old lady and they hugged tightly, both crying because Jay was gone, both clutching at each other with enormous love and understanding.

"You really did feel that way?" Julia asked in a choked voice. "You really did?"

"What am I, a dog in the manger?" Jay's mother asked. "I wouldn't want you to be happy again some day?"

"Well, but it's so difficult . . ."

"Of course it is, but listen. My Jay would want it that way," Nana Carolyn whispered. "You getting on with your life, a pretty woman like you, sweetheart."

"I love you," Julia burst out, with fresh

tears flowing down her face. "I've always loved you so much . . . and you know how much I loved Jay. . . ."

"I do know, Julia." Nana Carolyn's voice was soothing. "I do. And he looks like a fine fellow, that bearded man."

"Nana, you're a pip," Cristy declared, wiping away her own tears as she moved in to be included in the hug. "You're a classic example of a PIP!"

"I don't know what a pip is," Carolyn grumbled, "but I need a Kleenex, please, from someone."

"What's going on here?" demanded Nana Francie, just returning from the kitchen. "Did I miss something?"

"You sure did, Francie." Nana Carolyn drew Nana Francie into the hug along with Julia and Cristy—a four-way hug that spanned all three generations—and warmed a great many hearts of the family members looking on.

"I still don't know what's happening," Nana Francie said, frowning as she pulled away. "Somebody has to be practical here, after all. I was just checking the food for the brunch tomorrow."

"We're all set with that, Nana," Cristy said, grinning through her tears.

"No, I think we need more eggs. And more bread."

"So *I'll* do the cooking tomorrow," Nana Carolyn said. "I can make the food supply stretch, believe me." She had recovered enough to accept a tissue from Renee so she could wipe her eyes.

"You'll do the cooking?" Nana Francie looked horrified. "I'll be doing the cooking! Julia wants my famous pancakes for the brunch!"

"Oh for heaven's sakes, you'll both be cooking," said Bethany, smiling, hoping to prevent World War Three. "Nana Carolyn will make her famous scrambled eggs and bacon."

Julia stood there in silence and watched as the two ladies did their eternal squabbling. She herself was still in a state of shock.

As easy as that.

It was staggering. Cristy had spoken to Nana Carolyn and asked her to listen. Then, just as easily as that, the facts were now known and accepted by Jay's mother.

Julia looked down at her ring finger, left hand. She hadn't thought anyone would notice the absence of that wedding ring; of course she should have realized Jay's mother would.

But maybe it all worked out for the best because all the secrets were out. One thing a family shouldn't have is secrets, Julia had always believed.

He looks like a fine fellow, that bearded man. . . . Yes.

Forty-two

Late that night Julia managed to leave her overnight guests and slip out of the house. She walked through the rubble of the wedding scene—batted down grass, stray balloons in the bushes, wedding rice flung among the flower gardens.

Her yard was dark except for a sliver of a September moon that showed itself now and then between shimmery cloud layers. She could see enough, though, as she followed the path—she could see that most everything was folded and stacked, ready to be reclaimed by the rental company.

But how quiet it was out here!

Midnight had long since come and gone, and everyone in Julia's house had settled down in bed, as far as she knew.

The wedding gardens . . .

Oddly enough, the wedding gardens seemed still to reverberate with the festivities that had taken place there that day. Was that possible?

Or—now that she was writing a book—was her imagination working overtime?

Julia cupped an ear, positive she still heard traces of dancing music, silverware clinking, and the voices of her many guests.

There were echoes of the guests saying, "Come on, Cristy! Throw that bouquet!"

And the "Farmer in the Dell" song to which Jeremy and Cristy cut their wedding cake.

And Julia's cousin Adrienne, who had been so adamant against a garden wedding, saying at some point, "I must admit, Julia, you Maxwells put on a very fine party after all. Who would have thought you could do everything so well . . . outdoors?"

It had been a compliment . . . at least Julia chose to think so. She accepted it as an accolade because she felt in her own heart that the day had been a smashing success. Thanks to the help of many, many good people, the wedding had gone smoothly. And that was more than you could say about some fancy-schmancy weddings at the country club.

About the bouquet: Julia hadn't been standing in the single women's line for catching Cristy's bridal flowers. She hadn't wanted it. The bouquet had gone sailing across the gazebo and straight to Renee, who was delighted to catch it.

But as it whooshed through the air, Julia had caught a scent of perfumed roses. Somehow tonight, stumbling around in the dark, she imagined she still smelled those magical roses that were supposed to predict the very next bride.

Oh boy, Julia. Does the word "ditz" mean anything to you?

Anyway, here she was alone and tiptoeing across the property in hopes of seeing Ben, who had probably given up and gone home long ago.

"I really hoped you'd come." His voice whispered out of the darkness. Her heart thumped with pleasant anticipation—and more than that. Joy, as though she had just arrived home after a long, tiring day.

"Hi," she said softly, searching for him. She found him at the base of the gazebo, and stepped into the big, warm spread of his arms. She felt safe, and at peace. Somewhere, crickets chirped in trees and grass, while the heady scents of flowers gently perfumed the night air, but in Ben's arms all was quietness and sweet darkness.

She rested her face against his chest, marveling at the feel of him. His powerful torso seemed to consume her, blocking out the moonshadows, and tonight that was exactly the way she wanted things to be.

"I have a few things to tell you," she whispered into the folds of his shirt. Mmmm, he smelled so wonderful, like a fresh shower and clean-scrubbed skin.

"A few things to tell me?" He sounded worried. "Uh oh. This sounds ominous."

"Does it?" She angled her head so she was looking up at him. His beard glowed almost golden in the moonlight, and his eyes looked flecked with worry.

"It's not at all ominous . . . but give me a minute to think."

She ran a finger along the bridge of his dear, familiar nose, then down into the tangle of the beard. When she pressed her ear to his chest, she could feel the rise and fall of his heart within.

"Are you nervous, being here at your house?" Ben asked. "Too many possible eavesdroppers around? Want to walk down to my house?"

"Nope. I've got nothing to be nervous about anymore." She was grinning.

"What? What about the delicate little Nana-ladies?"

Moved by an impulse, she stood on tiptoe and touched his mouth with hers. She found it warm and sweet. "No problem. They very much like the big man with the beard. They decided he seems like a nice fellow for Julia."

"They did?" Ben looked staggered. "Even Jay's mother?"

She nodded. "Absolutely."

"You told them? That we could possibly be getting serious?"

"Cristy told them. She made Carolyn Maxwell listen."

He was silent for quite some time. "And what does Julia herself think?"

"Ah, that's what we need to discuss." She wriggled a bit in his embrace. "I've been thinking all day and—I remembered something you quoted to me a while back."

"What?"

"I looked it up tonight in my Bartlett's. Do you remember when you said: *'What's old collapses, times change, and new life blossoms in the ruins.'*"

His voice was husky. "Of course I remember."

"Ben, I don't know why it's taken me so

long to say this. I love you deeply. . . . I think I've loved you all summer long, but I was fighting it too hard—maybe to preserve my ghosts—to give in . . ."

"And now?"

"Now the ghosts are willing to move over. . . . They don't want to monopolize my life and my thoughts forever."

In the deep silence that followed, she could hear the rushing of night wind out back in the woods behind her property. She wondered what he was thinking, and then he gave her a bear hug that was positively crushing.

"I've been waiting a long time to hear that, Julia."

"I know." She backed away for a minute and stepped up two steps on the gazebo, so they could be eye to eye. "I love you, Ben. I love you so much I just want to tell the world."

"Then we will."

"Damn right we will," she said, grinning. "Tomorrow at my brunch, we'll make an announcement." She hesitated. "That is, if you want to do it that way."

"Julia. Of course I do." He hesitated. "Are we talking about an announcement of our impending marriage?"

She laughed. "Yes. Scary, isn't it?"

"Well, we have a lot of details to work out," Ben said. "Like—will you sell your house?"

"I've always intended to," she said.

"Could you be happy living in my log house?"

She couldn't resist teasing him. "That grungy old bachelor place? With all those mooseheads on the wall?"

He covered her mouth with his own, engineered a long and lovely kiss, and then said, "If you can find any mooseheads, you can take them down, Julia."

"That's a deal. So—yes, our marriage is the basic announcement we'll make at the brunch. And I honestly think most of the relatives will be happy for us."

"Even those Nanas, you say . . ."

"Oh, them, they'll be so busy cooking and fighting they wouldn't care if I ran away with Peewee Herman!"

"Huh?"

She chuckled softly. "Inside joke. Something Selena said."

He nodded. "There's only one big detail I care about, and I hope we agree on this one."

"The honeymoon?"

"You said it."

"Greece?"

"Athens, Mykonos, Crete . . ."

"Oh, Ben—I can hardly stand it! The Parthenon and the Royal Palace . . ."

"I can't wait either. Corinth, Mycenae, Olympia."

"Santorini . . ." She whirled around, giddy with anticipation.

Greece at last, traveling with this wonderful man—but he would be her husband!—whose interest was every bit as keen as her own. She felt incredibly blessed.

Now some cloud layers shifted. They were bathed in moonlight, surrounded by a sky full of sparkling September stars.

A leaf blew off a tree in a gusty little wind from the north, and that one gesture looked like the beginning of autumn.

"Summer is over," Julia whispered. Being up on the gazebo brought her close to the ear of the giant, which she loved.

It was all over . . . their magical summer of gardens and fragrances and preparing for Cristy's big day.

But autumn could also be a marvelous season. For them it would be a time for a new beginning, their journey to ancient Greece, their journey into a brand new marriage.

And they'd been given this autumn season just for themselves.

"I love you, Ben," she said again simply because saying the words—at long last—felt so wonderful.

EILEEN HEHL lives in Connecticut with her husband. Her first *TO LOVE AGAIN* book was *Earth Angel* in 1993. The author of many young adult novels, she's a member of the Connecticut Chapter of Romance Writers of America. She would love to hear from readers, care of Zebra Books.

Coming next month
from *TO LOVE AGAIN*

Moonglow by Sharon Wagner
Forever and a Day by Fay Kilgore

WATCH AS THESE WOMEN LEARN TO LOVE AGAIN

HELLO LOVE   (4094, $4.50/$5.50)
by Joan Shapiro

Family tragedy leaves Barbara Sinclair alone with her success. The fight to gain custody of her young granddaughter brings a confrontation with the determined rancher Sam Douglass. Also widowed, Sam has been caring for Emily alone, guided by his own ideas of childrearing. Barbara challenges his ideas. And that's not all she challenges . . . Long-buried desires surface, then gentle affection. Sam and Barbara cannot ignore the chance to love again.

THE BEST MEDICINE   (4220, $4.50/$5.50)
by Janet Lane Walters

Her late husband's expenses push Maggie Carr back to nursing, the career she left almost thirty years ago. The night shift is difficult, but it's harder still to ignore the way handsome Dr. Jason Knight soothes his patients. When she lends a hand to help his daughter, Jason and Maggie grow closer than simply doctor and nurse. Obstacles to romance seem insurmountable, but Maggie knows that love is always the best medicine.

AND BE MY LOVE   (4291, $4.50/$5.50)
by Joyce C. Ware

Selflessly catering first to husband, then children, grandchildren, and her aging, though imperious mother, leaves Beth Volmar little time for her own adventures or passions. Then, the handsome archaeologist Karim Donovan arrives and campaigns to widen the boundaries of her narrow life. Beth finds new freedom when Karim insists that she accompany him to Turkey on an archaeological dig . . . and a journey towards loving again.

OVER THE RAINBOW   (4032, $4.50/$5.50)
by Marjorie Eatock

Fifty-something, divorced for years, courted by more than one attractive man, and thoroughly enjoying her job with a large insurance company, Marian's sudden restlessness confuses her. She welcomes the chance to travel on business to a small Mississippi town. Full of good humor and words of love, Don Worth makes her feel needed, and not just to assess property damage. Marian takes the risk.

A KISS AT SUNRISE   (4260, $4.50/$5.50)
by Charlotte Sherman

Beginning widowhood and retirement, Ruth Nichols has her first taste of freedom. Against the advice of her mother and daughter, Ruth heads for an adventure in the motor home that has sat unused since her husband's death. Long days and lonely campgrounds start to dampen the excitement of traveling alone. That is, until a dapper widower named Jack parks next door and invites her for dinner. On the road, Ruth and Jack find the chance to love again.

Available wherever paperbacks are sold, or order direct from the Publisher. Send cover price plus 50¢ per copy for mailing and handling to Penguin USA, P.O. Box 999, c/o Dept. 17109, Bergenfield, NJ 07621. Residents of New York and Tennessee must include sales tax. DO NOT SEND CASH.

TODAY'S HOTTEST READS
ARE TOMORROW'S SUPERSTARS

VICTORY'S WOMAN   (4484, $4.50)
by Gretchen Genet
Andrew—the carefree soldier who sought glory on the battlefield,
and returned a shattered man . . . Niall—the legandary frontiers-
man and a former Shawnee captive, tormented by his past . . .
Roger—the troubled youth, who would rise up to claim a shocking legacy . . . and Clarice—the passionate beauty bound by one
man, and hopelessly in love with another. Set against the back-
drop of the American revolution, three men fight for their
heritage—and one woman is destined to change all their lives forever!

FORBIDDEN   (4488, $4.99)
by Jo Beverley
While fleeing from her brothers, who are attempting to sell her
into a loveless marriage, Serena Riverton accepts a carriage ride
from a stranger—who is the handsomest man she has ever seen.
Lord Middlethorpe, himself, is actually contemplating marriage
to a dull daughter of the aristocracy, when he encounters the
breathtaking Serena. She arouses him as no woman ever has. And
after a night of thrilling intimacy—a forbidden liaison—Serena
must choose between a lady's place and a woman's passion!

WINDS OF DESTINY   (4489, $4.99)
by Victoria Thompson
Becky Tate is a half-breed outcast—branded by her Comanche
heritage. Then she meets a rugged stranger who awakens her
heart to the magic and mystery of passion. Hiding a desperate
past, Texas Ranger Clint Masterson has ridden into cattle country
to bring peace to a divided land. But a greater battle rages inside
him when he dares to desire the beautiful Becky!

WILDEST HEART   (4456, $4.99)
by Virginia Brown
Maggie Malone had come to cattle country to forge her future as
a healer. Now she was faced by Devon Conrad, an outlaw
wounded body and soul by his shadowy past . . . whose eyes
blazed with fury even as his burning caress sent her spiraling with
desire. They came together in a Texas town about to explode in sin
and scandal. Danger was their destiny—and there was nothing
they wouldn't dare for love!